the
ice cream
girls

the
ice cream
girls

DOROTHY
KOOMSON

sphere

SPHERE

First published in Great Britain in 2010 by Sphere

A CIP catalogue record for this book
is available from the British Library.

ISBN 978-1-84744-364-9

Typeset in Bembo by M Rules
Printed and bound in Great Britain by
Clays Ltd, St Ives plc

Papers used by Sphere are natural, renewable and
recyclable products sourced from well-managed forests and certified
in accordance with the rules of the Forest Stewardship Council.

Mixed Sources
Product group from well-managed
forests and other controlled sources
www.fsc.org Cert no. SGS-COC-004081
© 1996 Forest Stewardship Council
FSC

Sphere
An imprint of
Little, Brown Book Group
100 Victoria Embankment
London EC4Y 0DY

An Hachette UK Company
www.hachette.co.uk

www.littlebrown.co.uk

thank you . . .

I would like to thank everyone who has been involved in this novel:

My family. Ever-growing and ever-wonderful, thank you for your unwavering love and support.

My agents. Ant and James, you're true diamond geezers. And, Ant, I forgive you for the newspaper article.

My publishers. Jo, Jenny, Caroline, Emma, Nikola, Kirsteen and everyone else who has had a hand in bringing *The Ice Cream Girls* to the shelves, thank you, thank you, thank you.

My friends. You know who you are and you know how much I love you.

MK2. You helped to make writing this book possible.

You, the reader. Thank you for taking the time to read my book. I hope you enjoy it.

And, to G: Thank you for being you.

For My Little Angel
You make everything worthwhile

part one

serena

AS COLD AS ICE CREAM?

Serena Gorringe, one half of the so-called Ice Cream Girls duo accused of killing popular teacher Marcus Halnsley, is expected to take the witness stand today in her murder trial.

Gorringe, 19, is the older of the two and is widely thought to have been the driving force behind the pair's cold-blooded plot to seduce, torture and murder her former History teacher.

Although Gorringe and her accomplice, Poppy Carlisle, went to the police after the murder claiming there had been an accident in which Halnsley was stabbed, evidence at the scene suggested he had been subjected to torture before he later died from a stab wound to the heart.

Both Gorringe, pictured eating ice cream and wearing a string bikini, right, and Carlisle deny torture and murder. They also both deny being the assailant who ultimately delivered the fatal blow to Mr Halnsley.

Daily News Chronicle, October 1989

3

serena

'Serena Gorringe, I love you.'

Oh my God! It's going to happen. It's really going to happen. After nearly 15 years of wanting this, hoping for this, *praying* for this, it's going to happen. He's going to propose.

Or, maybe he isn't. Maybe I'm having one of my 'moments' where I've so completely immersed myself in a fantasy, it seems real.

I glance around, searching for proof in my surroundings that I'm not making it all up. We're at a table for two outside our favourite Brighton restaurant – a small, family-run Mexican cantina that sits on the edge of the beach. It's a clear, warm night and the sky is teeming with stars. The rhythmic ssshushing of the dark sea mingles gently with the loud music spilling from inside the restaurant, while the smell of spicy food fuses deliciously with the salt air. To my left Brighton pier is adorned with hundreds upon hundreds of lights, and to my right Worthing pier's lights seem more demure than its more famous cousin's but are still pretty. This is such a perfect setting for a proposal, it can't possibly be real, I *must* be dreaming.

I focus on Evan again. He is down on bended knee, staring at me with a serious expression on his face. This is no fantasy. It can't be. Because in all my imaginings, Evan has never been prostrate in front of me – it's so far removed from his normal behaviour, I've never been able to conjure up what he would look like doing it. Big gestures with him are so few and far between that this one is like seeing a unicorn walking down Brighton seafront – I could only believe it if I saw it. So this must be real, because I am seeing it.

'Serena Gorringe, I love you,' he repeats, and I know this is definitely real. Only the real-life Evan would know that I would have flitted off into one of my 'crazy worlds' as he calls them, as soon as he got down on one knee and started speaking. Only the real-life Evan would know that I'd need to go into one of my crazy worlds to double-check this was actually happening. And only the real-life Evan would know that when I returned to this reality, he would have to continue by starting again.

'I want to spend the rest of my life with you.' He reaches out and takes my left hand in both of his large hands, holds on to me tenderly but securely. 'I don't normally say things like this, so when I tell you that you've made my life so much more than it would have been and I never want our time together to end, you know I mean it. So, would you do me the honour of marrying me?'

'We're already married,' I reply.

My husband's face softens from his serious expression into a huge, warming smile. 'Again,' he says. 'Will you marry me, again?'

I slide slowly and gently into silence to savour this. This *proposal*. I was robbed of this last time around. And this finally proves he wants to be with me for ever. Yes, he's already committed to it by marrying me, but he actually *wants* to do it. Last time it was all rather ambiguous and necessary when we decided to do it.

May, 1996

We lay fully clothed, side by side on the bed in his small London flat, staring at the ceiling. I'd just told him that the morning-after pill I'd taken after the condom split hadn't worked and I was pregnant. A missed period and three tests had told me so. (I'd waited until we were horizontal to break the news because I suspected he'd fall over.) 'Oh, OK,' he said, before sighing a deep, slightly mournful sigh of resignation and defeat. I sighed, too, knowing what he meant, how he felt. It wasn't terrible news, it wasn't even bad news, it was just life-changingly unexpected. I wasn't ready, I was sure he wasn't either. But here we were, ready or not. A baby was on its way.

'We should probably get married,' I stated.

'To stop our parents freaking out,' he replied.

'Because they would,' I said.

'Freak out. Yeah.'

'Yeah.'

Evan didn't realise that when I said 'should probably', I meant 'have to'. If it was just about me, I wouldn't have cared, I wouldn't have minded not getting married. But after what had happened to our family a few years earlier, what I had put my parents through, I could not do this to them as well – I could not add 'unmarried mother' to my list of crimes . . . I had to show them that I wasn't who the world thought I was, I was a respectable girl and I could do things the right way. I *had* to get married.

'It's not as if we weren't going to get married at some point, anyway,' Evan said, trying to rally, trying to rescue the situation by sounding positive. 'We might as well do it now.'

'Yeah, I suppose,' I replied. And six weeks later we were married and that was that. No romance, no story to tell and retell, there wasn't even an engagement ring to show off.

Ever since then, I've had a niggling doubt about where we would be if we hadn't been married at the wrong end of a shotgun. Without doubt, if he knew Serena Gorringe at the end of the eighties, if he knew the person who was all over the papers and who had been accused of something terrible, he would not have married me. But he did not know her. He met and got to know the real me. And I've always wondered if the real me was good enough. If the real me was the person he *wanted* to marry, instead of *had* to marry simply to satisfy ultra-traditional parents.

'Last time, we didn't get the chance to do it properly,' Evan says. 'I want that for us this time. I promised myself on the day we did that we'd do it again properly. Since our first wedding, I've been putting money aside so we could do it. Big church, white dress, huge party, honeymoon – the lot. We can have everything that we couldn't afford or didn't have time to do before, including . . .' He reaches into the inside pocket of his favourite suit jacket and pulls out a small, blue velvet box. He opens it up to show me and there, languishing on a silk bed, is a large, many-faceted, square-cut diamond on a silver band.

The air catches in my throat.

'An engagement ring. This time, an engagement ring as well as a real proposal.'

'Is that a real diamond?' I can barely form the words to speak in its presence let alone think about touching it.

'Of course. We can afford it now. And it's on a platinum band, from the same place where we got our wedding rings.'

My hands fly up to my face as tears fill my eyes and swell in my throat. He's thought about it, he's planned it and has done it all because I am good enough: he does want to be with me. He does want to be married to me, just as much as I want to be married to him.

I've never wanted to be with someone as much as I want to be with Evan. '*What about you-know-who?*' whispers my conscience. It is the part of my conscience that lives in the past; it worships the past, clings to it, is always determined to drag the past into the present. '*Wasn't you-know-who the love of your life?*'

My conscience is wrong, of course. Evan is The One. He's the only one.

'*Are you sure, Serena?*' mocks my conscience. '*Are you absolutely sure about that?*'

I'm sure, I'm one hundred per cent sure. There really is no one but my husband for me. What I had with *you-know-who* wasn't love, it wasn't like what I have with Evan. It wasn't even the same creature, how could it have been?

'Babe?' Evan says, in a way that suggests he has called me a few times.

'Sorry,' I say, 'miles away.' *Another life away.*

'I'm getting a cold knee and a little nervous,' he says.

'Nervous? Why?'

'You haven't actually said yes.'

'Haven't I?' I ask.

'No, you haven't.'

'Oh.'

He grins that grin of his. 'Do you want me to ask you again?'

I nod eagerly. Just one more time, especially now I know there's a ring involved.

'OK,' he says with a slight, mock-exasperated shake of his head. 'Serena Gorringe . . .' He pauses to slip the ring halfway up my finger, and I hold my breath, trying to remember every detail because I will recreate it for the kids, for my sisters, for my parents, for anyone who cares to listen. 'Will you make me the happiest man on earth by marrying me and becoming Mrs Gillmare all over again?' He pushes the ring into place beside my wedding band.

I almost forget to breathe as I examine the two rings. They slot together almost seamlessly, and they look like they were made for each other. Like nothing will ever tear them apart.

'Of course I will,' I say and leap up as he struggles to his feet. 'Of course I'll marry you again.' I throw my arms around his neck and he grins at me before he scoops me into his arms and then dips me backwards for a deep, show-stopping, movie-style kiss. Another unicorn-on-Brighton-seafront-type gesture. He is full of them tonight.

I immerse myself in it all. In the kiss, the proposal, the man. I'm only vaguely aware that we've had an audience and now the air around us is full of the sound of people clapping.

I'm going to hang on to this moment. I have to. I know how easily everything can be taken away. Everything is fragile, when you're like me. Very few things are permanent. I live on a precipice of falling into my past, of people finding out what I have been accused of, how I was publicly branded, and being judged all over again on that. I live with the constant fear that someone or something is going to tip me over the edge.

But not tonight, eh? Not right now. Right now, I am the woman who Dr Evan Gillmare wants to spend the rest of his life with.

Right now, I am the happiest woman on earth and nothing bad could possibly happen to me.

serena

I'm walking around my kitchen, opening cupboards and appliances, looking for the knives.

The dinner knives are safe but the sharp ones, the ones that can do serious damage, seem to be missing in action. Admittedly, that's my fault: I hid them last night, and I can't quite remember where. It wouldn't be a problem if the house wasn't minutes away from becoming a chaos of breakfast and day-organising and the usual family pandemonium. It wouldn't even be a problem if Evan hadn't made me promise not to do this again.

My fingers reach for the oven door for a third time and I yank it open really quickly, hoping that the knives will have materialised in there, the original hiding place, the favourite hiding place.

Every night, before bed, I used to collect all the sharp knives and put them on a baking tray and put them in the oven – just in case someone broke in while we were asleep and decided to use our own cutlery against us. Then I started doing it before we settled down to watch TV in the evening, in case someone broke in the back door while we were lounging in the front room. And then it was just after washing up because it was easier. After a while, I realised that hiding the knives in the same place every night, night after night, might not be a good idea if we were being watched, so I started hiding them in all sorts of ingenious places, places that a burglar with ill intentions would never think to look. Turns out, I wouldn't think to look there either because I'm constantly doing this: looking for the knives.

Evan, Verity and Conrad used to be very nice about it, accepted it as one of my little quirks, even though they had to hack away at cheese and tear bread some days because Mum couldn't find the knives. Then, Evan discovered them in his gym bag – at the gym – and had a total understanding melt-down. He came storming through the kitchen door, and started shouting at me in front of the kids. *'I could have been arrested for carrying multiple dangerous weapons, Sez!'* he'd screamed. *'And what do I tell them, I've got a crazy wife who hides the knives and then forgets where she's put them?'* I'd been so tempted to say, 'Yes, because that's the truth', but decided not to push it. I had to leave him alone for his temper to subside and then tell him I was sorry. After that, he made me prom-ise that if I insisted on hiding the knives, I'd write down where they were so it wouldn't happen again.

Obviously I'd crossed my fingers behind my back when I agreed because, *come on*, that would defeat the whole point, wouldn't it? I've been pretty good since then at remembering. But after last night, and the champagne and the celebration at home, my head is fuzzy, my senses are blunted and I can't remember much, least of all where I stashed the sharp stuff. Could've sworn it was the oven, would have put money on it.

I snatch the stainless-steel door open, for a fourth time, just in case. No. Nada. Nothing. *Damn it!*

Something being shoved loudly through the letterbox makes me jump. *'Shhh,'* I hiss at the door as I leap over the creaky floorboards, mapped out like uncracked paving stones in my mind, to collect the morning paper. *'Do you want to get me in trouble?'* I suspect Evan will take back the proposal, change his mind about wanting to marry me again, if he finds out that I can't locate the knives again. It's one of my many little foibles that niggle him.

November, 1990

At five minutes past 11 a.m. on the seventh of November, a tall, muscular man with a shaved back-and-sides Afro threw a pint of orange juice in my face.

I had been curled up, as usual on non-lecture days, in the big squashy armchair at the back of the college bar, beside the floor-to-ceiling windows that looked out over the college playing fields. I would sit in there, comforted by the smell of stale smoke, spilt alcohol and musty carpet, and read.

Until that moment, I thought I was safe, I thought no one knew where I was or who I was. I thought my shame had been buried and I could cautiously, carefully, start again, two hundred miles from the scene of my alleged crime.

But the splash of liquid on my face, hair and books told me otherwise. Told me to run before things got worse. People had spat at me in the street before, had written me hate mail, had crossed the road to avoid me, had threatened me with violence . . . and now it was starting up again. I leapt out of the chair and grabbed my belongings – my textbooks, room keys and purse – spread like a pack of splayed cards on the table, and ran. Not before I said, 'Sorry. Thank you. I'm sorry.' Not before I let him know that I wasn't enjoying myself, I hadn't forgotten, I hadn't really left it all behind.

'Wait!' I heard him call as I crossed the threshold. But I did not wait. I did not want to make it easy for him to finish off what he started.

Down the corridor, around the corner, out into the wide, paved courtyard, I ran. 'Please! Miss! Wait!' he called again but I sprinted on, heading for the safety of my room. I could hear his footsteps behind me, gaining on me, and I pushed myself harder, desperate to get to my room, desperate to shut and lock the door, to climb into bed and hide under the covers until he got bored and left me alone.

At the door to my halls, I worked as fast as I could to type in the five-digit code but as I hit the last number, his hand came down on my forearm, stopping me from turning the handle.

I tried to scream, but it was swollen and bloated from my run and stuck in my throat; then became firmly lodged into place by the fear of what was about to come.

'My God you can run,' he said, his chest heaving. 'Are you OK?' He pointed over his shoulder. 'I'm so sorry about back there.' He paused to catch his breath a little more. 'Whoa! Mad run! I thought . . . I'm sorry. I was coming over to see if you wanted a drink. I think of you as my reading partner because I always see you in there reading like I do. Thought I'd make contact. Turned into the wrong kind of contact, if you know what I mean.'

'You didn't do it on purpose?' I replied.

'Why would I do it on purpose?' he asked. 'What sort of sick person would do that on purpose?'

'You don't know who I am?' I searched his face for an answer that might be different from the one coming out of his mouth.

'Should I?' he asked with raised eyebrows.

'You don't know who I am,' I stated. I relaxed into that sentence, enjoying exactly what it meant: safety, anonymity.

'Tell me who you are, then, if I should know.'

'I'm nobody,' I said.

'Ri–ght,' he said carefully. 'So, are we cool? You're OK?'

I nodded at him. 'I'm OK.'

'Good. I can go back to my reading and not worry that I've traumatised you, yeah?'

I nodded again. 'Yeah.'

'Good. That's good.' He took a couple of steps away then said, 'What's your name?'

'Oh, um, well . . . um . . .'

'You don't know your own name?'

'I was just trying to work out if I should tell you my real name.'

'Fair enough.'

'It's Serena.'

'OK, Serena, I'll see you then.'

'Yeah, I'll see you.'

He'd walked a little distance away when he called over his shoulder: 'Oh, by the way, I'm Evan.'

'Bye, Evan,' I called. Under my breath I added, 'And thank you. Thank you so, so much.'

I tug the paper out of the door, knowing I should be grateful that the paperboy managed to get it *into* the door this time, mostly he stands at the gate and chucks it in the general direction of the door.

I go back to the kitchen, flicking through the paper even though Evan hates it when I do that. He likes to come to it afresh, without the pages mussed up by my fingers. On some level, that's probably why I do it: he tells me not to do something – asks, really – *asks* me not to do something and my brain tells me it wants to do nothing else but that thing. I can't help it. It's the same reason I've never been any good at diets – tell me I can't have a food and I want nothing but that food.

I'm halfway through the paper, flicking through the pages, when my eyes are dragged to the headline of the small picture-less square at the bottom of page five: SWEET TASTE OF FREEDOM FOR THE ICE CREAM GIRL. I lift the paper closer to my nose to be sure, to double-check I am really reading those words.

I stop in my tracks as ice-cold fingers with razorblade fingernails begin clawing at my heart, lungs and stomach. This is what it feels like when the past crops up unawares, when it will not stay dead and buried as it should be.

I read the words that go with the headline, and the tearing and ripping at my insides intensifies. This is what a heart attack feels like: what happens when your heart is overwhelmed by the secrets it carries and wants to let them out, hurting you in the process.

I read those words again and again and again. Life is all about scales, checks and balances, I sometimes think: every time something good happens, something awful will come along to even it out, to stop me being completely and blithely happy. I finally got my yearned-for proposal, so now she is back to haunt me.

Creak! of the top step sounds through the house, signalling the imminent arrival of someone I love and who does not know.

I can't be caught reading this. Even though there's no picture, there are two words that connect me to this, that would give me away and would unleash hell upon our small, ordinary lives.

I scrunch the paper in my hands and then run to the bin, hit the pedal and shove it in, down where it will not do any damage, down, down out of sight. I'll have to tell Evan the paperboy didn't deliver it or something; I'll have to go back on my promise to never lie – not to others, not to myself. But if it's a choice between a small white lie or the end of everything, I *have* to lie. Show me a person who wouldn't and I'll show you someone who has never lived through hell.

The weight of the tread of the footsteps tells me it's Evan. I pick up the stainless steel kettle, dash to the sink, and manage to turn on the tap before he wanders into the kitchen.

'Morning, wife-to-be-again,' he says. I'm sure he's smiling but I cannot turn to check, I cannot face him until I have composed myself, rearranged my expression so he can't tell something is wrong.

'Morning, you,' I say, bright and breezy. There is an extra forced note of happiness in my voice, but if he notices, he doesn't mention it. 'Ready for another day at the coalface?'

He sucks in his breath. 'Ooooh, not quite. Coffee, toast, smoothie. Then I might consider it.' I hear him rub the slight paunch that appears whenever he sits down or slouches. 'Actually, I could murder cheese on toast.'

Murder. The word echoes and pulsates in my mind and in the deepest recesses of my chest. *Murder, murder, murder.*

'Really thin slices of cheese. Dash of Worcester sauce.'

'You know where toaster is,' I say, playing for time. Knives. Where are the knives? *Where?*

'Sez?'

16

'Yes?' I reply.

'Look at me, please.'

I take an extra deep breath and turn to face my husband. He is a year older than me, on his way to forty, but with very few wrinkles to show for it, because, I often tell him, he's lived an easy life. His eyes are fringed by long black eyelashes, while his mouth is almost always ready with a smile. He has smooth, dark brown skin and has been through more hair-styles than me until settling on a close-cut shave all over. Once, Conrad convinced him to get an 'E' shaved into the back of his head. Our son, seven at the time, had thought it pretty cool, while I'd been amazed he'd done it. He was actu-ally going to keep it until I reminded him that most people don't expect their GPs to be walking adverts for dance drugs. The pair of them had looked at me as if I had named the drug ecstasy just to stop Evan being really cool and 'down with the kids'.

'Yes, how can I help you?' I ask him.

'Where are the knives?'

'Pardon?'

'I need to make cheese on toast; where are the knives?'

'They're um . . .' I stop speaking in the hope something else will take over and speak for me, that God will send an angel to put the right words in my mouth.

'You don't know, do you?' he says, as he observes me. I imagine that several patients who have tried to pull a fast one have wilted under the pressure of that look.

I sigh. Tut. Shake my head. All the while praying that some-thing will come to me. Or something will happen to rescue me. 'They're . . .'

Creak! at the top of the stairs interrupts me.

'Oh, is that the kids?' I say happily.

Evan's right eyebrow rises at me. 'Saved by the creak, huh?' he says.

Con wanders into the kitchen, rubbing one eye and tugging at the bottom of his red and blue pyjama top. My eight-year-old is usually a bundle of energy, constantly needing reminding to slow down. To look at him now, you'd be forgiven for thinking he spends most of his time asleep or slumped in front of the goggle box.

'Vee woke me up,' he complains as he rests his head on my stomach. 'She's singing. She's always singing, Mum. Make her stop.'

'I'll try, sweetie,' I say, running my hand over the smooth bristles of his shaved hair. It's good to hold him, to be able to anchor myself in the present with him. He is real. He is here. The soft shapes of him – his slender limbs and lean body – tell me this is my life, this is who I am. I am here, everything else is not.

'Your mother was just about to tell me where the knives are,' Evan informs our son.

Con lifts his head and rests his chin on my solar plexus so he can gaze up at me with eyes that are almost identical to Evan's. When he was a baby, people used to comment on the size of his eyes and the length of his lashes wherever we went. They are beautiful and large and open. Honest. 'Did you lose them again, Mum? Is Dad going to shout at you?'

'Noooo, Dad's not going to shout at me because I didn't lose them,' I say with a defiant look at my husband.

'So, where are they?' Evan counters.

'They're . . .'

Another creak sounds at the top of the stairs, this time followed by the skipping sounds of Verity coming to join us.

She has been unusually chipper these days. Skipping, singing, cheerily doing her kitchen chores – even offering to help Con with his. I suspect there's a boy involved, which does not make me feel good. Or happy. I'm waiting for the right time to broach the matter with her because she is too young for boys. She's not allowed to wear make-up, to stay out late, to go away with her friends, to have an email address that we don't have access to, to have a mobile phone number she can give to friends. But still, somehow . . .

The three of us watch her coming through the kitchen

doorway, tall and slender, hair pulled back into three connected ponytails that go from her forehead to the nape of her neck, wearing her pink dressing gown tied-up and nothing on her feet.

'What?' She stops just over the threshold. 'What have I done now?' she asks, aggrieved. 'Nothing, that's what. So why are you all staring at me like I've done something?'

'You haven't done a thing, sweetheart,' Evan says. 'We were just marvelling at how your arrival has stopped your mother telling us where the knives are.'

Verity's large brown eyes swing dramatically to me. 'Oh, Mum, you *didn't*!'

'Didn't what?' I ask.

'Forget where you put the knives, *a–gain*!'

'No, I didn't.'

'So, where be they?' Evan asks.

'They're . . . They're . . .'

'OH MY GOD!' Verity suddenly screeches. 'WHAT IS *THAT*?!'

We are trying to recover from the first screech when she continues, 'ON YOUR FINGER, MUM! WHAT IS THAT?'

Verity's screeches are up in the realms of dog whistles, and really quite painful to someone who is tired, hungover and under a serious amount of pressure.

'Oh, my engagement ring. Do you like it?' I hold out my hand for her to take a closer look. 'Your father asked me to marry him again last night and I said yes.'

'I was thinking we could do it on the twenty-fifth of June,' Evan says.

'Ah, so only one anniversary to remember? Yeah, good one,' I say to him. 'I'll still expect two cards and two presents, you cheapskate.'

'Wait, you're actually going to get married? With a ceremony and everything?' Verity asks.

'Of course,' Evan and I say at the same time.

'It's going to be huge,' Evan continues. 'Wedding dress, co-ordinated bridesmaids outfits, big cars . . . the lot.'

Verity rolls her eyes. 'Why can't you just be like other people's parents? They don't do this sort of thing.'

'Other people's parents clearly don't love each other as much as we do,' I explain, hoping she leaves it there, that she doesn't go over to the dark side of teenage stroppiness because she will be opening up a whole world of trouble for herself.

'You'll just show me up in front of everyone,' she says. 'Why can't this family just be normal for once?'

I feel Evan bristle a second or two after me.

'And that's the end of Verity Gillmare's performance of "Sulky Teen",' I say. 'We're going to get nice, polite Verity back now. And she's going to apologise for all the things she's just said.' I smile at my daughter. She knows that I've just stopped her from having her iPod taken away for a week, or having limited access to the computer. Evan has a zero-tolerance policy on backchat and rudeness, and I do not want the day to start with a battle between them. I just want this day to go back to being the lovely day after I was proposed to.

Verity stares down at her bare feet and starts to wriggle her toes as the atmosphere in the kitchen grows ever-thicker and more tense. Conrad has stopped breathing while his little heart is racing against my body. He's scared that if Verity is banned from television, has her computer taken away or is sent to bed as soon as she comes home from school, it'll mean the same for him; he'll be a victim of the fallout she caused.

'Sorry,' she mumbles.

'What was that? Did the little mouse speak? I can't hear her if she did,' I joke. 'Come on little mouse, squeak up.'

Despite herself, she smiles a little as she looks up and says, 'Sorry Mum, sorry Dad.'

'Good girl,' I say. 'Now come on all of you, sit down. We need breakfast and then to get this show on the road.'

'Knives?' Evan asks.

'Living room magazine rack,' I say without thinking. That was the problem all along, of course – thinking too much.

Almost imperceptibly, Evan's mouth and left eyebrow twitch.

He is thinking that Con could have found them, played with them, hurt himself.

'Before you say anything, the magazine rack is on top of the cupboard in the spare bedroom.'

'Of course,' he says and shakes his head in despair. 'Where else would they be? I'll go get them, shall I?'

'Right, so what do you want for breakfast?' I ask. 'Your dad will probably drop you off today on his way in.' I cannot leave the house to do my normal things for fear of someone seeing me and remembering. Those sorts of incidental news items in the paper are the things that jog people's minds; make them realise that you don't just 'have one of those faces', they really do remember you from somewhere. And that somewhere is somewhere you'd rather they forgot. 'And you can buy your lunches today, but no sugary or sweet stuff.'

'Mum, it's Saturday,' Conrad says.

Saturday? That's news to me. 'Oh,' I say.

'You did know that, didn't you?' Verity asks, her voice and attitude no longer surly, more incredulous and concerned.

'Course I did, just trying to keep you on your toes.' I give Con a quick squeeze. 'Come on, sweetheart, sit down at the table while I start breakfast. Dad's doing Saturday morning surgery.'

I turn back to the sink and try to calm myself. Forgetting the day of the week is normal after the heavy session of last night. Everyone knows I can't drink very much. So this . . . this memory lapse means nothing. It's not like before. That was then, this is now and this is nothing like then. All of us forget things every now and again.

All of us do it.

poppy

KILLER SMILE?

Poppy Carlisle, one of the teenagers currently known as The Ice Cream Girls, is to give evidence today at her trial for her part in the murder of teacher Marcus Halnsley.

Carlisle, 18, who gained her nickname after she appeared scantily clad, smiling and eating ice cream with her co-defendant Serena Gorringe, denies killing her former lover, Mr Halnsley. She and Gorringe allege there had been an accident following a fight that left Mr Halnsley with what they thought was a fatal wound. However, police revealed evidence that Mr Halnsley had several cuts to his torso, possibly the result of torture, and that he ultimately died from being stabbed in the heart.

Although Carlisle's fingerprints were found on the knife, she denies murder and is expected to claim, while in the witness box, that Gorringe returned to Mr Halnsley's house and killed him to frame her.

Daily News Chronicle, October 1989

poppy

The sky isn't a square of patchwork quilt. Sometimes with two or three black bars running down it, sometimes with wire mesh upon it. The sky is vast and deep and capable of smothering me.

For a very long time I thought the sky was that square of patchwork quilt because it was all I could see from most of the prison cells I've lived in.

Even when I went outside for exercise periods, to go from one part of the prison to another, to go to court for appeals, I would stop just to look up, and I would see how big it was. But at the same time, I would know it was just an illusion, a trick my mind was playing on me because I was allowed outside and everything *had* to look bigger because it seemed so small in the confines of my room.

Now, now the sky is a canopy that stops the planet falling against the sun and the moon. Now, today, I know the sky is immense and colossal, and I could drown in it. I'd forgotten how big the world is. And how blue the sky is. And how bright the daytime is.

I take my first steps outside Portslade station, on the outskirts of Brighton, and marvel at how crowded the world is. Titanic sky, gigantic world, dazzling daylight, swarming streets.

No one else notices these things of course, it is all absolutely normal to them.

★

'You're going to find it strange out there,' my parole officer had said. 'You haven't been to an open prison and had the chance to get out for a little while, like most people in your situation, so it's . . . it's going to be tough.' He was a surprisingly pleasant man – in his early fifties with a kindly nature. What he was saying without uttering the exact words was, 'Everyone is surprised that you, Poppy Carlisle, are getting out.' I would not admit my crime because I did not do it, I would not show remorse because I did not do it, and I would not beg any longer for someone to believe me. But, for whatever reason, they agreed my parole at the last minute, so the prison did not have time to put me through the usual procedures. I would be released into the big wide world as I was – unprepared and unaware. 'Here's my card, call me – any time – if you need help with finding work, or need a reference, or even if you're strug- gling. Any time,' he said. 'Any time.' He believed I was innocent, I was sure of it, but he couldn't say so officially, so he was trying to help in any way he could. Nice, but ultimately pointless.

Where have all these people come from? I ask myself as I wander past the level crossing beside the station and head for the sea. I'd love to head down to the beach, dip my toes in the water, feel the pebbles under my feet, but I need to do this other thing now. Any longer, any delays, and I might bottle it.

People think that prisons are overcrowded, but *this* is over- crowded. This is like being trapped inside a swarm of insects. Everyone so close and big and moving, moving, moving. When you're banged up, you expect to feel as if there are too many people encroaching on your space and you accept that you have no choice in the matter. Out here, people have chosen this. They've chosen this life.

'Sorry,' a woman says as she bumps into me. Immediately my hackles rise and I curl a fist, just in case . . . 'Really sorry,' she adds absently then rushes on without a second glance.

The house I'm looking for is quite near the station and even though I haven't been there for nearly two decades, I could find it with my eyes closed. Well, I thought I could. This street, Boundary Road, was here, but most of the shops weren't back then. There certainly wasn't a computer games shop, nor an organic bakery-slash-café. Nor *all these people*. At the bottom of the high street, I turn towards Brighton, towards Hove. It seems weird, being surrounded by all these buildings and cars and pavements. I've seen them all on the telly, of course, but they're different in the flesh. Bigger, smaller, more solid, less real – all of those things, all at once.

A woman my age, or thereabouts, walks towards me. She has the same mud-black hair as me, and hers is a crop like mine; she is my height and about my weight. She even has similar soft features to me. She is the real-life version of the reflection I saw in the train window every time we went through a tunnel. I watch her come towards me, and then pass me without even noticing me. I, on the other hand, stop on the pavement to turn to watch her.

I bet she chose her crop because she liked it, not because her life didn't allow her to shampoo, condition and look after long, shoulder-length locks. I bet her make-up came from a shop where the assistant helped her choose the right shade for her colouring – it probably didn't arrive in a clear plastic bag that was embossed with HMP Trembry Hall and also contained cigarettes, stamps and phonecards. I bet she's that thin because she's chosen it, not because years of prison food have drastically cut her weight. I bet that flimsy pink jacket she's wearing was chosen because it's pretty and suits her, not because it has to last several years and it's one of the limited number of outfits she's allowed. I bet those black shiny shoes with heels like spikes pinch her feet and make her miserable, but she wears them because they're gorgeous and she can – she isn't forbidden them because they're impractical and could be turned into a weapon.

I do not belong in this world any more, I realise as I stop staring at the woman who could be me in another life, and start to walk on. *I do not know how to be here, with all these things*. All these things that were like science fiction on TV are now real and life-like. And unsettling.

I make my way up to Surry Hills Street, and suddenly the nerves are at me again. They nibbled at me all last night as I waited for morning, and they started to take bigger bites at my last breakfast (which prison folklore said I had to choke down to make sure I never went back). As I took my first steps into the outside world the nerves sank their teeth right into my core and began ripping at my chest and stomach. I'd had to stand very still and let them feast on me as I looked around, at the grey-yellow bricks behind me, the steady grey road ahead of me, wondering if I should turn around and knock on the gate and ask them to let me back in.

Once I decided there was no going back I'd wrestled the nerves into submission, then concentrated on getting myself across London and down to the coast.

Now that I am here, my mission has been achieved, the nerves are back, jabbing and biting into every square inch of my body.

I stop outside number thirty-four, stare at the sage-green door with its shiny brass knocker and black and white rectangular doorbell.

I am terrified of what is behind the green door. About what will happen when I knock and the door is opened. I am terrified, but I *have* to do this.

There are thirteen steps from the pavement to the door.

I raise the knocker and hit it.

It takes sixty-seven seconds for the door to be answered.

And it takes one second for the look of recognition to appear.

'Poppy,' she says.

'Hello, Mum,' I reply.

serena

Everyone gasps when I push aside the pink velvet curtain and step out into the viewing area.

Everyone – the saleswoman, her assistant and a couple of other brides-to-be – except Verity, who wouldn't dare be that expressive. She simply glances down after studying me for a few seconds, but I spotted the pride and delight in her eyes. She can't hide those sorts of things from me – from everyone else, maybe, but not me.

'You look . . .' The saleswoman's voice fades away. 'There aren't words,' she finishes. Then, somehow, finds them: 'White is so gorgeous against dark skin, don't you think?'

Her assistant nods in agreement. Although still looking down, I see Verity's fresh, young face scrunch up as she goes, '*Huh*?!' in her head. She's so young, I remind myself. She does not know that people say that sort of thing all the time. I like that she's innocent, untouched and still able to be surprised by the world at large. I'd like my thirteen-year-old to stay that way for as long as possible, if I'm honest. Book smart, street stupid. But then, being street stupid is how people are able to take advantage of you.

She's come round to the idea of us getting 'married' again: after a few days of sulking she decided that it wasn't so bad, especially since she could choose her own dress.

In the wall of mirrors in the bridalwear boutique, I am

reflected back at myself ten times – 360 degrees of me. I've never seen myself so completely before. No matter where I look, there I am. My tall, slenderish frame, my straight black hair pulled back into a low ponytail at the base of my neck, my make-up-free face. There I am. It's unnerving. Especially as I can also see the blood on my hands. It's dripping off my hands, off my fingers on to the beautiful top layer of satin silk. Everywhere it drips it leaves a little rosette of red, creating more and more flowers, until the slim-fitting skirt that is gathered at the back is like a field of snow, topped with poppies. Each one is a pure and unrelenting red; each one a stain on my soul. Poppies are the sign of remembrance, aren't they? And this blood on my hands is saying that: *remember me*. It's as if *he* is standing beside me, dripping his blood on to my hands so it trickles on to the dress, while his deep, slightly gravelly voice is whispering through the smile on his face, 'Never forget, Serena. Always remember me.'

I wonder if the saleswoman will mind if I rip this thing to shreds to get it off me? I wonder if Evan will mind if I say I don't want to jinx my life any more by getting married again?

June, 1992

For nearly two years Evan and I were on nodding terms after he threw his drink on me. We'd see each other in the bar on Friday nights, in the corridors, in the pubs in town, sometimes just in the street. We'd nod and mutter, 'All right?' at each other as we passed, never finding the need to stop and talk. Then, one day, he stopped when we passed each other on the high street.

'I'm leaving in a couple of days,' he said at me to get me to stop.

'Leaving?' I replied, surprised that he'd initiated conversation.

'Yeah, I've finished college. I'm going to medical school in London.'

'Right,' I said. 'Well, good luck.'

'Thanks.'

We stood in an awkward silence for a few seconds. He hadn't thought it through when he spoke to me, hadn't formulated an escape plan when he opened his mouth and now we were both stuck, like flies on flypaper – desperate to get away but unable to free ourselves.

'So . . .' he said.

'So . . .' I said.

I linked my hands together and started to pick at my left thumbnail with my right thumbnail. *'Just walk away,'* a voice inside my head said. *'I can't,'* another voice replied. *'That would be rude.'*

'So's murder,' the first voice said.

My head snapped up to look at him, our gazes collided and a spark ignited between us.

'You know,' he said. 'I've been trying to work out for ages if I fancy you or not.'

'Right,' I replied.

He shook his head. 'I don't think I do.'

'OK,' I said, thinking, *That's a good thing, because as sure as eggs is eggs I don't fancy you. Apart from a minute ago.*

'Shame really,' he said. 'Because I think we'd really get on if we got together.'

'OK. How do you know that, then?'

He shrugged. 'I just get that feeling. You seem like the sort of girl I could take home to meet my mother.'

'Why does that sound like an insult?' I said.

'It's not. You just seem nice, that's all. Bit of a laugh, good personality, nothing offensive about you. My parents would love you.'

'Well, that's good to know – some random boy's parents would love me. I can rest really easy now that I know that.'

He smiled and something lust-like somersaulted in my stomach, then danced lightly up and down my spine.

'Do you want to give it a try?' he asked me.

'What, meeting your parents? No thank you. I'm sure they're perfectly lovely, but blind parent-dates really aren't my thing.'

'I meant going out together. Do you want to give going out with me a go?'

'No, not really,' I replied.

Evan looked taken aback, and marginally offended. 'Why not?'

'Just not that interested in going out with anyone.'

'Bad break-up?'

'Probably the worst break-up of all time,' I said.

'Oh.'

'And I'm sort of staying away from all that for a while. A long, long while.'

'Right.'

'And, just so you know for the next girl you ask out, saying that you're not sure if you fancy her and then saying you think your parents would like her probably won't pass for sweet talk. Some women might like it, but most of them would be offended.'

'Yeah, you're probably right. But you're sure I can't change your mind? Not even for the sake of my poor parents who think I'm never going to make them grandparents?'

I laughed as I shook my head. 'Especially not for them.'

'OK, well, if you change your mind, you can always . . .'

'Knock on the door of every medical school in London and ask for Evan?'

He laughed, a smooth, throaty laugh that sent the whooooo-hooooo feeling up and down my spine again. 'I'll see you, Serena,' he said, a smile still on his face.

'I'll see ya.'

'And every time I think about missed opportunities, I'll think of you.'

'OK,' I replied and, this time, I had no problems walking away.

'Why are you getting married again, Mum?' Verity asks as we head back home in the car. She is sitting up front and could easily pass for being my younger sister she is that grown-up looking. Often, I try to remember what it was like to be thir-teen, to try to tap into what she might be feeling and thinking, but my memory – fuzzy and haphazard at the best of times – lets me down, it blurs itself into a haze of waving my older sis-ters – Medina and Faye – off to uni, watching *The A-Team* and doing a paper round. I cannot remember how I felt about any-thing, how I felt about my parents, what big secrets I was determined to hide. I remember what it was like to be an older teenager, though, and sometimes I have to stop myself from tarring Verity with the brush of those experiences.

But then, aren't most teenagers more grown-up more quickly these days? Shouldn't I be extra vigilant now because she might fast forward to being me a little bit earlier? This is the battle I have with myself, trying to balance protecting her as a mother should, and protecting her as *this* mother knows from experience she should.

I take time to consider her question as I pull out of the roundabout on to the A26, the road back from Uckfield to Brighton. *Why are we getting married again?* 'Because we can, I suppose.'

'Don't most people just renew their vows and have a party? Why are you almost pretending that you're not even married?'

'Because we're not,' I say jokingly.

I feel Verity's eyes widen, I hear her heart almost leap out of her chest as she gasps. 'You're lying!' she screeches, almost burst-ing an eardrum. Somewhere nearby dogs are whining. 'Tell me you're lying!'

'I'm not lying, I'm joking,' I say to end Vee's sonic mode before it brings on a migraine. 'I'm joking, I'm joking.' I want to ask her what would be the big deal if we weren't actually married, but that's a conversation I should not get started with a teenager. *Especially* not a *teenager.*

'I suppose we're getting married big this time because we couldn't do it on this scale before,' I say. 'We couldn't afford to. We were so young, but we really wanted to get married, so we did it. I suppose it was an unspoken thing that that one was the first wedding and at some point in the future we'd do the big one.' I'd love to tell her the whole truth, but how can I tell her that we only got married when we did because I was up the duff, and I was up the duff because we'd had a contraceptive malfunction? How can I tell her that and not expect in, say, two years' time for her to come to me asking for my blessing to move in with her older, tattooed, long-haired boyfriend who plays drums in a band and who is expecting her to leave school and get a job so she can support his 'art' while they live in a glorified squat in Kemptown? And how can I not expect, when I protest, for her to throw, 'Well, you were pregnant before you got married and only got married because you had to' back in my face?

When it comes to my teenage daughter, I am a hypocrite and I don't pretend to be anything other than that.

I continue, 'And, besides, you get to be there,' *even though you were technically at the last one*, 'and so does Con. We have the chance to get married with all our family there. So, in that sense, we are actually doing it for the first time. You know?'

From the corner of my eye, I see her nod.

I check the rear-view mirror and my blindspot before I indicate and pull out into the right-hand lane. I hit the accelerator to get past the blue Micra proudly displaying a green 'P' on its rump and keeping a steady ten miles below the speed limit. New drivers like that make me nervous. I always suspect they're going to do something crazy for no other reason than that they don't know any better, so I always speed past them and get away as soon as possible.

I check the rear-view mirror again to make sure there's nothing too close behind me as I go to pull back into the left-hand lane when I see the blue lamp of a police car. As always, even after all these years, anxiety spikes in my chest cavity. I cannot help it, the police make me nervous. Always.

The light flashes on suddenly, and I have to tear my eyes away from it in the rear-view mirror to concentrate on the road ahead.

'They're coming for you, Mum,' Vee says, copying what her dad says every time we see the police. If Con was here, he'd say it too. None of them have ever noticed that I *never* laugh, I never even smile. I tug at the corner of my mouth and say nothing, allow the joke to wash over me and pretend I don't know that the police may very well be coming for me.

I hold on to the steering wheel for dear life, and concentrate on the road and pulling safely back into the left-hand lane. *It's all right, they're not here for me,* I think to calm myself, even though the siren is whipping up the anxiety that darts around my chest like a bird that's accidentally flown through an open window and can't find its way out again. *They've got an emergency to get to; a real criminal to arrest.*

The police car surges forwards, but instead of speeding off down the road, it keeps level with our car. *Oh God.*

I risk a look across and the policeman in the passenger seat points to the side of the road. *'Pull over,'* he's indicating. *'At the first safe spot, pull over.'*

'Mum,' Vee hisses in alarm, her eyes probably wide like saucers.

'I know,' I say, sounding calm and in control. Not at all as if I'm contemplating putting my foot down and making a run for it.

I look over again, hoping that he's made a mistake.

The finger is still pointing to the side of the road, still ordering me to pull over. His face is a little more set, a little more angry now, the shape of his mouth an unimpressed line, his eyes hard, unamused pebbles in his face.

Oh God.

I can almost feel the handcuffs closing around my wrists again; the smell of a police cell is not one you can ever forget.

I hit the left indicator and start to look for a place to pull over. Once I do, once he comes striding over to me and asks for my licence and then types my name into his computer or says it over the radio, the truth will come out. He'll find out who I really am. And so will Vee.

poppy

Where am I?

I have been waking up every hour or so all night and each time I think the same thing: *where am I?* It's the quiet that wakes me. Drags me from sleep, wondering what is wrong, what is amiss, what has happened to stop the world being so loud.

My eyes would dart around the room, looking for familiar shapes – the sink in the corner, the metal toilet, my locker, my noticeboard, the window high up on the wall – and each time I didn't see them, my heart would flutter and panic. Then the memory would settle on my mind that I was out, I was free, there was no need to panic. I've been doing that all night. Maybe not even every hour, probably more often. I didn't think I'd ever get used to prison when I first got there, but now the world feels weird not having all the noise and the creak of metal, the permanent chill that hangs in the air. Cotton sheets, a thick mattress, curtains on the windows, carpet under foot – all luxuries I've practically forgotten exist to everyday people.

October, 1989

It was so loud.

Everything seemed so loud. Even from the hospital bed where they put me first of all – suicide watch, apparently – everything seemed so loud. And now, in my single cell, which

I got because I was as notorious inside as I was outside, it was so loud. Every second crammed to its brim with noise, even in the dead of night it did not stop.

I lay on my bed with my eyes wide open, the blackness of my tenth lights-out in this room sitting on my chest, swirling in my throat, scoring at my eyes. I reached up to touch my eyes, just to reassure myself that they were open, because I could not always tell. Sometimes I would think I had fallen asleep, and that the darkness was a part of that. Sometimes I would think that if I had my eyes open and it was this black, I could close them and open them and everything would be back to normal. I would not be in this box, I would not be drowning in blackness.

'Ohhhhhhhhhhhhhhhhh,' it was a loud keening, this time. My eyes had been drifting shut and they snapped open at the sound that was tearing through the landings and crawling through the sliver of space at the bottom and around the viewing hatches in the doors. This time keening, other times sobbing, other times the shouting of friendships separated by bang-up at the end of the day, other times the slam of prison vans, other times arguing, other times the sound of flesh on flesh, other times the dull swallowing of anti-depressants. Always there was noise and always it went straight through you, stampeded to your core and reminded you where you were in case, for a brief moment, you managed to forget.

'Ohhhhhhhhhhhhhhhhhhhhhhhhhhhhhhhhhhh,' the keening continued.

I wanted to tell the silly cow to shut up. That we were all in the same boat. That just because she had children she wasn't going to see for a while, or maybe she was innocent, or maybe she'd gone to court not expecting to be sent straight here, didn't mean that she was worse off than the rest of us. Didn't mean she could cry and wail so loudly that everyone in the prison could hear her.

'Ohhhhhhhhhhhhhhhhhhhhhhhhhhhhhhhhhhhhhhhhh,' she persisted, so loud and constant I had to raise my hands and slam them on my ears. I often did that when I heard someone telling how she'd hurt the person who was abusing her children, or abusing her, and now she wouldn't be seeing her children outside of these walls for years; or someone was saying that she'd just not paid a fine and now she was stuck here for six months and her other debts would be building up. I never wanted to hear that because I had only just begun my life here and I did not want to hear how other people had been wronged, too. And I did not want to hear this cry of a wounded animal. It was probably reality setting in. That hideous moment when they finally realised that even if they were innocent, or were going to appeal their sentence, they would be here for a long time. It's a moment you never forget. And it makes you cry out in pain. Or turn inwards, and think about doing yourself harm to make the reality an unreality.

'Ohhhhhhhhhhhhhhhhhhhhhhhhhhhhhhhhhhhhhhhhhhhh-hhhhhhhhhhhhh,' the noise went on. 'Ohhhhhhhhhhhhhhh-hhhhhhhhhhhhhhhhhhhhhhhhhhhhhhh.' I pressed my hands harder over my ears, but I could still hear this woman, this wounded animal, whoever she was. And her noise was filling up my cell. 'Ohhhhhhhhhhhhhhhhhhhhhhhhhhhhhhhhhhhhhhhhhh.'

'OI! ICE CREAM GIRL!' bellowed a voice from somewhere. 'SHUT UP! Some of us are trying to sleep.'

'Ohhhhhhhhhhhhhhhhhhhhhhhhhhhh.' It was me. I was making that noise. I was the wounded animal. It was me who had been hit with reality. It was me showing the outside world inside these prison walls that I was in agony and I was scared and I was here for ever.

It was me being so loud.

It was me. And I didn't know how to stop.

Water falls on my skin like a hundred thousand little kisses, each one firm and warm and perfect.

I lather my arms again – the third time – and immerse myself further in the extravagance of a shower with temperature control and strength above a dribble. It beats down on me like a relentless rain, the type that used to clean the windows in Trembry Hall, and I am revelling in it. I could spend the whole day in this cubicle, reacquainting myself with the finer points of washing. Sometimes we weren't given access to the shower for three or four days; we had to make do with the sink in the corner, using our towels as flannels and washing over ourselves as quickly as possible to stop from freezing to death.

Staying in this shower, washing off the last twenty years inside, is helpful, too, because I don't really know what I'm going to do next. I mean literally, after this shower, what do I do next? Every day for more than twenty years has been structured, regimented, with a time for everything. Now I am free, I can do as I please. And I'm not sure how. In my head, in my wildest dreamings, I had thought I would spend the day with Mum and Dad. We would sit down and talk, eat, drink, catch up on all the missing years. They'd even call my sister, Bella, and my brother, Logan, get them to come over and we'd catch up as a family. In my reality, in the life I was *actually* living . . . I shudder as I think about yesterday.

When Mum opened the door, I expected a rush of emotion from one of us. I expected to want to throw my arms around her, to hold her close in the hope that she would do the same to me. I expected to want to bury my face in the soft crease of her neck and cry. Really cry. Cry my aches inside out. Wash away the years with tears, have her dry them with sympathy and understanding and being my mum.

Instead, a barrier rose between us the second she opened the door.

'Poppy,' she'd said.

'Mum,' I said. The word was unfamiliar in my mouth, since I had not said it in so very long.

'What are you doing here?' she asked. Her eyes scanned behind me, and I realised she was checking to see if any of their neighbours in the identical thirties semis along the road were looking, and she was checking to see if the Old Bill were lurking somewhere ready to haul me back to the nick.

The barrier, wide and solid and invisible, rooted itself even more firmly into the ground and thickened. Not only did she think I had escaped, she also thought me to be stupid. If I had done a bunk, this would have been the first place the Old Bill would have looked so why would I turn up here?

'They let me out. Remember? I wrote to you? Told you I was coming out? Asked if it was OK to stay with you until I got back on my feet?'

'I don't think I got the letter,' she'd said. Her face said, *'Did you really write to me or are you lying to me, which will lead to me being arrested for helping you?'*

'It wasn't returned to me, so I presumed you'd got it.'

'You should have called to double-check,' she said.

'I would have if, when you changed your number ten years ago, you'd given me the new one.'

The wrinkled skin on her neck and the smoother skin on her high cheekbones coloured up at that, while she dropped her gaze from looking just left of my head to down at her feet. She was hesitating, waiting . . . Waiting, I realised, for me to leave. She would not ask me to, but she was hoping I would. I had nowhere else to go, except possibly under the arches down on Brighton seafront. 'You'd better come in,' she eventually said.

I'd stepped in, and experienced a rush of memories of tearing over this threshold as a child on a visit to my nan, barrelling into the living room and almost knocking over Granny Morag I was so excited to see her. She was my favourite person in the world after my dad, and coming here was always the biggest treat on earth. When she had a fall fifteen years ago, my parents had moved in to take care of her, and then stayed after she died two years later.

'You can put your things upstairs,' she said, unable to disguise her disgust at the clear HMP Trembry Hall plastic bags and the tatty holdall I'd got from a prison volunteer that held all my worldly possessions. 'You can stay in the room you used to sleep in.'

Her voice did not prepare me for what I found in 'the room I used to sleep in'. It was *exactly* the same as I left my bedroom at the end of the eighties, when I was still a stupid teenager who wanted to be Madonna and thought she'd marry Don Johnson. Except it had been transported from London to here. Everything was exactly as I remembered leaving it: the single bed with the blue-sky-white-cloud pattern over brown nylon sheets; the hulking, mahogany veneer wardrobe that sat to the left of the window; the tatty white with gold edging dressing table that had a neat line of unicorns with coloured manes along the back edge under the mirror; my Madonna-inspired chunky silver crucifix that hung over the corner of the mirror, next to a picture of the lady herself, all in black, chains and chains around her neck, a black bow tying back her shaggy hair. Even the posters – Madonna, *Miami Vice*, Michael Jackson, Prince, Adam Carrington from *Dynasty* – seemed to have been put up in exactly the same place.

This is what they would have done if I had died, I thought to myself as I moved slowly across the room and sat on the bed, looking around, trying to take it all in. *This is what they have done because, in their minds, I did die.* When the verdict was read out in court, and I was found guilty of murder, I died to them. I had been slipping away from them as the trial unfolded and they found out more and more about me; more and more that told them I was no longer their little girl. And when the word 'guilty' was proclaimed, I flatlined. I passed away. I was gone, but the little girl who had created this room lived on, and they could survive quite happily with these things because they belonged to the girl who wasn't a slut, who wasn't a liar, who wasn't a murderer.

As I discovered more and more things that had been replaced exactly as they had been twenty years ago – the LCD clock radio on the gold-edged white bedside table, my line of mix tapes on the shelf in the bedside table, my stainless steel digital watch hanging on the corner bedpost – I thought: *this is what it feels like to be dead to someone.*

Soft white towels that smell of flowers. They have to go on my ever-growing list of everyday extravagances. I wrap this giant one around me, breathing in and breathing in and breathing in until I become high on the scent of the towels.

I'd had a shower yesterday, but a quick one, feeling guilty for being in their house when they weren't expecting me, feeling unnerved to be back in that room. I also wanted to go down and try to talk to Mum. If I left it too long to try to break through that barrier that had arisen between us it might become stronger, harder to traverse. By the time I had found something to wear that wasn't so obviously from the eighties it told the world I had been 'away' for some time and fit my now-thinned frame, and wasn't from my prison bags, and descended the stairs, Mum had gone. She left a note saying she and Dad were out for the rest of the day and all evening – it'd been planned for a while – and they'd see me in the morning. And PS, I could have the shepherd's pie that had just finished cooking in the oven for my lunch and dinner if I was hungry.

The half-drunk cup of tea on the kitchen table, the half-folded laundry sitting in the washing basket by the washing machine, and the open door of the dishwasher all told me that she had left in a hurry. She was that desperate to escape from me, the dead daughter who was not meant to come back, she had left her housework unfinished.

I eventually found the plates, heaped on the shepherd's pie, and then took my meal outside. The temperature had dropped dramatically since I had arrived, but I still settled myself at the mildew-covered white plastic table at the bottom of the garden, and ate the too-hot food. Then I sat and smoked a pack of cigarettes, watching the sky, watching the climbing vines on the walls, listening to the neighbours going about their business, immersing myself in the outside world until my fingers and limbs were so cold and achy that I could hardly move them, and the only light came from the rectangles of orange-yellow thrown out by the kitchen door and window.

Eventually I stubbed out my last cigarette and went inside to go to bed, deciding to change the sheets on the bed for cotton ones. Still achy and cold, I washed up my plate and cutlery and water glass, then climbed the stairs feeling a little more like Poppy Carlisle again and a little less prisoner EX396798.

On the landing outside the bathroom, beside the huge picture window that lets light flood into the upstairs areas, I bump into him. Not literally – he is leaving their bedroom – I am leaving the bathroom, but our worlds have converged at this point.

He looks old. There is no other word for it, no other way to describe him. Mum had looked older, but he looks old. As if time has paid particular attention to him, ravaging him over and over until he is sixty-one but looks old.

His hair, although still neat and short, has thinned and disappeared on top, what is left is now almost completely white, with only a few darkish grey spots here and there. His handsome face has been softened and lined; his eyes, the colour of bluebells, are heavy and sad. Incredibly, painfully sad. A sadness that affects the set of his mouth, and hollows out two wells in his cheeks. His body always upright and strong – he was a muscular man who didn't seem to be physically intimidated by anything or anyone – now he seems to have shrunk, his shoulders hunch forwards a fraction and his limbs seem less solid. The shell of him, the man who he was, is different, but he is still him, still Dad. Mum used to tell me that when I was just learning to talk and he would leave the room, I'd stare at the door for ages, waiting for him to come back. And when I heard a noise outside the room, I would, in my baby voice, call, 'Daaaaaa!' Asking him to come back, asking him where he was and what he was doing without me. That was one of the few things she could accurately recall from my childhood, and I knew she was right because, in the entire world, the person I loved the most was my dad.

I have not seen him in twenty years, since the day of the verdict. In my heart, in my soul, I feel a tug, a desperate need to reach out and touch him. I want to feel his arm under my fingers so that I can confirm that he is real, I have not imagined him, and I am not going to lose him again when reality comes back to me. I smile at him, hesitantly, waiting for him to respond, react, notice me. While I was 'away' he could pretend I was not around, but here, in front of him, he has to at least acknowledge me – even if it is just to tell me to put some clothes on. The smallest contact is all I need.

However, I am a ghost. I am insubstantial and unreal. He looks straight through me, his eyes focusing beyond me, and then he continues on his path to the stairs and moves down them, out of sight.

I thought I had felt it when I saw my old room magicked down here, but really that feeling was nothing. *This* is what it's like to be dead to someone. *This* is what it's like to be a spectre in your own life.

serena

'Can you step out of the car, please, Madam?'

His voice is professional, but clipped. I didn't pull over soon enough and he's not happy. Maybe he thinks I was being defiant instead of just plain terrified. *How often do the police mistake terror and anxiety for criminal behaviour?* I wonder as I reach for the door handle.

My hands work remarkably well, all things considered. I can tell Verity is on the verge of bursting into tears. She's scared because I am, and she doesn't like to get into trouble or to see someone else in trouble. And I am, clearly, in trouble. My legs don't shake, my knees don't knock, as I swing my jeans-covered legs out of the car and plant my feet on to the concrete on the hard shoulder of the A26.

I'm only an inch shorter than the six-foot policeman and that surprises him for a minute.

'Licence?' he asks, his voice a little more clipped, I think, because I am not a small woman. As his eyes meet mine, I see a flashbulb of recognition pop in his eyes. He knows my face from somewhere, but he can't quite place me. I lower my head and reach back into the car.

'Pass my bag, please, love,' I say to my daughter who is trembling like a newborn foal.

She does as she's told and from my purse I produce my licence. It's not a new, photographic one – which would give

47

him more time to study my face, work out where he knows me from, if I am a fugitive on the run – but it does have my parents' address. This is the one thing I never got around to changing in all this time. I am an idiot.

He slips it out of its plastic wallet and unfolds it. He doesn't speak as he studies the green paper, only the buzz and whoosh of cars driving on by, going about their business, surrounds us. I think he is waiting for me to say something, to ask what the problem is, to confess to something.

Silence is the best way forward, I've found. I do not have to say anything, at least I didn't the last few times I was arrested, and I'm going to exercise that right. Even if it makes me look guilty as sin, I'd rather not say anything that can't be taken back. Silence can always be explained away, erased almost with a single word; the wrong words in the wrong combination at the wrong time can damn you to hell. Or, at least, to prison.

The cars continue to whiz by and I find myself comforted by them, allowing myself to float on the sound of them as they hurry by.

'Do you know how fast you were driving, Madam?' the police officer eventually asks because I haven't thrown myself on my knees, begging for mercy and I obviously have no intention of doing so.

'Um . . . no,' I reply. 'I speeded up to overtake the blue Micra. But only for a few seconds.'

'You were travelling well over eighty-five miles per hour for at least ten minutes.'

I was? 'Oh,' I reply. 'I didn't realise. I thought I was only going that fast to overtake. I never speed. I always try to drive safely.'

He is still studying my licence, still reading and re-reading my name, trying to join up the dots in his mind. When all the dots are joined, when he gets to the end of the puzzle, the policeman's face gives him away. It freezes in its inquisitive expression as everything falls into place and he connects the dot of my old name with the dot of my general description with the dot of my alleged crime. And there he has it: who the woman he's just pulled over is.

He recovers quickly, hides his shock behind a professional mask again, but, when he looks up at me from the licence, his eyes are piercing. They want to slap handcuffs on me and cart me off to jail where he – and quite a lot of people – think I belong. He appears, in the short time I have known him, to be the kind of man who would not advocate simply throwing away the only key – but melting it down, freezing it in liquid nitrogen, shattering it into a trillion pieces and having those pieces scattered all across the world's oceans just to make sure that they were never found, even accidentally, so one such as I could never be released.

'Is this your licence, Madam?'

'Yes. I haven't got around to updating it with my new address,' I say.

He raises his left eyebrow a little. *And new name?* he's trying to ask.

Correct, I think back at him. I will not say it, though. If he wants to know what I'm calling myself these days, he's going to have to work that bit harder.

He hands the licence back to me. 'You should get it updated. It's an offence to drive without a valid licence,' he says.

I nod at him. 'Yes, officer,' I say.

'I could breathalyse you and have you come down to the station for driving over the speed limit,' he says, just to watch me squirm, I'm guessing.

'Yes, officer,' I say. He is getting a thrill out of this. He's only human, after all. In his shoes, I might do the same thing. I might get some enjoyment out of 'paying back' someone I thought beat the system.

'I won't, *this time*.' He knows how to be professional and menacing in just the right proportions and it would worry me if not for Verity. My concern for her overrides my fear. She must be scared of this skin-deep Jekyll and Hyde impersonation he has going on. It's bound to be even more terrifying

49

because she doesn't know what is really happening here. 'I'd better not have occasion to stop you again,' he says. 'You won't be so lucky next time.' We both know what he means by that.

'Yes, officer,' I say. 'Thank you.'

As I shut my door behind me, I feel safe again. Protected from the prying outside world by a simple metal shell. I was lucky that time. If he had been the true menacing type, I would be heading for a cell. For a breathalyser, for a urine sample, for what feels like a catalogue of small humiliations only to receive a metaphorical slap on the wrist and to be sent on my way with no charge, not even a few lines scrawled on a page ripped out of a notebook. No record. That's happened to me about twenty times. I've been stopped in a car and recognised and then 'put in my place'. After each time, I vow to change my licence details, to make myself inconspicuous, but each time I forget. My defences kick in and I try not to think about it. I can't tell anyone – least of all Evan – about it, so I end up pretending it didn't happen . . . until next time.

This is the first time it's happened with someone else in the car. And poor Verity is still trembling.

'It's all right, sweetie,' I say, trying to hide how much I'm shaking as I slot the key into the ignition. 'Just a misunderstanding.'

'But why did he say all those things?' she asks, distressed. She looks every one of her thirteen years; no longer older and a little mature, now she looks like a little girl who needs a hug and a mountain-load of reassurance from her mother.

'He was just doing his job,' I say.

'But he said he was going to arrest you!' she wails.

'No, he didn't. He said – quite clearly – that he could arrest me, but he wasn't going to. It's fine.'

'It's like he knew you, Mum,' she says. 'It's like he knew you and he didn't like you. Why?'

I shrug my shoulders and shake my head. 'How could anyone not like me?' I say as I check my rear-view mirror and blindspot then indicate to pull out. 'I'm lovely.'

April, 1995

I was lost. Properly lost. I had parked my car around here somewhere while I went to the house to pick up the material for
Medina for her dressmaking course – although why she couldn't
do it herself was still a mystery – and now I couldn't find my way
back to my car. The material, which was light and floaty when
made into a chiffon dress, was heavy, bulky and unwieldy in
my arms in the quantities she'd bought it. The seller who had
put the small ad in the paper was obviously feeling aggrieved
with the hard bargain she had driven on the phone because he
hadn't offered to carry it to my car for me – he hadn't even
offered me a black binbag. It didn't surprise me – Medina rarely
paid full price for anything. I'd seen her try to haggle in super-
markets! According to her, the price on the ticket was just a
starting point. She had a way, too, of making the person feel as
if they were in the wrong for wanting the price they asked for.

I struggled on down the backstreets of Kensington. In this
fading light, they all looked the same to me – big imposing
houses and blocks of flats, narrow windy roads.

A tall man came striding towards me and, as always when I
was alone in a street with a man, my heart did a frightened
little jump. It was momentary and reflexive, I'd had that for
years. I should probably ask him for directions, but he seemed
to be in a hurry, his long legs striding out, and I didn't want to
get in his way. He gave me a brief nod, and smile; the dark
acknowledgement, Faye, Medina's twin, calls it – the way black
people acknowledge each other when they're in a predomi-
nately white area. I gave him a brief smile and nod back, and
he strode on. After a second, I stopped, turned back to look at
him. He had stopped too.

It was, it was him.

'It is, it's you,' he said.

'It is, it's me,' I replied.

He came back the few steps to me, and without even asking,
he took the bundle of material out of my hands.

'Thanks,' I said.

'Thanks?' he asked, confused.

I pointed to the material that now filled his arms. 'For lightening my load.'

'Oh, don't mention it,' he said. 'You look exactly the same.'

'Wow, that didn't take you long, did it? Less than three minutes to start the insults.'

'What insults?'

'You said I look exactly the same.'

'You do.'

'And, the last time we met, you said you didn't fancy me. I assumed it was because you didn't find the way I look particularly attractive. So if I look exactly the same, that means I'm still unattractive to you.'

'You deduce far too much from far too little,' he said. 'And talk a lot.'

'Only around you, actually. Most of the time, I'm pretty quiet.'

'I don't believe you.'

'OK, I suppose that is your right.'

'And you're wrong, anyway. I do find you attractive.'

'*Now* you might do, but then you didn't.'

'Would you rather I found you attractive in the past and not now? Especially since back then I seem to remember you had sworn off relationships.'

'Well—'

'Answer carefully, little one, for the wrong answer could bring all this rather fine flirting to a screeching halt. And wreck any chance we may have of getting together.'

'No pressure then.'

'There is a vast amount of pressure, didn't you understand that from what I just said?'

'I was being sarcastic.'

'Nah, I don't think you were.'

'You're incorrigible,' I said.

'I've always wanted to be incorrigible. Are you going to

come for a drink with me then? Or are you still off all men, for ever and ever amen?'

'I am. But I might make an exception for you, seeing as you're so incorrigible and so pleased to be incorrigible. When were you thinking?'

'No time like the present.'

'Ah, can't, I have to get this material to my sister.'

'Where does she live? Maybe we can drop it off then go for a drink. It'll be nice to meet the future family.'

'Don't be starting all that "my parents would love you" stuff again. Actually, my sister lives in Bethnal Green, not far from me.'

'Right, so where are you going? The Tube station's nowhere near here.'

'Oh, that – I'm lost. I've been wandering around for ages. My car's parked near here somewhere. Well, I think it is.'

'How about this for a plan?' he said, smiling as though I was one sandwich short of a picnic, but quite liking it. 'I help you find your car, you drive us to your sister's and then we go for a drink afterwards?'

'It'll be quite late.'

'Is that a no?'

'I did not say the word "no". Nor did I imply it. I just suspect we're going to get to my sister's house and you'll go, "Oh, it's a bit late for a drink, how about we just go back to yours?"'

'Do you want to know the tragedy of this situation?'

'Yes.'

'That never occurred to me. I *really* wish it had, but it didn't. I thought it'd be nice to do something together. I live and work just a bit beyond Bethnal Green, so I could go on afterwards, but damn it, I can't believe I didn't think of trying to get into your place. You'd make a good man, you know?'

'Why Ewan, you say the nicest things.'

'Thank you, Serena. So, is it a goer?' He remembered my name. After all these years, he remembered my name – there was something special about that.

'I suppose so.'

'Right, so what road did you leave the car on?'

'I can't remember.'

'You can't remember.'

'No, my memory's a bit fuzzy, all over the place.'

'Really, wow. Think I lucked out there, most women I know are elephants – never forget, even the smallest transgression. If you've got a fuzzy memory, I think we're really going to get along.'

'Yeah, don't bank on it, mate.'

'Were there any distinguishing marks about the road? Anything, anything at all?'

'Not that I can remember. Except, I think there was a blue house on the road. Although I might have just walked past a blue house. No, no, I think there definitely was.'

'Blue house, right. I know exactly where your car is. Come on, follow me.' He turned in the direction I had just come from and started striding down the road. I didn't have too much trouble catching and keeping up with him.

'If you don't live or work around here, what are you doing here?' I asked, as we turned the corner I had just navigated to get on to this street.

'Ah, well, I was meeting someone for a drink. A girl. A friend of one of the nurses at the hospital. This nurse has been trying to set us up for ages. She was convinced we would get on.'

'And you didn't?'

'Well, I thought things were going OK, until she excused herself to go to the loo. She didn't even go in the direction of the loos, she went to the foyer and picked up the payphone. I sat there, watching her. She speaks to someone for a few minutes, laughing, joking, comes back, sits down. Five minutes later, the restaurant phone rings and the manager comes to tell her she's got a call. She goes to the phone, comes back and deadpan says, "Something's come up, I have to go." I ask her what's come up and she just looks at me, all startled because she obviously wasn't expecting me to ask. She just shrugs and goes, "I don't know, something" and off she trots. Leaving me with two half-eaten meals, an empty bottle of wine and the bill. And of course, all the people at the nearby tables have heard this and are looking at me.'

I burst out laughing. I had to stop in the street and hold my sides I was laughing so much. 'That's one of the funniest things I've ever heard,' I managed between breathy laughs. 'How boring must you be?'

'I know, that's what I've been thinking all this while. She'd told her friend she thought I was the most gorgeous man she'd ever seen. So now, she's got an awful date story to tell, with me as the bad date. Me. She'll tell people I'm nice to look at but dull. How is that fair?'

I started on a fresh crop of laughs.

'She wasn't exactly a barrel of fun, either, but you don't see me dumping her, do you?'

'That isn't the worst part, you know, Ewan,' I said to him, still laughing but walking while I did it.

'It isn't? What could be worse than that?'

'At some point, you're going to hear your story again but it'll be a million times worse as it's told back to you. Your bad date stories – being told by someone else – always come back to haunt you.'

'Ah, great, thanks for that.'

'No problem.'

'You have to promise to tell me if I become boring though, OK? Don't just dump me at the table and leave – tell me I'm being boring.'

'You could never be boring.'

'I'm glad you think so,' he said as we came to a road where I could see LC, my white automatic Micra. (LC was short for Little Car.)

After I dropped the material off at Medina's, he and I had a quick drink before closing time because he had to rush to get his train back to Essex.

'It's Evan, by the way,' he said as he brushed a kiss on my cheek. 'I'm Evan, not Ewan.'

'But I've been calling you Ewan all night. Why didn't you say?'

'I've already had one woman walk out on me tonight, I didn't need to ruin things with another woman.'

'OK, *Evan,* I'm sorry I got your name wrong. But I had a fabulous time and you're not boring at all.'

'Thank you,' he said, and cupped my chin in his hand, then leant towards me and kissed the end of my nose. 'I'll see you soon.'

'Yeah.'

As I lay in bed that night, I knew it was going to work out with Evan. Fate had brought us back together. And he was gentle. Good looking, nice, funny, but also gentle. I had teased him and he hadn't slapped me in return. He hadn't shouted at me or sulked or made me feel afraid. People I knew often told me that was what men were really like – my sisters told me, too, but I never completely believed them. How could I, when the only man I knew in that way was not like that? He was not tolerant, he was not gentle, he had a very limited sense of humour.

Evan wasn't like *him*. Even when I got his name wrong he didn't seem to mind. He could laugh at himself, he could laugh at me, he seemed like one of the gentlest men I'd ever met. That was why my conscience was unsettled. My conscience knew that with a gentle man that Fate had returned to me, I could probably be happy.

With a gentle man, I could start to dig my way out of the prison I had been living in.

Verity is quiet and nervy the whole drive home. Her eyes keep looking in the rear-view mirror and the wing mirror and out the back window just to be sure there aren't any more police around. That's the problem with age: you start to see more things to worry about. If Conrad had been in the car, he would have thought it was cool to be stopped by a police officer, it wouldn't occur to him until it actually happened that it could end with me being thrown in prison. And even then he wouldn't take it that seriously until he was told that he wouldn't be seeing me at home again for a very long time. Verity, unfortunately, knows what the police mean and she can also decipher the nuances of conversation. Which is why Evan and I now row – mostly – in the car when the kids have gone to sleep. Even sarcasm upsets her because she can tell there's something going on.

As soon as we get home, she kicks off her trainers and leaves them scattered under the coat rack, wrenches off her burgundy denim jacket and slings it on top of the trainers and runs upstairs. Probably to write in her diary, maybe to cry, definitely to find an outlet for what happened. I would go after her if I didn't suspect it would cause more harm than good. I don't know what to say to her that would make her feel any better about what happened.

Con and Evan are in the kitchen, eating ice cream over the island.

'I can't believe you eat that stuff,' I say to Evan, feeling my stomach turn as I watch the white mounds on their cones slowly disintegrate. 'It's basically just sugar and lard.'

'Oh yes, I know,' he says.

'I can't believe you let my children eat it, either,' I say. The sight of it, right now, after what just happened is stomach-wrenchingly disgusting.

'It's the best thing in the world,' Evan says, through a mouthful of white filth. I want so much to slap it out of his hand, snatch Con's away and dump them both in the bin. Out of sight, out of mind.

'I'm going to wash my hands,' I say, and turn to leave the kitchen.

'Hang on, where's Verity?'

'Upstairs,' I say. I had been hoping to break the news to him gently but now . . .

'Did you two have a row?' Evan asks, his voice full of concern, even though he only has eyes for the ice cream in his hand. Watching it ooze and melt all over their hands makes me want to vomit.

'No, but she is a bit upset.'

'Why? What happened? Hideous bridesmaid dress?'

'No . . . On the way back we . . . kind of . . . were stopped by the police.'

'You were *what?*' he asks, finally able to tear his attention away from the confection in his hand.

Con's eyes widen in awe. 'Wow,' he breathes.

'Apparently I was speeding,' I say. 'I was overtaking and didn't slow down soon enough. So the police car that seemed to appear from nowhere pulled us over. And Vee got upset because he said he could take me down to the station or breathalyse me.'

'*You* who barely makes it over thirty, even in a fifty zone, were speeding? Now that's one for the record books. Poor kid must have been terrified. I'll go see if she's all right.' He stands up and comes towards me, still holding that *thing* in his hand. 'Here,' he shoves it into my hand, 'hold this.'

I stare at it: the feel of it under my fingers, the sweet vanilla smell of it in my nostrils is turning my stomach. 'I haven't washed my hands,' I tell him. 'I'll have to bin this now, you can't eat it.'

'Don't you dare, woman!' he calls from the foot of the stairs. 'Con, you're in charge – if she tries to bin it, come and get me.'

'OK, Dad,' Con calls back.

Any second I'm going to throw up on it. I'm going to cover it in bile and lunch's Spanish omelette, and then he definitely won't be able to eat it.

'Here,' I say, thrusting it at my son, 'you look after it for your dad, I really need to wash my hands.'

I rush to the sink, turn the hot water tap on full, hoping for enough stored hot water to cleanse away the stickiness it has slicked on my hands, and the near-invisible stain it has left upon my skin.

'What did the handcuffs feel like, Mum?' Conrad asks through a mouthful of ice cream.

I stop for a minute, wanting to ask him what he knows, who told him that I'd ever had handcuffs linked around my wrists – then I remember what he means. 'He didn't handcuff me, sweetheart,' I say, scrubbing again and again at my hands.

'Oh. What's it like in a police car?'

It's like being buried alive, and knowing you're being driven to a place where they'll bury you alive again. 'He didn't put me in a police car.'

'Oh. Did he at least talk on his radio thingy about you?'

Not while I was there. I'll bet he'll mention it to a few others, though. I'll bet they'll all be on the look out for my car after this. 'No, love. But it did crackle a bit.'

'Oh.' My eight-year-old is deflated, disappointed – for one moment in time he thought I was exciting, that he'd have a good story to tell his friends about his boring mum suddenly becoming interesting. I am not. I am dull and I am proud of that fact.

I am still trying to get the ice cream off my hands. Physically it is gone, but it is still there in other ways, staining my flesh in the same way that blood does by hiding down in the little ridges of the skin.

I often think that my hands will never be clean, that no matter how long I wash them for they'll always look how they did in the continuous reflection I saw in the bridal shop: they'll always be unclean and drip-drip-dripping in *his* blood.

serena

October, 1985

History is the most boring subject on earth. *On earth.*

It has nothing to do with me and I really wish I didn't have to do this lesson. '*Srrenna, Srrenna,*' Veronica Bell, who sat behind me in History, kept calling at me under her breath. She wasn't even saying my name properly. She wanted to me to take the note she'd written out of her hand and give it to Liam Ruthers who sat in front of me. I wasn't going to do it. I wasn't going to get involved in her trying to get Liam to notice her. I knew I'd get caught, and end up in detention or something. I'd seen it happen to other girls who'd tried to help Veronica. The teacher always got the note, read it out to the class, Veronica pretended she knew nothing about it and the note-passer got detention. That wasn't happening to me. Especially not in this class. Veronica didn't even like me. Most of the time she ignored me or called me names behind my back: like maps – spam backwards – because, according to her, I had a big, shiny forehead that was just begging to have someone hit while they yelled 'SPAM' in my face. She wouldn't dare try it, though. She wasn't sure what I'd do in return. She was all talk when I wasn't there, but nothing to my face. And despite all that, she wanted me to help her to get Liam to go out with her.

I stared down at the page in front of me, shutting out Veronica's hisses. I was so bored I could yawn. I hated this classroom as well.

It was smaller than the others, the windows weren't as large and Sir never opened them, so we all seemed to be crammed in here, and the boys smelt. They all wore their dads' aftershave even though most of them didn't shave. And most of them kept a can of BO basher in their lockers so they could have a quick spray between classes. 'Girls like boys to smell nice,' that's what Medina told me when I asked her why they did it. The girls were just as bad with their Yardley and Charlie, but the boys sprayed on loads and loads and I always felt sick afterwards.

'Miss Gorringe, perhaps you would care to tell the class why policemen are sometimes called Bobbies?' asked the new History teacher, out of the blue. He wasn't like other teachers. He was only a little bit older than us. And all the girls said he should be a film star because he was good looking. His class was the worst for the smells: all the girls rushed to their lockers to spray on perfume before his class and the braver ones put on make-up and wore their jewellery, despite it being forbidden. I'd even seen Veronica pull up her skirt so her legs above her knees were on show.

I didn't like him much. He was always picking on me. Always asking me questions, like there was no one else in the class whose name he could remember so if there was a question to be answered, he called mine.

'Because they were created by Sir Robert Peel. And Bobby is a shortened version of Robert.'

'What year did he form the police force?' Sir asked.

'1829, Sir,' I replied.

'What else was Sir Robert Peel famous for?'

'Abolishing the Corn Laws.'

'Year?'

'1846.'

'*Show off,*' Veronica hissed loudly and a few people in hearing distance laughed.

She didn't understand: I had to do extra reading because Sir was always picking on me and this was the only way to not give him a reason to give me detention.

'Miss Gorringe, I'd like to see you after class,' Sir said. My heart sank. If I got in trouble, they'd tell my parents and that was when the real trouble would begin.

'But, S—' I began.

'After class, Miss Gorringe,' he insisted.

'Lucky cow,' Veronica hissed, causing more laughter around me.

'What was that, Miss Bell? You want more detention? What?' Sir cupped his hand around his ear. 'You're desperate for it? OK, if you insist, Miss Bell. If I hear another word from you, I'll make sure you have detention with the head for a month.'

Everyone in class laughed, and Veronica kicked my chair when Sir had turned back to the blackboard. 'I'll get you,' she hissed.

'I'm really scared,' I replied. You didn't grow up with two older sisters and not know how to stick up for yourself. I was quiet, I was shy, I did not have that many friends, but I wasn't an easy target. Medina and Faye had made sure of that.

'You should be,' she said.

I turned to her, not caring if Sir saw, since I was staying behind after class anyway. 'No, Veronica, *you* should be,' I replied. From the way she immediately put her head down and stared at her textbook, I knew she'd got the message.

Everyone had filed out and I had stayed in my seat with my stomach tumbling and tumbling over itself like the washing machine did during a long wash. This wasn't fair. I hadn't done anything. 'I'll get right to the point,' Sir said, sitting on the edge of the desk in front of me. 'You're a bright girl, Serena. But you're easily distracted and I don't like the people you hang around with. That Veronica Bell is nothing but trouble.' I decided not to mention that I wasn't friends with Veronica Bell. There was no point, teachers saw what they wanted to see. That's why Veronica had never been caught for passing notes. No teacher ever saw that although the person caught passing the note might be different, they were always sitting behind or beside or in front of Veronica. 'You're getting Cs and Bs in my class when clearly you have the knowledge to do so much better. You could be an A student, Serena. I've been testing you, these past few weeks. That's why I'm constantly asking you questions. I wanted to see if you would do what I hoped you would and start doing extra reading, and you did. Not many students would do that. You're a gifted pupil. I want you to do better.'

'How, Sir?' I asked.

'I want you to start taking History a bit more seriously. It's a great subject if you try.'

'OK, Sir,' I said.

'Look, how about I give you a couple of extra lessons after school, give you a chance to see what History is really all about? And then we'll take it from there. I'll talk to the head, let him know that I want to tutor you, and if you decide you can like History a little better, I can tutor you up to your O'Levels next year. Help you get an A. What do you think?'

'OK, Sir,' I said. Did I really have any choice? When he talked to the headmaster, he'd most likely ring my parents. And once they heard that I could possibly get an A in an O'Level, I'd have to do it whether I could like History or not.

'Oh, come on, Serena, sound a little more enthusiastic than that. It's going to be fun. Trust me.'

January, 1986

'I want to take care of you for ever,' *he* said, stroking his thumb against my cheek.

I was a little unsure what to say. I'd never had a boy tell me something like that before, and certainly not a man, a teacher. The closest I'd ever come was when Tommy Marison had grabbed me and pushed his lips on mine and said I had to be his girlfriend. (Medina and Faye had what they called 'a nice little chat' with him and he never bothered me again.) Sir was nothing like Tommy Marison, and I liked being around Sir. In the last three months, I'd started to like History a little more thanks to our after-school tutorials. I liked sitting in his classroom and listening to him explain history in a way that I could understand. When he talked about history, away from the other pupils, it wasn't the most boring subject in the world about a group of dead people that had no relevance to my life. It was jam-packed with exciting stories full of danger and hope, intrigue and betrayal. And love. Always there was an element of love. I'd grown to like class, but I *loved* our tutorials. I could even call him by his first name in tutorials – 'It's more grown-up, don't you think?' he'd said.

This was the first time he said something like that or touched me, though.

'Oh God, I'm sorry,' he said and leapt up. 'I should *not* have said that or done that. I don't know what's wrong with me.' Red in the face, and shaking with nerves, I guessed, he moved to the other side of the classroom.

'I'm so sorry,' he said. 'I'm so, so sorry, I don't know what came over me.' He stumbled over a few chairs as he went to the blackboard, picked up the chalk-powdered eraser and started to rub out the things he'd written on the board earlier that day. 'I'll, I'll, erm, talk to the Head. I'll find you another tutor. I'll say it's not working out.' He cleared his throat, moving the eraser back and forth over the same spot, even though it was clear of his spidery writing. 'I'm, erm, thinking of leaving at the end of the term anyway, but once you tell your parents and the school find out, I'll probably be asked to leave before then.' He stopped what he was doing, then turned to me. 'I want you to know that it wasn't your fault. I'm the adult, I shouldn't have crossed the line like that. Blame me for doing something so wrong, OK? Not yourself. You have done nothing wrong here, OK?'

I nodded.

'Good girl,' he said with a smile. 'Now, you'd better go. Tell your parents that I'll more than understand if they want me fired.' He smiled at me again, then turned to the blackboard. 'Goodbye, Serena.'

'Bye, Sir,' I replied, deciding I needed to be formal again. I slowly got up, started to pack my books away. I took my time shutting each book and then putting them carefully in my brown satchel. When I was finished, I swung my bag on to my shoulder. He hadn't turned around at all: he stood at the board, rubbing it clean over and over.

When I was at the door, he said, 'Have a good evening, Serena.'

'Thanks, Sir,' I replied.

I walked home instead of getting the bus and along the way, I kept reaching up to touch my face. His touch had been so gentle and soft. And the way he said he wanted to take care of me made my stomach tingle upside-down every time I ran it through in my head. He wanted to take care of me. That must mean I was special. Someone thought I was special. Someone as clever and grown-up as him thought I was special.

'Hello, Serena,' Mum called from the kitchen as I opened the front door and dropped my bag and took off my school blazer, hooking it over the globe of the banister.

'Hello, Mummy,' I said, as I ambled into the kitchen.

Mum was stirring something on the stove and the whole house smelt of tomatoes and oxtail and onion and garden eggs. I wasn't hungry, I realised. My stomach had been rumbling after school but the hunger left me after he touched me – that one, quick touch had taken away my hunger and left in its place . . . I couldn't properly describe what I felt.

'Are you all right?' Mum asked as I pulled out a chair at the dinner table and sat down.

I nodded. I was more than all right.

'How was your History lesson?'

'It was OK.'

'Are you going to get an A for your O'Level, then?' she asked. She asked me this after every lesson.

'I hope so,' I said, stroking the place setting at the table. 'I just have to keep working really hard.'

'Good,' Mum said. 'Now, go and get changed and start your homework before dinner.'

'OK,' I said.

I climbed the stairs feeling as if I could float up them, and as I changed I wondered if Sir would like my stonewash jeans and big white T-shirt? If he liked my hair in a ponytail or if he'd prefer it loose? If he would like me to wear mascara and lipstick like the other girls at school? I couldn't concentrate on my homework. Instead, I flicked on the radio part of the tape player that I'd 'borrowed' from Faye and Medina's room when they went off to university two years ago. Sade's voice sang out, explaining about the sweetest taboo.

I lay back on my bed, listening to her sing, listening to her words, and when she had finished, I spent the whole evening writing his surname after my name. I wanted, desperately wanted, to be a part of his life for ever and ever.

poppy

'These are for you,' Mum says as she slides what she has been holding in her hand for the last few minutes across the wooden kitchen table towards me.

She has managed to sit down at the same table as me for more than three seconds. She didn't make herself a cup of tea, so I knew she wasn't staying, but it was a start. She actually came into the kitchen and didn't immediately walk out again. We can build on that. Dad being shut away in his study is something I do not know how to work on so I will not think about it for now. Now, I stare at what my mother has given me.

Keys.

She has given me five keys on a metal loop. Keys. For nearly twenty years I've only ever heard the sound of keys in locks, and seen them hanging on the belt loops or sitting in the hands of screws.

Heard them, seen them, not held them. Certainly never *owned* them.

Carefully, as though they are a potentially rabid animal that could snap venomously at me at any second, I extend my hand and stroke my fingers over the top of them. When they do not bite me, I pick them up, hold them in the palm of my hand, reacquainting myself with the coolness of metal and the delicious jagged edges.

'Two are for the front door,' Mum says. 'The smaller three

are for the padlocks to Granny Morag's beach hut,' she says. 'She left it to you.'

'And you're actually giving it to me?' I ask.

'Of course, Poppy. It's what she wanted. It would be *illegal* not to give it to you.'

Why don't you just add, 'Some of us aren't criminals like you' and be done with it? I think at her. I stare at the keys. Gosh, not only do I have keys, I have property.

Granny Morag always believed that 'the system' would come to its senses and would see the truth, would see I'm innocent and let me out. So, in her will, she had left me beach hut number 492.

Mum's eyes are intently watching me, although I do not know what sort of reaction she expects. 'Your father has been painting it twice a year, he changes the locks and keeps an eye on the place,' Mum says as I continue to caress my keys. 'He's kept it nice for you.'

'Bless Granny Morag,' I say. 'Just bless her.'

Mum smiles. A sad, wistful thought is clearly clouding her mind, and I suddenly feel how difficult and harrowing it must have been for her to live without her mother all these years.

'Do you miss her?' I ask.

'Every day. You get so used to someone being there, and I suppose you take for granted the time you have because you forget to say the things you want to say until it's too late. I miss her wit and her sharp eye. I miss her grumpiness in cold, damp weather and her false teeth in a glass beside her bed. I miss—' Mum comes out of her reverie and, blinking quickly, realises she is talking to me. 'But you get used to living without people, don't you? If you don't it will eat you up whole. You find a way to put them to one side and carry on.'

'If you say so,' I reply and run my fingers along the jagged edges of the keys. I feel like putting them in my mouth to find out what freedom tastes like.

'Well, the beach hut is your responsibility now,' she says rather ominously.

70

'Could you make that sound any more threatening?' I say to her. 'You sound like the Big Luv during a bollocking.'

Her mouth tightens and colour creeps up her neck into her cheeks at my language. 'What is the Big Luv?' she asks tersely.

'The Governor, the main governor. It's rhyming slang – Guv to Luv.'

The tension in her mouth increases, her colour, usually a pinky-red, is now red and high. She obviously doesn't like being compared to someone from prison.

'I just don't want you letting down your gran's memory by allowing her beach hut to fall into disrepair. Or wasting your father's hard work. Your gran believed in you right until the end. Don't dishonour her.'

'You think she was silly to believe in me, don't you?' I say, despite my decision three seconds ago to stay silent.

'Misguided,' my mother says. My mother thinks me capable of murder. It's incredible that she can. I'm innocent. I wish they would believe that. I didn't do it. How could I?

I loved him. Right till the end. Even when I was scared of him, and he acted like he hated me, I could not stop loving him.

'Thanks for the keys,' I tell my mother. 'I'll go and have a look at it in the next few days. I'll make Granny Morag proud.'

Her silence as she leaves the room says it all: 'You couldn't do that even if you tried.'

'I'm going to prove to you that I am innocent,' I tell her even though she has gone to hide upstairs. 'Do you know how? I'm going to find Serena Gorringe, and I'm going to make her confess that it was her, not me. I'm going to make her confess that, after the accident, she went back and she murdered him.'

serena

'Can I tell people that the policeman put handcuffs on you?' Conrad asks on the way to school on Monday morning.

All weekend he has been questioning me about the incident and questioning Vee, just to make double-triple sure that I hadn't forgotten that the policeman actually did put the cuffs on me. The novelty has worn off for me, and for Vee, but for the two who were not there it has been a non-stop source of amusement.

'No, sweetheart, because it's not the truth.'

'But no one will know,' he protests. 'Please, Mum. I'll tell them the truth later, but can I say it just for a little bit?'

'Con, you know the difference between lying and telling the truth, and you know which one is right and which one is wrong, don't you?'

'Do you, hypocrite?' asks my conscience.

'Yeeesss,' Con replies.

'Which one do you think is the best thing for you to do?'

'Hypocrite, hypocrite, hypocrite.'

I know he is sticking out his lower lip in indignation. 'Tell the truth,' he says.

'Always tell the truth,' I say. 'Because you're a good boy.'

'Does that mean you're a bad girl?'

'OK, Mum.'

'The truth's better, anyway,' says Vee who is supposedly in another world, listening to her iPod and reading a Judy Blume

73

book. 'You can tell everyone that your mum was speeding and then it turned into a high-speed chase with the police. Because that's basically what happened.'

'Wow,' Conrad says. 'Thanks, Vee.'

'Yeah, thanks, Vee,' I say through gritted teeth. 'Thank you very much.'

Conrad receives his usual hero's welcome when I walk him to the gates. I do this every morning I drop him off. No matter how late or how harassed I am, I always walk him to the gates and then drop to one knee, give him a hug and a kiss and tell him I love him, then kiss him again on the forehead. I know the day is coming when he won't throw his arms around me, and say, 'I love you, Mum' before running off to join his friends who have abandoned their games to come hang around the gates, waiting for him. The countdown is on to the day when he'll be mortified to have me even walk him to the school gates, so now, when I still can, when he doesn't care that all his mates watch him tell me he loves me every morning, I do it. I hang on to my baby, I wear his words and his touch like the precious coat of diamonds they are.

As usual, I walk away from Con feeling like I did on his first day at nursery – very close to rushing back through the gates, grabbing him and running away while calling over my shoulder, 'Sorry, I made a mistake, he shouldn't be at nursery, I'm not ready yet.'

Vee is still plugged into her world of music when I return to the car. She has her feet up on the dashboard, her book has been discarded face down on my seat while she sings with her eyes closed and her head thrown back. I stand at my driver's door and watch her, watch the curve of her throat contract and expand as she sings, watch her lips work their magic around the sounds she makes. Although she is the image of me at that age, she is striking in a way I never was. And here, in her own private universe, sheltered and protected from the world, she is all the more radiant. Really rather beautiful. But I would think that, I'm her mother.

As soon as I open the door, she snaps out of it – she takes down her feet, snatches up her book, and fixes on her seatbelt – almost as if the interlude did not happen.

'You should just drop him off in the car at the gates, you know, Mum,' she tells me when I start the ignition. 'It's not like he hasn't got any friends who he can stay with until the bell goes.'

'I know,' I say happily.

'You baby him all the time,' she says.

'I know.'

As I navigate through the streets towards her school, I am on the verge of asking her if her recent near-permanent good mood and round-the-clock singing is boy-related. My eyes slide over to glance at her, working out if it is a good idea or not.

She reaches up to scratch her earlobe while concentrating hard on the book. This is not the time. I need to do it at home, where she has nowhere to run and no excuse to remove herself from me with the question unanswered.

I don't turn off the engine as Verity unloads herself from the car. 'Have a good day,' I say to her.

'You too,' she says. Unlike Conrad, she doesn't have a gang of people waiting for her to arrive: Verity, like me at that age, has a limited number of friends and she doesn't seem to mind. I may not be allowed to walk her to the gates, but I always wait and watch for her to walk through them and hold my breath, praying that there is someone there for her to stand with and talk to until the bell. Zephie, one of her friends, approaches her and I breathe out. It's OK, she's safe, she won't be on her own, she won't be an easy target for bullies and others. I won't spend the drive to work and the rest of the morning worrying about what happened after I drove away. She has left behind her iPod and her book on her seat and I reach across to put them away in the glovebox as usual.

When I was twelve I read every Judy Blume I could get my hands on. It wouldn't occur to Vee to ask me if I'd read them –

I'm just not that hip in her mind. I turn the book over to see the front, to see which one in the host of books she's reading. *Forever.* I stare at the cover for a long, long time, not allowing myself to panic. I will not panic until there is reason to panic. I shelve it in the glovebox with the silver iPod and put my seat-belt back on, adjust my driving glasses and set off for work.

So what if my daughter is reading a book about teenage love and sex? It doesn't mean she is actually doing anything. I read that book, I read a lot of other books.

'*And look how well things turned out for you,*' snipes my conscience.

It's all going to be fine. I'm going to have that 'boyfriends' chat with her and it'll all be fine.

'*Of course it will,*' says my conscience. '*Because history never, ever repeats itself, does it?*'

I drive to work with my heart in my throat, trying not to think that when evil comes a-knocking on your life, it very rarely looks as horrible as it is.

serena

February, 1986

I couldn't understand why *he* didn't like me any more.

Since that first touch in the classroom, he stayed away from me. He was still tutoring me twice a week after school, but he always sat on the other side of the desk and didn't even look at me for too long, let alone anything else.

I thought he liked me. I thought I was special to him. The way he used to talk to me, to look at me as an adult, an equal, made me *feel* special. But he'd been acting as though I was just another student to him. I had to call him by his surname again, I had to listen or pretend to listen, and I had to sit near him remembering the touch of his hand on my face, knowing I'd never feel it again. Because he didn't like me. I didn't understand what I'd done wrong, what had changed.

Every school day started with me feeling sick as I wondered if he was going to show me again that he liked me. At home, I would lie on my bed, staring at his handwriting in my exercise book, wondering if he had ever written my name over and over and over, like I did with his name. He had started to mark harder, as well. I'd been getting Bs and A minuses, now the highest mark I got was a B minus. He'd write: 'You can do better' at the bottom of each grade and in our tutorials he'd go through my essays, explaining what I had done wrong. Never anything other than schoolwork.

'How do you get a boy to notice you?' I asked Medina on the phone during the third week of being 'just' his pupil again. I was hunched up on the fourth step of our pattern-carpeted staircase, with my eyes fixed on the living room door while I whispered into the phone. I didn't want Mum and Dad to hear – they would not be happy to know I was even thinking about boys let alone . . .

'That depends on what you want them to notice about you,' Medina replied coyly. She was at university in Oxford now, and I was sure that all sorts of men were running around after her. She'd had her pick of boys when she'd been in school – they were always trying to get her attention, giving her gifts, writing her bad *bad* poetry, offering to give her lifts. She was a boy magnet and Faye wasn't, even though they were identical. If I wanted to know how catalysts worked, I'd ask Faye; if I wanted to know how boys worked, Medina was the one.

'I want to make him like me,' I whispered.

'I'm not sure I'm all right with you wanting to make a boy like you. You've got exams coming up and you're my little sister – you're meant to still be playing with dolls and speaking with a lisp. You're swottier than Fez, you're not supposed to be interested in boys.'

'Please, Mez. I just need to know how to make him like me.'

'Who is he?'

'Someone at school.'

'Hmmm, someone at school.'

'So? How do I get him to notice me and like me?'

'The thing is, Sez, and you need to remember this, it's not about getting him to like you, it's about whether you like him.'

'But I know that I like him!' I wailed as quietly as I could.

'No, I mean, look, you'll always meet boys you like and who don't like you back. That's natural. Not that it's happened to me, but moving swiftly along. What you've got to be careful of is trying to change yourself to make him like you. If he's worth your time, then he'll notice how wonderful you are without you having to do a thing.'

'But I thought he liked me: he was all nice to me and now he's just nice to me.'

'If he's still being nice to you, what's the problem?'

'He was *nice* nice to me and now he's just nice to me.'

'You're making my head hurt and I'm a girl, I'm supposed to be able to follow complex reasoning, and *your* reasoning, but I don't.'

'Look, just tell me what I have to do and I'll stop making your head hurt. Do I wear make-up?'

'Yeah, but not too much. Actually, very little. In fact, nothing at all. You're beautiful as you are. And anyway, I'd love to see you get make-up past Mum and Dad.'

'I'll put it on in the toilets at school and take it off before I come home.'

'Urgh! I hate that you've learnt these things off me.'

'What about a short skirt?'

'No!' she almost screeched. 'Stay well away from them. And the same with flashing cleavage. You're giving him the idea that you want to go further than . . . well, just further. And you're still young, you're not ready for all that. And don't even think about customising your uniform – Mum and Dad would hit the roof. Even I didn't do that.'

'You haven't told me anything,' I complained.

'That's because you're perfect as you are. Stop being in such a rush, all of that will come in its own time. Sez, honestly, you're perfect. And if he can't see it, then he's not worth it. I promise there'll be someone better out there.'

It wasn't often that I ignored the advice of my older sisters. I might fight with them, 'borrow' their clothes without asking, but I'd always listen to their advice. In this instance Mez was dead wrong: he was definitely worth it and there was no one else out there for me. There never would be.

I started to wear lip gloss. It was the best I could do. I didn't get pocket money and I'd have to save up a lot of lunch money and bus fares to be able to afford make-up, so I had searched Faye and Medina's room and found some lip gloss and mascara. The mascara was dry and the brush was caked in black cement-like gunk so I had to throw it away, but the lip gloss was brand new and only slightly tinted, so Mum and Dad didn't even notice. Neither did *he*.

I thought I saw his gaze linger on my mouth but it was just my imagination. The whole thing was my imagination. I was being silly, anyway, because he was a teacher after all. And I was a pupil and he would never do anything like that. Especially not with someone like me. Maybe Mary Lachmere, because she was popular and pretty and she'd been told off so many times for shortening her uniform but she didn't care. She even wore jewellery – earrings and rings – and put them on as soon as she finished the numerous hours of detention she got for wearing them. She just didn't care. She was the sort of girl he would like if he ever decided to do something like that with a pupil. Not me. I really was swottier than Faye. That's why Mum and Dad were so keen on the after-school lessons – anything to ensure I got as many A grades as possible in my O'Levels. He might even like De-De O'Brien. She was really pretty but clever with it and her family had loads of money so if they got married, they'd probably live in a house that her parents bought.

'Who would?' Sir asked.

I stared at him, wondering what he was asking.

'Who, if they got married, would live in a house bought by their parents?' he asked.

Oh no, I'd done it again. I'd said what I was mulling over out loud. In *front* of the person I was mulling about. In front of *him*. I stared at him, wide-eyed and scared. I had no idea what to say. The truth wasn't likely to come out of my mouth and I really didn't like to lie. Not even to save myself from major embarrassment.

'You're not concentrating on History at all, are you?' he asked gently.

I stared at the book in front of me, ashamed to be caught.

'Oh my, look at the time!' he suddenly exclaimed. 'I'm not surprised you're not concentrating – it's way, way past your home time. Your parents will have my guts for garters! Right, come on, pack up, and I'll drop you home. Don't tell anyone because it's not really allowed, but if I don't make sure you get home safely and soon, there'll be even more trouble.'

My heart started to pound forcefully in my chest, like a hammer trying to bang nails into a steel surface. I was going to be in his car. *Alone*. He could kiss me and no one would see. I knew he wouldn't, but he could. If he wanted to.

Across the dark school car park, we walked side by side with Sir carrying my books and my bag. He even opened the door for me. In the car, on the drive home, I kept pretending . . . I kept pretending that we were boyfriend and girlfriend, that he was taking me home after we'd been to the cinema to see an eighteen film and we were going to go to his house and we were going to kiss and *everything*. I hated to admit it to anyone, but I wasn't entirely sure what 'everything' was. We'd had sex education lessons in school when I was about thirteen, but I couldn't work out where all the bits on the diagrams were now. That picture of the man's thing looked weird as a cross-section, I couldn't imagine it as a whole thing. And the pictures of the woman's bits were just as strange with the man's bits in it and not in it. I couldn't work out how they got together.

Did he have to ask you first? Did you always have to be lying down? Where did the rest of your body go when you were joined down there? That was the sort of thing you talked about with friends, but since I'd started the lessons after school, I didn't have that many friends left. They would all go home together, and do stuff on the way back and then talk about it the next day in break and in lunch and, because I wasn't there in the evenings, I had no idea what they were talking about half the time. Elouise sometimes called me, but I wasn't allowed to speak on the phone until my homework was done and after dinner, and by that point it was her dinner and both our parents said it was too late for phone calls. So I'd slowly sort of lost my friends. I still sat with them in the canteen and in break, but I wasn't really a part of it any more. Certainly not enough to ask about *that!*

'Remember, this is our little secret,' Sir said as he dropped me at the end of my road. 'I'll stay here to make sure you get in OK, but don't tell anyone that you were alone in my car with me.'

'OK, Sir,' I said.

He reached out, stroked the side of my face. 'You're a good girl,' he said. 'You're a very good girl.'

All through dinner I kept reaching up to touch my face, remembering the lightness of his touch, the way his eyes had stayed on my lip-glossed mouth as he spoke, the way his eyes seemed to sparkle as he looked at me. I was only fifteen, but I knew, without a doubt, this was love.

March, 1986

Sir sat with his feet up on his desk, staring out of the classroom window. He looked worried and concerned and my stomach dipped – had we been found out? Had someone seen me in his car and now we were in trouble?

'Hello, Serena,' he said quietly when he heard me pull out a chair.

'Hello, Sir,' I replied. I didn't want to hear that we'd have to stop our lessons, or that he was going to have to leave school because we'd been caught.

'Sorry,' he said, as he took his long legs off the desk and slowly stood up. 'Not feeling that great today. I had some bad news.'

He looked so hurt that I ached for him, I hurt because he hurt.

'My ex-wife, Marlene, was meant to let my son come and visit this weekend. She moved him to the Midlands so that I couldn't see him regularly. She lied and lied in court, said some awful things about me and the court believed her so I can only see him when she decides. This weekend he was meant to be coming to stay for the whole weekend – but she called the school earlier and said she'd changed her mind. I had all these things planned and she's—' He physically sagged where he stood. 'I'm sorry, I don't mean to burden you with all these things. Can we skip today's session? Is that OK?'

I nodded. His ex-wife sounded awful. Really awful. How could she do this to him? He didn't deserve it. He was always talking about his son, about how he did this and did that, how he missed him. I didn't realise that his ex-wife was making him suffer so much.

'Come on, grab your books, I'll still drop you off at home.'

In the car park, he didn't start the car straight away, instead he said quietly after a while, 'I don't want to be alone right now. After I drop you off I'll be on my own until Monday.'

Monday. That was two whole days away. More if you counted this afternoon. And he didn't want to be alone. And I didn't want to be without him for all those hours – they'd feel like weeks.

'I can come to your house, if you like, Sir. We could study there, if you want? Then you won't be alone.'

He shook his head, sadly. 'I couldn't ask you to do that, Serena. Your parents wouldn't be too happy if they found out. And the school could sack me.'

'We won't tell them,' I said. 'I won't tell anyone. Not even my sister, Medina. And I tell her everything. But I won't tell her this.' I was talking quickly, trying to make him understand that I knew what was at risk. 'I haven't told her about you giving me lifts home every day, I haven't told anyone. And I won't tell anyone about this.'

He thought about it, stared out of the front windscreen, frowning with his mouth set in a heavy, straight line. 'Only if

83

you're sure, Serena. Only if you're absolutely sure. And you're certain you can keep it a secret.'

'Yes, I can, I promise I can.'

'OK, it'd be great if you come over. Keep me company for a while. We'll work on your History, of course, but it'd be great having you there.'

He reached out and stroked my face. A string of tingles thrilled up my spine. *I hope he strokes my face again,* I thought as he started the car. *I hope he strokes my face again and again and again.*

March, 1986

On the Wednesday, he kissed me.

He leant sideways towards me, where I was seated on the right of his kitchen table, and he gently pressed his lips against mine. It was to say well done for managing to understand and explain a complicated History theory. It was a brief little kiss, but I could not breathe afterwards. I thought about it the whole time we continued to work, even though he was acting as if he'd done nothing out of the ordinary. I thought about it as he drove me home, I thought about it in bed that night, I thought about it on the way to school.

On the following Tuesday, he kissed me the longest he had ever done. Each little 'well done' kiss every day had been getting longer, and he still acted as if nothing was different, but on the Tuesday, as soon as we entered his house, he shut the door behind us and took my school bag from me and dropped it on the floor. Then his arms were around me and he stared into my eyes for a few seconds before he dipped his head and kissed me. His tongue moved slowly into my mouth and I wasn't expecting that, so I tensed up. He broke away. 'Relax, OK?' he said. 'I'm not going to hurt you. Just relax, I'll show you what to do.' The second time he pushed his tongue into my mouth, it was all right, actually.

On the following Friday, he led me upstairs after kissing me at the front door, and I found out the answer to all those questions I had about 'everything'. Afterwards, he dropped a light kiss on my mouth and told me how much he had longed for this to happen. 'You're special to me, I hope you realise that. This was very special to me.'

He fell asleep and I lay very still in his bed with him beside me. *Is this what being a woman feels like?* I wondered. I hadn't felt it when I grew breasts and my periods started, I just felt different, achier. This felt a little bit the same: I ached in the same sorts of places and I felt different again. *Maybe different is what being a woman is.* I couldn't tell anyone though, so I couldn't ask anyone if this was it. Was I now a woman because I'd done *it*? Because I'd touched a man's thing? Or was it completely separate? It must be, because even though I'd done *it*, if I had to live my mum's life, the life of a woman, I wouldn't know what to do.

I continued to lay very still, trying not to disturb him. I wasn't sure I'd liked *it*. I wasn't sure I wanted to do *it* ever again.

He opened his eyes, looked at the clock and groaned. 'It's six,' he said. 'We'd better get you home before your parents start to worry.'

Putting on my green school uniform skirt, yellow shirt, green jumper, yellow-and-green tie, and green blazer was odd and made me uneasy. I'd just done something with a man I was in love with, something that women did with the men they were in love with. But I didn't feel like a woman. Women didn't wear school uniforms, or know that they had their Maths and RE homework in their bags. They didn't wear brown leather shoes that their parents bought half-price in the Clarks sale. They didn't have their name in their underwear, underwear their mothers bought them. They didn't wear green bobbles in their hair.

I loved him, but doing that hadn't made me feel more like a woman, more worthy of being with him. It just made me—

My thought was interrupted by Sir pulling up at the top of my road. He turned to me, then looked around briefly before he leant over and kissed me on the mouth. The first time he'd ever done that outside of his house. 'I'll see you Monday, OK?'

'OK,' I replied.

'I had a great time.'

'Me too.'

'Good.'

I got out of the car and was about to walk away when he waved me back towards him. I leant in the car window that he had wound down. He was going to tell me he loved me. And then I'd know I was definitely a woman because girls didn't have men saying they loved them. I knew he felt it – he would not have done that with me otherwise – and he was finally going to say it. 'Don't forget to get yourself down to the doctors as soon as possible and get yourself on the Pill. We don't want you getting knocked up, do we?' he said. 'See you Monday.'

And with that, he wound up the window and then drove away.

I didn't mind. Not really. I knew deep down that he loved me. And I loved him. That was all that mattered. We loved each other.

April, 1986

'It's me,' the woman's voice said on the square black answerphone thing next to *his* phone. The phone had started to ring while he was in the bathroom and I had sat patiently on the sofa waiting for it to pick up the call. She sounded like a grown-up and was slightly cross. 'I'm just ringing to say can you please hurry up and find yourself another naïve fifteen-year-old virgin so that you can go back to leaving Jack and me alone? I'm sick of you being interested and interfering in our lives when it's convenient for you, and ignoring us when you've found yourself another pupil to relieve of her virginity. Don't make me come down there to say it to your face again, OK? Just get lost. LEAVE ME ALONE ONCE AND FOR ALL! Oh, and just in case you haven't found yourself someone new, it's your son's birthday on Saturday. A card would be nice. But I'll buy one and a present from you, as usual, just so your son doesn't think you're a complete scumbag who only keeps in touch to make my life a living hell. And, by the way—'

He came running back into the room, snatched up the phone and put it to his ear. I decided to leave the living room, to go and wait in the corridor until he had finished talking to her. His ex-wife.

I had a tingly feeling all over my body. Why did she say those things? Were they true? Had he been out with other pupils? I stood very still as the tingling got worse. It couldn't be true. Could it? It just didn't seem like the sort of thing he would do. But the veins of anger threaded through her voice sounded so solid, certain, *sure*. Very few people would sound so concrete if they were lying.

'I'm sorry you had to hear that,' he said when he reappeared. 'You see now what I have to put up with? She's a complete nightmare. You'd think having sole custody of our son would be enough for her, wouldn't you? But no, she has to torture and abuse me as well.'

I nodded. He was right, of course, she was a nightmare. Ever since I'd known him he'd been grieving over the loss of contact with his son, how she used their boy to get at him. You couldn't make up those emotions.

'Oh, babe,' he said, and took me in his arms. As usual, the world's worries started to melt away as he held me. 'I can imagine what you're thinking. I'd be thinking it too if I was you.' He held me at arm's length so he could look into my eyes. 'It's not true, none of it. She only said those things because, as a male teacher, I've had my fair share of girls having teenage crushes on me. I would never act on them. *Never.* This, what we've got, is special. The first. The only.'

I nodded.

'She . . . I think she was having an affair. I can't prove it, of course, but I think she was cheating on me and to make herself

87

feel better she tried to make out that I was doing it, too. Please believe me. I don't know what I'd do if you didn't. We're risking everything to be together, I don't want you to have any doubts. If you have any doubts about this, then we can end this right now.'

No! I couldn't let that happen. It'd been six weeks since we'd first done *it* and I couldn't end it with him. He was like the air around me: without him, I'd suffocate. I'd go back to being the boring little girl who preferred books and revising to going out to the park or watching grown-up foreign movies. I wouldn't know who I was without him; I wouldn't survive.

'You do believe me, don't you?' he asked.

I nodded. Of course I believed him. Between the man I loved and his jealous, cheating ex-wife who else could I believe?

'Good girl,' he said, pulling me into his arms, snuggling me up tight, making me his all over again. I always felt safe and loved when he held me. I always felt that no one and nothing could hurt me. 'Good, good girl.'

I hugged him back knowing that soon, very soon, I'd feel like a woman and not just a schoolgirl playing at being a grown-up.

poppy

It's probably one of the most beautiful things that I have ever seen. And it's mine.

I haven't had much that is mine in my life. Up until you leave home, I reckon most kids don't really have much that isn't connected to their parents. Since I left home to go to be taken care of by Her Maj and her prison service, my opportunities to acquire *things* – status-defining possessions – were pretty much zero. I have not had much I could call my own.

Except, as of this moment, I have a beach hut. I have a green and red wooden shed with burnt orange doors that sits on the tarmac on the promenade on Hove Seafront. I am the owner of property. Thanks to Granny Morag.

Granny Morag was the only one who cared enough to send me the things I needed inside: a battery-operated radio, a Walkman, tapes, stamps and writing paper. She also sent me clothes and shoes on a regular basis, up to the limit that was set by the prison, and money for phonecards and anything else I might need. There was nothing I wanted for when Granny Morag was alive except for visits, which she found hard to arrange transport-wise by herself. One time, when I was sent to Cheshire for what turned out to be only a year, she came all the way in a taxi, bringing boxes of homemade biscuits with her, and a coffee and walnut cake. That was the time before everyone and everything were viewed as potential drugs mules and anything that wasn't hermetically sealed and then opened and gone through with a fine-tooth comb was not allowed.

We spent the hour talking and talking like we were in her living room in Brighton, eating cake and drinking tea. It was only as she was leaving that she said, 'I'll get you out of here, Poppy lass. I won't rest until I do. I know you would never kill someone and I'm going to make sure the world knows it too.' That was the last time I saw her – she died three years later of a massive stroke.

She wasn't like my gran at times, she was more a friend than anything. She used to come up from Brighton to London to help Dad look after me when I was little, and sometimes I would stay with her in her house for the weekend. I regret not telling her about Marcus. About what he was really like and what was really going on in my life. She knew I had a boyfriend, and she knew I wasn't always happy, but she didn't know the ins and outs, the depths my 'relationship' with him plummeted to. She didn't know about Serena. Maybe if she had she would have convinced me to leave, to let Serena have him and to walk away. Run away, knowing how forthright and outright blunt Granny Morag could be. Maybe she would have been the voice of reason in the madness that surrounded Marcus. Or maybe I wouldn't have listened. Because that's why you don't tell those close to you things, isn't it? You don't want them to do what good friends and loved ones are meant to do – tell you the truths you don't want to hear, the truths that would dismantle all your reasons for doing crazy things.

My hands are shaking as I try to push my key into the first circular lock on the beach hut. It's rusty. I'm not sure the last time Dad came down here, but it's rusty and I have to use the tip of my key to scrape away the disintegrated pieces of lock until I can see silver metal. Then I try again. The key finds its way through the rust and other blockages and comes to a rest in its natural home. I jiggle it a little, and then turn. It's creaky as it moves, but it rotates and the latch it was holding in place slides back. I watch it intently, immersing myself in the experience of freeing a latch, breaking its solid link. Undoing each latch is a sweet experience, something to savour, something to remember. I am making something free, opening it up to the world.

If only the judge who sent me down me could see me now.

'Never have I seen such a blatant disregard for human life. To torture and then to violently butcher a man of impeccable reputation, who was devoted to his young son and dedicated to teaching is reprehensible. Your attempts to paint your victim as some kind of monster – although ultimately unsuccessful – have not gone unnoticed by the Court and it will be taken into account when it comes to sentencing,' he boomed at me across the court. The haze of shock at the verdict, at Dad's departure, at even being there had not cleared so I could only vaguely process what he was saying. 'In sentencing you, I deem it necessary for you to have the time to understand the gravity of your crime. I hereby sentence you to life imprisonment with a minimum term of twenty-five years. If I were able to disallow early release for good behaviour, I would. You have robbed the world of a talented, gentle, kind man, in return you are to repay society with your life.'

Days, or maybe it was even weeks, later when what he said had sunk in, when the smell and sounds of prison were so overwhelming and I realised that I would be surrounded by this for ever, his words came back to me. Stored up as they had been in my brain until I could understand them. He had not only been carrying out his job, he was actually judging me. He thought he had seen the truth despite everything that had been presented to him in court, he thought he knew 'my type' and was making sure he sent a message to all other teenagers out there who thought it a good idea to seduce and murder older men. He thought he knew best and so wasn't judging the crime, but me. It must have stuck in his craw that Serena got away with it. That there was nothing he could do to throw her away with the rest of society's trash, too. I bet he had a nice little speech all polished up to deliver and damn her as well.

Well, he might still get the chance, if things work out for me the way they're meant to. The way they're going to – because I've found her. I've found Serena.

The hinges creak as I unbolt one door and then push both orange doors wide open, letting in the light, illuminating the dark place into something bright and light and beautiful.

Fuck you, Mr Judge, look what I've got. His little speech, his damnation of me, was indeed too personal and too smoothly delivered within minutes of the verdict being announced so my stretch was reduced to eighteen years minimum. Apparently that was good. That was taking into consideration that it was a first offence, I'd had no other dealings with the police before-hand, and I was of good enough character to have stayed out of prison on house arrest until the trial. When my solicitor passed on the information and I nodded at him, I could tell he thought I was being ungrateful, that having seven years shaved off a life stretch was cause for celebration. 'Only if you're not innocent,' I wanted to say to him, but kept quiet because I knew he wouldn't understand.

My palace is dusty, the smell of rust and emptiness and the sea have become trapped in the grain of the wood inside and slowly diffuse into the air around me. This isn't much smaller than most of the rooms I've lived in since 1989. It's a hell of a lot more welcoming. I run my fingers over the rough, marine-treated wood, with its coats of stark white paint, and allow the smell, the history of the place to seep into me. I close my eyes and smile as I remember the picture I saw of Granny Morag and Grandpa Adam sitting outside here on their stripy deckchairs, metal cups in hand, proudly smiling at the camera.

On hooks behind the door are two deckchairs. One red, one blue. If any more than one person other than Granny Morag came down here, they'd have to sit on a blanket. It takes a little manoeuvring, trying to work from memory and against natural instincts, before I manage to put the red one up. Then I put up the blue one beside it on the tarmac. I sit on the blue one – the red one was Granny Morag's. When I stayed for the weekend we'd come down here and I'd sit on the blue deckchair and she would sit on her red deckchair and we would stare at the sea, wave at people walking past and eat the picnic she brought. I thought life couldn't get much better back then. Being with her here was the best thing on earth.

I look over at her seat, remember her as she was: the big curls of her grey-white hair framing her face; her soft features brightened even more by her smile; her large, friendly eyes; her small, perfect little mouth. She always wore small pearl earrings in her ears, and her engagement and wedding rings on her finger. Even though Grandpa Adam died a year after I was born, Granny Morag never married again. She was popular with the old fellas of Portslade, but she never went beyond a spot of companionship. 'Why would I want to be messing with all that again, lassie?' she'd say to me. 'You know when you've met the man you're meant to be with. I don't see the bother of trying again.'

I close my eyes for a second, fancy that I can feel sun on my face, even though it's an overcast day and there is a slight chill in the air. I prefer the outside when it's like this. The sky does not look so scary and threatening and huge, but something to be ignored while I spend as much time in the fresh air as I can. It looks manageable again; only slightly bigger than the snatches of it I used to get.

I'm going to paint the inside of the hut an off-white. Maybe even a cream-white. Sew a new cover for the boxseat – I know how to do that now. Get myself a new kettle and a camping stove. A flask. Maybe even a picnic set. I'll repaint the doors, keep it Granny Morag's deep, dark orange but freshen it up. I may even get a rug for the floor, and a picnic blanket. And I'll have to get myself a big woolly blanket so I can wrap up warm, drink tea and watch the sun go down.

I reach into my pocket and take out my cigarettes and lighter. I'll need to get a job, of course, to be able to afford all that. That might take some doing, but I'll have to find the money somehow. Granny Morag has given me this place and I want to make it my own and make her proud at the same time.

I inhale life into the cigarette, drawing in breath to make the tip take the flame and glow, while I look over at Granny Morag's chair.

'Thank you for this,' I say to her. 'Thank you. I'm going to make you proud. I'm going to look after this place. And I'm going to clear my name. I'll make you proud of me again, you'll see.'

I've found Serena. Three days in the library, going through old microfiche films of the publications from that time to find out where she went afterwards and then on the library's Internet, looking for as many Serenas in the Leeds area who even vaguely matched her description. I looked and looked until I came across a photo on a social networking thingy website of a college reunion. She was trying to avoid being in the picture, but they still caught a partial of her – enough for me to recognise and enough for them to bother 'tagging' her with her new name.

I blow out a long plume of smoke, feeling for a moment like the villain in a black-and-white movie with a long cigarette holder and nefarious cackle.

Fate is on my side. Fate knows I'm innocent because I've found Serena and she lives less than two miles from here. With her so close, virtually a heartbeat away, it's only a matter of time before I get my life back.

serena

'I'm incredibly proud of you, Verity,' I say to my daughter. 'You're the cleverest girl in the world and you're a lovely person.'

Evan and I have just swapped children for the goodnight portion of the evening.

'Thanks, Mum,' she mumbles, embarrassed. Today, three days after I found that book, we had a note from her form tutor saying that in all her subjects to date Verity was doing outstandingly well, and if they were still conducting Key Stage 3 exams, she'd be expected to achieve an 'Exceptional' in all her subjects. All of them! In other words, my daughter was a big girly swot.

'Well, she's always been talented like that,' Evan had said to me as he re-read and re-read the note, almost bursting with pride. 'We've worked hard to encourage her studies.' He'd obviously forgotten that it was me who taught her to read before she went to nursery, and that it is me who checks over her homework every night. In fact, Evan seemed to have forgotten that when she was going through her 'why?' stage it was me who ended up, more often than not, pulling out encyclopaedias and dictionaries to get the answers so she would stop. He did everything but slap his hands over his ears and run away screaming 'Lalalalalalalalala, can't hear you,' until she ended the question onslaught.

'Yes, *we* have,' I'd said, pointedly, but it was completely lost on him. He'd refolded the note and slipped it gently into his inside breast pocket, patting the pocket afterwards like it was a precious item and it was safe there, beside his heart, keeping him warm.

Verity unhooks her iPod from around her neck and carefully winds the earphones around its slim, silver body before placing it gently on the bedside table.

'I always knew you were clever, but it does well for the school to realise it, too.'

'Dad said I get it from you,' she says. 'He said you had the book smarts and he was good at reading the streets.'

I roll my eyes at her father. Once, on an episode of *Starsky and Hutch*, one of them had said that in police work it was always important to 'read the streets' to fight crime. Starsky or Hutch meant that on a blazing hot day, he'd seen a man in a big overcoat going towards a liquor store, as they call them in the US. And, sure enough, it turned out that the man was going to rob the store with a shotgun stashed under his coat. Ever since he saw that episode, Evan has been going on about 'reading the streets'. If he's trying to find a parking spot, he 'reads the streets'; if he's trying to find the shortest line in the supermarket, he 'reads the streets'; if he's trying to find the quickest route to anywhere he 'reads the streets'. I've said more than once that if he's not careful, he's going to read the streets right into the spare room.

'He said since you'd already passed the book smarts on to me, he was going to teach me and Con how to read the streets,' she adds.

'I'm going to pretend I didn't hear that,' I say. 'I'm going to pretend your father doesn't have some really annoying sayings.'

I lean forwards and kiss her forehead. Her skin is soft and warm. I remember how soft and warm she was when she was a baby. I used to love to cuddle her, and would leave her to sleep for hours on her feeding cushion on my lap, just to be near her. Simply to hold my baby. I sometimes want to hold her now, but it would cause a major incident if I did. She didn't seem to be a baby for long enough. One day she was lying still, her eyes following me wherever I went as I tried to spruce up the place before Evan got home, the next she was walking and then talking and then she was a teenager who had died a million deaths when I sat her down to talk to her about the birds and the bees and periods. It all seemed to rush so quickly by, I sometimes feel like I missed it. I want to go back and do it again. I wouldn't change any of it, I would simply pay more attention. Remember what it was like when she was light enough to lift with one hand. Remember how it felt to see her roll over in her cot for the first time and stare at me. Remember the look on her face when she realised that she could get from here to there by moving her feet.

'Vee, do you have a boyfriend?' I ask.

Her face twists in alarm and shock, with a liberal dose of disgust sprinkled on top. Each emotion was too quick and too briefly on her face for me to work out the real answer. 'No,' she says.

'Be honest, would you tell me if you did have a boyfriend?' I ask.

She doesn't say anything. I don't really blame her – as we'd recently had confirmed, she is not stupid – there is no possible good answer to that question. If I was her, I would keep it to myself. I did keep it to myself. 'Mum, I can't answer that question without getting into trouble.'

'You can,' I say, smoothing the covers that lie in crumpled folds over her biceps and chest. 'I'm not going to get cross. I promise you I won't.'

'I don't have a boyfriend, Mum.'

'OK, I believe you. But I'm asking because I want you to talk to me. I want you to know that you can talk to me about anything.'

Vee rolls her eyes, and snakes down a little further under her covers. 'It's because of that book, isn't it?' she says. 'You think because I'm reading *Forever* I've got a boyfriend.'

That book, your singing, your near-permanent good mood. 'That's part of the reason.'

'Just cos I read a book about *that* doesn't mean I'm doing what's in it. I read a book about a flying horse the other week, doesn't mean I'm going to try and put wings on a horse, you know?'

'Yes, I know.'

'I just like to read, you know?'

'Yes, I know. But it's not just about the book. It's . . . well, you're at that age. Boys might notice you, you might notice boys, and I want you to know that you can talk to me. I don't want you to keep things to yourself. Even if you think I won't like it, I still want you to tell me. It's not good to have secrets like that.'

'Did you tell Grandma about your boyfriends?'

'No,' I say. 'No, I could never have told her stuff like that. I told your aunts, though. You haven't got an older sister, so I want you to talk to me. And if you can't talk to me, then maybe one of your aunts. They are your godmothers, after all. I just want you to always have someone to rely on. I'd love for you to talk to me, but if you really can't then talk to one of them. OK?'

'OK,' she mumbles.

'Promise?'

'I promise.'

'Great. Goodnight, gorgeous clever girl.'

'Goodnight, Mum.'

I kiss her on the forehead again, resisting the urge to kiss both cheeks, too, like I used to when she was a baby.

After I switch off the light, I make a mental note of the places she glanced at — suitcase on top of the wardrobe, the gap beneath her chest of drawers, the area where her laundry hamper sits — when I was talking to her. That's where she's hidden things, that's where I need to look to find out what I need to know. She is a teenager, she can't help keeping things from me. I couldn't help myself, either. I know what can happen when a teenager hides too much from those who love her. I let it happen to me, I won't let it happen to Verity. She'll be angry with me for a while if there is anything to find and I confront her with it, she might tell me in not so many words that she hates me, but I'd rather that than the alternative. Anything is better than the alternative.

June, 1986

'But I don't want to wear them,' I said to him.

He had bought me a pair of fishnet stockings and a suspender belt, to wear with a black-and-white two-tone skirt he bought me. But I didn't want to wear them. They looked complicated and silly and like something an old woman would wear. I was only fifteen, after all. I really didn't want to do it. In the three months we'd been together he'd brought me so many things – a lot of it underwear I had to keep at his house so that Mum wouldn't find them – that I didn't really like, but I never said anything because I didn't want to hurt his feelings. This was the worst, though, and I really didn't want to wear them.

They would be difficult to put on and I didn't like stockings or skirts.

I used to wear leggings under my Lycra skirts, but he said they made me look like a man and I shouldn't wear them around him. Then he said I shouldn't wear them at all, even if I wasn't with him in case we met up spontaneously, then I'd be wearing them around him. Then he said I wasn't to wear leggings ever because they were ugly and they made me look ugly. 'I suppose you're right,' I'd said about the leggings. But I didn't think stockings were the answer – I'd just stick to tights.

'What did you say?' he asked me, conversationally, as I held up the suspender contraption, trying to work out which bit of pale pink lace went where. I couldn't believe women actually wore these. They looked like a cross between a cat's cradle you made between your fingers with a length of string and a slingshot. The pale pink fishnet stockings were horrible, too.

'I don't want to wear them,' I said.

'That's what I thought you said.' He put down his paper and took his legs off the squashy, square leather pouf, then put his feet down. He stood up and went to the window and looked out over his front garden. 'Make us a cup of tea, there's a good girl,' he said, his back to me.

As I made his tea, I started to worry that I'd upset him. He'd left the school a month ago, because things were serious between us, and he was struggling to find supply teaching work, so he wasn't very happy sometimes. He'd probably paid good money for those things. Normally I wouldn't say anything, but they really were horrible and I couldn't imagine wearing them. Especially not in pink!

'Thanks,' he said with a smile as I handed him his mug of tea. I'd wiped the dribbles from the side, just like he liked it. He took a sip and smiled at me. 'Ohhh,' he said, still smiling, 'good cup of tea that. Ohhh, yeah.' He carefully settled the mug on the wide windowsill and then turned back to me.

It flashed up in his eyes a second before the pain exploded in my right cheek, knocking me backwards off my feet on to the floor. I sat still on the floor, wondering for a second what had happened, and if he had felt that jolt too as the world rocked under his feet. But his feet were still planted firmly on the ground, he did not look as if he had moved. It must have been just me then, it must have only happened to me.

My hand went to my cheek, but my eyes did not raise themselves immediately to look at him. I sat on the floor, clutching my face and trying to breathe, trying to remember how to breathe.

'Put on the suspenders and stockings, there's a good girl,' he said. 'And don't ever tell me you don't want to do something again, OK?'

I sat still, staring at the floor; the fear twirling around and around my heart made me too scared to raise my head to him.

'OK?' he repeated.

'OK,' I replied with a nod.

I scrambled to my feet, the imprint of the back of his hand still burning its embrace on my face, my heart cantering in my chest as I went back to the suspenders, lifted my skirt and started to work out how to put them on.

I heard him take another sip of tea, even though he hated noisy drinkers – and eaters and breathers. 'This really is a good cup of tea, thanks.'

'What would you do if Vee had a boyfriend?' I ask my husband, who obviously finished his goodnight a lot quicker than I. He has cracked open a bottle of beer and has his bare feet up on the coffee table and his eyes on a taped episode of *Match of The Day* that he's already watched.

He lowers the bottle on its route to his open mouth as his eyes slide over to where I have flopped in an armchair. I need to get to the kitchen to wash up and hide the knives, but I want to sound out Evan first. I want to make him aware of what I am worrying about. I hadn't expected it, but he uses the remote to stop the recording, and to switch off the TV.

'What would I do or what would I say?' he asks.

'Both,' I reply.

'What would I like to think I'd do or what would I probably do?'

'Both.'

His broad shoulders and chest move upwards and down-wards in a sigh. He stares at the marble fireplace, empty and benign but still guarded by a bronze grille. 'OK,' he says. 'As Dr Evan Gillmare I would sit her down, ask her to tell me about this boy. I would ask if it was serious, if he was nice to her, and when she thought she could let me meet him so I could judge for myself. I would also ask again if it was serious and what precautions she was taking.

'As Verity's father I would probably shout as loud as I could about not letting some pleb near her, I'd find out who he was, would lock her in her room and then hunt him down to explain that not only did Verity have an age of consent around the thirty-five mark, he still wasn't allowed near her, even then. Then I'd never let her out of my sight.

'The reality would probably lie somewhere between the two, although much closer to Verity's father.'

'Pretty much how I'd react then,' I say.

'So, has she? Has she got a boyfriend?' He is holding his breath, his body is tense. I wonder what he would do right now if I said yes?

'She says not.'

'Do you believe her?'

'She's never given me any reason to not believe her. And you know she spends most of her time here, filling up that big brain of hers. I just worry that if she has got a boyfriend she's going to hide it from us. I'd rather know, than not know.'

'I'm probably not the best person to reassure you, Sez, I'm sorry. I see girls all the time who are getting up to stuff their parents have no idea about,' says Evan. 'They come to me for the Pill or the morning-after pill, or they get condoms from the nurse. Some of these girls are not much older than Vee. I always ask them if they've talked to their parents. Almost all of them haven't, of course, and I'd be lying if I said I wasn't thinking of Vee when I'm tempted to send them away and tell them to come back once they've spoken to their folks. But I know they won't, they'll just find someone else to give them what they want or even do it without any kind of precaution or protection. I always say to them to think about waiting, or to come back with their boyfriends so the three of us can talk through all their options.'

Agitated and a little sad, Evan runs his hand slowly over his close-shaved head, then rubs his head back and forth, quickly. He takes two large swigs of his beer before he speaks again. 'They never bring them back, of course, but I try. I hope it sinks in that if a guy isn't willing to be man enough to come with them to sort out contraception and STI protection, then he probably isn't right for them. But let's be honest, by the time a girl walks through my door for contraception or advice on an STI, it's pretty much too late, nothing I say is going to stop her.'

'You never know, they might think twice.'

'Think twice, still do it. They think they know, they think they're ready. I mean, how old were you when you first did it?'

'Fifteen,' I mumble as the heat of shame burns another permanent mark on my already-scarred soul.

'Could anyone have stopped you?'

'No, I guess not.'

'Did he come with you to—?'

'No,' I say.

'There you go.' Evan swigs some more beer. 'I see it all the time.'

He does, doesn't he? He sees it all the time and he is understanding, he is empathetic, he is open minded. This is the time. The time I should tell Evan everything about *him* and what happened. He'll understand then why I'm worried and why I want his help to keep an extra eye on Vee.

Not telling Evan about *him* is something I've sweated blood over for years. Since I met him, in fact. It's easier on my body and mind if I try to shut all that out. When I think about it, I feel the world closing in on me: I find it impossible to breathe, things start to get blurry around the edges and that thing happens to my memory where I can't remember everyday things. Like I couldn't remember it was Saturday a week or so ago. When I think about the past, I lose time and I lose myself. Who knows what talking about it would do? But time is not on my side right now. That piece in the paper . . . All it'll take is for another snippet to appear and for him to see and then, not only will I have to deal with the fallout of him finding out, I'll have to explain why I didn't tell him.

'I need to tell you something,' I say.

'That's the second time someone's said that today,' Evan says, his lips had been on the lip of the bottle and now they are away again. 'It's a secret, so when you see him, don't say I told you. Act like you know nothing, OK?'

'OK.'

'But he's got to know I'd tell you, right?'

'I guess so.' I really wish I knew what he was talking about, why it has stopped me from telling him this huge monumental thing I have been carrying with us every day of our relationship.

'He's always calling me a girl cos I tell you everything.' Ah, Max. He calls every bloke who isn't constantly drinking ten pints a night, and chatting up women who aren't his wife, 'a girl'. Better a girl than being a sad, short accountant from Portslade, but that's by the by. Evan plays football with him and they get on, so I mostly ignore it. 'But why wouldn't I tell you everything? I have nothing to hide. And you have to stay with me, for better or worse, right?'

'No,' I say, 'I have to stay married to you because I love you. Anyway, what's the big secret?' *What is the problem so I can get on with what I really should be doing?*

'Max came to lunch with me and Teggie today. And he told us that his missus was married before,' Evan says.

'What? June?'

'Yup. Did the deed in Vegas a while back, apparently. And that scar she says she got falling off her bike? Actually the scar from removing the tattoo of her ex's name from her shoulder. And the bike she didn't fall off was actually a Harley.'

'This is June? Mousey little June?' The woman who I've always thought deserves a medal for putting up with Max.

'Afraid so. Max is gutted. He thought the reason she was so cool about the wedding being a registry office job and a small do was because he'd been so firm about not wanting a fuss, she knew her place because he's the man and she's the woman when, really, it just made it easier for her to cover up the previous marriage.'

My secret isn't that bad. Not really. I haven't done anything to actively hide my secret, I have just avoided telling him. So have all my family.

'I told him, it's his own fault,' Evan mumbles.

'That was supportive of you.'

'Well, it's true. You treat someone like a second-class citizen, you say to her things like, "I'm the man so you have to do what I tell you" and what do you expect? I've always said he should treat June better. Acting like she should be grateful to have him is what got Max where he is. Why would she tell him the truth about herself if he's being that disrespectful?'

'Maybe it had nothing to do with how he treats her.' I cannot *believe* my secret is making me stick up for an eejit like Max. 'Maybe it's just that she was scared of losing him so she kept it to herself. I mean, we know she loves him, why else would she put up with him? And if she loves him, then she knows telling him about her past might ruin things. Maybe she thought keeping quiet was the best way to keep her relationship going.'

'Maybe. He's gutted, though. He reckons she only told him because she's planning on leaving him. Which makes him feel worse because she obviously won't care what he says because she's going anyway. He hasn't actually talked to her, you understand. He hasn't found out why she lied or why she's suddenly told him, he's just not talked to her. Idiot. Especially when he doesn't want her to leave. He's gutted.'

'I'll bet he is.'

Evan swigs his beer, and I marvel at the arc of his profile from his forehead to his chin, how beautiful he is, how sometimes I fear that he is too good for me. I don't deserve him. I don't deserve him, I don't deserve this life. 'You know what he said after I said it was his own fault?'

'What?'

'He said it to me and Teggie, actually. He said we should watch our other halves. Cos women are devious and we never know what they're hiding.'

'Devious is your middle name, isn't it Serena?'

'That's when Teggie said I was right, and that it was all his own fault and he was a fuckwit. I said he could sleep in the spare room till it all blew over, if he wanted.'

'You *what*?'

'It's OK, he said no. He doesn't like being away from home too long in case he comes back to find her gone. All this has only shown him how much he loves her.'

'Revelations can do that,' I say.

'Too much drama,' Evan says. 'Just be honest and then there's no revelations and no drama.'

'It's not always easy to be one hundred per cent honest one hundred per cent of the time,' I say.

'Yeah, maybe. Hang on, how did this conversation start? We were talking about Vee maybe having a boyfriend and now we're on to honesty. That's some ground we've covered in the space of five minutes. Do you want a beer?' He stands up to leave the room.

I shake my head, I don't want a beer. I want to go back to the start of this conversation and see, for the first time in months and months, the best window of opportunity to tell him sitting open and have the chance to climb through it – not watch as another thing slowly closes it and then welds it shut again.

'Come on now, be honest, you do want a beer, don't you?' Evan says. 'Come on, tell me the truth.'

I shake my head again, smiling before he leaves.

'OK,' I whisper. 'I'll be honest. Once upon a time I was arrested and tried for murder. I was tried for murder and I almost went to prison.'

poppy

I'm still having trouble sleeping. Getting through a night without waking up, wondering where the noise has gone, is still impossible.

Laying here in the relative dark, I'm constantly bombarded with pieces of the past; memories of Marcus and how he did this to me. They fall from nowhere on to my mind, and play themselves out whenever they hit.

May, 1986

'Wow.'

That was the first thing he ever said to me.

He looked me over with those eyes as big as saucers, as clear, blue and deep as the sea after a storm, and said that one word.

Sitting on the park bench, eating an ice cream – a 99, my favourite – I had not thought anyone would notice me. Let alone someone like him. My mouth dried up as my heart started to thump too loud in my chest and ears. It was exactly like I read about in *Jackie* and *Blue Jeans* and *My Guy* and *Photo Love*. Exactly. My heart was racing, my head was all fuzzy, my knees definitely felt weak, and my mouth was dry. The best-looking boy in the whole world had just spoken to me and I thought I was going to melt.

The girls in the stories I read would know what to do, what to say, but I couldn't remember anything that they said to the boys they liked. How they got him to keep talking to them. So I stared at him.

'I've never seen anyone make eating ice cream seem so sensual.' He put his head to the side, then gave me a small smile. He was better looking than Don Johnson and Michael J. Fox, and loads more gorgeous than the boys in my magazines. What was that word they used sometimes? Sexy. That was exactly what he was: sexy. 'You really look like you're enjoying that.' His smile spread across his face sprinkling tingles, like a million trillion little stars, all over my body.

I was aware, of course, that my tongue was hanging out; I'd been about to lick my ice cream when he spoke to me, so I'd frozen with my tongue there for him to see. 'It's the thing you do with your tongue,' he said. 'I don't think I've ever seen anyone do that.' More smiles from him, more tingles for me. 'You're obviously special.'

He reached up, ran his hand through his blond-brown hair and smiled some more. His smile was bright, and soft, and friendly, and everything good in the world. It was perfect. He was perfect. Like no one I'd ever met.

'I'll see you around?' he said.

I slowly nodded when I realised it was a question, not just a thing to say to someone at the end of a conversation. I still had my tongue hanging out when he threw another smile at me before walking away.

I lie in the dark, in the room from the eighties, and another memory bomb explodes in my mind.

May, 1986

I hung around the park at the same time every day for nearly two weeks before I saw him again. He just happened to be walking through and his face creased up into that beautiful smile when he saw me on the same bench – this time with an ice cream and a book. It'd got boring after the first time, waiting there for two hours, just in case.

We saw each other in the park a few more times, just talking about nothing in particular: he told me he was a teacher, he asked me where I went to school, and when I told him he said he'd taught supply there a few times and vaguely remembered me. We just talked and talked, until one day, three weeks later, he handed me a piece of paper.

I looked down and on it was scrawled a phone number.

'Ring me,' he said. 'Anytime. If you need help with your school work, or even if you want to just have a chat.' He got up, looked around and then gently stroked my cheek while smiling down at me. 'I'd really like to hear from you.'

And then he was walking away without looking back. I stared at the number, knowing I was going to call him the very next day. Even though he mentioned that he had an ex-girlfriend called Serena who wouldn't leave him alone, I knew I had to call him. I stroked every single digit on the page, imagining they were somehow connected to him. Slowly I lifted the piece of paper and pressed my lips against it, imagining I was kissing him. I had to call him. I just had to. I was completely and utterly in love with him, so I had no choice, I had to call him.

And another.

June, 1986

'It's not serious between us.' Marcus was telling me about Serena. He'd say this a lot – every time I'd been to his house he mentioned her in some way. I had seen her once: I'd arrived half an hour early to see him, and had spotted her leaving. She was glamorous and gorgeous and all the things I wasn't. Tall, and well dressed and completely confident. I was surprised that I hadn't noticed her that day in the park, and I was even more surprised that he'd look twice at me when he had her. Not that anything had happened between us. We were just friends, nothing more. Heartbreakingly, nothing more. 'I stay with her because she's quite vulnerable.' She hadn't looked vulnerable when I saw her, but I didn't say that. He didn't know that I'd been so excited to see him that I'd arrived early that one time, and had spotted her. I had a feeling he wouldn't like it – it would seem a bit like spying on him – so I hadn't told him. Which meant I definitely couldn't tell him that she didn't look vulnerable to me. 'I don't know what she'd do to herself if I dumped her. I'd never forgive myself if she took a load of pills or something. That's what she said she'd do if I ever thought about leaving her. She's trapped me.'

Poor man, I thought. I reached out and touched his arm, just to let him know I was there. He was so brave, having to take care of someone who was that unstable. He reached out and cupped my face in his big strong hand. I always felt so safe with him. Safe and wanted – I'd never felt like that with anyone. Being with my dad made me feel safe, but this was different. This was love. The kind of love that I'd longed and longed for, that I read about and dreamed about. This was it, true love.

'You're such a good friend,' he said, staring straight into my eyes. I went all bubbly inside – that always happened whenever he looked at me like that. 'I don't know how I'd get through all this without you.'

I managed to pull up the corners of my mouth into a smile but only just. I felt like I was drowning. I couldn't catch my breath properly, my head was buzzing and swirling, my body was trembling. He could probably feel me shaking under his hand. He'd probably felt it every time he touched me because that's what happened.

'You make everything worthwhile,' he whispered.

I stopped breathing.

'When I'm with you, I feel like I can do anything.'

That's how he made me feel. When I was with him, I was

pretty and funny and clever. Not having many friends at school meant nothing. Not really getting on with my mum wasn't important. When I was with him I had everything I needed. And he was saying that he felt the same way about me. I did that for him. He was saying he was in love with me, too.

He leant forwards, his hand still on my face, and I felt my whole chest tighten. He was going to . . . His mouth touched mine and everything exploded in my head and chest and stomach and down below at the same time. He pulled away a little but was still close enough for me to feel his breath on my face. 'Relax,' he whispered with a gentle smile. 'Haven't you ever been kissed before?'

I nodded, even though I hadn't. I didn't want him to think I was a silly little schoolgirl.

The corners of his soft, pink mouth curled up into another gentle smile. 'You don't have to lie to me,' he whispered. 'Poppy, sweetheart, you have to be honest with me. I'd think it was sweet if you hadn't been kissed before. It'd make this all the more special. I don't get to have a lot of special "firsts" any more.'

I just stared at him.

He smiled some more, moved a little closer. 'Was that your first kiss?' he asked.

I nodded.

'You're my special girl,' he said and kissed me again. This time for a little bit longer. I didn't know how to do this – I'd seen it on TV but it was different in real life. It wasn't as easy as they made it look; how was I meant to breathe? Where was I meant to put my hands? How would I know if I was doing it right?

'Relax,' he said, his lips resting on mine. 'I'm not going to hurt you. Just relax, OK?'

I nodded a little.

'Good girl,' he said. He pushed me back on to the bed as his hand went up my top. We were in the spare room at his house where he'd taken me to show me the view over the back garden. It was where his young son slept when his ex let him come over, which wasn't very often, he told me. It was a single bed, like the one I had at home, and there were a couple of Paul Gascoigne and Gary Lineker posters taped to the walls, and a Gary Lineker bedspread on the bed. We'd sat down to have a chat and now we were lying down, with him on top of me, his hand up my top. He started to kiss my neck, while his hand stayed under my top and over my bra, and I didn't know what to do with my hands. Was I meant to put them on his back like on TV or behind his head? Or leave them on the bed?

'You're so cute,' he said as he paused in kissing me. 'You really don't know what to do, do you?' He was staring down at me, looking at me as though I was incredibly important.

I shook my head, a little panicked that my inexperience would put him off.

He kissed my forehead and smiled. 'Don't worry, I'll take care of you. I won't do anything you won't like. I won't hurt you.'

He pulled my batwing top up over my head and threw it off the bed. I was slightly scared then. No one except the girls in PE, Bella (my sister), and Mum, had seen me with only my bra on. I shrank in on myself, crossed my hands over my chest.

'It's OK,' Marcus said, soothingly. 'You don't have to hide from me.' He pulled my arms apart and a small smile danced on his lips as he looked down at my plain white bra. I wished suddenly that Mum had bought me something a bit nicer, more grown-up – maybe with lace. He expertly unhooked my bra and threw it off the bed, then his hands moved over the mounds of my chest as his eyes took them in as well.

Then his hands went to the top of my leggings and he tugged them down over my hips. As his small smile became a wide grin, I groaned inside. My knickers had the day of the week written on the front. Worse than that, it was Tuesday and I was wearing Friday's white knickers with red writing.

'You could not get any cuter,' he said before pulling off my leggings and knickers together.

My stomach lurched with fear and uncertainty. I'd only just had my first ever kiss. Two kisses and now we were naked. Except I was naked, Marcus wasn't. I was bare and exposed, he wasn't. He sat back on his heels on the end of the bed and stared at my body, his eyes running over every curve and line and roll of puppy fat.

The longer he stared, the more uncomfortable I got. The more scared. Does he expect us to . . . ? He shed his pastel jacket, with its rolled-up sleeves, and threw it to one side, then went his white T-shirt.

His belt jangled as he unbuckled it, then he unbuttoned the top button of his jeans and unzipped himself, his eyes never straying from my naked body the whole time.

I wasn't sure I wanted to do it. It was all happening so fast and I wasn't ready.

'Marcus,' I said. My voice was wavering, shaking with fear. 'I don't want . . . Can we wait?'

He stopped pulling his jeans down. 'What?' he asked, looking at my face for the first time since he pushed us down on to the bed. His eyes weren't focused on the here and now, with me, they looked as if they were somewhere else; as if he didn't recognize me.

'I . . . I want to wait,' I said, my voice still fragile and shaky. 'Please?'

'Wait,' he stated, frowning at me. 'You want to wait.'

I managed a small nod, hoping he'd understand. Hoping he'd still like me. I snaked my arms around my bare chest, suddenly cold under his glare. He climbed off the bed and angrily snatched up his T-shirt and jacket from the pile of clothes on the floor.

'Get dressed,' he said, and marched out the room without looking at me again.

He was so angry he wouldn't speak to me, wouldn't look at me as he drove me home. As we got closer and closer to the spot around the corner from my house, where he always dropped me off so that my parents wouldn't see, I was hoping he would say something. Anything that would mean he still wanted to see me and would show I hadn't driven him away by not going through with it. He slowed his white Ford Escort and then pulled in, and still he didn't speak. Still he kept the wall of frost between us.

I was scared then. Scared that he would never forgive me, never speak to me. I couldn't live with that. I couldn't live without him speaking to me. He stared straight ahead, his body tense, his hands clamped to the steering wheel. He was waiting for me to leave and he was going to let me go without saying another word. He was going to go back to his life with Serena and have no one to support him when she threatened to kill herself. He was going to forget about me.

'Will I see you again this week?' I asked.

He gave a short, silent laugh as he continued to stare out of the windscreen, shook his head slightly and muttered something that sounded like 'unbelievable' under his breath.

'Marcus?' I asked, desperate.

'Get out of the car,' he said.

'I'm sorry, I was just sc—' I said.

'Just get out of the car,' he cut in, his voice as cold and hard as steel. I'd never heard him speak like that before. 'Get out of the car and leave me be.'

'I'm sorry,' I whispered, moments away from tears. My hands were like slabs of meat that I couldn't get to work as I tried to open the car door. His irritation was growing the longer it took me to open the car door. I finally managed to get it working and it sprang open, letting some of the pressure out.

I'd barely got on to the pavement when he leaned over, and pulled the door shut again. Then he sped off, his tyres squealing as he drove away from me. I stood on the street watching him go, terrified that this was the last time I'd ever see him. Terrified that I'd never feel the same way about another person

114

as I did about him. Terrified of what I'd have to do if I did see him again.

I've had enough remembering. Enough, enough, *enough!* I throw back the covers – new ones I found in the airing cupboard – and reach down to pull on some socks before I reach for my old dressing gown. It's not ideal, wearing the old blue-and-red striped thing, but it's better than nothing and better than the things I had in prison. I still have to wear them because almost all the clothes in the wardrobe are twenty years old and too big for me now I'm prison-thin. And hideous. Let's not forget they're hideous. There are some gems in there, but most of them are just plain hideous.

I creep down the stairs, avoiding the creaks of the floorboards that I have learnt off by heart now. A glass of water, and maybe a few biscuits will help me to settle again. They've helped these past three nights of freedom.

I don't switch the light on, instead I get the water and a few biscuits and sit at the table to eat them. Normally I would have taken them upstairs to my room, but that room is . . . unsettling. I can't help but think about Marcus when memorabilia from that era assaults me from every angle. But I can't just dismantle it. Either Mum or Dad took the time to put it together; I can't rip it down as if I don't care about the trouble they went to.

Creak! on the stairs has my heart skipping a little, and raises my hackles. Seconds later, I watch Dad walk into the kitchen, heading for the glasses cupboard. He is in his dressing gown and slippers, and has obviously not been able to sleep, either. He does not see me at first. He doesn't see me until he has poured his glass of water and turns away from the sink with the glass at his lips. He jumps a little and stops drinking as his eyes make out my shape, sitting in the dark at their table.

'I couldn't sleep either,' I say, indicating to my glass of water and biscuits.

In reply, he puts down the glass of undrunk water on the

edge of the sink, not seeming to care that it could easily slip off and break, then walks out of the room without looking at me again.

'Daaaaaaaaa,' I say softly. 'Daaaaaaaaa.'

July, 1986

Three weeks.

It'd been three weeks and I still hadn't heard from him. He didn't wait for me outside the school gates. He didn't wait for me in the usual place by the park. He didn't come and wait near the clothes shop where I worked all day Saturdays and Tuesdays and Thursdays, during the holidays. He didn't ring my house and hang up if someone else answered. Nothing. For three weeks, nothing. In six weeks the last golden rays of summer would be fading, autumn would be just around the corner, which meant I'd start back at school soon and we couldn't meet more often like we planned. I was too scared to just turn up at his house in case he shouted at me – or worse, ignored me.

I was frantic. Going out of my mind. I cried myself to sleep every night. I stopped eating – it just made me feel sick. I didn't want food, I didn't want to watch telly, I didn't want to read, I didn't want anything but to have Marcus back. He loved me, he'd practically told me he loved me, and I'd let him down. By not going through with it I'd let him down, made him feel awful. I'd really hurt him when he needed me and now I'd lost him for ever.

'What's the matter, love?' Dad eventually asked me. He came to my room where I was lying curled up on my bed.

I hurt. My stomach was hollow, but full of lead; my head felt like a helium balloon – all light and ready to float away – but banging with a dull, heavy ache; an elephant was sitting on my chest and my eyes would not stop leaking tears. I wanted to scream his name out loud, just so someone would know that he had been mine, that I loved him and now I'd lost him.

'You've been like this for more than two weeks. We're all so worried about you,' Dad said. 'I don't like to see you like this, Pepper, love.' Dad had called me Pepper since I was tiny. ('That's my little Pepper,' he'd always say with pride, no matter what I did. 'The cleverest girl on the whole street.')

'He doesn't love me any more, Dad,' I said into my pillow.

'Who?'

I couldn't tell him everything because Dad would NEVER understand, so I shrugged.

'Have you got a boyfriend?' he asked. I could tell he was hoping that I would say no – the last thing he wanted was for me to have a boyfriend.

'He doesn't love me any more,' I said.

'Pepper, love,' Dad said, stroking his hand over my hair like he used to do when I was sick, 'he's not worth it.'

Dad didn't know him. Marcus was worth it. He was worth everything. He was everything.

'Any lad that can make you feel like this is not worth it. No one should ever make you feel like this.'

'But what if it was my fault?' I asked. 'What if I did something wrong and now he won't speak to me?'

'What could you have done that would make him stop speaking to you?' Dad asked.

'I don't know, but it was all my fault,' I said, sounding almost hysterical.

Dad put his arms around me, and rocked me back and forth. 'Don't upset yourself, Pepper. It'll all be OK, I promise you. You'll forget about this lad soon enough and there'll be someone else. Someone who is nicer to you and who doesn't make you feel like this. I promise you.'

He didn't understand: I didn't want anyone else, I wanted Marcus.

'Should I try to fix things?' I asked into Dad's chest.

He shook his head so hard it shook his body and me in his arms. 'No, Pepper. No. You could do more harm than good. Sometimes it's best to let things be. They have a habit of working themselves out for the good of all concerned.'

I knew what was best for the good of all concerned. I knew what I had to do.

'I'm ready now,' I said to Marcus, two days later, on his doorstep. He had opened the door and almost snarled when he saw me. 'I don't want to wait any more.'

'Sure?' he asked, the snarl waiting to be slipped back into place if I even wavered.

I nodded quickly and said 'Yes' just as quickly, so he wouldn't think I was about to change my mind – and so that I wouldn't change my mind.

A grin spread itself across his face as he stepped aside and used his hand to sweep me in.

It hurt. He hurt me. I don't know if he meant to, but sometimes it seemed as if he enjoyed hurting me. But afterwards it didn't really matter because he took me in his arms, he kissed my forehead and he told me it was worth the wait. I was worth the wait.

'Aren't you glad you changed your mind?' he asked.

I nodded and said yes, quickly, so he wouldn't question if I meant it.

'You deserve a gold star,' Marcus said as he pushed me back on to the bed again. I didn't even bother to ask myself if I wanted to do it again, especially when I hurt below and inside and when I hadn't particularly enjoyed it. He did, and that was all that was important. *Isn't your first time supposed to be like this?* I thought to myself. *Doesn't practice make perfect?*

'You're a good girl, really, aren't you?' he said. 'You're my good little girl.'

I'm drifting off now. My eyes are growing heavy and my body is sinking down into the unfamiliar spaces in the mattress, settling itself to sleep. I'm going to sleep. Now that I've stopped fighting it, now that I've let those memories play themselves out, I can relax and allow myself to drift away.

I'm wrong, of course. There's one more. One more unexploded memory bomb ready to detonate. As my grip on this reality finally loosens, it goes off, ushering me into the land of nod.

'Poppy, this is Serena; Serena, this is Poppy,' Marcus said, standing between the two of us. She was tall and slender, and even more glamorous close up. I had been with Marcus officially for three months and he said I should meet her so that we could relax when we were together, so we wouldn't always be on edge in case she found out.

I had wanted to ask him why he was bothered if they weren't together any more, but I didn't. I decided to leave it for another time, and just meet her. See what she was like for myself.

She forced a smile on her face and held out her hand to shake mine. Dumbstruck and nervous, I took her hand and shook it back. *She doesn't seem vulnerable*, I thought. *She doesn't seem the type who would kill herself if he dumped her properly*. But there was no reason for Marcus to lie to me about that, was there? She was just probably very good at hiding how crazy she really was.

'Good to meet you,' she said, even though her face said otherwise.

'You, too,' I said.

'We're all going to get on famously,' Marcus said. 'I promise you, the three of us are going to have a really good time together.'

serena

I reckon that paperboy gets some enjoyment from doing things like this. From making me leave the house in my dressing gown to get the paper from the other end of my front garden, from leaving it where it'll get wet if it rains, or – as he's been doing for the past week – putting number thirty-nine's paper through our door and putting ours – number ninety-three – through their door.

Thankfully, the people at number thirty-nine are OK: Ange, the mother, is nice and Ryan, her eldest son, is Con's age so they play footie in the park together if we're ever there at the same time. Ryan is in a posh private school so they aren't schoolmates, but I like that Con has someone his own age to play with outside of school. I like them, but not enough to read their paper.

In my hallway, I slip my feet into Verity's too-small trainers – all my shoes are neatly put away on the shoe rack at the other end of the hall, then shrug Evan's big overcoat on top of my dressing gown – I'm only going up the road and it's early, so no one will see me.

Feeling like a spy or something, I dash down the road to Ange's to swap them over. Usually I'm able to just pick it up from by their gate and drop theirs in its place, but today the little so-and-so has actually pushed their paper halfway through the door.

'You'd better pray I never get to meet you, boy,' I say to myself as I open the gate and creep up the path to get it.

Just as my fingers make contact, the paper is yanked through the letterbox and the door is suddenly snatched open. Ange stands in front of me in her pink fluffy dressing gown, her hair a sleep-induced blonde mess, and a ring of black, blue and purple around her left eye.

Internally, I draw back, a little shocked but not as much as I probably should be. She is always perfectly made-up with just a bit too much foundation no matter what time of day it is; she always wears long-sleeved shirts no matter what the weather; she always looks on edge whenever she mentions her husband. Those are the clues, those are some of the many, many clues.

We stare at each other for a moment then, without a word, we exchange papers and she turns away, shutting the door firmly behind her as she returns to her house, to her life.

poppy

I have a letter postmarked HMP Colfrane.

It's from Tina. I wrote to her with this address, but I didn't think she would use it. I sit down on the third stair and eagerly rip it open. I expect to see lots of black 'censored' lines on it. She used to write lots of dodgy things in her letters when she wrote to me, just to have them censored, just to wind up the screws. And to make me laugh, of course, always to make me laugh.

October, 1989

'Well, aren't you a special lil' ray o' sunshine,' the woman said, sitting opposite me at my lone table.

I looked up at her, not really comprehending what she was saying through the general haze that surrounded me, and her strong West Indian accent – I wasn't sure if it was from Jamaica or somewhere else. I couldn't understand a lot of things. This was my first trip to the dining hall, I usually just ate in my room, but I had ventured here and now sat at a table, all alone. Until this woman showed up.

'Come on darlin', smile, it not dat bad.'

Where do you think we are, in a café? I asked her silently. *At the Queen's garden party? How could this not be 'dat bad'?*

'M' never taut m' see da day, y'know?' she said. 'Black girl go free, white girl bang up.' She knew who I was, most people in here probably knew who I was. 'We all waitin' to see your friend, not you.'

I stared down at my plate, prodded at the grey mush in front of me with my plastic fork. I wasn't hungry, but a part of me was telling me to eat. To eat, to sleep, to try to keep going as normally as possible because there was always the appeal. There was always the chance that I wouldn't be here for long. The truth would be revealed and I could get out of here. That part of me had my dad's voice. Although I had not heard from him since the guilty verdict – and only Mum had dropped off a suitcase of hastily packed clothes and belongings at the prison gate, then left – the voice inside that was telling me everything would work out and I'd soon be free was my dad's.

'It not so bad, y'know.'

I scowled at her in my head; on my face I wouldn't dare. She was terrifying. Everyone here was terrifying. I should not be in this place with these criminals and I knew, in deep down places, that I was going to come to some harm here.

'M' call Tina. Call me de welcoming committee,' she said. She smiled, showing yellowing teeth that looked like they had once been straight and white and strong.

'Led me give you some advice,' she said.

I continued to prod at the mush on my plate. I hadn't even attempted to cut the bread roll to butter it – it looked like a slab of brown marble and sounded like one when it had been dropped on to my tray.

'You be awright, y'know, if you keep your head down. Don't budder no one, and no one budder you. Y'hear?'

I nodded without really listening. 'An' Poppy da Ice Cream Girl be careful who your friends are, y'know. M' talk to everyone who talk to me, me have no friends, friends, y'know.'

No, I don't know, I thought. *I have no idea what you're talking about.* But I nodded all the same. I nodded because she might leave me alone quicker if I did.

'You keep yourself to yourself, it safer dat way, m' promise you.'

That I understood and agreed with. I wasn't going to befriend anyone in here. I was nothing like these people, they were not the sort of people I'd be friends with. I wasn't going to be here that long anyway. What did I need friends for? Especially when they were all criminals.

'You tink you better dan all of us, eh?' Tina asked.

My cheeks flushed that she'd been reading my mind.

'You not, y'know. Not in da eyes of da law. Dem screws, dey make sure you know it every single day. And dem udders, dey won't like you lookin' down on dem. You tink you better dan everyone else, fine, jus' hide it better, girl. Hide it deep, for you own good.'

She was right, I had to be careful, I had to be really careful in here about what other people found out about me.

'And listen carefully now, dis important: stay away from drugs.'

Drugs? Is she pulling my leg? Even if I was into drugs, how would I get them in here? I looked up at her, confused and sceptical. I thought she had some good advice, but she was clearly a bit doo-lally.

'Girl, you face!' she leaned forwards and lowered her voice. 'Dere more drugs in here dan out dere, y'know. Jus' be careful. When someone offer it to you, say no. It's hard. You get so lonely and sad and scared in here, dat you want any-ting to make it feel better, to kill da bird. An' dere udders who give you drugs first for free. To help you out, dey say. Dey jus' want you to owe dem. Den they'll be wanting you to get people to smuggle it in. An' you do it, too. Once you got a habit, you do any-ting to get it. Any-ting. I seen nice gals, y'know? Like you. All nice and prim, wouldn't say boo to a goose when dey get here. Den drugs get dem. And den, dem decrutching udder girls to get de drugs out and beating dem friends, making dem maddas smuggle in money and jewellery an' tings to get de drugs.'

'What's decrutching?' I asked.

'You don't wanna fin' out, trust me. Jus' stay away from de drugs. Dey is bad news all round, man, bad news.'

125

'I'll try to remember that.'

'I mean it, y'know. An' don't do no favours for anyone. They be all nicey-nicey, tell you some sob story, ask to borrow you phonecard, for you to get dem som-ting from da canteen. Don't do it. Everyone got a sad story. You start to do favours, dey take advantage. Or dey start to get you ready to smuggle drugs in for dem. Jus' say no, to everyone and every-ting. Y'hear?'

I nodded. If I was to trust no one, then why was she helping me? I asked her this.

She smiled that wide, tarnished smile of hers again. 'M' tell all de new girls who look as scared as you do dis stuff. It's what m' want when m' first got here. But, girl, dey never listen. Dey forget, dey don't believe me, dey tink dey know better. At de end of de day, dey stupid. Are you stupid, Poppy da Ice Cream Girl? Dat is de question you have to ask yourself. You get yourself a job, keep ya head down, you be fine.'

'What are you in for?' I asked. She seemed so nice, kind, gentle. Like me, she was probably innocent and she didn't belong here.

'Dat's anudder ting m' mean to tell you, never ask dat. If someone gonna tell ya, dey tell ya. Not everyone as famous as you, y'know. But you hear tings, you always hear tings, and you find out eventually. Don't ask doe.'

'Sorry,' I said.

'Ain't no ting. Me? M' grow up with strict parents, m' dada die, m' madda and m' we start rowin'. We row an' we row an' den me run away. M' tink m' big grown woman, m' can survive on m' own. An' den me start up really nice, find a new yard, small job. M' get involved with a man, nice white boy him, put m' on drugs, put m' on streets. Nice boy, rich parents. When m' get arrested first time, him parents take care of him, bail him out, give de judge de speech about how he was corrupted by dis dirty black girl. Him walk. Me? Two stretch. Den in and out of prison. But dis time . . . I get five stretch for trying to smuggle drugs into the country. And life for killing the bastard that rape me to get his drugs out of me.'

126

Nausea rose like a tidal wave inside me, threatening to spill out of my mouth on to the table. I was sitting in front of a murderer. A real-life killer. She had killed someone, removed them from this earth and she didn't seem ashamed of it. She said it, just like that. She seemed so nice, so innocent. But she was a drug addict, a prostitute and a killer. And I thought she was just like me.

'Don't look so shock dere Ice Cream Girl. M' know m' business. De man beat me an' rape me. Even when he got him drugs he rape again and again. And me know de poe-leece no do nuffin'. I a prostitute, right? I do what I do so me don't deserve to say no to a man. Me know de risks, right? I know all dis. I take it. He rape me an' rape me an' me take it. Den, he go and den he come back, he say he gonna fix me so no one ever look at me again, and I never have chil'ren. He try to hurt me, and m' say no more. M' no take it no more. M' hit him, catch him off guard, m' take him knife, m' stab him to save m'self. Self-defence.'

'Self-defence?' I echoed.

'Self-defence if you a nice rich, white girl, but not if you ex-prostitute wid accent. Dey only know abou' de drug smuggling cos m' tole dem. M' try to be honest.'

What am I doing here? I asked myself. I was tempted to stand up on the table and scream it at the top of my lungs: 'WHAT AM I DOING HERE?'

'Poppy da Ice Cream Girl, don't look so scared. You be fine, as long as you no stupid. And you no look so scared. De strong ones dey feed on you fear. Even when you strong yourself, you show fear at start, dey pick on you. Hide you fear, hide it good. You have you own room, dat easier.' She stood up, picked up her tray. 'Don't be stupid Poppy da Ice Cream Girl, dat how tings work in here. You don't be stupid, you stay safe. See ya.'

She walked towards a table of other black women, who all greeted her with a smile and they started chatting, the sound of their voices blurring into the general noise around me. The haze I'd been living in the past few days, ever since I left the hospital wing, descended again. I felt calm again. But Tina's words stayed lodged in my head. 'Don't be stupid.' She was a drug addict, a prostitute and killer. If there was anyone that would know how things worked in here it was her. I should listen to her.

Dear Poppy The Ice Cream Girl, (she's written)
So, come on then, what's it like out there? Is it as AWFUL as everyone says – haha!
*   Things are absolutely wonderful in here. Everything is exactly the same. And, of course, I wouldn't have it any other way!*

March, 1990

'But why do I have to move, Miss?' I asked the screw who had dropped a couple of black binliners on the floor of my room and told me to pack up because I was being ghosted. Not out of the prison, though – out of this room, off this level, down to somewhere else.

I liked this landing – as much as I could like anything to do with this place. It was quieter up here with the other lifers, even though I was the by far the youngest of them on this level. Although, technically, I was a young offender and should have been with other offenders my age, they had no single rooms on that wing, and being famous and a lifer meant I was allocated a room of my own. My room – small and cramped and hideous with its cockroaches and creeping damp – was still my own space. It still meant I could dress alone after a shower, I could put things wherever I wanted. I could do whatever I wanted. All the rooms on the four landings below this one were shared rooms, a few dormitories on the lower level. I thought that being notorious had this going for it at least – why was that being ripped away from me too? They already had my freedom, why were they taking away something else as well?

'Don't ask questions, EX396798, just do as you're told,' she replied in her gravelly smoker's voice.

My hackles rose at this screw's use of my number. She loved doing that; loved to remind you that you don't officially have your name any more, that since the moment you walked in here, you became a number. On every piece of paper that relates to you, that number has to be written. If they so chose, they could forgo noting down your God-given name at all and just use your number. This screw in particular also loved to use your number so you never forgot she had a long and detailed memory. Oh, and to remind you that she was a fucking bastard.

Sometimes I would be stopped short by how quickly I started to speak and think like the other prisoners: how easily I'd started to resent the prison officers, how quickly I started to swear, how I picked up the lingo. I had been here six months, was allocated to stay here, and sometimes I felt like the girls who'd been here years.

'I haven't done anything wrong, Miss,' I stated, 'I don't see why I should move.'

'I'll be back in ten minutes, anything you haven't packed gets sent to the incinerator. Got that?' she said, her voice sounding more gravelly than it had two minutes ago. I was going to sound like that if I didn't stop smoking. I'd only started since I'd been in here. But cigarettes were something to do, a silent but constant companion, another way to kill bird. I understood now what Tina meant about drugs being appealing. After a few months, when it dawns on you that even appeals can take years to come through, you start to look around for other things to occupy your time, your mind, your body. You look for escape routes wherever you can, anything to kill that bird called time.

'Yes, Miss.' I snatched up the bags then began to unpeel all the pictures and magazine pages I'd stuck with little globules of toothpaste to the noticeboard and walls of my room. That bastard screw wouldn't even tell me where I was being ghosted to.

I soon found out: 'Welcome, welcome to the party room,' Tina said, flashing me her less-than-perfect smile and opening her arms wide to show me my new quarters. 'I'm so glad we are going to be sharing,' she said.

This, this move, was all down to her. In general, prisoners did not dictate such things, but I had a feeling this was down to her. She seemed to have some sway with the other prisoners but that obviously extended to the Big Luv, because look where I was. Away from my welcomed solitude to this. I'd never even shared with my sister when I was at home, now I was expected to do so with her, a complete stranger. An ex-tom, ex-smackhead, and murderer. Don't get me wrong, I had a lot of time for Tina, I had a lot of respect, but that didn't mean us sharing would be a good idea. Especially not when I had my appeal coming up and I had to prepare myself mentally for it. It'd probably be the first time I would see my dad since I'd been in here. Mum came to visit every so often, so I'd seen her, but not Granny Morag. And Granny Morag probably wasn't going to be at the appeal because she'd be taking care of Bella and Logan who certainly wouldn't be coming. I would see Dad, though.

I needed time and space to prepare myself, not this. Not this sharing nightmare.

Tina already had her bed picked out, her locker beside her bed had a few cosmetics on top, all neatly lined up, and a Good News Bible resting proudly on the edge of the locker closest to her bed. The sink in the corner had her toothbrush and a tube of Crest toothpaste sitting in a tin mug. Her noticeboard was covered in postcards from Jamaica and photos of her family. I only had a few photos of my family. A few I had hastily packed the night before the last day of the trial, when something in me told me to at least pack a bag in case. I packed it, but had left it at home. Serena's family, apparently, had a bag with them. She'd been ready to go down, which is maybe where I went wrong. I stupidly believed that being innocent meant I'd be sent home with the Court's apologies.

The metal-framed bed on the opposite side of the room to Tina's was neatly made up, with hospital corners and the white sheet folded down at the top over the thin, grey, scratchy prison-issue blanket. I was touched: she'd obviously done it – there was no way in hell a screw would do anything like that.

'I don't understand what I'm doing here,' I said, sitting down on my new bed with the two binbags of my belongings slumped beside my feet.

'Poppy the Ice Cream Girl, sometimes it's better not to question these things. Sometimes it's better to just embrace it.'

'How can I embrace something that's basically a loss of privileges?'

'Did they say you were losing privileges?'

'No, but this isn't exactly good, is it?'

'People would kill to be in here with me. Even when there's overcrowding they don't put just anyone in here because they know what an honour it is to be with me. Stop complaining or I might think you're not really my friend.'

'You were the one who warned me off being friends with people in here, now you're saying that we're friends?'

'Every young girl who comes in here for the first time needs to be told to stay away from "friends". It stops them making stupid mistakes and it makes them take their time to suss people out before they get to know them. Otherwise, you would all become friends with the first person who smiles at you. And a snake's smile can be very pretty. Very pretty indeed.'

I flopped back on the cardboard-like mattress, stared up at the grey-cream ceiling with its cracked and peeling paint. My appeal had to go well. They had to quash my conviction and set me free – I couldn't take much more of this.

'Let me tell you the rules for this room,' Tina said.

Rules, of course there were rules. Everything had a rule in here. 'We don't sleep too late, we get up, sweep the floor, mop it with bleach every other day – that helps to keep the cockroaches away. Tidy your bed, keep your things neat. You wash up anything you use straight away. We can take it in turns to get Sunlight soap from the canteen to wash underwear. We try to get as much time outside as possible – it's good for the mind and soul to be outside in God's fresh air. We don't play the radio too loud. And we have as much fun as possible.'

'This isn't a holiday camp, and we're not here for fun,' I said.

I heard Tina rustling around in her locker and then, after a fashion, the click–click of plastic on plastic. She was probably knitting, a lot of women did that in here to keep sane and to keep them off the fags. I could not summon the energy nor will to lift my head to see what she was making.

'You know what your problem is, Poppy?' she said. 'You want to be rescued. You long to be rescued but you're not willing to do it for yourself. And you cannot see a good rescue when it hits you over the head.'

'You've rescued me?' I asked. 'How? Because all I can see are four walls and a window with bars on it and a metal door I'm not allowed a key to.'

'You're so pathetic sometimes, I wonder why I like you,' she replied. She obviously avoided answering my question because we both knew she had not rescued me. She had probably just called in some favours to get herself a roommate. 'Tell me what your favourite colour is so I can make you a blanket for your new bed.'

'Green,' I said.

'Baby blue it is then,' she replied, and the clickity-click got faster.

'Hang on,' I said to her, lifting my head to watch her sit cross-legged on her bed, knitting, 'what happened to your accent? You don't sound West Indian any more, you sound like Northern Shona, like you're from Yorkshire.'

'I am,' she said with a grin as she scrutinised the line of stitches she was creating. 'Would you have listened to a word someone with my real accent was saying? Would you heckers! To someone like you, a Jamaican accent is probably a bit scary, but definitely unforgettable. And before you ask, yes, everything I told you about my story and why I'm here is true. Every word. Every bleeding word.'

I rested my head back on the mattress again. Shamefully, she

132

was right, her real accent would have been lost in the white noise in my head – her Jamaican accent, being so alien to me, kept repeating in my head when I got into a situation that she had warned me against.

'And by the way, you say "Caribbean", not "West Indian".'

'OK,' I said. After a few seconds, I raised my head again. 'I really don't like blue that much.'

'It's only a scarf,' she countered. 'I'm sure you'll love it.'

'A scarf? You said a blanket a minute ago.'

'Girl, do you think I'm going to use up all my spends on wool to make a blanket? Are you mad?'

I've managed to knit myself a new roommate. She's much quieter and neater than you, but she doesn't seem to get it when I tell her to wash my smalls, too. So, in that way, you were far better. Not that I want you back, or anything.

April, 1990

'It's true,' one woman said to the other.

'Really,' said the other.

'Yes! Alicia was cleaning the Big Luv's office and she heard Black Tina tell him he'd have blood on his hands if he didn't move the Ice Cream Girl into a shared room before her appeal. After the appeal would be too late.'

'Alicia ought not to be listening at doors like that.'

'I told her, she won't listen. But she was right, cos Black Tina's got the Ice Cream Girl as a roommate.'

'Black Tina always calls it right, though. She can see who's going to top themselves a mile off.'

'Yeah.'

'Yeah.'

The two other women, older than me and older than Tina, were standing in the corridor that led to the showers and didn't know I was standing just around the corner, listening to them. I'd been on my way to get another shower in after spending the day getting all dusty while helping out in the library, when something in the way they were talking just around the corner made me stop where I was out of sight and listen. You got to know which conversations were worth listening in on very quickly in here. You found out the best gossip, the real news and, of course, you found out how vicious people could be about other people. Now I knew why Tina and I were sharing. She thought I was weak enough to do that. She thought I was like the other women who had done that. I wasn't. Of course I wasn't. I hadn't even done any cutting up in about three months and the scars on my arms were starting to heal. There was no need to. I didn't need the release I'd discovered in here from cutting up any more. I knew my appeal was going to be heard and my conviction quashed, worst-case scenario I'd be given a new trial. Tina really had no reason to worry about me. I didn't mind that she'd been grassing me up, because it was out of concern. And she really had nothing to worry about.

In your last letter, you said you'd come and visit me when you got out. Girl, I say when you're out, stay out. It's the worst thing in the world walking through those gates again, as I'm sure you'll remember.

November, 1990

The world is a vicious, vicious place.
 There is no justice. Nothing is fair.
 Nothing is fair and I do not want to be here any more.
 I stared up at the window of the cell: the bars looked thicker, more solid now that I was going to be here longer. Now I was going to be here for ever. They had strengthened themselves because with my current need to escape, I could probably bend them with my bare hands. I could pull them clean out of the wall like Wonder Woman. I could rip apart the steel door and push aside every single person who stood in my way to get out of here. That was why the bars looked stronger, that was why

the door seemed more solid – they were preparing themselves for a fight.

'You would do well, young lady, to concentrate on paying your debt to society, to stop wasting the Court's time with appeals and to admit what you have done. There is a certain grace in admitting your failings, and it will help you in the future when it comes to release if you confess and face up to what you have done.'

This time, I did not need a few days for the judge's words to sink in, to assimilate the knowledge that no one believed me, that they weren't going to quash my conviction, nor give me a new trial on the basis that the original verdict was unsafe. This time I had heard everything that was said when it was said. And I knew it was the final nail in the coffin. No new evidence meant no chance of anyone listening to me. All they had to do was listen to me. I wasn't a liar. Yes, I had lied a couple of times, only to do with Marcus and to make sure no one found out about us. And I had hidden the clothes I was wearing that night because I was scared. But I was not a liar. And I would never lie about something as important as this.

No one believed me, though. Not even the two people who were meant to love me more than anything: Granny Morag had shown up at the court every day for the three days of the appeal because Mum and Dad did not need a babysitter. They did not come to the appeal. They thought I was liar, too, apparently. They thought I had got what I deserved. Only Granny Morag believed in me.

The image of her crying as the judge gave his verdict branded itself on my mind, on my corneas, like red-hot metal on flesh. Only the two of us in court knew the truth. Everyone else was there to see me get sent down again or to cover it for whichever publication or show they worked for. No one was interested in the truth.

Even my solicitor and barrister hadn't been able to look me in the eye after the verdict. And when I mentioned another appeal, they had both exchanged looks and advised me to take

135

some time to reassess what I wanted to do. In other words, you can appeal again if you want, but without us.

I am here, for ever.

I am here, for ever.

I am here, for ever.

The thought kept playing in my mind.

Tina came back to the room after being somewhere else. She had tried to comfort me when I came back but, when I would not let her touch me and would not speak to her, she had wisely decided to leave me alone. As I would be properly, if it wasn't for her interfering.

'Come on now, love, you've got to get up,' she said. 'Get changed out of your suit and put on some civvies. Seeing you all dolled up like that gives me the willies.'

'This is your fault,' I said to her, quietly, but forcefully. I wanted her to know that I knew what she had done. How she had taken a part in this conspiracy against me. 'You jinxed me. By getting me moved in here, you jinxed me.'

'I wish I were that powerful,' she said, calmly. 'Pops, I've been around a long time, I've seen this time and time again. Very few people, especially those convicted of murder, get out on the first appeal – especially if someone else hasn't come forward and confessed to doing it. I didn't want you to be alone if it happened to you.'

'Who died and made you my mother?' I asked nastily.

'You say you're innocent, so don't let this be the end of it. You have to get up, and get back to trying to prove you're innocent. Write letters to people who can help you, find a new brief – because most of them jump ship after the first appeal fails – and get back out there, fighting. Don't take this lying down.'

'I don't see you doing any of that,' I said. 'I don't see you "out there" fighting. I see you just sitting back and taking it.'

'But I'm guilty. I did what I did, and I'm being punished for it. Self-defence or not, I broke the First Commandment and I deserve to be punished for it. Would I rather my sentence was shorter? Yes. But could I cope with being told over and over

136

again that I got what I deserved – not only from him but also from the courts? No. But if I hadn't killed him, not even in self-defence, as you say you didn't, then nothing would stop me fighting.' I felt her shrug across the room. 'But that's the difference between you and me, isn't it, Ice Cream Girl? You're still waiting to be rescued. I know that no one can rescue you until you've rescued yourself.'

'Fuck you,' I said, simply.

'And fuck you back,' she replied happily. I heard her climb off her bed and then come across the room. She yanked back the covers and took my hands in hers. I had never noticed before but the backs of her hands were a mass of scars, deep cuts and cigarette burns. They looked old, ingrained in her skin like they were always there. She gently pulled me upright, but didn't let go until she had tugged me to my feet.

'You're not allowed to be depressed about this now. Now, you go out there with your head held high and you start thinking about how you're going to fight this. When the time is right, and you'll know when, I'll leave you alone to get depressed. And when that's over, you can apply to be on your own again. Because then you'll be ready for it and I can stop worrying about you.'

'What if I don't want to fit in with your little plan for my life?' I asked.

'Of course you'll want to fit in, because you're still not ready to rescue yourself, are you?'

I shrugged a little because she was right. I wasn't ready to rescue myself – but only because I didn't know how. I defy anyone who had led a life like mine up until eighteen to know how to rescue themselves from a high security prison. I defy anyone, no matter what sort of life they'd lived, to know how to rescue themselves from a high security prison.

So, have you got yourself a jump yet? Was that the first thing you did, picked yourself up a willing bloke who didn't look like the wart on my bum and screw him senseless? That's my plan. I

didn't tell you, did I? My parole board review is coming up soon.
I might be out there with you before long. And we can go for that
drink we always talked about.

May, 1991

'I think it's time,' I told Tina six months later.

It was the middle of the night and we had both been quiet and still in our beds, while music and shouting and screaming and laughing raged in the world outside. Those were the sounds of the post-bang-up hours: the sounds of people connecting and escaping in any way possible by projecting themselves noisily into the atmosphere around their rooms. If you listened carefully, you could hear the sadness and tragedy, too. The sobbing into pillows and towels, the deafening peace of hearts breaking, the silent din of minds collapsing.

I had learned to tune it out. All of it: the loud racket and the quiet chaos; I shut it out so I could sleep, so I could survive.

'I know, sweetie,' she said.

'I'm going to miss you,' I said to her.

'More than you realise,' she said.

'What do you mean?'

'I'm being ghosted, to begin the next stage of my sentence. I don't know where I'm going, but it'll probably be back up north. I hope so. I've been getting on better with my mum recently. If I'm up there, then she might be able to afford to come and see me.'

'God, I hope so. I don't want you to go, but if it helps you and your mum get back together . . . I just hope so.' Because if her and her mum can overcome that, then I could, too. I could get my parents back in my life as well.

'I probably won't see you again, Ice Cream Girl.' I hated it when people called me that, except when she did it. Tina, my best friend, the only real friend I'd ever had, could probably call me anything and I'd be fine with it. Marcus had made sure I didn't have any friends, because – he said – they might have told about him and me. When, really, it was to make sure I only had him to depend upon and I had no one to stand back and say, 'Get out of that thing with him, get out of it now!' It took coming here to meet someone who I could get on with, someone I could trust.

The thought of never seeing her again . . . it cleaved my heart in two. 'Don't say that,' I begged her. 'Please don't say that.'

'It's true. It's best to prepare for that, then anything else is a gift.'

'Thank you,' I said to her, after waiting for the news to sink in, 'for the rescue.'

'It ain't no ting,' she said in her 'Jamaican' accent. 'It ain't no ting at-all at-all at-all.'

'Yeah, well, we both know it was everything.'

'Keep in touch, OK?'

'OK,' I replied.

We both knew we'd try, but if it'd work was another matter. Once this place got hold of you, once you accepted that you were going to be there a while, you found it hard to make connections with the outside world. Because every connection, every tiny touch from them was a reminder of what you had lost. What you hold dear. What you may never have again.

Look, I'm running out of things to say. I'm hoping things are good for you out there. Tell me what it's like out there. Tell me if I'll like it.
I miss you.
(But not enough to have you back, OK?)
   Love,
     Tina xxxxx

I refold the letter after reading it several times. I can't wait to tell her that I've already found Serena, which means I'm well and truly on my way to clearing my name.

part two

poppy

At 7 a.m., the bright blue front door opens and, wrapped up in a silky blue-and-red, knee-length kimono, with a silky red scarf around her hair, she leans forwards and reaches for the rolled up newspaper on the 'You're sooooo welcome' doormat. Her lips move in a curse upon the head of the paperboy as her long fingers close around the daily newspaper – *The Chronicle*, I checked – and pulls it towards herself.

She checks, as she always does, the space by the door where milkmen leave the milk and as always she seems surprised to see it empty. She does not order milk from the milkman, so I can only guess that it's a reflex left over from childhood.

At 7:55 a.m. the front door opens and he appears. As usual, he is wearing a suit and carrying a black bag that looks like a satchel, but probably contains a computer. He pats his left pocket with his right hand, before turning to call inside the house, then uses the brass knob at the centre of the door to shut it. He walks a few feet down the road and uses the keyfob in his hand to unlock his car. He dumps his bag in the boot, then climbs into the sleek, silver beauty, sticks on his sunglasses – even if it is raining out – and drives away.

At 8:05 a.m. the front door opens again. She herds out the children, a triangle of toast in her mouth, her arms a chaos of coats and bags and sandwich boxes, then asks the son to shut the door. The daughter, her spitting image, strides ahead, earphones

143

jammed into her ears, while the son sticks beside his mother, chatting and chatting as they walk even further down the road to her car. She's got the family car that has seen better, cleaner days on the inside. The son takes her keys and unlocks the car door, and the daughter climbs into the front seat. The son happily jumps into the back, while she dumps the things in her arms on to the backseat of the car beside the son. She takes glasses from the glove compartment on the dashboard and slips them on. She checks they are all strapped in, then does her mirror and signal checks – twice – before pulling out of her space and disappearing in the same direction as her husband.

Every morning it is the same; sometimes the paperboy puts the paper in the door, sometimes one of the children runs back inside for something, sometimes the husband leaves five minutes after the rest of the family, but mostly this is the way it happens. This is the way Serena Gorringe, now Serena Gillmare, lives her life. This is the way Serena lives a life that should have been mine.

serena

'Ow!' I yelp as I'm jabbed for the umpteenth time. 'Will you stop doing that? It blinking well hurts.'

'Ah, well, if you will be having those fancy-smancy nerve things all over your body, what do you expect but pain?' Medina, my sister, replies.

Our other sister, Faye, smirks from behind her magazine. My sister who is jabbing me – on purpose I suspect – is going to make me a wedding dress that is a fraction of the cost of the ones I tried on last week. Evan said that was defeating the point of 'going large' this time, but I couldn't face another excursion to a bridal boutique, where I'd have to look at myself in full-length mirrors and maybe have that blood vision again. As it is I'm still feeling sick from having held an ice cream the other day. *He* would be laughing his head off if he could: 'What, the Ice Cream Girl doesn't like ice cream any more? How funny!' Besides which, it'd be far more special this way – I haven't worn a Medina Bryse original in years.

Medina – Mez – who is on her knees, has been pinning pieces of white material all over me for hours now, and treating me like her own private voodoo doll in the process. She is thirty seconds younger than Faye, or something like that – I should probably know, having had two kids and being married to a doctor but it's the sort of thing that's only really important to Faye. She, having used all other arguments at

145

hand, rolls out the ubiquitous, 'I *am* the oldest' when she needs to try to get us to fall in line. (She'd be gutted to know that Mum once told me that she's not all together sure that Faye *is* the oldest. She just assumed because Faye looked like she wanted to be first when they were both lying in their cribs.)

If it wasn't for Faye's need to wear glasses (to make herself look more intelligent and more like the chemical scientist she is – they are the weakest prescription above plain glass) and Mez's habit of radically changing her hairstyle every time I see her, you could not tell them apart physically.

'I'm so glad Evan's decided to make an honest woman of you at last,' Mez says. 'Marrying you this time because he, like, actually wants to.' (I'm sure somewhere out there Verity would be spinning in her seat – a forty-something woman is probably not legally allowed to use 'like' in that way in a sentence.)

'Excuse me!' I protest. 'I think you'll find he wanted to marry me the last time. That's why we've been together for so long. That's *why* we're here today, with you doing this.'

'But he had to last time, didn't he?'

I shake my head, trying – and failing – to look convincing. 'No!' I am aiming for 'aghast at the very idea!' but come off slightly camp and ineffectual.

'No?!' exclaims Faye from behind her magazine. 'Oh, come on, Sez, no one – not even Mum and Dad – bought that whole "honeymoon baby" story.'

'What?'

'Purlease!' Mez rocks back on her heels so she can look up at me, her long shocking-pink fringe falling backwards as she looks up. 'We're all older than you, remember, we've all been there – did you really think we'd believe that nonsense? That wedding had "shotgun" all over it.'

'If you cut it in half, it'd have shotgun written through it,' Faye chimes in.

'If you held it up to the light, it'd have a shotgun water-mark.'

'In fact, didn't your wedding licence actually have a "shot-gun" watermark?'

They both start laughing. Once they start their double act, nine times out of ten I'm the butt of their jokes. I curl my lips into my mouth to express my indignation and try to rise above it, as Mum used to say I should.

'It was his idea to get married, actually,' I say.

'Oh, *purlease*,' Mez begins again. 'He only did it so that he was the one holding the shotgun rather than having it aimed at him – I think he rightly guessed that it was more likely to go off in one of our hands.'

'And we'd all be pleading "accidental discharge, guv",' Faye says.

'Because the first one got our sister up the duff, the second discharge was more deadly,' Mez adds.

'Sorry, m'lud, we didn't mean to kill him, it was an accident!' Faye says. Time stands still and we all stop breathing, trying to pretend she didn't say that. It's happened many, many times over the years. A harmless joke that reminds us . . .

Faye clears her throat, and opens her mouth to apologise, I think, then she changes her mind and closes her mouth again. She draws her long, slender legs up into the chair, and adjusts her glasses on her face before she returns to the magazine article in front of her. Every so often she'll reach up and brush a lock of her long, sweeping fringe aside, like she does when she's in deep thought or is nervous.

Mez is now focused on one part of the 'dress'. She's pin-ning and re-pinning the wide hem without looking up, and without 'accidentally' jabbing me. The pins have multicoloured heads on them that look like tiny ball-bearings against the shim-mering pearlescent of her nail polish.

One of us is breathing very loudly. As if she is running a race. As if at any moment she is going to run out of oxygen. I try to focus on the dress. My dress. My wedding dress. At my last wedding I wore a cream skirt and jacket over a white blouse. This version of the dress is floor-length, with minimal fullness,

147

gently flowing out from the wide waist, a deep V at the chest with long sleeves. It's going to be a triumph, the best thing Mez has made yet.

The loud breather is still struggling for breath, struggling to get air into her lungs and not freak out.

'She's coming out soon,' I say. I do not to need to use her name, they know who I mean. 'She might already be out, actually.'

Faye and Mez both sigh at the same time, both have the same inflection in that sigh: relief, exasperation, disbelief. Even after all this time, still disbelief.

'I know,' Faye says, still skulking behind her magazine.

'We saw it in the paper,' Mez says.

I bite the skin on the inside of my lip; my breathing isn't as loud as it was, but it is not calm, either.

'Do you think she'll try to contact you?' Faye asks.

I shrug, more in despair than ignorance. 'I don't know. I hope not. God, I hope not, but I don't know.'

'You haven't heard from her in all this time?'

'No. I've moved a lot, and it's not as if we were ever friends.'

'I'm sure she won't,' Mez reassures with a tone that suggests she isn't that convinced about what she is saying.

My anxiety about her release is not exactly well hidden. I cannot sleep, I find it hard to eat, and every little thing seems to bring me back to that time: the dress in the wedding shop, being stopped by the police, the talk I had with Verity. Evan thinks it's wedding nerves that have stopped me sleeping through the night; have me waking up at the crack of dawn to go and sit in the kitchen, watching the world get brighter and brighter after the darkness; and have me hiding the dinner knives as well as the sharp ones.

'I take it you still haven't told his nibs?' Faye asks.

'It never seems to be the right time.'

'Yeah, right,' Fays scoffs.

'Stop being a bitch, Fez,' Mez jumps in. 'It's not like it's something you just bring up, is it? "Oh, by the way, honey, I

148

was once tried for murder, and I didn't go to prison, but the girl I was tried with got life. And there was lots of bullcrap written about me in the papers for weeks. Oh, and could you pick up a pint of milk on your way home?" I mean, *come on*!'

'I'm not saying it'd be easy, but he is going to being seriously pissed off when he finds out. Wouldn't you be? After all this time, finding out something like that about him?' Neither Mez nor I can disagree with that. 'It's not exactly the best way to start a marriage. Not the first time, and definitely not the second time,' Faye says.

'What would you know about marriage?' Mez says, effectively sticking a knife in Faye's back. Faye wants to get married but Harry, who she has been with for nearly as long as I have been with Evan, doesn't see the need for it. They've been together so long, he says, that it'd be a pointless exercise, a waste of money. God knows what he's said about Evan and me doing it twice; God knows how much it must hurt Faye that Evan and me are doing it twice.

'Enough to know that your marriage isn't as strong as you make out if you're not telling your husband such a major thing about your life, or if your husband likes to holiday without you and the kids at least once a year.' I wince on Mez's behalf as Faye plunges the knife into her back.

This is why it's not good to talk about those times. It always ends up in an argument, in a slanging match that reiterates in all our minds that we haven't forgotten the pain of then, and we're still living with the scars now. We haven't forgotten, we haven't healed, we've simply carried on with day-to-day life.

'Just because we don't live in each other's pockets, doesn't mean there's something wrong with our relationship,' Mez snaps. 'But that's something you wouldn't know about, isn't it? I mean, how is Harry? I'm surprised he hasn't been on the phone asking when you'll be back to cook his tea.'

'Ha! Shows what you know,' Faye spits, 'Harry does all the cooking.'

'That's because he hasn't got a wife to do it for him.'

'I'm sure that's what Adrian tells the women he meets when he jets off to paradise without you.'

'All right, stop now!' I say. 'Stop. I don't want Evan and the kids walking into this.'

'She started it!' Mez screeches.

Faye and I both stare at her with our mouths open.

'Did you, a forty-two-year-old mother of four really, *really* just say that?' I ask.

'No!' Mez replies, obviously embarrassed. 'It was my evil twin.'

'You loon,' Faye says. She sighs, and tosses her magazine aside, aiming for the coffee table, hitting the floor instead and not seeming to notice. 'Look, I'm sorry, but . . .'

'"But" doesn't make an apology, it makes an excuse of your behaviour,' I cut in, repeating what Mum used to say to us when we fell out as children.

Faye smiles. 'OK, I'm sorry. Full stop. I'm sorry for saying those things.'

'Me too,' Medina says.

'Me three,' I add, even though I didn't technically say anything. I was sorry for the rest of it, though, for causing all of this.

'Excuse me,' Medina says and scrambles to her feet. She grabs her bag and, pausing to rub her knees, she hobbles and walks out of the room. Faye leans over and scoops up her magazine and seems to engross herself in the article straightaway. I stand, immobile and almost non-human, like a mannequin as I wait for Mez to return.

Superficially, that was just a sisterly spat that has passed as quickly as it started; realistically that was another vicious reminder that we never fought like that before all the stuff with me and the courts and the press and the murder.

No one outside of our family unit – no one who would look at us in court, who would read about us in the papers – would ever guess that away from prying eyes, we were systematically tearing ourselves apart. Away from the outside world, everyone in our family started to fall to pieces, and never really recovered. Even though our times together are always fun and laughter-filled, the closeness we once shared is gone. In its place is guilt, regret, the ability to say the nastiest things and, for the longest minute on earth, mean every word of them.

August, 1986

'I swear to God, Serena, if you don't stop moping around this supermarket, I'm going to scream,' Faye said.

This was all her fault. I was meant to be at *his* house, spending the better part of the school holiday with him before I started sixth form college, but Faye had come back early from her holiday with her Loughborough uni mates and had come home. Which was wonderful because Medina had gone to France, and I'd been missing them both. Having one back was almost as good as having them both here. I'd just been about to get ready to go out when Faye offered to do the weekly shopping down at the Co-op and said to Mum, 'Serena'll come to help.' *Then* she turned to me saying, 'You'll come, won't you?'

'I–I–I'm meeting someone,' I'd stuttered.

'You can call them and cancel, can't you?' Faye had said.

I gave her a one-shouldered shrug. I *could* cancel if I wanted to. But I didn't want to. I wanted to see him. The way he had been talking lately, and the way he was looking at me . . . I was convinced he was going to tell me he loved me. It'd been almost eight months and he hadn't said it yet, but he was getting close. And when he said it, all the other worries – tiny little worries really – would melt away. He wouldn't shout at me sometimes, he wouldn't question me obsessively about the boys from my school we saw in the street or park. Things would be better between us. Not that they weren't great, super, as they were. They'd just be that extra bit great, that teensy bit more super.

'Come on, just ring them,' she'd encouraged, heading for the corridor. 'And if there's a problem, I'll speak to them and say that I hardly get to see my little sister so I'm demanding quality time together now.'

There was no way she could talk to him. We were still – rightly – keeping it a secret. He'd explained that even though he'd stopped being my teacher people would still have a problem with us. They'd go looking for dirt on him and Marlene, the ex-wife, would happily give it to them. All made up of course but, as he said, mud sticks. It would destroy his chances of getting supply teacher work as well when term started.

'It's all right, I'll call and cancel,' I'd said reluctantly. He would not be happy. He was looking forward to seeing me as much as I was looking forward to seeing him and this would upset him, and I didn't like upsetting him. It was just easier and nicer between us if I didn't upset him. Because when he got upset, it was my fault what happened next. It had to be. He wasn't like that normally, was he? So it must be down to me.

When I'd called, he'd listened in silence to my explanation as to why I couldn't make it. It was the sort of silence that put me on edge, knowing he was not happy and therefore . . . After I finished explaining, saying over and over again that I had no choice and that if I didn't go with her she'd get suspicious, he hung up without saying a word. A streak of terror tore through me, settling in my stomach as a pool of sicky-fear. He only ever hung up when he was extremely annoyed. I'd closed my eyes for a moment before I resettled the phone in its stand. I did not think about what was going to happen the next time I saw him. I *couldn't* think about what would happen the next time I saw him.

As I shopped, I couldn't think about it but the pool of sickness, of fear and dark dread, was getting slowly and slowly bigger, a drip-dripping of anxiety that could not be plugged. Faye was wrong, I wasn't moping. I was wishing that this hadn't come up, and I could be with him and everything could be OK between us. I felt awful then, wishing away time with my sister. Wishing away time with one of my best friends.

'Oh, I get it!' Faye said, throwing a can of tomatoes into the trolley. 'It wasn't a friend, it was a *boy*friend.'

I said nothing, just examined Mum's list, searching for what was next.

'I take it Mum and Dad don't know about him?' she said, not moving. She'd folded her arms across her chest, rested her weight on her left hip and was raising her eyebrows above her glasses. When I did not reply, she continued: 'Of course they don't. You haven't been shipped off back to Ghana, have you? Who is he then?'

'Just a boy I know,' I mumbled into my chest.

'Hence the lip gloss, the long plait extensions and slightly smarter dressing. Does Mez know you've been "borrowing" her clothes?'

'No!' I exclaimed. 'And you mustn't tell her, either.'

'I might not,' she replied, 'if you tell me about him.'

'He's just a boy I know,' I replied. Mez would exact many levels of revenge upon me if she knew I had been dipping into her wardrobe so that I looked nice for him.

'Is he older than you?' Faye asked.

I nodded. I couldn't tell her how much older – that he was technically old enough to be my father, but only on paper. In reality, in those moments we were together, he was nothing like my father. There was absolutely nothing dad-like about him.

'How much older?' she asked.

'Only a couple of years, eighteen months.'

'*Serena*!' she said, as if in pain.

'What?' I replied. 'He doesn't seem like it. He seems my age.'

'Is he at college or starting college?'

'No, he works.'

Her eyes widened. 'Oh, Sez, he sounds a bit too grown-up for you.'

'He's not, I promise you he's not.'

'Look, I want to meet him.'

'No,' I said, 'you can't.'

'Serena, you're not going to introduce him to Mum and

Dad, so I want to meet him instead. I want to make sure he's OK.'

'He is. I promise he is. If you meet him now, you might scare him and he might dump me. *Please*. I just, I don't want anything to go wrong. He's really nice to me and everything. I . . . I love him. I really do. If he ever stops being nice to me, I'll finish it. I promise. Please don't make me let you meet him. *Please*.'

'OK,' she finally agreed. 'But I'm going to keep an eye on you, and the moment I suspect you're not happy, I'm going to tell Mum and Dad, or make you introduce me.'

'Thank you, thank you,' I said. Relief cascaded through me, almost washing away the sicky fear. But, after the relief, came . . . a feeling that sat like a heavy, cumbersome stone upon my heart.

I had changed. I had become a different person. Was *this* what being a woman, being a grown-up, was about? You lied to the people who loved you? You lied to the people you loved for the good of someone else? I had lied to Faye. I had never done that to either of my sisters before, and I had lied to her for him. I had given up that part of myself for him. And he'd never know. But I would know, I'd always know that now there was no going back. I could never tell them the truth about our relationship, not all of it. I'd always known that, but doing this, lying about it, meant it was definite. I was finally adult enough to see that there was no way out.

'Are you OK, Fez?' I ask.

She has been sitting with her feet under her and her eyes scanning the same article for a while. In fact, I don't recall seeing her turn a page even once since she got here. Out of the three of us, she has always been the most sensible, the most level-headed, but she never reacts like this to our falling outs. Even if we have said near-unforgivable things, while Mez will keep up an indignant exterior and I will desperately think of new ways to apologise for *him*, Faye will be forging ahead, trying to get back to normal as soon as possible. Not in this instance. There is something sorrowful wrapped around her, and it is keeping her apart from us. It's not simply the row: she arrived with it clinging to her shoulders like the first fall of snow.

My oldest sister sighs, then looks up from her magazine. 'Not really, no,' she says. That, I was not expecting. I was expecting the usual 'fine' you get when you ask someone how they are, or even to hear some of it after a little prodding – I was not expecting an outright 'no'.

'What's the matter?' I ask, gathering handfuls of the white calico in my hands and bobbing down at her feet, so I feel more like her sister and less like the Queen. I want her to know that I am someone she can rely on and trust to listen to her problem.

'I want a baby, Sez,' she says, looking me in the eye. 'I know it's not cool and everything to say that and that I should be grateful for what I've got, but I want a baby.' Every one of her forty-two years seems ingrained into her smooth, mahogany skin, while her eyes are misty and swim with sadness behind her glasses. 'It's worse at big family events or birthdays and stuff, and for me both are coming up in the next four months.' The corners of her mouth move downwards. 'I never thought I wouldn't have kids. I never expected to have them, but I suppose I just thought it would happen when the time was right. And it's not going to happen. I've run out of time. At my age, it's now or never time and it's going to be never. And . . .' She presses the palm of her hand over the centre of her chest, pressing down on her heart, as if to stem the pain glugging out, 'it hurts.'

'Have you talked to Harry about this? Does he know this is what you want?' Despite how much we rib Harry for renaming us the Witches of Ipswich when none of us have even been there, he's a good man. Solid. Dependable. The kind of man you'd want your daughter to marry. I'm sure if he knew how much she wanted this, he'd think about it again. He'd have to, or lose her.

155

'Yes, I've talked to him and neither of us have changed what we want. He doesn't see the point in ruining things by getting married and having kids. He doesn't see the point in settling down.' What, apart from being a forty-two-year-old marketing executive with the most gorgeous woman on earth as your partner and the potential mother of your kids? Apart from that, no, there aren't that many reasons – or even any reasons – to settle down. 'To him, we're fine as we are.' She takes her glasses off and presses her fingers in the corners of her eyes. 'That old saying about the milk and the cow, you know: "why buy the cow when you can have the milk for free"? I've lived it.' Her laugh is a bitter, sour sound that falls like lead on my ears and makes my heart turn over and over in my chest. I do not want someone l love to be 'laughing' like that, nor to be feeling like this.

'Oh, Fez,' I say and move to hug her. She is so soft and warm in my arms, it's hard to believe she could have made the sound she just did with that laugh.

'I'm being silly,' she says. 'I have a good life. A great life. I have a man who loves me and an amazing career. And I choose to stay. But still, I can't help how I feel. And I love him. He's a prat sometimes, but I love him. I chose that.' She pulls away from me, and gives me an almost real smile. 'It's fine, really. It's fine.' Unconvinced and still concerned, I sit back and watch her avoid making eye contact. 'The thing is, Sez, for better or worse, he knows everything about me. And that's why I don't leave. It'll take a forever to have that with someone else. It pisses me off that you've got this happy marriage that's not one hundred per cent honest.'

I grind my top row of teeth into my bottom row as my defences kick in and I remind myself not to react. She is upset, so I cannot react.

'Sometimes I feel like you married him under false pretences. And you've stayed married because of those false pretences. And that's not fair.'

'I married him because I love him and I stayed married because I

worked hard at it. We have both wanted to leave and give up over the years, but we didn't. That's why I'm still married, because both of us have made it work.' The me in my head, the one who is free to do as she pleases, says that to my sister. The me in the room, the one who has felt guilt every day for more than twenty years, says nothing. I take it from her. I take almost all those comments from anyone who knows about *him*. Because knowing means they are in a position to judge. Not the right position because no one else was there apart from me and her and *him*, but it's a position of power. And when you wield that sort of power, the power that could destroy my life with a single misspoken word, I do not mess with you. I do not argue, I do not snap back, I do not censure. When you have power over my life, I let you get away with everything – including murder.

'You need to be honest with him,' she says. 'I don't know how you can live with yourself when you're not being honest with him.'

I give a vague nod. I find it hard to live with myself in many, many ways, this one isn't particularly special.

Mez's heels clatter down the stairs. 'You had better not have moved, Serena Gillmare, or there will be trouble,' she calls.

Faye smiles 'I'm fine' at me and waves me back to my position by the dining room window. I stand then scuttle back as she returns her line of sight to the magazine.

Mez dumps her bag in the chair by the door, the waft of freshly applied make-up and perfume coming before her. Her head is slightly lowered as she comes towards me. She picks up her discarded tape measure and drapes it around her neck again, then picks up her red velvet pincushion and twangs it into place around her wrist. As I watch her, I spot the red rivulets running through the pearly-whites of her eyes. That's why she was gone for so long – she has been crying.

'You moved, didn't you, Gillmare?' she accuses jokily in an over-bright falsetto. 'You moved and now I'm going to have to redo the waistband and refit the skirt.'

'That's OK,' I reply, matching her tone but not sounding as

shrill, 'it was feeling a little tight around the middle, anyway. It'd be a struggle to sit down, so this time you can maybe have it give a little more, well, give.'

'O. M. G!' she says in a mock American accent. 'You want an *amazing* dress and you want to be able to sit down as well? Why don't you just ask for painless childbirth while you're at it? In fact, why don't you just ask for other impossible things like never-melting chocolate? I hear Father Christmas is taking requests.'

Faye, still hiding behind her magazine and for intents and purposes still uninvolved in the dress part of the proceedings, laughs. It is a warm, sweet laugh, one that is so unconnected to the one of a few minutes ago, I'd be forgiven for thinking I'd imagined the other one. And that I'd imagined the quiet but damning tirade she'd rained down upon me.

Mez starts to remove and replace pins at an alarming speed.

'Ow!' I yelp as she jabs another pin into me.

'There you go again – why don't you add, "fewer nerve-endings" on to your fantasy wish list for Father Christmas?' Faye laughs again and the tension between them starts to decrease, as if a pressure valve has been opened.

The new-found tension between Faye and I won't be so easily dissipated. And there is something bothering Mez that is making her like this. She wouldn't normally go away to cry, she wouldn't normally use Faye's longing to get married against her, she wouldn't even be using her pins to get at me. Something is driving her to be like this, and I suspect it's got something to do with the wedding. Or rather, it's got something to do with me going through with the wedding when I haven't told Evan about *him*.

Since all that stuff exploded twenty years ago, everything seems to come back to *him*. Back to the decisions I made as a fifteen-year-old. If I had known that falling for the wrong man when I was still really a girl would all but destroy my family, I would have chosen differently.

But at the time, I was fifteen. I did not know that when you drop a stone of a stupid choice in the pool of your life, it can cause a tidal wave to surge outwards, destroying everyone and everything in its path. I did not realise that falling in love would set about ruining the lives of everyone I knew.

poppy

'Can I buy you a drink?' he asks.

I look up from the pint glass of orange and soda in front of me, look him right in the eye. 'No,' I say. I find that, out here, looking someone in the eye as you say 'no' is the best tactic. They realise that you mean it. They realise that you're maybe not the giggly girl who'll be impressed because they've deigned to talk to you. They realise that you know that just because they've looked at you, fancied a shag and want to make it happen, you don't necessarily have to go along with it.

Every night this week I have come to the Lonely Ploughman pub near Mum and Dad's house after working on the beach hut to get something to eat and to have a drink. Mum and Dad are still 'uncomfortable' having me around. Every time I walk into a room, one of them – usually Dad – leaves, the other – usually Mum – stays as long as they can before making an excuse and leaving. Meals, which used to be such a family affair, are now rationed out and it is each person for themselves to finding a quiet space to eat it in.

If I sit at the table, they eat in the living room. If I take my plate into the living room, they go upstairs – despite the rows we used to have about food and plates in the bedrooms. It's just easier all round if I'm not there, if I stay away as long as possible until I've done what needs to be done with Serena and they can see that I am not the monster they believe me to be.

161

This pub, one I never went into as a child, is nice and quiet. Mostly men come in here, from what I've seen this week, and mostly the type of men who have no qualms about approaching a woman sitting on her own. I'm pretty sure they don't think I'm a prozzie, not when I dress in the old jeans and shirts and cardigans of Dad's I found in the black binbags in the garage. (They're too big, too mannish, and slightly dated, but they're not from the eighties and they're not from prison, so they're the best I can do until I find a job.) So they must think I'm lonely, desperate and on the look-out because every night at least two different men have asked if they can buy me a drink.

Like this man in front of me. Admittedly, he is better looking than the usual ones who come over, convinced they're talking to a woman who is 'up for it'. He has dark hair that is combed back off his face, a square jaw, smooth forehead, straight nose, nice lips. In short, a good looking man. If I was interested.

'Please?' the man asks.

'No,' I reply. Short. Simple. Unambiguous.

'Go on, let me buy you a drink. What's the worst that could happen?'

I am not answering that question because that would give him an 'in'. I would be engaging with him on his level and once I start answering questions, it's only a short step before he sits down. That's happened almost every night this week, too. If I start to engage with the conversation the other person has started, I end up with them staying far longer than necessary. If I avoid giving them an 'in' things progress a lot faster. 'I don't want you to buy me a drink. I want to sit here and have this one all on my own.'

He sits any way.

'I'm Alain,' he says.

It sounded as if he said his name was 'A Lon' but I'm not going to ask, because that would be engaging. He holds out his hand, expecting me to shake it, I think. I stare at it for a few seconds, then refocus on his face.

162

'I'm not interested in your name or you,' I reply.

'Wow, that's blunt and to the point.'

I continue to stare into my drink – I am still not going to give him an 'in' by continuing this conversation.

'Whoever he is, he must have hurt you pretty bad to make you so . . .'

'No one made me anything. I am just not interested in you. Please leave me alone.'

'I guess that's me told.'

'Yes, it is.'

He stands up again. *Finally!* He's got the message. He's not very persistent, and I like that. Most of the persistent men this week have to be *told*. And when I say the words, it's like watching cockroaches scurry when a light is turned on as they more often than not walk away without uttering another word. I'm surprised word hasn't got round yet.

'You're beautiful, you know?' A Lon says. 'Despite the harsh words, you're really quite beautiful.'

'Thanks,' I mumble. He is a different kind of persistent. He uses compliments and flattery as well as normal conversation to try to wear you down. 'But I'm still not interested.'

'I'll simply have to work just that much harder to change that,' he says.

'Don't bother. There's nothing you can do that will change my mind.'

'We'll see.'

'I've just come out of prison,' I say. This is what I have to say to get rid of the persistent ones, the ones who do not skulk away mumbling 'frigid bitch' or 'lesbo' when I tell them to leave me alone. Those words are my equivalent of a can of man repellent.

'Oh?' he says, joining the ranks of the extremely persistent ones. The ones who think I am either winding them up or trying to turn them on. They hear 'prison' and an image of women in skimpy pyjamas chained up together, getting it on at every opportunity, starts to dance in their minds. They then start to fantasise about him and me and a friend – another woman who is, like myself, gagging for it – getting it on.

'Yes, I have just come out of prison and I would very much like to be left alone.'

'What were you in for?' A Lon asks, right on cue. His hand is curled around the top of the chair he has just vacated, and he is ready to pull it out and sit down. He is hoping for a confession as well as a jump.

I stare him straight in the eye so that he knows I am not joking. 'For killing my boyfriend,' I say.

This is the point where they run. Some straight away, scurrying like filthy cockroaches back to the cracks they crawled from once the light has been shed on them. Some pause. They weigh up the possibility of sex with a gagging-for-it-bird such as myself with the probability that I am a psycho, and I will do the same to them if they dare to even contemplate messing me around. *Then* they run without uttering another word.

A Lon pulls out his chair and plants his jeans-covered behind on it, settles his sweating pint glass of lager on the knobbly wooden table and then rests his bare elbows on either side of it and his face in his hands. 'Tell me *everything*,' he says.

'Why would I do that?' I reply.

'Because I've never met a real-life killer before. Not up close. I'm fascinated.'

There's always one. Always one cockroach that's bigger and braver than the rest. That decides to stand its ground when the light comes on and the human lumbers into sight: they decide not to go legging it for the safety of the damp, fusty corners in the cell, they decide they are up to any challenge a human might present. After all, they're the only things that will survive a nuclear war.

I've always thought that those cockroaches are the most stupid. Not brave, stupid. What's most likely to occur – a nuclear explosion, or the size five foot of a prisoner? *Exactly*. I told any such cockroach so when I squished it: 'It's all about probability – and you're more likely to die this way than to experience a nuclear war.'

This man in front of me is a stupid cockroach. He has no idea that when I was inside, my disgust and fear of those creatures wore off pretty quickly – it became a simple case of me versus them and I *always* won.

'Seeing as you don't seem to get the message that I want you to leave me alone, I'll do the decent thing – leave you alone.' I stand up, wrap Dad's cardigan around myself and turn towards the door.

My legs are as shaky as a newborn animal's as I stride away from him, out of the gloom of the pub into the clear night outside. I have to stop, just beyond the entrance because I am shaking so much.

Why? I wonder. I'm not scared of him, and he didn't come across as frightening or threatening in any way. I have known fear and terror and this is nothing like that. But none of the other men who have approached me every night for the past week have had this effect on me.

'Maybe you like him,' Marcus says. I was wondering when he would show up. I turn to my left, he's there. He's often there, beside me, watching me. Listening to my thoughts, observing my life, giving me a hard time. Even if I can't make out his tall, slender form, the light bouncing off his mousy-blond hair and glinting in his blue eyes, I can still hear him. You'd think he'd haunt the person who killed him but, no, it seems I have that honour. Maybe because he blames me: if it hadn't been for the accident, she wouldn't have been able to do what she did.

I ignore him, and instead turn my face upwards to the dark sky. It is black and it is clear and it is where I want to be right now. My fear of the sky has worn off, and has been replaced by a desire to be a part of it. To dance and jump from cloud to cloud, to string together the stars, to swim in the pitch black ocean of a starless night. I want to be up there.

'You do, don't you? You like him,' Marcus persists as I start to walk towards home.

165

'Shut up,' I say to him in my head.

'*You really, really like him. Don't know why, he is an idiot. Eyes too close together, teeth too straight. Too pretty by far.*'

'He's better looking than you.'

'*Not possible, my dear.*'

'Go away, Marcus.'

'*No.*'

'Fine. Don't go away. I'm just going to ignore you.'

'*You can try, but you won't succeed.*'

I'm not shaking any more; focusing on ignoring Marcus has had the effect of calming me down.

'*Poppy, talk to me,*' he begs. He used to have this voice, did Marcus, that he would use afterwards. It was as smooth and gentle as baby's skin, perfectly pitched to touch that part of me that might be looking to escape. '*Please talk to me, Poppy, please.*' It hit its target every time, every time I would forgive him, wouldn't consider leaving because I *knew* it wouldn't happen again, I *knew* he could not be sorrier, I *knew* that things would be OK if I tried a little bit harder as well.

I start back towards Mum and Dad's without Marcus in my head. I don't know who he thinks he is, but he can't control me any more.

serena

August, 1986

Every time I came and left home, I would look at the space up the road from my house, where *he* would pull up and drop me off – 'our' spot. I would always look at it if I walked past, I'd imagine seeing his car, imagine what I'd think if I was a stranger walking past and saw a white Escort, parked there, with two people in the front. I'd imagine what I'd think about the two people, if I would assume they were boyfriend and girlfriend, or if I would think it strange that they were together and wonder if they were just friends, or even teacher and pupil.

As I walked on the opposite side of the street approaching 'our spot' I glanced across at the place as usual and there was his car.

But surely, it couldn't be. I was meant to see him tomorrow, not today. And he never risked coming to pick me up, just dropping me off when it was late. It had to be another car that looked like his. I carried on walking, carried on staring and as I drew level with the car, I realised it was his car. And he was in it.

Not alone.

Beside him was the girl from the park. The one who had been eating ice cream and he had gone to speak to, about three months earlier.

He had his fingers tangled up in the long strands of her black tresses and was smiling at her as she spoke.

He leant forwards and kissed her. Brief but significant. Then he sat back and looked right at me. Almost as if he had been waiting for me to come home so he could do that and I could see.

That was why he hadn't said a word two days earlier when I had to cancel him to go shopping with Faye. He hadn't said a word, hadn't reacted, because he didn't care whether I was there or not. If I didn't turn up, there was always someone else who could stand in for me. There was always the ice cream girl.

August, 1986

'Serena, what do you expect? You can't keep cancelling on me and expect me to sit in on my own, can you?'

I had only cancelled on *him* the once. Once. I did not say that, though. It was not worth the trouble it would cause for me to point that out.

'Why were you kissing her?' I asked quietly, careful to strip my tone of anything that even resembled anger or jealousy. He would hate that.

'Are you questioning me? Saying that I can't do something?' he asked defensively.

'No. No,' I replied quickly, trying to calm him, stop him . . . 'I was wondering . . . Is she your girlfriend?'

'I don't have a girlfriend, you know that, Serena. You know that I can't have a girlfriend when I've got you.'

I didn't understand what he meant, whether he was saying I was his girlfriend or not, but I couldn't ask. 'OK,' I said, quietly. 'OK.'

We sat on opposite sides of his living room, him on his big leather settee and me on the hard, wooden chair he kept by the telephone table. He got up from the settee and my heart bolted to my throat, my body tensed. With every step he took, the more rigid my body became. I braced myself as he came to a stop in front of me, braced myself for it. For that moment. He reached out, took my hands in his and then pulled me gently upright.

Slowly, gently, he enveloped me in a hug, took me in his arms. 'You know I love you, don't you?' he said.

It took a while for me to realise it wasn't going to happen. Then it took me another second to realise what he had said: 'I love you'. I had been waiting to hear those words since the moment he stroked my face in the classroom, and now he had said it and I had almost missed it.

I nodded quickly, in case he thought I didn't know he loved me.

'I'd hate to think you didn't realise how special you are to me. How much I love you.'

I relaxed a little. He really did love me, after all. It'd been worth it, it'd all been worth it.

'I only went with Poppy because she's a virgin and you weren't, the first time.'

My body tensed again and he held me tighter, almost as if trying to hug away my body's anxiety. 'I was,' I said quietly. I was. I honestly was. I hadn't done that with anyone else. I couldn't. I hadn't met anyone else I loved as much as him.

'A complete virgin? No one had ever kissed you or anything like that?' he asked.

When I was thirteen, Tommy Marison had grabbed me when we were alone in a classroom together and pushed his mouth on to mine. It lasted for all of three seconds and I hadn't even wanted him to kiss me so I didn't think of that as a kiss.

I'd told *him* about it, of course – I told him everything about me – and at the time he'd said it wasn't a kiss. Why had he changed his mind?

'Tommy Marison pushed his mouth on to mine. That wasn't a real kiss,' I said.

'Real or not, a kiss is a kiss is a kiss, baby, and Poppy had

169

never been kissed before. She isn't damaged goods. I needed that. To be with someone pure. You understand, don't you?'

'*Please hurry up and find yourself another naïve fifteen-year-old virgin.*' Isn't that what Marlene had said in her message? Her words, the conviction in her voice, whirled around my head like a battery-operated spinning top.

'Please tell me you understand, baby. I need for you to understand. I didn't do it to hurt you, it was what I needed. Tell me you understand.'

'I understand,' I stated. *I understand a lot of things. I understand that this is not my fault. I understand that I did nothing wrong. I understand that I cannot say to you I did nothing wrong.*

I understand that I am scared of you.

There, I have thought it: sometimes I am scared of you and you should not be scared of the person you love.

'Thank you, baby, that means so much to me. You mean so much to me. Poppy, she's nothing. I can't get rid of her just yet – me being her first means she's really attached to me. It'd break her heart. I don't know what she'd do to herself if I ended it now. I'll keep her around for a bit longer and then let her down gently, OK?'

'Yes,' I replied.

'You make it so easy to love you,' he said.

I have to get away from you, I thought. *You are going to keep hurting me if I stay.*

The day I got my O'Level results, after I had opened them to show my parents, I had come over to his house and had handed him the envelope. He'd pulled out the slip of paper and had screamed with joy.

'My God, Serena, you've done it!' he shouted, then scooped me up in his arms and spun me around. 'You've done it, you've done it! You're amazing! Seven As and four Bs. I couldn't have hoped for better for you.' He kept spinning me round and round until we were both dizzy with happiness. 'You can do anything you want now, you know that, don't you? The world's your oyster.' He put me down then, telling me to wait where

I was, he sped out of the room and upstairs, then came back with a box wrapped up in gold paper.

'I got this for you, but it doesn't seem enough now, after you've done so well.'

I carefully opened up the paper and inside was a Walkman. My very own Walkman. I'd been saving for one of them and now I didn't need to because he had got me one. It played tapes on both sides, as well, so I wouldn't have to keep taking the tape out to turn it over, and it was a beautiful blue colour.

He pressed a kiss on my mouth suddenly. 'I'm so proud of you,' he said, quietly, seriously. His voice caught in his throat and tears filled his eyes. He looked away for a second, composed himself. 'I don't think I could be more proud of you than I am at this moment.' I had to leave to go home for a family lunch but on the doorstep he'd smiled at me and said, 'No one deserves these results more than you.' And I'd floated on air all the way home.

That was only three weeks ago. Three weeks ago he thought I was the most amazing person on earth. Things had only really started to go wrong between us when he met this girl. They hadn't been perfect before, but they were a lot better. Maybe I should give him another chance. I wasn't scared of him all the time. Maybe if I just let him deal with this Poppy in his own time, afterwards, we could be together properly. We could even go public. All I had to do was wait for him to get rid of her, then things would be good between us again. Good. Solid. Wonderful.

After all, he said he loved me. And that was what I'd always have over her. He would never love her, not when he was with me.

Not when he'd said it not once but three times.

September, 1986

She was smaller and curvier than I expected. Of course she was pretty, and it was hard to believe she'd never been kissed before *him*.

171

I wanted to ask her how she could live with herself when she was sleeping with someone else's boyfriend. I wanted to ask her if she knew how much it hurt me to know he had been with her. I wanted to ask her why she couldn't find someone of her own. Instead I stuck out my hand for her to shake and said, 'Good to meet you.'

'You too,' she said.

And I fancied for a moment that I heard the faint click of a key turning in a lock; the moment destiny set the lock of the shackles that would bind me to Poppy for ever.

poppy

'Well, well, well, fancy meeting you here,' he says.

It's that idiot from the pub the other week. He cuts a striking form along the promenade which is packed with people, even on a Wednesday afternoon.

I was in the middle of a painting break, munching on an apple rescued from Mum and Dad's fruit bowl and drinking from a bottle of water filled from the tap, when he appeared. Although there are many, many people on the seafront, all out here trying to soak up their own little piece of sunshine, he stood out. His frame, tall and wiry, was sheathed in an eye-catching Hawaiian shirt that was a mass of green, red and yellow palm trees, beige knee-length shorts and Jesus sandals. I recognised him even with his wraparound sunglasses on – because there was something forced and purposeful about the way he sauntered down the promenade.

'You're the cock from the pub,' I say, without removing my sunglasses. I picked up these sunglasses for just over a fiver in the markets in the old post office in Brighton the other day. Marcus would have pitched a fit if he caught me wearing these: they would have offended everything about looking polished and finished he held dear. I started to get like that, too. It wasn't worth the pain, the consequences, not to pay close attention to how I looked by following what he said I could and couldn't wear. Nothing was worth that. But these black plastic things are all I can afford and, honestly, not so bad. They do the job, keep the sun out of my eyes, and that's all that I can ask for, really.

'No, I'm Alain,' says the man in front of me with a smile.

'That's what I said, you're the cock from the pub the other day.'

'And, like I said, I'm Alain.'

This could go on a while and I have no interest in partaking any further. As it is I've broken my 'do not engage' rule twice in two minutes. I return my gaze to the sea, a blue that I have never seen anywhere else before, and my breathing immediately falls in time with the rock and roll, the to and fro of the waves. I had been captivated by the surfers who were sitting astride their boards, paddling further out in search of bigger waves; and I'd been fascinated by the yachts and boats bobbing around casually as a backdrop to the swimmers and paddlers who have ventured into the water. Every day I am astonished by the world. Every day, I remember that I had forgotten that these sorts of things existed. When my life was grey and boxed in and regimented, this was going on 'out there'. This and a hundred million other amazing moments. I take another bite of the apple, sighing to myself as its delicious tart juice fills my mouth.

'Lovely day for it,' A Lon says. I thought he'd rightly guessed I had no intention of speaking to him again.

A feeling slips down from my head to my stomach, filling me with an icy dread. I turn back to him, and instinctively shade my already shaded eyes so I can see what his face does when I ask, 'Have you been following me?' I stopped believing in coincidences a long time ago and this is one coincidence too far.

A Lon does not dismiss my question straight away and more chilling dread creeps through me. He bobs down to my height and curls his top lip in to chew on the right side of it. 'Not exactly,' he says, eventually.

'What does that mean?'

'I saw you a week or so ago, here. You were painting the side of the hut and you looked . . . Your fringe was getting in your face and you kept doing this really cute thing of blowing it away. You had the tiniest splatter of paint on your face, and lots of little spots of paint on your arms and hands. I just thought you were so beautiful. I wouldn't have dared speak to you, then I saw you again in the pub and I thought, "It's Fate, I have to give it a go".' All the time he is speaking, his head is bowed, like a man in prayer, his gaze focused downwards where his prayer book should be. He is avoiding eye contact because he is lying.

'And, I kind of recognised you. I kept thinking I'd seen you somewhere before, you seemed so familiar.' Now he glances up, dares to look me right in the eye. 'Then you said that thing about being in prison so I typed in lots of different things on the Internet about women who kill their boyfriends, until . . .'

'You found my picture.' I swivel back to stare at the sea.

'I found your picture. And I kind of remember some of the stuff from that time. I was about eighteen then.'

'So, what are you doing here? Most men would have run a mile.'

'I like you,' he says.

'Right,' I reply with a sigh. Fetishist. Probably wants me to dress up, beat him, hurt him, pretend I'm going to kill him. I had many, many letters in prison from people like that, people asking for that; people who didn't seem to realise I was locked away from the world.

'I do,' he insists, 'I came for a walk today hoping you'd be out here.'

'Right,' I say again.

'All right, I'll come clean.'

This is more like it. 'Yeah?'

'I've always wanted access to a beach hut. You've got one, I have to pretend to like you to get access to it.'

My head snaps round to stare at him. He grins and raises an eyebrow. 'Which reason are you gonna believe, huh?'

I shake my head and look away, to hide my ever-so-slight amusement. No one has gone out of their way to make me laugh in a while. To give him his dues, he is funny – but he is a man. And I do not have the best track record with men. The first was my last for twenty years. The first has probably broken me.

He sits back, rests on his arms.

'I didn't say you could share my beach hut space,' I remind him.

'No, but I have the feeling you're going to.'

'You know, A Lon—' I say, not looking at him.

'That's *Alain*. Alan with an "i" – it's the French version, my father's French,' he explains.

'Right, I see. *Alain*, I was in the library the other day.'

'That's good, you should always use your local library.'

'Yeah, you should. Especially if you can't afford books.'

'True, true.'

'Like I was saying, I was in the library the other day and I came across this book called *He's Just Not That Into You*.'

'I know it. There's a movie too.'

'*Really?* I never did! You know, the title offended me so much I couldn't actually make myself reach out and pick it up.'

'OK,' he says cautiously.

'"Who do these people think they are," I was thinking to myself, "letting men get away with all sorts of poor behaviour and telling women to accept it because they're 'just not into them'?".'

'Right . . .'

'Turns out I was wrong.' I fix him with a beady-eyed, hundred-yard stare. 'It's a great line. Because, you know what, I'm just not that into you. Please leave me alone.'

'Go on, give me a chance, you might find you grow to like me,' he asks. 'What have you got to lose?'

I curl my lips, salty from the sea air, into my mouth and shake my head. He goes to speak, a protest on his lips, but I speak to halt him. 'I've lost half my life already, don't you think I'm entitled to at least have myself heard when I tell someone I want to be left alone?'

He sighs a little. 'You're right, of course, you're right. I'll leave you alone. But is it OK if I drop by every now and then to visit the beach hut? I'm going to miss it so.'

'It's a free country, or so I'm told.'

He jumps to his feet, makes a big show of patting gravel off the palms of his hands. 'I'll see you?'

Replying to him with a sort of head shake/nod is the best I can manage at the moment. I do not want to encourage him, but of course I'm disappointed by what I had to do as he walks away. He is someone who wants to spend time with me, even knowing where I have been and what the world thinks I did. Ghost Marcus was right: I do like him, I could grow to like him even more. I'm sure if I spoke to someone more worldly-wise about these things they would probably say it was perfectly normal to want to have . . . *that* with him. I don't mean just sex, I mean the whole lot. That is what I have missed. When I had it with Marcus it was fabulous. It was like floating on air and believing you'd never touch solid ground again. He knew how to make me feel like there was no one else in the world but me.

Marcus knew about the other stuff as well – he knew how to make life far too real. He knew how to twist pain and fear and terror into the strands of everyday moments.

It's that 'real' stuff I do not want any more of. I've had about as much reality as I can take. Alain seems nice. He looks like someone off the telly. He has a sense of humour. But he could still turn. And that is a risk I'm not willing to take.

BANG! CLASH! BANG! behind me on the road has me leaping out of my seat and ready to stand well back from the door before I think what I'm doing. My head swings around, wildly, looking for the prison van, waiting for the silent screams of the first-timers as they are uncuffed and herded like frightened cattle into the holding area. On the street beyond the green behind my hut is a man unloading a couple of deckchairs and a picnic hamper from a campervan. It is not the prison van. I am not still in prison.

When will that stop? When will I stop jumping to attention every time I hear the shutting of car doors or the jangle of keys or the smell of cheap, watered-down bleach? When will I get back to normal?

I must look a little silly standing here like this, gawking at the campervan couple who are oblivious to the anxiety they've sent spiralling through my veins. I recap my water and wrap my apple back in its plastic bag for later. I need to get back to painting the beach hut. I need to get back to doing something I know I can do and I can focus on.

I need to concentrate on this and forget all about the man with the Hawaiian shirt, dazzling smile and tight ass who I sent walking out of my life.

serena

I'm being followed.

At least, it feels that way.

I can't be sure, and I don't know who would or why they would, but it's a feeling I've been having a lot recently. One of being watched. One that someone is encroaching on my personal space from a distance. It used to happen to me all the time, after everything.

Notoriety of the kind I managed to garner does not go away overnight. It is not fleeting and forgotten, wrapped indelicately around someone's fish and chips the next day, even after I was found not guilty of murder. It sticks around, waiting impatiently for someone to discover something else new, or someone to remember a story that might just prove my guilt. Then it would start again, and I would have that creeping sensation of someone trying to learn a little bit too much about my life by watching me.

I have that feeling now. It is Thursday and Evan and I have an appointment with the priest at the church where we're going to get married. There are so many things left to do that I'm having to work ridiculous flexi-time hours, but my boss is all right. I've been his personal assistant for many years and as long as I get all the work done and he never misses a meeting or family birthday, he doesn't mind how I structure my hours. When I first applied for the job, he'd said that someone who had eleven O'Levels, three A-grade A'Levels and a first-class Honours degree would be under-challenged in the role on offer. I'd proved him wrong. I had applied to do a doctorate in English Language, but I now had a baby and she had to come first. Also, Evan and I needed the money, especially after stretching ourselves to buy the house in Preston Park as part of his move to work at a small surgery down in Brighton.

I quite enjoyed organising someone else's life and, all these years later, I still enjoy it, and I'm still grateful it gives me the flexibility to leave whenever I need to. Which is why having the creepy feeling of someone following me today, when I am leaving work at a time I would normally be here, is even more worrying. Maybe they sit here all day and wait.

I usually park in the underground parking spot in our building, but today I was in a rush and couldn't find my pass so had to park in the public car park a few minutes away.

During that time of our arrest and then the trial, when she and I were nicknamed The Ice Cream Girls, I learnt what it was like to be watched and followed and basically stalked, and it is happening again. Someone is watching me. Regularly.

I stop in the car park and look around, trying to see who is watching me, who is causing the hairs on my neck to tingle and my spine to shiver. People are milling around: getting out of cars, pulling into spaces, climbing into cars, loading boots up with shopping. Everyone looks normal. As if they should be there, as if they are going about their daily business like I was until I felt someone's eyes on me again. Someone who is closely, *deliberately* watching me.

After that little snippet in the paper, maybe someone has tracked me down and is trying to start it all up again. But they'd be more unsubtle, I think. After a few days of watching me go about my basically boring life (which I love), they'd need something else to keep their interest going. So I don't think it's the press again. It could be *her* but I don't know how she would have found me since I have a new name and I don't live in London. No, it must be someone else.

I unlock my car door and climb in, knowing that all the while someone is observing me. Someone is scrutinising my every move. I hate the not knowing. If I knew who it was, then I wouldn't be so worried. I'd be worried, yes, but not like this. This is so frightening because it makes me feel powerless. And everyone I pass in the street, every car that seems to be going in my direction for just that bit too long, is a suspect. A potential assailant. The person who is going to hurt me, hurt my family.

Pulling out of the car park and on to the main road, up on to the road that leads me out of town, I feel the eyes drop away, the scrutiny lessen. It's got worse over the past few days, I realise, my heart skipping up a few beats as I admit this to myself. Before, the chill would come over me fleetingly; the past week or so it has been happening much more often. In different places at different times. Sometimes when I am picking Con up from school, sometimes when I am getting the paper in the morning, sometimes, like today, when I am leaving work.

I want to tell Evan about it, but it's like a lot of other things in my life I can't share with him because they are all interconnected by the same poisonous web, and if I tug one cord all the other cords will fall apart too – if I explain part of it, I'll have to explain the rest of it, and that isn't how I want to tell him.

If I just knew who it was, then I'd feel a little better. Who is stalking me? And why? *Why?*

May, 1987

'Are you OK?' *he* asked when I had not been moving for a while.

I wanted to speak but I could not, because my mouth could not form the words and my chest detonated with agony every time I breathed in too much or breathed out. I could not get enough breath together to form even a word. One simple word. One word: 'enough'. 'Stop.' 'Please.' 'No.' Whatever the word, it would not be yes. Because I was not OK. This was not OK.

'I'm sorry, Serena, but you made me do this.'

'"But" doesn't make an apology, it makes an excuse of your behaviour,' I heard Mum say in my head. Mum. *I want my mum. I want her to hold me, to tell me it's going to be OK, to make all of this go away. I want my mum to turn back time so I never did this. I never got involved with this.*

'You made me. Why did you have to smile? What's wrong with you? Don't you love me any more? You're everything to me and sometimes I think you couldn't give a fuck what happens to me. If I died tomorrow would you even cry? Would you even notice?'

I want my mum.

I tried again to move, to uncurl myself from the ball I had turned into when he'd started to kick me. Not quick enough, not fast enough, and I had cried out when the steel in the toe of his new shoes connected with my ribs. Through the shooting stars of pain, I managed to curl up and tried to breathe even though it was agony. I tried to breathe and hold on and wait for it all to be over.

'God, Serena, you know I love you. Why do you make me do these things?'

I want my mum.

'I wouldn't have to if you didn't make me.'

I tasted blood in my mouth, and felt pressure on my side. I still could not breathe properly. The air was being stained with the sound of how I felt: inhaling was an agony of shrieking, gasping sounds and stars behind the eyes, exhaling was a silent cry of suffering.

'Serena? Why are you breathing like that? Serena?'

His hands made me wince, even though I could tell they were trying to be gentle.

'Serena? Stay with me, baby. Stay with me. I'll get you to the hospital, OK? It's all going to be OK.'

I want my mum, I thought at him as he gently lifted me into his arms, catapulting the agony like stabbing knives through every nerve in my body.

I want my mum, I want my mum, I want my mum.

Evan has already booked St Catherine's church not far from us in Preston Park for the date he suggested because he knew you have to do these things months, sometimes years in advance.

We lucked out, he'd said, with the church being free on our anniversary when he rang on the off-chance, so he'd booked it and decided we'd find everything else to fit in around it.

I like it that Evan has become more romantic and involved in our relationship since the proposal. He takes my hand after he's held open the car door for me. He kisses my neck when we're standing in the supermarket queue – much to the horror of Con and Vee. He has just become affection personified.

We're holding hands as we enter the restful, gloomy interior of St Catherine's. It's a beautiful building with a sand-coloured bell tower and an arched oak wood entrance.

Despite the reverence we usually feel when entering a church, we don't walk in so much as almost fall through the doors, giggling at each other.

'Shhhhh,' I hush him as we stumble towards the aisle, 'we need to be respectful.'

He responds by tickling me, causing me to wriggle away, trying to get his hands off me while stifling a giggle. 'Shhhhh,' he hushes me. Evan stops trying to tickle me and instead pulls me into his arms, and automatically I wrap my arms around his neck and smile up at him. If someone had asked what I wanted from Evan that I wasn't previously getting, it would be this. Overt displays of affection. The public part isn't important, it was knowing he could do it and would do it if the mood took him. His obsessive tidying (which excludes the kitchen for some reason), cigar smoking and sports watching I can more than live with: they form the man I married – he wouldn't be him without those bits. But this, this new him is a bonus I would never dare have wished for. It might have come true and I would have had to lose something else about him to make it right. To balance things up. And it seems that my wish came true anyway. I not only got a proposal, and a wedding, but also this man who has no problems showing he loves me.

'Just imagine, in three months we're going to be doing this right here,' Evan says quietly, adding to the hushed, calming atmosphere of the church. He kisses the end of my nose, something he does when he's feeling particularly affectionate.

'I know,' I whisper back. 'I'm so excited I can hardly breathe.'

'It's good to see two young people so obviously in love,' a man's voice cuts into our loved-up bliss.

We jump apart, embarrassed and guilty, like two children caught with their hands in the biscuit jar – or two adults caught canoodling in the house of God.

'Oh, God, Father,' I say, then realise I have just taken the Lord's name in vain – in his own house – and stop talking.

'We're sorry, we were just . . .' Evan begins.

'Practising?' the priest says. 'It's fine, this is God's house after all, and God is love, so I am hardly going to object to you showing love. Had you removed clothes, however, I might not have been so understanding.'

Evan and I both relax and smile at the priest. He is a solid man, whose girth has obviously seen one too many cream teas and biscuits. His white hair is scattered with grey and black, as is his full beard. He has a smiley mouth and striking brown eyes that seem kindly and astute at the same time.

'You must be Mr and Mrs Gillmare,' he says, holding out his hand.

It's that small action – reaching first for Evan, then for me – that does it. It catapults me back through time and I seek out the priest's eyes again, his face, the curl of his mouth. My body seems to be turned inside out all at once, and I am woozy and lightheaded as I raise my hand for the priest to shake. He does the shaking because I have lost control of my limbs as I stand here in God's house, talking to one of his representatives.

'I'm Father Gabriel,' he says. 'Not to be confused with the angel of the same name. After all, he is rather higher up in God's hierarchy than me. But I like to think I can hold my own.'

I've met many Father Mikes, Matthews, Davids and Martins over the years but not any other Father Gabriels.

'Old Father Mike and I are always arguing over which one of our namesakes is higher up God's hierarchy,' Father Gabriel continues. 'I call him old, he's only two years older than me. He just seems older. I think the Angel Gabriel is more important – after all, without him, Mary might have thought it was just something she ate.'

Evan is liking Father Gabriel's patter, he must trot it out many, many times a week but he makes it sound original. When I first met him, he was a lot thinner and younger. His hair was black and his face more angular. He was new to the priesthood, only ten years or so older than me. But he had the same striking gaze, the same kindly manner. I was sitting in the pews at a church in London, shaking and trembling and trying not to cry or throw up. I could not go home, I could not stay where I had been, the light in the church was on and the door of the church had been open so I had come in and sat at the back, trying to work out what to do.

June, 1988

My terror was like barbed wire twisted around my heart, entwined around my stomach, coiled around my mind. I did not know what to do with myself. My parents weren't expecting me home so no one would really miss me, but home is where I wanted to be. Except I could not go there.

'Are you hurt?' the priest asked.

He had walked softly because I had not heard him approach.

'S-s-sorry,' I said, trying to rise from the seat, but finding it hard on my rubberised legs. 'I-I-I go.'

'No, no,' the priest said, sitting down in the pew in front of

185

me. He didn't look so scary, all dressed in black as he was, when he sat down. Standing over me as he had been he reminded me of the Grim Reaper, coming back to finish the job that he'd started earlier that evening. 'Sit, sit. Don't feel you have to rush off anywhere. This is an open place for anyone.'

I stopped trying to stand and sat, still. Waiting. Waiting for the answer as to what to do to come to me.

'Are you hurt?' the priest asked again.

I shook my head.

'Your clothes, they have blood on them,' he said. 'Are you sure you're not hurt?'

I looked down at the white top I had put on earlier that evening. It was scattered with red, like hundreds of poppies of all different sizes. I pulled my jacket across my top to hide the stain, to hide the evidence.

'I'm Father Gabriel, can you tell me your name?'

'S-Serena,' I managed. My lips felt numb, as if they were not connected to my body so I could not work them properly.

'Serena, that's a pretty name. Are you in trouble, Serena?'

I was in big trouble. I had done something terrible. Something so very terrible, I wanted to throw up every time I thought about it.

'Can you tell me what has happened, Serena?'

I shook my head. I could never tell. Never.

'Are you Catholic, Serena?' he asked.

I nodded.

'Well, that means if you ask me to hear your confession, I can listen to what you have to say and I will never tell anyone what you have told me.'

'N-n-not even t-t-the police?' I asked.

'No one, not even the police. Not even my superiors in the church. It stays with me.'

I nodded again.

'Do you want to tell me what the matter is? See if I can help you?'

He couldn't help me, no one could help me.

'You don't have to talk, Serena, we can sit here in silence if you want. But if you want to talk, I will listen and I will never tell anyone else.'

I covered my face with my hands, tried to normalise my breathing. I was so scared. This shouldn't be happening.

'You . . . you swear you can't tell anyone? You swear on God?' I asked.

'I swear on God. It is one of my sacred vows.'

Anxiously, I tapped my fingers on my lower teeth. *Should I tell him? Will he be able to help me? Will he be able to tell me what to do?*

I looked up at him. He was quite young for a priest, and he seemed so kind; his eyes looked like they wanted to help, instead of condemn me like some of the priests did when they gave a sermon on those Sundays my mum would make me go to church with her.

'Would you like me to hear your confession, Serena?'

I braced myself and nodded.

'Tell me,' he said softly.

'I . . .' My voice faltered. 'I think I just killed someone.'

Father Gabriel is so affable and friendly and funny, Evan is feeling very comfortable in his room. It's becoming obvious that he doesn't recognise me. Why would he? It was twenty years ago. He must have seen a million people in that time. Well, maybe not a million but enough to render me simply another stranger to him.

I am on edge, though. This is another coincidence about the past that is connected to the wedding. Another occurrence that is warning me that I should tell Evan before it is too late. Giving up after the other night was a stupid thing to do. It could all so easily go wrong. If Father Gabriel had recognised me, I would have had to explain it all to Evan right there and that would not be a good way to start a meeting about getting married in front of the priest we want to marry us.

The priest continues to crack jokes, to tell us that he wishes more people would come and get married again after a registry office job because it made him feel important, as if they needed him to make a marriage seem real. 'Imagine the numbers we'd get coming through these doors if everyone thought like you did. The diocese would have no reason to question whether to close us down or not.' He starts to nod, sagely. 'Of course, your marriage is all about me and how it will benefit my church.' Evan laughs and so do I.

'After fifteen years, I think it's safe to say you two don't need to come to our pre-marriage classes,' he says. 'Out of interest, why have you decided to get married again?'

'Erm, well,' Evan begins. He has been doing all the talking: I have been too shaken to speak. 'We, erm, kind of did it in a rush last time. This time, we wanted to do it properly.'

Father Gabriel nods. 'Quick and necessary, was it?'

'Hmmm . . .' Evan replies.

'Ah, well, it obviously worked out for you both. And who am I to judge what brings two people together? The Lord moves in mysterious ways, after all. Well, it's been awfully nice to meet you both. I look forward to seeing you again on the big day. If you could pop in for the odd service or two between now and then, it would look so much better in front of the other people who run the church. Me, I'm just happy to have people come here, but others aren't so "free thinking".'

'Will do,' Evan says. 'We'll bring the kids to Sunday service as well.'

Ass-kisser, I say in my head.

'It was good to meet you, Evan.' He shakes my husband's hand. 'We can get together nearer the time to discuss the order of service and the such like. And we can do a dress rehearsal the night before if you're not too busy.'

'That would be great,' my ass-kissing husband says, beaming away.

'Good to see you, too, Serena. You'll make a lovely bride, I'm sure.' He takes my hand in both of his and, smiling at me, shakes my hand, holding on a bit longer than necessary at the end.

He remembers me. How could he not? There can't have been that many people who confessed to killing someone to him. He is still smiling at me when he drops my hand. He never did say anything to anyone, even though he had many, many chances to do so. Even today, more than twenty years later, he hasn't even given an indication to Evan about me.

On the way back to my car, walking on shaky legs, I can hear the clock ticking, reminding me that I am living my current life on borrowed time, and very soon it is going to run out.

poppy

He still walks out of any room that I enter. He still looks through me when he bumps into me on the stairs and on the landing. He still behaves as if I am dead to him. If he carries on, he may get his wish because every slight, every time he pretends I'm not there, is a slice into my heart, a wound that I find it hard to recover from.

I cannot take much more. I have decided to try and talk to him. To get him to talk to me, to let me back into that space in his heart that was always there for me. During Mum's long stretches of illness, he taught me to walk, he used to dress me and change me, he used to give me my milk. He was the one who brushed my teeth, combed my hair, he had Granny Morag teach him to make braids so he could put two in my hair. Even when I was twelve it was him, not Mum, who sat me down on my bed and stuttered and blushed and hmmmed and ahhhhhed his way through the talk about periods. We were a team, a unit, but now he ignores me. Now he pretends I do not exist. I am not there. I do not understand how he can. I could never do it to him, no matter what anyone said he had done. I don't think, even if I was presented with irrefutable evidence and a confession, I would believe he had done it.

So I don't understand how he thinks I could have done this.

I knock on the door of Dad's study. I haven't ventured in there since I have been here, not even when they've been out and I have gone searching through their rooms for the things of mine that are missing. It used to be Grandpa Adam's study and when he died Granny Morag kept it exactly as it was, until her death, I guess.

There's no reply. I know he's in there, and he knows it's me because Mum is off doing some shopping. I want to talk to him. Just talk to him and have him connect with me verbally. Even if he tells me he wants me to go, I would prefer that to the silence, the blank stares, his equivalent of exiling me to Siberia.

I miss him. If he would let me, I would tell him that. I would tell him I'm sorry for not being his perfect girl. I would beg him to love me again.

I knock again, wait again.

I knock a third time, this one half-hearted and desultory. After the same reply, I turn away. Dad is not there. Mr Carlisle is in but my dad has left the building. Has left my life.

October, 1989

'Guilty.'

The word sounded hollow and heavy at the same time. Hollow, heavy, final. I did not sway, I did not faint with the vapours, I did not burst into tears. I turned to seek out Dad, sitting in the upper rafters of the large court. He had been saying for weeks, months, in the whole run up to this day that it would be OK. That I would not be sent away from them because I was innocent and innocent people were not found guilty. Dad, my dad, the greatest man in the world, the man who was always right, stared back at me. He met my eye and I met his and I felt the world open up between us; a fissure in the universe that was going to separate us.

Of all the people in the world I did not want to be separated from, it was him. My dad. My hero.

He held my gaze and then his blue eyes fell away as he shook his head.

He thought it was true. Everything that had been said, everything that had been written, he thought it was true – that I was capable of that. Of murder.

'Ah, Pepper, love, why? Why, why, why?' I could hear him saying in my head. He stood up and Mum immediately stood with him. *Scritch scritch* came from somewhere behind me and I realised that the court impressionist was capturing this moment. The moment where I turned to my dad to help me make sense of what was about to happen to me and the moment, with disgust in his eyes, he turned away. He and my mother climbed the short flight of steps to the exit and then they left without a look back.

'Dad?' I whispered deep down inside where no one would ever hear. *'Dad?'*

'I'm not going away, Dad,' I say to him when he enters the kitchen fifteen minutes later.

I tricked him. Only a little trick: after his silent reply to my knocks, I opened and closed the front door to pretend that I had gone out. Then I crept back into the kitchen and waited. It was two: he would need his post-lunch coffee, and thinking I had gone out would make him leave the safety of his study and venture into the kitchen.

He stops in the doorway, surprised to see me. In front of me I have two mugs of coffee, the milk in a jug, the sugar bowl with a teaspoon and a plate of his favourite biscuits – ginger snaps. I've done all this as quietly as humanly possible so he wouldn't know I was still here.

He observes my handiwork with a steely silent stare, then glances so briefly at me it stings like a quick, unexpected slap. Then he turns to leave.

'I'm not going away, Dad,' I repeat. 'Even if you want me to leave, even if you ask me to leave, I will keep coming back until you talk to me.'

My dad, my big strong father, doesn't move from the spot he is standing on. This is his olive-branch of hope. Possibility.

This is my chance to tell him everything I have wanted to say all these years.

'None of it was true,' I say to him. 'What they wrote in the papers, what they said on the news, it wasn't true. That wasn't me. You know I wasn't like that. You know me. Please, believe me, it was all made up.'

He takes a step, he is slipping away again. I had him for thirty seconds.

All those nights, all those days, alone in my cell, alone and surrounded in a shared cell, I wanted my dad. I wanted him to make it all better. I need him to know that.

'I cried for you,' I say. He stops. 'Almost every night, I cried for you. I wanted you to make it better. To tell me it was going to be all right. You were the only person on earth who could do that.' I sent him visiting order after visiting order. 'You never came to see me,' I say. I keep thinking I'm angry about that, but I'm not. I'm terrified. Because if he could not see me for twenty years, that means he stopped loving me. 'I was your little girl, and you never came to see me. Why, Dad? Why?'

He shakes his head in slow motion.

'All I ever wanted was for you to come and see me. In twenty years, you never came. And I'm not a little girl any more. I grew up and you never saw me. Didn't you want to see me?'

He takes another step away, still shaking his head in a slow, precise manner.

'Talk to me, Dad. Please tell me what you're thinking. Please, just talk to me. *Please.*'

His head shaking stops, suddenly and brutally. Then he shakes his head, once.

'Dad, talk to me.'

'*Can't.*' The word is so quiet, it is barely a whisper. '*Can't.*'

He walks away and I hear the door to his study slip into place behind him, and then the turn of the key in his lock ricochets like a stray bullet throughout the silent house.

It's not only me who was the prisoner. He was too. That's

what they say, isn't it? When you send someone to prison, rightly or wrongly, you sentence all their family, too.

I knock over the chair I am sitting on to dash to the closed, white panelled door of his study. I press the palms of my hands against it, lay my head between my hands. 'I'm sorry,' I murmur to the wood, hoping it will carry the message to the man inside. 'I'm sorry, and I love you.'

As I walk towards my beach hut, I try to pretend I did not hear him crying on the other side of the door. I try to pretend that I did not hear the bravest man in the world crying because he is still serving his prison sentence. For him it will never end, and it's all my fault.

part three

serena

Medina's house is in order when I arrive, unannounced, for a visit.

I wouldn't normally do such a thing and anyone who did it to me would get a more than frosty reception. However, things are not right with my sister and if I rang her she would fob me off, pretend that she was fine and that I was worrying over nothing. But she wasn't fine the other day. We all laughed and joked after the spat at my dress fitting, but her eyes, sad and heavy in her otherwise beautiful face, were still ringed a post-cry scarlet. It wasn't simply to do with our row. There was more, and I had to find out what.

'This is a nice surprise,' Medina says warmly as she steps aside to usher me in. She has one of her wide, relaxed smiles on her face and I can tell she means it. Her twins and two non-twins are in the large living room of her Georgian 'mansion', as I call it. One of the twins and the oldest non-twin are in front of the television, glued to a repeat or DVD of *Doctor Who*. The other two are further back in the room, sitting on the floor with one reading a book, the other drawing on a large piece of paper. Everything is so serene, I wonder for a moment if she has a switch that she flicks that puts everything in place when the doorbell goes: the kids are deposited in specific places to carry out specific activities, the floor flips upside down and everything that was on it is dumped underneath, while the top part that's on show is clear and tidy and neat. And the volume in the house is set at 'four' instead of 'eleven' like it is in my house, most of the time.

I hate that expression 'I don't know how she does it' but in Medina's case it is entirely appropriate. I don't. I can't even begin to fathom it. My house with two children, one of whom is a teenager, is chaos more than ninety per cent of the time – Mez has four children under ten and she lives in serenity by the look of it. The kids are so engrossed, *absorbed* in what they are doing, they do not even notice I am here. Probably a good thing since I want to talk to Medina uninterrupted.

'I was in the area,' I say to Mez as I follow her rounded little bum, confined in tight jeans and topped with a floral home-made gypsy top, to the kitchen.

'Really?' she asks. 'What were you up to?' She immediately goes to the kettle, flicks it on.

'Nothing,' I say. 'I wasn't in the area at all. I wanted to see you.'

'Oh, OK,' she says. She moves to the fridge, takes out a half-bottle of wine. 'Would you like a glass?' She waves the bottle of pinot at me. 'Seeing as you've come all the way to see me?'

'Nah, I'm driving.'

'Oh, yeah, sorry, didn't think.' She rehouses the wine, reaches instead for a four-litre bottle of milk and a box of Belgian chocolates. 'What's the matter?' she asks as she retrieves two mugs from the cupboard by the kettle.

'Nothing,' I say.

'Why the special visit, then?' She makes tea quickly and deftly – in half the time it takes me to do most things. She does most things quickly – quick and efficient is my youngest older sister, even though she is creative and flamboyant. If I had been making the tea, I'd still be dithering as to which mugs to use and why Evan doesn't check that stuff from the dish-washer is clean before he puts it in the cupboard and whether I should open that new packet of biscuits or finish off the chocolates in the fridge.

Mez takes a seat opposite me at her round wooden table. She has put the cups in front of us and pushed the chocolates over to my side of the table, although she is beadily eyeing them – I suspect she will slap my hand away if I reach for one of her favourites.

'I wanted to see if you were all right after the other day.'

'The other day? What was the other day? Oh, you mean the day of the fitting? Gah!' She waves her hand away dismissively. 'That was nothing. You of all people should know that.'

'There was more to it, I could tell. I noticed you'd been crying up in the loo. I want to help, if I can.'

Mez shakes her head, her hair bouncing as she shakes. The pink fringe has gone, it is now black and short and straight. 'I was just tired or something. You have nothing to worry about, little sis, I promise.'

'Mez, I know something's wrong. And I'm not leaving until you tell me what it is. Evan's taking the kids out for pizza tonight so I can literally stay here all night if necessary.'

All of a sudden she sags in her seat, sits back and throws her face up to the ceiling. She has a striking profile that is, quite strangely, different from Faye's. Most of the time you could not tell them apart – they are identical twins, after all – but when you look at them sideways on, you can see subtle differences. Medina's jaw is slightly squarer, Faye's nose is a fraction flatter at its tip.

She shakes her head as she stares up at her ceiling. 'I'm in trouble with the police,' she says quietly.

I do not know what to say. I am so shocked, I opt for my default setting and stay silent. It really is the best policy when you are in trouble. Or in shock. Opting for silence stops you from saying something that will at some point be used against you. I'm pretty certain that choosing silence in most arguments I've had with Evan has probably saved my marriage. I am too shocked to speak right now. Medina is so sensible, how can she be in trouble with the police? But then, wasn't it I, the original goody two-shoes, who was on trial for murder?

She lowers her head to continue shocking me. 'I was speeding a little, just a little, but the police were doing stop-checks.'

'Speeding a little isn't too bad,' I offer.

'No, it isn't. But, I'd been for lunch with a couple of people I used to work with. I'd had a couple of drinks. Well, maybe three. I failed the breathalyser. Only by a little, but it was enough of a little to make them arrest me and take me down to the police station. I admitted guilt so I was cautioned and released on bail.'

There's a sick feeling you get when you know you've done something wrong; it lodges itself under your ribs and won't allow you to do much of anything – especially not breathe or sit comfortably – because what you have done is going to hang over you for the foreseeable. Probably for ever. I have this feeling now, listening to my sister. This is bad – actually, this is something that 'bad' doesn't even cover.

'I'm going to lose my licence, there's no two ways about it. The arresting officer told me that. She was really sweet, really nice about it because I was obviously so oblivious to how much over the limit I was and I held my hands up to it straight away. But she said, with the speeding as well, there was no way I wouldn't lose my licence. Minimum twelve months loss of licence, maximum prison.'

I do not know what to say, I really don't. I cannot form a thought, let alone offer comfort. I remember what it is like in prison, in cells. The fear and the loneliness. The fear of being alone, the fear of being with other people who might be dangerous. I do not want that for Mez. She can't go to prison. But she might. She might have to do what I did until the courts could be persuaded to let me out on bail under house arrest. She might have to experience what I did until the courts could accept that I was not a flight risk and, after telling me to hand over my passport and requiring my parents to put up their house as collateral, they let me go under curfew for nearly a year.

'That's not even the worst part,' Mez says, her eyes flicking briefly to the door, checking to see if any of the kids are hanging around and in earshot.

'How can this get any worse?'

'I haven't told Adrian.'

'Why?' I ask, trying not to be shocked and openly horrified. It is difficult, though. But then, I haven't told Evan, have I?

'You of all people have to ask me that?' she replies, hotly. She is about to shout at me for being a hypocrite, I can tell. She's done that several times over the years — not as many times as Faye, though.

'I can understand why you wouldn't, but I presume, as this is something that isn't going to go away and you'll have to attend court, he'll have to know soon enough. Why haven't you done the deed already and softened the blow? And got some support, even. I hate to think that you've been going through all this on your own.'

'Support? Adrian?' She snorts in ridicule at the very idea. 'I can barely get him to look at me nowadays let alone support me.'

'What's happened?' I ask.

'Life,' she says, pushing out her chair and standing up. She rubs the palms of her hands on the front of her jeans, leaving small trails of sweat. 'Life is what happened. We both have one, but they're not exactly merging at the moment. He's out working all hours, I'm working all hours here with the kids and never the twain shall meet.'

'But he'd want to know that you're under so much pressure, that you're in a bit of trouble, surely.'

I feel, rather than see, the 'would he?' expression pop up, like done toast in a toaster, on her face. She moves to the dishwasher, pulls it open and starts to unload it. 'A few months ago,' she says, as she quickly but neatly starts to replace the glasses in the wall cupboard to her right, 'I had a bit of a "moment". I was shopping in the supermarket and I picked up a bar of chocolate for Adrianna, but didn't put it in the basket. I completely forgot about it and almost walked out with it. Luckily at the last minute, something inside reminded me about the chocolate bar and I paid.

'I came home, told Adrian about it – you know, as you do, wife to husband.' She swings round suddenly, clutching a white china mug in her hand and pointing it at me as though she was about to accuse me of something sordid and tea-related. 'Do you know what he said? "God, Mez, isn't it enough that we've already got one crim in the family, or is it something genetic?"'

I thought Adrian liked me. I thought, because he knew me, because he was around at the time of the trial and the stuff in the papers and the aftermath, that he knew I didn't do it. I thought, like everyone else in our family, who stood by me, who were supportive and strong, that he knew I wasn't capable of such a thing. Obviously I thought wrong.

'He was joking, he said, when I burst into tears. But not that much, eh? So, that's why I don't tell him. Imagine what he's going to say now. What other "jokes" he's going to come up with. I can't handle it at the moment.' Having seen the hurt and horror on my face, Mez hides her face in the cupboard. 'I will tell him, just when I feel better about it. When I know what to expect exactly, I'll tell him.'

'Do you want me to come to court with you?' I ask the back of her head.

'No,' she says emphatically. 'I'd never put you through that again. Thanks for the offer, but no, I'll be fine. Adrian will probably have to come, show them I'm a respectable woman with a supportive – ha ha – husband and a young family, who made a mistake I've owned up to and who they can't throw the book at. I'll be fine. Everything will be fine.'

'What about you and Adrian?'

'We'll be fine, too. We just need to sit down and talk for a change. It obviously doesn't help that he's off on holiday with the boys every two seconds. Trying to "blow off steam". That's why I blew up at Fez. That crack she made really hit home. And hot on the heels of Adrian's remark – it all just got a bit much. But it'll all be fine. Everything will be fine.'

Why is it that each time she says everything will be fine, I believe her less?

'Let me know if there is anything I can do,' I say to her. She won't. I know her, she's like the others in my family; we won't ask for help no matter how bad things get. We continue until breaking point; we soldier on until we cannot march any more. It doesn't matter though, I know exactly what I have to do to help her.

'OK,' she says, from inside the cupboard. 'Will do. Do you want to stay for dinner? There's plenty.'

'No, I, erm, have a couple of things to do before I head back to Brighton. I'll just go play with the kids for a while and then go.'

She finally stops unloading the dishwasher and while carefully avoiding eye contact with me, she turns her head to look at me. She smiles the saddest smile I have seen in years and my heart starts to break. 'See ya, then. I'll let you know what other ideas I've come up with for the dress.'

'Oh, no, don't worry about the dress, I'll buy one. You've got enough on your plate.'

'I've said I'll make it and I will. I *want* to make it. It'll take my mind off everything. I'll email you some sketches.'

'Fantastic. See you, love.'

'Yeah, see ya.'

My sister is still smiling her sad smile as I leave the kitchen.

I know how to help her all right: to give her husband a kick up the backside.

July, 1989

'I don't understand why you were at this man's house, anyway,' Mum said.

Unusually, the police, who had just arrested me, let my parents and my sisters visit me in the police cell. They were being generous because, they said, in the morning, after the hearing, I would be sent to Holloway without the chance to go home in between to see them. I could be on remand there for up to a year until the case went to court. They were going to recommend no bail because of the nature of the attack, they were going to tell the Court that I was a dangerous criminal and that I should stay behind bars until the Court could put me away for good.

That was how they told it to me, before they led me to the cells, and that was probably what was going to happen, my solicitor said, because I admitted being there. It was no wonder the police could be generous with my visitors: from now on, they said, it'd be two people at a time for the rest of my life.

My father had his arm around my mother, while Faye and Medina, I'm not sure they were aware, were clutching each other's hands, like they used to do when we were small children. Faye had a face of stone on her; Medina looked like she had been crying. They'd both been called away from their lives in other parts of London to come here to see me. To see me like this, sitting in a dank, tiny room on a hard metal bed garnished with a wafer-thin mattress, and with a metal toilet in the corner.

'He's my boyfriend,' I said to Mum, knowing that I had to tell them everything before the police told them. 'I've been going out with him for a couple of years.'

Faye and Dad both frowned deeply, not wanting to take in what I was saying; Mum and Medina's eyes widened in alarm. Yes, that would mean I was fifteen when it started.

'He was your teacher,' Faye said. 'Your History teacher. And you were going out with him?'

I looked down at the floor in shame. 'Yeah.'

'But, Serena, how could you?' Medina asked.

'He . . . he said he loved me.'

'He's not allowed to love you,' Faye said angrily, 'he was your teacher. He raped you.'

'No, no, it wasn't like that. He didn't force me or anything.'

'If you were under sixteen, then he raped you,' Faye said. 'You're not old enough to give consent. He should know that. Whether you said yes or no, he's not allowed to do that with you.'

'I know, but . . .'

'But, what?' Medina said. I'd never heard her so angry, so enraged. 'What? How can he love you when he's an adult and you're a girl and he's meant to be looking after you? And now he's dead.'

'I didn't do it.' My eyes swung round wildly to each of them, trying to make them see and understand. 'I didn't. I couldn't. No matter what the police say, I didn't do it.'

'But you were there,' Faye said.

'I didn't do it,' I said. I could feel the tears building up behind my face. 'Mummy, I promise, I didn't do it. I didn't.'

'I know,' she said, breaking away from Dad and coming to me. She put her arms around me. 'I know you didn't do it, Serena. I know you couldn't do that. That's not how we brought you up. You couldn't.'

I held on to my mother, knowing that I wouldn't get hugged like this again in months, maybe years. The other three watched us, looking slightly removed from the situation.

I knew I had to get them to believe me. Because I didn't do it, not in the way they were saying. I did not murder him.

Adrian holds up a 'one minute' finger to me as I enter the plush cocoon of his office because he is on the phone. His office is decorated in warm reds and burgundies with sumptuous furniture fabrics and thick-pile carpet. His office always reminds me of a womb, what it must look like to a baby, all red and soft. I've always privately thought that it's a sign he never wants to grow up, but that's the sort of thing I'd never say to anyone. Why would I? You don't make mean jokes about the loved ones of the people you love. I like Adrian, womb-like office and all, which is why the whole journey over here to his management consultancy office in West London has been difficult. I cannot believe he thinks I am a criminal. What else has he said about me behind my back, what else has he thought about me and what I was accused of?

'Sez,' Adrian says, standing up as he throws the phone back into its cradle.

Don't you 'Sez' me, I think at him. *Not when you think I'm a criminal.*

'Haven't seen you in ages,' he says.

Like Judas, he comes to me and kisses me on both cheeks. I feel his touch like a burn of accusation, like the nicks of the knife he has inserted into my back. I stiffen at his warm greeting and allow him to move away before I relax and take the seat opposite his desk that he indicates.

'I know, Adrian, it's been a while – we really should get the kids together.'

'I hear congrats are in order,' he says. He claps his hands together and rubs them hungrily, as if in anticipation of the party we're going to have. 'You're doing it all again, I hear. From scratch.'

'Yeah, we are.'

'Is that why you're here? To ask me to be in the wedding party?' He pushes a hand through his blond hair, temporarily moving it off his face, showing his fine-boned features and smooth-skinned forehead. 'I know Mez is making the dress, and I'm assuming she and Fez will be bridesmaids, so I guess Harry and I will be groomsmen? I'd be honoured. Truly. Honoured.'

Adrian's job as a senior management consultant – hence his own office and never being able to turn off his mobile – means that he can sometimes take over. He anticipates what a person (client) wants and needs then tries to fulfil that want and its corresponding need. However, when it's not work-related, he often doesn't actually take the time to find out what the person he's dealing with really needs or wants. He makes assumptions and then takes over.

'No, that's not why I'm here,' I say, gently. 'I'm actually here to ask you to stop being such an arse to my sister.'

He sighs and deflates all at once. 'It was only a matter of time before you showed up, too. You can't have one Gorringe bollocking without the other.'

'Too? You mean Faye's been here already?'

'Of course. The second Medina starts moaning to one of you, I know you're bound to turn up shouting the odds. No wonder Harry calls you the Witches of Ipswich.'

'Yes, and no wonder Harry gets the living Michael taken out of him at every opportunity. And am I shouting?'

'No, I guess not, at least that's something.'

Faye when riled, when she thinks someone is taking advantage of a family member, is a monster. I can well believe she gave him a verbal kicking he won't forget in a hurry, but it clearly hasn't worked. Subtlety is the way to get Adrian to admit he's being a dick, that he is a father not a single man and he cannot live the single lifestyle any longer. Or rather, he can but can't expect to have his family there waiting for him at the end of it. I need to kick his arse so gently, he has no idea that it's been kicked.

'What's going on, Ades? And, for the record, Medina didn't come moaning. She hasn't said anything that wasn't dragged kicking and screaming out of her. She is one hundred per cent loyal.' I leave the 'unlike you' bit hanging there like a ripe, red apple on a tree – he can take it and swallow it if he chooses or he can ignore it, but we both know the accusation, the fruit, is there, waiting for him.

'You tell me,' he replies. 'I have no idea what's going on in my marriage any more.'

'Why are you either working all the time or running off on holiday with "the boys"? Why don't you want to spend time with Mez and the kids?'

'It's not all me,' he says defensively, spinning on his chair to stare out of his window at his uninspiring view over the hotchpotch black and grey of rooftops in this little square of London. 'I just can't talk to her any more. She's not . . .' He raises his hands and moves them towards each other as if he is holding a ball and trying to jam his hands together, but the invisible ball is stopping his hands from making contact. 'She's just not there.' Another jam at the ball. 'She's not the woman I married.'

209

'Well, of course she's not – you married a single, working woman, now she's a stay-at-home mother of four children. How can you expect her to be the same? Has it occurred to you that you're not the man she married? The man she married would talk to her if there was a problem, not hide behind work or his mates.'

'Serena, you have no idea what it's like.'

'Tell me then.'

'I love her, of course I love her. I don't think I'll ever stop loving her. And the kids. They are my world. But . . . Medina's got . . . She's . . . I can't talk to her. I come home after a busy day and all she wants to talk about is what the kids have done and the bread she's baked and this new dress pattern she's found. I don't have a wife any more, I have a 1950s housewife who, for all I know, is doped up to her eyeballs on happy pills. It's like Medina's not there any more and in her place is this strange woman who has nothing beyond the home to talk about. I spend time with my mates so I get some stimulating conversation every now and again.'

'How dare you.' I keep my voice low and calm, let the words do the talking. If I do not shout, maybe the shame he should feel will be more acute, more effective. 'She is bringing up four children – *your* children. What exactly do you expect? For her to take care of the children every day and then to go rushing to you when you come home and take care of your every need and provide you stimulating conversation and a good shag while she's at it?'

'You don't understand,' he says.

'Well, then make me, because you're not presenting a very good image of yourself here, Ades.'

'Oh, Serena,' he says on the crest of a sigh. 'All of that wouldn't be so bad if it wasn't for the rest of it. Her obsessions.' He glances over to see if I am listening, which I am, avidly. 'She sees danger everywhere. Sometimes I'm surprised she lets the kids go to school at all – she was actually thinking about home-schooling them at one point until I put my foot down.

She's scared of what will happen to them at school. Not with the other kids so much as, well, with the teachers.'

That knot of sickness, the one that comes from having done something wrong, tightens in my stomach again. Tugs itself so taut, I almost have to double over from it.

'And every time the kids are out of the house and out of sight, she thinks something's going to happen to them. That the world is full of people waiting to prey upon them. I can't convince her that it's not true, no matter what, so I've kind of given up. Because, you know, she thinks I don't care enough if I don't buy into all her paranoia.

'Then of course, things always get that little bit worse for us when you do something.'

'When *I* do something?'

'Yeah. When you got married the first time, when you had Verity, when you moved to Brighton, then when you had Conrad, now this wedding. Every time something good happens to you, she starts to obsess that the police will find that missing piece of evidence that will send you to prison.'

'But there's no evidence to find.' I am confused. 'How can they find evidence that isn't there? And why would . . .' My words fail, drain right away as Adrian becomes flame-red from the line where his forehead meets his hair probably right down to his manicured toes in his expensive shoes. 'She thinks I did it,' I say. 'She thinks I'm guilty.'

'She worries about you. She just—'

'She just thinks I'm a murderer *and* a liar.'

'No, she thinks that you were scared and that it was self-defence and that you knew no one would believe you—'

'So I lied.'

This is too much new and unsettling information for my brain to process at this current time. Medina, my sister, thinks I am a murderer. She's always thought that. She thinks I have killed someone, that I have taken a life.

'Sez,' Adrian begins, sounding troubled at my silence.

I hold my hand up to stop him talking. 'No, no, don't say

211

anything. This isn't about me, we're talking about you and Medina. If you're right, and she has got these obsessions, then it sounds as if she's traumatised, not crazy. And if you love her—'

'Of course I love her. Even when it's not easy to be around her, I love her.'

'If you love her, you should be supporting her rather than running off with your mates all the time. Seriously, how is that going to help? And how do you think the kids are taking it? If, as you say, their mum won't let them out of her sight and the rest of the time their dad's not there, what are they supposed to think and feel?'

'She won't let me get involved with the kids,' he says. 'If I try to do something with them, she has so many things on the list of dos and don'ts it's not worth it.'

'Oh, don't be so pathetic. These are your kids you're talking about. Not worth it? Ades, are you seriously telling me that if you cancelled one of your "holidays" and took that time off work and every morning you said to Mez that you'd give the kids their breakfast and take them to school, she'd say no? Cos, you know, even when Verity and Conrad were really young and I was still convinced they would break if the wind blew too hard, on Saturday mornings when Evan would get them dressed and take them out, I thought it was a blessing. I mean, he'd give them chocolate pastries and juice drinks that were full of sugar for breakfast, and he'd dress them like they'd fallen into a pile of jumble, but that was just his way of doing things. And you could not get a more paranoid mother than me, but I could relax because they were with him, the only other person on earth I'd trust them with.'

Adrian says nothing, he is staring into the mid-distance, and ever so slightly sulking.

'To be perfectly honest, the only reason I trusted Evan so much, bad as it sounds, is because he proved over and over that the kids are the most important people on earth to him. More important than me, even. I know he'd never let anything happen to them. Yes, yes, I should be able to entrust them with him because he's their father, but the simple fact is I couldn't at first. I was so worried and paranoid, but Evan reassured me that he cared about the kids as much as I did. How can you prove to Mez that you love the kids as much as she does and stop her being so paranoid if you're always jetting off on your hols? How can that do anything but prove to her that she's all alone in this and that she needs to be doubly vigilant because the person who's meant to have her back hasn't?'

'You're probably right,' he mumbles.

'Try to get her some help, too. Maybe get her to talk to someone? See if they can help her with her obsessions and her worries. But do it in a way that says you love her and you're worried about her, not that she's a crazy person you can't bear to be around.'

'I don't think she's a crazy person.'

'You've got to prove that to her, not me.' I stand up, ready to walk away from this meeting enlightened. I came to kick his ass – I am walking away knowing that he and my sister think I am a killer. 'And stop feeding her paranoia by telling mean "jokes" about having criminals in the family.'

Adrian colours up again and looks down at his desk in shame. Or is it embarrassment? Shame would mean he feels bad and knows he was wrong; embarrassment would mean that he feels bad because I'd been told what he said – he meant it, but I wasn't meant to know. 'Serena, I—'

I shake my head at him and hold my hand up again to halt his words. 'Sorry' isn't going to change this, or make either of us feel any better. 'I'll see ya, Adrian. I'll see you soon.'

'Yeah, bye, Serena.'

Don't you mean, 'Bye, Murderer'? I think as I walk out of his office.

I am having trouble walking to my car.

My legs will not move one in front of the other as they are supposed to; they feel like they are on springs and that my body is bouncing and swaying as I move.

My entire family think I am capable of committing the ultimate crime.

If Medina thinks that, then Faye definitely does. And so do my parents, because they are the only people who could convince them that their sister is innocent. If they haven't managed it, then they must think it too.

Four of the seven people I care about most in this world think I am a murderer. Four of the seven people I care about most in this world think that I should have spent the last twenty years rotting away in a prison cell.

poppy

It's Fate.

It's meant to be. I am supposed to clear my name. That's the only way I can explain the fact that she is living down here, too. The two of us are still linked and we will be until I have made her confess.

First though, I need to find out everything I can about her so that I can work out how to approach her. What to say that will get her to tell the truth. And when that happens, Dad will be able to look at me, *talk* to me – I will come back to life and he will love me again; Mum will stop looking so nervous around me, as if she is waiting for the time when she will catch me sneaking into her room to put a pillow over her face. When Serena confesses, I'll be a free woman. I might even get a special letter from the Queen, apologising for my lost years.

I'll get my life back. This part of it, anyway. No probation appointments, no having to tick the previous convictions box. I could even commit a petty crime and not worry about being sent back to prison for the rest of my days. And I can finally, *finally* stop waiting for my new life to begin.

'Ms Argyle, room five,' says the voice over the tannoy system. 'Ms Argyle, room five.'

I rise from my seat and carefully replace the magazine I have been flicking through back on the low wooden table in front of me. That's what Penelope Argyle is like: neat and tidy; doesn't like to make a mess, doesn't like to cause a fuss.

I walk along the narrow corridor and check the numbers on the doors until I reach room five. I knock and enter without waiting for an answer.

The man inside stands and smiles. It's a warm, friendly smile and I almost falter. Then the picture on the desk catches my eye: husband, wife, two children. All grinning.

'Hello there, I'm Doctor Evan Gillmare. Take a seat and tell me how I can help you.'

I had to come here, because this is another piece in the jigsaw of the life she stole from me. I could have married a good-looking doctor. I could have had two children. If she hadn't done what she did, all this could have been mine. And I need to get as close as possible to this life before I speak to her.

Dr Gillmare is reading the form I filled in so I take the opportunity to scrutinise his room. It is crammed with books on oak shelves, and all around the room are dotted photos of his family. Him and his wife. Him and his children. The wife and the children. My eyes keep coming back to the photo on the desk. For some reason, it is the one that needles me the most. The four of them, the parents with one arm locked around each other, one around the shoulder of a child, are all laughing – *laughing* not merely smiling – at the camera. Maybe it's because they look so complete. As if nothing can tear them apart because they are four and they are perfect that way.

'So, Ms Argyle, it says on the form that you've just moved to the area.' Dr Gillmare makes me jump by speaking to me.

'Yes.'

'Are you from here originally?' His voice is rich, warm, deep. I could bathe in his voice, float in its beauty and never come out.

'No, I'm from London. I have family living down here, I need to be near them.'

'OK. You know it's a little unusual for me to see patients

without their notes or without them being registered here, but you said it was an emergency and you asked for me by name.' He is good looking, of course. *Of course.* Serena wouldn't go for anyone ordinary or plain. First it was Marcus, now it's Dr Gillmare, and I'm sure in between there have been a host of men who have all been tall and handsome, if not dark. Dr Gillmare has empathy to top off his looks. If I was a real patient, I would feel comfortable talking to him about virtually anything. He has that kind of face, that kind of manner. No wonder he wears the widest wedding ring I have ever seen on a man and has a picture of his family on every free inch of space – he wants patients to know he is very married because I'm sure they fall in love with him with alarming regularity.

Even though I know who he is, I could easily see myself joining the Dr Gillmare fan club. And if Serena gets sent down . . .

'Ms Argyle?' he asks.

I jump slightly because that's me, isn't it? 'Yes?' I ask, flushing slightly at the thought that was unwinding in my mind.

'You asked for me by name.'

'Erm, yes. Someone I met a while back said you were the doctor to see.'

'OK. As I said, it's unusual to see a patient without their notes or them being fully registered here, but as it's an emergency, I've made an exception. What is your emergency?'

'Oh, yes, I . . . um . . . I . . . need the morning-after pill,' I stutter. That's the best emergency I can come up with.

'OK,' he says, swivelling back to his desk and tapping on his computer. 'When did you have the unprotected sex?'

Damn it! How long is it before it's too long? Forty-eight hours? Seventy-two? Ninety-six? I can't remember. I spent so much time convincing the receptionist to let me see him that I forgot to do the other part of the research.

'Um . . . yesterday? Yesterday morning.'

'OK.'

'At about eight o'clock.'

'Right.'

'Well, eight till about eight-thirty.'

'OK.'

'Actually, eight-forty-five.'

'Uh-huh.'

'Actually, you know what? Let's just call it nine. It was virtually nine. So let's just call it nine.'

'All right, nine it is. We could even say nine-thirty if it makes you any happier?'

'No, no, nine's fine.'

'Good. But you do know that you can get it from most chemists now?'

Really? No one told me. When did all these things change? From what I remember before, you had to practically have a note from your mother saying you were allowed before anyone would even say the words 'the Pill' in front of you, let alone give you the morning-after one. Now you can just wander into a chemist and ask for it? Has the world gone mad?

'You didn't have to wait to see a doctor.'

'Oh, um, right, yeah. It's just, that I . . . I mean, of course I knew that. I just . . . I just wanted to see a doctor to be sure. You know?'

'Better to be safe than sorry,' he says.

'Yeah.'

'Right. If you roll up your sleeve, I'll check your blood pressure before I give you the prescription.'

He has soft, gentle hands that brush my skin as he slips the armband around my bicep. I watch his hands, with their square nails and fine wrinkles eased into the smooth, dark brown skin.

'Your blood pressure is a little high,' he says. 'Nothing to be worried about, though.'

'I get nervous around doctors,' I explain. *Especially ones married to people who had me sent to prison.*

'I understand. OK, I'll prescribe you one dose of emergency contraception. It is only one pill now, so take it as soon as possible. If you are sick or vomit, the pill may not work so you

218

should come back and see us. Your period should arrive as normal, but if you are late do come back as there is a chance – a small one, but still a chance – that you may be pregnant. Is that OK?' He has been typing away while talking and then printing out the prescription rather than writing it, but he's managed to make me feel as if I am the most important person in the whole of the surgery.

'Yeah, that all sounds fine,' I say, feeling mollified. I have taken advantage of the good nature of this man; it's not his fault he is married to a murderer. He probably doesn't even know.

'Is there anything else you wanted to discuss, Ms Argyle?' he asks in a kindly voice.

'No, why should there be?' I wave the prescription at him to show that I have everything I need.

'I couldn't help but notice the cuts on your arm,' he says.

I'd almost forgotten they were there. They are from such a long time ago and the scars have faded, almost blended in to my skin. Or so I thought. I hadn't even noticed that he had seen them. He certainly didn't react to them. And now I have to dream up some more lies.

'Don't feel you have to explain. Or talk about it,' he says before I further add to my list of misdemeanours. 'But if you do want to talk about it, about anything, you can always come back to us here, or we'll help you find a counsellor.'

I say nothing because I do not know what to say. He clearly doesn't think I am a freak – he is being professional and caring without prying. He is empathy personified.

'We're here to help,' he says.

I nod and stand. 'Thanks, doctor,' I say, feeling *horrible* as I open his door and close it behind me.

serena

'Mum, is Dad your best friend?' Conrad asks.

'I suppose he is,' I say. 'Why do you ask?'

'If Dad broke something, would you get cross with him even though he's your best friend?'

Ah, I see. My crafty son has come out to join me in the garden. I had been staring up at the stars, waiting patiently for a shooting star to streak across the grey-black night. *If I see a shooting star I'll tell Evan tonight,* I'd thought as I tugged my coat around my body and settled down to watch. *If I'm meant to tell him tonight, the shooting star will be my inspiration.*

Con had come out about ten minutes ago and had climbed on to my lap and, grateful to have him behaving like a baby for a while, I'd pulled him in towards me so he could be protected from the cold by my coat, too. He'd sat so still for so long I thought he'd nodded off to sleep, when instead he was using this quality time to lay the groundwork for confessing what he had done.

'Yes, I'd be cross but if he was sorry and told me what he had broken, before I found out what it was, I wouldn't stay that cross for long.'

'OK,' Con says and slips off my lap to run back inside.

'Hey, hey, what did you break?'

He shakes his head, confused. 'Nothing.'

'So why were you asking about if Dad broke something?'

'Because Dad dropped your hair straighty thing down the toilet when he was being a famous rapper in the bathroom and he asked me to ask you if you'd be cross with him.'

'He *what?!*' I reply, leaping up out of my chair.

'He said to say he was sorry.'

'He will be! You tell him he can sleep in the spare room tonight and buy me a new pair.'

'OK,' Conrad says happily. He goes towards the house and stops just short of the back double doors, looks up and cups his hands around his mouth. 'MUM SAID YOU CAN SLEEP IN THE SPARE ROOM TONIGHT AND YOU HAVE TO BUY HER MORE!' he bellows.

The bedroom window, which overlooks the garden, immediately opens and Evan leans out, tapping his finger on his lips, trying to hush up our son. Evan taught Con to do the 'Shhhhhhh' tapping his finger on his lips thing when he was ten months old.

'AND SHE SAID YOU'RE GOING TO BE SORRY!' Conrad adds for good measure.

'Right,' I say to Conrad, putting my hands on his shoulders, 'now that all our neighbours know our business, let's go to bed, shall we?' I guide him towards the house.

'OK, Mum,' he says happily.

It's not until much later, when everyone in the house is asleep and Evan is snoring gently beside me, that I remember the shooting star promise. I did not see one, so I do not have to tell. But, I want to. I shift across the bed, curl up into the shapes left by my husband's well-built solid form and loop my arms around him.

'I did a really stupid thing once upon a time, Evan,' I say into warm, soft creases of his neck. 'And I want you to know about it.'

poppy

Glancing at my watch, I realise that I am late for my Tuesday job.

I have two jobs now: on Mondays, Wednesdays and Fridays, I clean for a woman in Hove. I'd got that job through Raymond Balaine, an old friend of Mr Fitch, my probation officer. I'd met Raymond at the end of last week, in his office above a shop in Brighton town centre, and instantly disliked him. It wasn't simply because he looked very much like a sun-burnt, overweight, gout-ridden tomato, nor that when he spoke he sounded only a couple of evolutionary rungs above a grunting animal; it was mainly that he was at pains to tell me that he didn't like ex-jailbirds, he wouldn't piss on me and 'my kind' if I were on fire, and I'd better not mess up. In an ideal world I would have walked out after telling him what to do with his job, but in that world I wouldn't also have to explain the twenty-year gap on my CV. Miraculously, he'd found me a three-morning-a-week job almost straight away – 'I'm desper-ate, so you'll do' – and paid weekly. On Tuesdays and Thursdays, I do my other job – I watch Serena. I study her life and learn everything I can about her to learn how to approach her. How to get her to confess in the quickest way possible.

I am going to be late to see her this morning, though, because the bed was too snugly. Too comfy and cosy. And when the alarm started to buzz away on the bedside table I reached out from under the covers and hit the snooze button before I even thought about what I was doing. I pulled the cream cotton sheet higher above my head and snuggled down, waiting for Mum to come in and remind me that if I was late it'd be my own fault. She'd then be followed five minutes later by Dad, often with a glass of orange juice, telling me the last one to breakfast wouldn't get any bacon or sausage, depending on which one Mum was burning that morning.

I'd stayed in my cosy, rosy memory for longer than was decent, clinging on to the sheet and the fuzziness of sleep as I waited and waited for the creak outside the door.

After a few minutes, feeling slightly embarrassed and surprised that I'd tumbled so willingly into the memory, I'd pushed myself further into the centre of the single bed, curling myself up tighter beneath the covers, allowing the foolishness to dissipate. No one would know that I thought it was twenty years ago. No one would know that I'd gone back in time and had basked in what it was like to be loved and wanted by my parents, instead of having my father ignore me and my mother fear me.

'I'll know, Poppy,' Marcus had said in my ear.

'Like I care. And who are you going to tell?' I said to him.

He appeared lying beside me, his face pushed right up to mine, so close I jumped a little. 'You, of course,' he said simply. 'And you'd hate that more than anything. Being reminded that you're not as hard and resilient as you pretend. You'd hate to be reminded that you're just a bit soft girlie who cried for her daddy every night.'

'Oh, get lost,' I'd said and threw back the sheet and the covers to leap out of bed to get away from him.

Glancing at the red LCD numbers of the black clock radio that I'd had since I was fourteen, I realised how late I was. I'd definitely missed the paper grab, I'd miss the school run, I'd miss him leaving for work. I'd probably have to skip straight to work. Watch her go into the offices of the large insurance brokers just behind Brighton Station that she worked for. I hadn't managed to find out, yet, what she did. Whenever I rang their switchboard and asked for her job title the disconcertingly efficient receptionist would say, 'Just putting you through' and before I could say, 'No, I—' I was being whisked into the phone system. The Internet hadn't told me, meaning she was either too lowly to be mentioned or too important to have her details given out to the general public. With her big house and big car, two adorable children and husband, I know which one it will be. I'd hurried down the road, and came round the corner on to Boundary Road just as I saw the bus coming.

I had to run a few feet to the bus stop, but I caught it. It was quite full, which I wasn't used to. The bus I usually get is empty, only a few people who need to be somewhere early struggle on to it. I am surrounded, right now, by people in suits, people with bags, people who read with one hand while holding on to the poles with another, schoolchildren whose chatter spills down the stairs and babbles through the bus, punctuated by the tiny tinny sounds of the new versions of Walkmans. It's like being back in the mess hall, a bit. So many people, all crammed together to do the same thing, but not really communicating outside of their own little worlds; each spinning in their own orbit in the same solar system.

As the bus trundles down New Churchington Road towards town, I pretend for a few minutes I'm like each of the adults on the bus: I have somewhere to be, I have a job or a class to attend, I am a valued member of society. No one would ever know any different. Maybe my hair is a bit different, cropped as it is to be easy to care for, maybe my clothes of skin-tight jeans and fringed suede jacket are a little too authentically retro, but that's the beauty of Brighton – you have to try *really* hard to stand out or look out of place.

I bend a little to look out of the window so I can count the beach huts up to mine. I do this every morning: counting up to eleven from the end, right near the exit from the promenade to the street.

'One, two, three, four,' I count under my breath, moving

my lips as the bus moves slowly along. 'Five, six, seven, eight, nine, ten, el—' I almost cry out loud.

There is someone standing beside my beach hut, doing something. Doing something that looks like scrawling graffiti.

It takes a few seconds for the rest of my mind to catch up: my beach hut is being vandalised.

The part of me that's been paying attention reaches out and rings the bell. Several people look up, frowning – the bus obviously doesn't usually stop here at this time of the morning. There are no schools near here, nor offices. Just flats and houses on the roads running up off New Churchington Road and on the other side of the road the sea, the beach, and the line of beach huts with their backs turned towards the road.

''Xcuse me, 'xcuse me,' I throw at the other passengers as I struggle to get to the front and to the doors. My heart is racing and my mind is galloping beside it, both of them desperate to convince me that I counted wrong. That my beach hut isn't being defaced, that someone isn't in the process of doing this to me.

Because it would not be a random attack. It would be . . . No. It's not my beach hut, it can't be. I leap off the bus and wait for it to pull away before I step out on to the road. A car horn blares at me and I remember that I need to check the road before I cross. I search and search for a break in the traffic. There isn't one. Everyone is eager to get to work or school or wherever. They don't understand what I am going through.

In desperation I dash out, the sound of horns blaring causing my heart to clamour up into my throat, but I don't care – I need to get across the road. I make it to the central island in one piece, and pause for a few seconds. The traffic is less heavy on this side, fewer people are going the way I have just come from. *After this blue car*, I decide, and dash out like an athlete heading for the finish line once the car has passed me.

I run down the path from the street to the promenade and dash the short distance to my hut, surprised the vandal hasn't

226

left. There is a buzzing sound – like a large demented bumble bee is trying to get into the hut beside the vandal, whoever they may be.

'What are you doing?' I shout from a distance away, above the buzzing. I am not scared, but I am not stupid. Until I know who I am dealing with, it's best not to go right up to the person and start a confrontation. Let them show themselves so I can decide what the best course of action is. 'What are you doing to my beach hut?'

The buzzing sound stops just before the person appears from the gap between my beach hut, a white mask on his face and big goggles over his eyes. But I know who it is before he strips his face of its protective gear. Alain.

'What are you doing?' I ask.

He is wearing paint-splattered clothes and in his hand he carries some kind of tool.

'Sanding,' he says. 'You said I could visit the hut and, when I did, I noticed this edge was a little uneven. So I decided to sand it down. But once I did that bit, the rest looked tatty, so I had to carry on.'

What do I say? I can't make him put the uneven ridges back on the hut. I'd noticed them but had decided to leave them, to just paint over them and leave them for another time – when I could save up and buy the right tools, or even pay someone to do it. I have to engage with him now and I'd already decided not to do that.

'I'm going to have to buy the paint for the sides now, and I can't afford that at the moment,' I say.

He raises a 'wait a minute' finger then disappears back into the gap, before coming back out with two paint cans. 'They're the right colours,' he says. 'I rang the Seafront Office and checked. I've even got primer and undercoat back there.' He is staring at me, and expectation fills the gap between us. He's nervous, I realise. Wondering if I am going to throw his good deed back in his face and tell him to leave me alone. Or if I am going to accept this act of kindness for what it is – an act of kindness. He is persistent. More persistent than any cockroach I have encountered: the ones I used to crush in my prison rooms always stayed dead after they were crushed. I learnt, though, that they played dead sometimes, and I had to make sure they were properly crushed. I had done that with this man, and he still came back.

Maybe he isn't a cockroach after all. Maybe he is . . .

'Shouldn't you be at work?' I ask.

'Day off. That's why I thought I'd make a start on this today. I've got a spare paintbrush if you're free?'

I search in my pocket for the familiar ridges of my keys and pull them out. I'll go to see Serena on Thursday. She's not going anywhere, is she? 'I've got a few bits of the inside to finish off first,' I eventually say to him. 'Good thing I leave my painting clothes here, isn't it?'

Alain smiles a smile that flips my stomach upside down. 'Yeah, it's a good job,' he says. My stomach flops back the other way. *Stop it*, I tell myself. *You're not allowed to fall in love with him. You're not allowed to do anything until you've made Serena confess.*

Even as I'm telling myself this, I know my face is softening into a smile, my eyes are matching the expression in his eyes, and my heart is gently opening up, ready to let him in.

poppy

'You look incredible,' Alain tells me. 'Simply . . . incredible. Beautiful.'

'Thanks,' I mumble. I want to smile, but I feel a bit strange doing it. It's been so long, I forget how to take compliments. He is full of compliments, not only for the way I look, the things I say, the way I paint, even the way I hand him coffee. He notices little things about me and then comments on them with a compliment. It's hard not to be caught up in it, not to want to hear those lovely words aimed at me trip off his tongue.

It's been a bit of a natural progression to where we are now. Weather permitting, he would come by after work – he's a college lecturer – or whenever he had free time and continue to sand and prime and paint the hut with me. Then we'd go for a drink or two afterwards. Last week he suggested we just go for a drink, and we did. Ten days later, we've been on a series of 'dates', like they do on the telly.

'You don't look so bad yourself,' I say to him. He is *wearing* a white collarless dress shirt with the top two buttons open, black suit trousers and that is it. He is *wearing* them because he looks so fit in them. It's the simplest outfit but, *God*, he looks tasty in it. There's a hint of smooth collarbone and muscular chest visible through the open shirt buttons; that shirt flows inviting down his body, disappearing into the top of the trousers. The trousers fall in such a way that they emphasise his slender hips, rock-hard arse and muscly legs. I'm guessing about the details of his body, of course, since I've yet to see anything beyond the odd flash of chest and the smooth skin below the fair hairs of his forearms. He is freshly shaven, while his dark hair has a just-washed glisten, all coming together to give him a youthful, scrubbed-up look. Beside him on the pub sofa is his suit jacket, with his silky bow tie peeking out of the top pocket. We're going to the theatre, so I'm dressed up too.

I have rescued a blue silky gown my mother had hidden in the back of her wardrobe. I used to try it on when I was twelve – padding out the breast cups with toilet roll and climbing into her heels. Whenever she caught me in it, she used to tell me about the parties she and Dad used to go to, wearing it along with her pearls and diamonds (paste and plastic). She'd tell me how much fun they had, how this dress had become her favourite of all the others she had. She gave it to me when I was fourteen because, she said, she wasn't going to be wearing it again and I looked so sweet in it. Then she obviously took it back.

When they moved and recreated my bedroom, they seemed to have removed some vital pieces – namely the things they'd given me that were theirs. This dress, some of Mum's jewellery, a 1950s edition of *Peter Rabbit*, a classic Mini V car model in a glass box Dad had given me – he'd always planned to give me a Mini like that for my eighteenth birthday but never got the chance. I found the items in their room, stashed away at the back of their big old wardrobe, as if they'd been trying to hide those little tokens of affection from me, hide them in Narnia where I'd never think to look.

The wardrobe was, in fact, the *first* place I looked because people are incredibly unimaginative when it comes to hiding even their most precious items. Maybe I was just naturally paranoid, but I didn't hide anything to do with Marcus in my wardrobe. I hid them under the two loose, creaky floorboards in the corner by the window. I hid the underwear he gave me, the picture I had of him I'd taken from his house without him knowing, I hid some of the clothes he gave me, I hid my diary there. I also hid the clothes I was wearing *that* night, the clothes that had his blood on them, there.

So when the police came and searched the house and my room, and tore it apart, they found nothing. They found no evidence that showed them I had killed him. I don't know why I didn't give them the clothes. The items – a pair of high-waisted long black trousers, a plunging-necked pink top and a pink jacket – probably would have backed up my story, showed them that I *was* innocent. But, by that point, they weren't listening to me. They had decided they knew what had happened and anything they found was to back that up, not to prove who really did it. I took the stuff under the floorboards out the day before the trial started and hid my diary in a suitcase of old clothes, and the underwear and the bloody clothes I stashed in a black bag, in the early hours of the morning, under the black bags in the metal bin outside because it was bin day and I knew they would be taken away.

Serena gave them her clothes. And they almost crucified her because of it. It was me who went to jail, but with the clothes and other things they found of hers that linked him to her, she almost went down. It was a dangerous game she played. She acted innocent, she behaved innocent, she behaved as if she had nothing to hide, nothing to fear because she hadn't done anything wrong, when we both knew she did. We both knew she did.

I'm getting worked up. This happens all the time. In prison, I found equilibrium: I had to focus on the day-to-day, on getting through every day, on finding ways to make those days turn into weeks, those weeks turn into months, those months turn into years, those years into decades. I had to find ways to wish my life away. Out here, it only takes the smallest of things to drag me back to Serena: what she did; how she escaped. Everything seems to ignite the heat of anger I feel when I think of her.

I have to stop thinking about her. Enjoy this evening with Alain.

'Would Madam care for a glass of champagne before the car arrives to pick us up?' Alain asks, as he takes my hand to help me into my seat. He is the perfect gentleman, always standing when I arrive or leave the table, always opening doors for me, always buying the first round, never attempting to kiss me . . .

The touch of his hand is electrifying. I want to move my fingers to rest between his, I want his hand to rest on the small of my back and pull me close to him, I want him to dip his head and kiss me on the mouth. I want so much to have real, physical contact with him. Body to body, skin to skin. I have fantasises of being held by him. Being held by anyone would be nice, but by him it would be . . .

'An orange and soda for me, please,' I say. 'The champagne bubbles tickle my nose and throat.'

'Oh. I've asked for a bottle to be put in the back of the car. Shall I cancel it?' he asks.

'No, no, it's very sweet of you. You drink, I'll watch.'

His lips part in a little laugh and my eyes are transfixed by that mouth. It is so sensuous, I'm sometimes desperate – achingly so – to trace the outline of his lips with the tip of my tongue. 'Call me strange, but I like the idea of you watching me,' he says, flashing one of his heart-stopping half-smiles.

'Strange,' I say to him.

He laughs again before taking his wallet from inside his jacket and heading to the bar. It's a good thing he likes me watching him because, even if I tried, I doubt I could remove my gaze from his divine body as it walks away.

'Do you want to come back to my place?' I ask at closing time. I have my legs curled up under me, I am resting my head back against the smooth, butter-soft leather of our sofa in the Maid Marion. Alain has his feet up on the other end of the curved sofa. The place has cleared out, as it often does during the evening when there is no football on, and it is literally just Alain and I, dressed up to the nines for our theatre date. 'My parents have gone to London for a few days to visit my brother and sister – two days with one, two days with the other. I have the house – and the biscuit tin – to myself. If you're very good, I might even let you have a jammy dodger.'

'Do you mind?' Alain asks, suddenly serious, his forehead a mass of concerned lines, his head slightly dipped so he can see all of my face as he questions me. 'Do you mind that they've gone to visit them without you?'

I turn my head away from him to stare at the bar, inhaling as I do so. I hate that you can't smoke in pubs any more. I'm just the wrong side of lazy to keep going outside for a fag, and conversations like this *need* a fag to accompany them. Instead, I pick up a beer mat and start to spin it through my fingers while I scrutinise the bar that I've seen every time we've been in here. Along the top of the bar is a row of glasses, all hanging or sitting upside down, waiting to be used. Imagine the carnage if that shelf ever fell, if the screws holding it into the bar frame one day just gave way and the whole thing came tumbling down? It'd be somewhere equal to the carnage left behind after you're sent to prison, only with more blood.

September 1988

Bella's face was buried in her ragdoll's body most of the time; Logan's eyes were wide and white with fear. They watched the police tear through the house: feet trampling around our home, hands pulling things off shelves, upending furniture, ripping things apart, leaving behind a hideous debris. Mum held Bella, Dad held Logan, and I sat alone with them at the kitchen table, all of us trying to weather the chaos raging around us. None of us spoke as the soundtrack of things falling, thudding, occasionally smashing, orders to look here and there seemed to play on loop. The officer in charge, Detective Inspector Grace King, came into the kitchen and fixed me to the spot with her most fearsome look. They hadn't found anything, which had probably annoyed her even more. I don't know what they expected to find – maybe a detailed written confession because they had the murder weapon, and I'd told them I had thrown away the clothes I was wearing because they were ruined – but they still insisted on searching the house.

'Take her away,' she said to the two uniformed officers who had come into the room with her. I was on bail and under house arrest, the only reasons they would need to arrest me again would be if I broke my curfew conditions or they found new evidence. Or to scare me, it seemed.

Bella began to cry and Logan anxiously shook his head as the officers wrestled me to my feet and roughly put the cuffs on behind my back. It was all for show, to scare my parents or the kids into saying something that would incriminate me. I knew it was for show, but Bella and Logan didn't and their horrified, terrified faces as I was led out of the kitchen became scored into my mind, onto my heart. Their fears didn't go away for that whole year leading up to the trial. Bella would wake up at night, crying for me because she was scared I would be taken away; Logan insisted on sitting beside me at dinner, when we were watching TV, even if he came into my room while I was reading.

They didn't really understand what was happening, just that someone said I did something bad and I hadn't done it.

'Yes,' I say to Alain, 'I mind. I mind very much. My brother and sister were six and seven when I was sent down. I tried writing to them but my mum asked me to stop because they were too young to understand I wouldn't be back for years and years, so my letters were confusing and upsetting them.

'I still sent them birthday and Christmas cards but I never heard anything, which I guessed meant they never got them. Then, when they were older, I started writing to them again, but the letters came back unopened, along with the cards. Well, opened by the prison staff, but you know what I mean.

My family didn't want to know. All these years I've tried, but now they're old enough to think for themselves and they still don't want to know. Mum all but said so when she mentioned the visit to London – she kind of hinted that as long as I was in the house, they wouldn't be coming down.' I shrug at the futility of the situation. 'What am I supposed to do? I can't force them to want to know me. They've just listened to all the crap that was said about me and believed it, I guess. Without bothering to ask me.'

October, 1989

I hugged Bella first, then Logan. 'I'll see you when I get home later, OK?' I said to them on the last day of the trial. I truly believed I would. That's why I'd had to hastily pack a suitcase of belongings last night just in case. They both hugged me back extra hard and ran to Granny Morag, who was staying at home with them. They moulded themselves to her, holding on for dear life, it seemed; holding on in case she went away like I was about to. 'I really will see you later,' I told them. I was innocent, I was bound to be found not guilty – why would what I was saying be a lie?

Alain nods, staring into space, as though considering what I have said. I don't want to kill the mood: we've had a buzz going all evening.

'Are things even a little better with your family?' he asks.

I have told him all about Mum walking around pale and shaky, as if scared of what I might do, and Dad just not being anywhere that I am. I have not told him that the only reason I stay, the only reason I don't walk away from them now and try again when my name is cleared, is that here I get to be near *her*. I have not told Alain anything about her – he hasn't asked, either. I assume he's read all the articles, that he knows what I was accused of, but he never brings it up directly. He talks around it, acts as if he's not bothered a lot of the time. I'm not sure if it's because he isn't or because he feels he has to act that way.

'Let's not talk about that,' I say. I cannot deal with all that at the moment. I want to go back to the buzz we'd had earlier. When we'd had our 'theatre date', when we talked and acted as if we were about to go to the theatre any second; then, between eight and ten we talked about *Hamlet*, the play we were 'seeing'. And then, from ten to the ding–ding of the last orders bell, we talked about how nice it was to get out of the house and watch live performances.

'Do you want to come back to mine then?' I ask again.

'Want to? Yes. Should? That's another matter.'

'What does that mean?' I ask. From what I knew of men, and admittedly it wasn't much, if they liked you in *that* way they generally didn't need asking more than once to come home with you. They certainly didn't debate the shoulds and shouldn'ts of it.

'It means I'll think about it as I walk you home. Come on.' He is on his feet, shrugging on his jacket and picking up my wrap to slip around my shoulders.

Think about it? I ask myself, as I allow him to slip the thick material around my shoulders and pick up my fancy bag. *What the fuck does that mean?* 'If you don't want to come back to my place then say so,' I tell him as he holds open the door for me, nodding goodnight to the bar staff as we leave. 'I'm not desperate or anything. I thought we were getting on well, I didn't want the night to end. I'm not saying we have to do anything. We just—'

He stops walking up towards Westfield Road, the road that leads back to Hove and Portslade, and faces me. His hands are buried deep in his pockets and he is staring at the pavement. 'I'm trying to be a good guy here, Poppy,' he says.

'By making me feel small and unattractive?' I reply. We are standing close to each other, so close any other couple would be kissing right now. I would be in his arms, his mouth would be on mine, the world would melt away and we'd be falling into each other, falling into the kiss, becoming one in the easiest, smallest of ways.

'I don't want to take advantage of you,' he says. 'You're incredibly vulnerable at the moment and it wouldn't be right of me to do anything, to make a move on you when you're this . . . fragile.'

Fragile? *Fragile?* 'You just don't fancy me, do ya?' I ask him. 'It's the prison thing. You thought you could get over it, but you can't and now you're feeding me all this shit to try to hide it.'

'It's not the prison thing,' he said. 'Not in the way you think. I mean, yes, it's not great to think you were in prison, but that's not it. You've just come out into a whole new world: you need time to assimilate being out, not have someone try to get you into bed.'

'Why haven't you asked if I did it?'

'What?' he asks, cautiously.

'We've spent all this time together in the last fortnight and you've never asked if I did it. Why not?'

He raises his shoulders to his ears, blows air out of his mouth in exasperation and confusion but he doesn't say anything.

'Ask me.'

'What?' he asks, alarm on his face. He's drawn back from me, afraid all of a sudden.

'Ask me.'

'Poppy—'

'Ask me.'

'No.'

'Ask me.'

'No.'

'Ask me.'

'No. I'm not going to do it.'

'Why, because you're scared of the answer?'

'Because if I'd wanted to know the answer, I would have asked. I'm not going to ask because you tell me to.'

'What are you doing with me?' I ask. 'Why are you bothering with me? Is it because I was infamous a few years ago?

Because no matter what you think, I am not that girl. I am not an Ice Cream Girl. I never was, I never will be.'

'I like you, Poppy. It's that simple. I like you and I want to get to know you.'

'I don't think you're being completely honest with me.'

'It might seem old fashioned to you, but I like to wait, before all that. If I didn't like you as much as I'm starting to I'd, well, you'd have come back to mine before now and I probably wouldn't be seeing you as much. I just like to wait. Is that so crazy?'

Is it? I don't know. When I wanted to wait with Marcus, it became a big thing . . . It became an impossible thing. I do not know if men wait. I do not know what men do. To be honest, I don't know what women do. I only know that this one is saying the things I wanted to hear twenty-odd years ago; he's talking the words that I wanted to come out of Marcus's mouth.

I am starting to think that maybe he is my do-over, my chance to reset the clock and start again with a man. Maybe I can try to have a relationship again, this time without the ex-girlfriend who isn't an ex, and the other stuff. Maybe Alain is my chance to get it right. I would love to get it right. Even if it's with someone I have just met.

'Do you want to come back to my house and just have a drink?' I ask him. 'It'll be the first time I've slept alone in a place for more than twenty years. I'm a bit—'

'Scared?' he supplies.

'Yeah, that. I'm a bit that.'

'OK, no problem. I'll even sleep on the sofa, if you want.'

'You will?'

'Yeah, course. That's what mates do for each other, isn't it?'

'I suppose so.'

'Come on,' he says with that trademark grin of his. He reaches out and circles me with his arm, pulls me closer.

I snuggle into him as we start to walk back towards my parents' place. 'I didn't think much of the second act denouement, did you?' I say, affecting the posh accent I had to work hard to stamp out in prison.

'No, I didn't, so clichéd and obvious.'

'I know, who on earth do they get to write these things?'

poppy

Dear Tina, (I write in my head)
It's not that I've forgotten about Serena, or that I don't want to clear my name, it's just that life has kind of got in the way.

Mrs Raines, the woman I clean for three times a week, recommended me to some of her friends, and they all called Raymond and asked for me by name. He was actually nice to me when he called and asked what days I wanted to do. So now I work all day Monday and Wednesday, and until lunchtime on Friday. Which means I have money. Not stacks, but money. I have bought new clothes from the markets and from second-hand stores: I no longer look like a cross-dresser or someone stuck in a time-warp.

And I have Alain. I have a boyfriend. Things have progressed between us to kissing and the occasional fumble, but nothing more. He still wants to wait and I adore that about him. I adore that he respects me and doesn't want to rush things. I'm scared sometimes that I've fallen for him too quickly, that I don't know him but I feel so close to him I hate to be away from him. And I get scared that this is all going to go horribly wrong and I'll mess up at work and get sacked. But I'm trying to do what you taught me: focus on the now, focus on the things I can do and can change and do them well.

How are you? I miss you. I can't wait for you to come out and for us to get together. I'm putting money away in a 'Tina fund' so that I can come up to Yorkshire when you get out, and visit. I wish you'd let me visit you now, though. It won't be weird for me going back into a prison, I promise it won't.

I have to go now, but take care of you.

Love,

Poppy xxxx

part four

poppy

I'm assuming most couples shag when they're alone together, that they cram their private hours with as much physical intimacy as is possible, leaving the soft moulds of another's body on theirs. Alain and I usually lie on top of the covers, kissing and cuddling. More cuddling than anything else.

Occasionally we go a bit further – 'second base' they call it in the American TV shows – where he slides his hand up my top and I have a fumble down below, but nothing more. He doesn't seem so keen sometimes. Something stops him – he physically wants to, but he can't seem to get over the hurdle of actually taking it further. It's probably better this way, and when he's ready – and if I'm ready at the same time – then we'll go all the way. I sometimes think I'm ready, then a shudder of Marcus will run through my body – chilling and nauseating – and I'll be grateful Alain was wise enough to make us wait.

'I always thought you were pretty fabulous, actually,' Alain says out of the blue.

We have been laying side by side, our bodies barely touching, and staring at my bedroom ceiling, not speaking as we listen to classical music on the radio. My parents are out until late tonight, Mum told me in a note, so I had to find my own dinner.

'Erm, what are we talking about? Have you had one of those conversations in your head that you've only let me in on at the end?'

245

'Kind of. I was just thinking about the other week, in the pub, when you said you think your siblings listened to all the crap about you.'

'Yeah, what of it?'

'I listened to it, I had no choice because I didn't know you personally, and I thought you were pretty fabulous.'

'Fabulous? Me?'

'Yeah, you. You . . . you as one of the, you know . . .'

'One of The Ice Cream Girls?' I say, filling in his blanks.

'Yeah.'

'Fabulous?'

'Yes, *fabulous*. What's wrong with that?'

'Nothing, I suppose, it's just very *Sex and The City* of you.' I turn my head to him as he has done to me. 'I'd expect a man like you to use words like "sexy" or "fit", not "fabulous". That's something you'd hear someone say on *Sex and The City*.'

That look reveals itself on his face. Tina told me about this look a while back. Since she'd been in prison the first time, when she was out, if she ever mentioned something that was of the moment, modern, people would look at her funny. Wondering how she knows something that they know, wondering just how easy she had life on the inside to be able to quote episodes of a TV show. Alain wears that look: a slight frown wants to break through his expression, a pursing of the lips as they twitch, wanting to ask me a million questions about how truly difficult my life inside must have been for me to know about *Sex and The City*.

'Why are you looking at me like that?' I ask.

'You know *Sex and The City*?'

'What, someone like me isn't meant to know about *Sex and The City*?'

'No, it's not that, it's just . . .'

'I was in prison, not on the moon. We do have this thing called "television". I believe it was invented before I went away.'

'No, it's just . . .'

'You're not sure how you feel about me being able to do

normal things like watch television? Well, let me assure you, television and reading were probably the only two "normal" things about my life. Everything else was . . . the hell people want it to be. Well, for me it was. Because for me, not having my freedom was punishment enough. Being banged up sometimes twenty hours a day with nothing to do but stare at the walls or read a book that I've read a hundred times was another layer of torture. The food, the noise, the hygiene, the not knowing who your friends are, the having to beg to see a doctor if you're ill were another deep layer of torture. Having no visitors except the odd solicitor or my uni tutor until they cut funding so I had to give up my Open University course that they suggested I do – the final layer. Not being able to go to my gran's funeral – the icing on the cake. So, you know, I reckon being able to watch television and even watch programmes that the rest of the free world watches and enjoy them is a small thing in prison. But then, I would say that, I was a prisoner. Maybe I'd feel differently if someone had hurt me or mine and they'd been put away. Maybe I'd advocate making conditions even worse.' Maybe I'd want Serena to suffer more than I did because she's had twenty years of freedom, and normal living. Maybe I'd want Serena to live through hell every second of every minute of every day.

He licks those lips that were minutes ago twitching to ask me questions. He probably would have been more subtle, more delicate and discreet, would certainly never have said that upfront, but he'd have been trying to say that. I have no time for subtlety any more. Like so many different parts of my personality that were eroded over the time I was 'away', I cannot remember when I stopped being subtle, when I started to ask people outright what they meant, as well as stating what I saw and thought and felt. I cannot remember what I was like before, nor when the change happened. And I cannot remember if I prefer the new, less subtle me or the old one. It's hard sometimes to think that I do not know who I was and that I may never remember. I have memories, but not experiences. That's

247

what 'life' means. That part of me has been removed. A life for a life. What, though, if you don't deserve that punishment? What if you don't deserve to have your life taken because you didn't take the life you are being punished for?

'I was actually going to ask why you thought my word was a "chick" word.'

We both know that wasn't what he was going to ask, but I decide not to call him on it. I don't want to ruin this moment. They are so rare because Mum and Dad don't go out at the same time very often, and I've never been to his place. I roll towards him, trying to get close to him, to make my body a part of his and his mine. That is the best part of cuddling, the lingering closeness you create. 'I told you,' I say to him, 'I expect a bloke like you, one who says "chick" without a hint of irony, to say something like "sexy" or "shaggable" not "fabulous".'

'Sexy and shaggable or fit don't really sum it up,' he replies. 'It was more than about looks. Me and my mates, we used to talk about it. That picture, it just said everything about you. You were sexy, yes, but there was this dangerous side to you both. The way you're grinning at the camera, it's like you're both saying "Come hither . . . but you're taking your balls in your hands if you do." You were the ultimate poster girls. I had that picture up of you both in my room for ages. My mum hated it. She couldn't beli . . .' His voice fades away while a look of extreme discomfort descends upon his face, infecting his body. *'She couldn't believe her son had a picture of a couple of cold-blooded killers on his wall when there were so many other nice girls out there,'* I finish for him in my head.

I used to get letters in prison that said virtually the same thing about that photo. I never knew how they found me, but I would get letters from 'fans' – a lot from haters, but far more from 'fans'. Almost all of them male. Almost all of them asking me to send them something personal, something intimate, sometimes even worn underwear. Every one of those poison-pen letters went in the bin and over time their numbers dwindled to virtually nothing. This confession of his is surprising in lots of different ways. I did not think he was like that. And I did not think he had remembered me that clearly, but then he didn't. Like everyone else, anything he felt – good, bad or disgusting – was about the girl in the picture, the smiling killer the papers wrote about. Not me. I am not her. I never was.

'You want to hear something ironic?' I say, just to shatter any illusions he might have. 'We never got to eat those ice creams. We were branded these killer vixens because we allegedly did nothing but eat ice cream and look good and Marcus died, but we never got to eat those ice creams. Marcus wouldn't let us.'

'Wouldn't let you?' His voice is sceptical, wondering how anyone could stop a woman from eating ice cream.

'It's hard to explain if you weren't there, but he wouldn't let us do lots of things. He just had this way of making you decide not to do something he didn't want you to do. Like the ice creams – he said we should both get one for the photo, he thought we'd look good in our swimsuits, all dolled up with an ice cream. After he took the photo, he said, in this really sweet voice, to think about the damage us eating the ice creams would do to his arteries.'

'*His* arteries?'

'Yes, *his* arteries. "It'll break my heart, girls, if you both got too big to look pretty any more. Poppy, sweetheart, you're on the edge, and Serena, my love, you know how you balloon at the drop of a hat." That's all he had to say to get the doubts going in our minds.'

'*I'm only saying it because you both mean so much to me. I wouldn't bother, otherwise. And if I don't say it, who else will? But, hey, don't let me stop you. If you really want that ice cream you eat it, as long as you know what you're doing as you eat it,*' Marcus adds in my head. He had that look in his eye, the one that told me I could eat it but I would pay for it. Not just with him not loving me any more, in other ways. In other, more painful ways.

'What did you do?' Alain asks.

I used to love ice cream. When I was younger I used to

sneak an extra one in – my own special ice cream – when I went down the road to buy them. I wanted that ice cream. I didn't want to not eat it, but I didn't want Marcus to stop loving me or to be angry with me. Because that was what he was saying. If I ate the ice cream, I would get fat and he would stop loving me. As it was he was already thinking that I was on the cusp of losing what beauty he saw in me; this would push him the other way. Away. Out of love. I wouldn't have been able to bear that. I know I loved him that intensely I was willing to share him and willing to put up with the other stuff. If I couldn't bear to give him up to another woman, why on earth would I give him up to a load of lard on a biscuit?

'I'd love to tell you that I argued, or even took a tiny defiant lick, but I just accepted he was right and binned it. I spent the whole afternoon thinking about the ice cream, disintegrating in that bin. Serena tried to disguise that she was doing what he wanted by pretending to trip and dropping her ice cream so she couldn't eat it . . . So, do you still think I was fabulous? Or, as is much closer to the truth, a pathetic little schoolgirl?'

'Fabulous. Always, always fabulous.' He draws me closer and kisses my forehead. 'Always fabulous.'

I didn't tell Alain what happened afterwards. That part of that day, the part I could talk about, was bad enough, but everything to do with Marcus had parts that I could not repeat, parts that had to stay hidden. And what happened at the end of the ice cream day was one of them.

August, 1987

When it was time to leave the beach, Marcus went to get the car while we got dressed. I waited until the last possible second, trying to soak up as much of the sun's rays as I could – it didn't seem to shine the same way in London, didn't make me feel as relaxed and warm and content. Eventually I reached for my clothes, sitting in a neat, folded pile beside me on top of my bag. They had to be like that, everything had to be like that.

Always. Neat, orderly, tidy. If anything was ever out of place . . . it wasn't worth thinking about the consequences. It was easier, simpler if things were always neat and tidy.

I saw the spot before my hands touched the soft fabric of my dress. A spot of white ice cream, the size of a pea, staining the front skirt of the pink dress he had bought for me. My hand froze mid-air.

No. No. No! There can't be a stain on my dress. There just can't.

I stared at it, not knowing what to do. There was no way I could hide it. There was no way I could wash it off and dry it before he came back. This couldn't be happening to me. I'd been so careful for so long, I hadn't made any mistakes or said anything stupid, and now this . . .

All ready to leave, Serena came closer to me. She was zipped into her knee-length yellow dress, the pristine version of mine, her feet in her heeled espadrilles. She'd removed her big straw sun hat and had her big straw beachbag on her shoulder. She'd got dressed the moment he left because she knew what would happen if we kept him waiting.

With panic whirling around inside, I looked up at her while she looked down at what I had been staring at. She briefly closed her eyes, curled her plum and gold lipsticked mouth in on itself and shook her head slightly. She understood the enormity, the gravity of what I'd done.

Without saying a word, because she rarely spoke to me unless she absolutely had no choice, Serena dropped her bag and hat, reached under her arm and unzipped her dress. Then she slipped out of it, threw it at me so it landed in a heap on my lap, and then snatched up my dress and put it on. I sat and watched, watched as she zipped it up, watched as she picked up her bag and hat again, watched as she took a few steps away from me, and stared off out to sea.

We both knew what she'd done, what it meant, what would happen when we got back to London.

I dressed quickly, and picked up my belongings, too, and waited for Marcus to return. He didn't come back down to

251

the beach, he hung around on the promenade, and we both made our way over the shingles, our headway hampered by the heels on our espadrilles.

He frowned when he saw that we were wearing each other's dresses. The frown was replaced by a flat-mouthed glare when his eyes alighted on the spot of ice cream on the front skirt of the dress Serena was wearing. He moved his gaze to her face, and she stared back at him, defiance was in her eyes, on her face, in the way she stood up straight and tall. She rarely stood straight – if she did she was nearly the same height as him and he hated that. She was doing it for me: gently challenging him so that even if he did guess that I had done it and she was trying to take the blame – which would make it worse – he'd be far more occupied with her current behaviour.

I understood what she was doing, but not why. She didn't like me, I didn't like her – she had no reason to save me. Especially when I wouldn't do it for her.

Marcus's face closed in tight, barely containing his rage as he turned on his heels and stalked away.

She followed and I brought up the rear. I wanted to speak up, but I couldn't. My voice had been quietened by incremental degrees over time. And I couldn't speak, I couldn't confess. I shouldn't have let her do it, but I was too scared to do anything else.

I kiss Alain and he kisses me back. I was anything but fabulous that day.

And I'm ashamed every time I think about it.

serena

Even though it's crazy, I do this.

It's almost compulsive. At least once a year, I come to the library and look through the microfiche about myself. And her. And *him*.

Most of it is online nowadays – the librarians always tell me this. But I do not want to use the Internet at home or at work to look at this stuff. On the Internet you are like Hansel and Gretel in the woods – leaving a trail behind wherever you may go. Unlike Hansel and Gretel, nothing gobbles up your path and others can find out very easily where you have been, what you have looked at. I do not want anyone in my life to know I look at this.

I had to take a half-day today to come here because I need an outlet. I need to be able to think about those times without losing the plot completely. Having my behaviour censored by being in a library is the best way.

My family think I'm a murderer, and I have to remind myself why. The fear I have of that time, the gaps in my memory it has caused, mean that if I try to think about it, I lose myself. Every defence I have kicks in and I start to fall apart.

They think I am a murderer.

Adrian obviously told Medina and she obviously told Faye, who obviously told Mum and Dad, because they have all been ringing me for days. Trying to get me to talk to them, I think.

I do not know because I cannot speak to them. How can I speak to any of them knowing what they think, what they feel?

Evan has caught me crying in the kitchen at 4 a.m. a couple of times and has slipped his arms around me, held me and hushed me and told me it would be OK. He thinks it's normal for sisters to fall out, that we'll fix it soon. And I feel my throat start to ache because it wants to tell him, but the words and the fear expand so much they cannot break through. And all I can do is cry, and let him hold me and try to think of ways to fix this. Try to think of ways to rewrite history so I never met *him,* and I never let him ruin my life. Like he always promised me he would.

Working slowly and methodically, I go through the newspapers from that time. From our arrest after our confessions, the run-up to the trial, the trial and afterwards. I should know word for word what they say now, I have been through them enough. But some headlines are more eye-catching than others.

ICE CREAM GIRLS CONFESSION! Veronica Bell did indeed get me back. She went to the newspapers and told them that *he* was a great and gifted teacher and he would show an interest in the brighter pupils. But she knew something was wrong because I threatened her. 'He wanted to help me after class, but even then Serena had her sights set on him and told me to stay away from him. She told me that I should be scared of her.' She is reclined along the bottom of the two-page spread, wearing a school uniform with the shirt knotted above her belly button, the buttons open to the knot, and her breasts barely contained by her pure white bra. Her skirt almost covers her bum and she has bunches in her hair. Did Mum and Dad, Faye and Medina believe that? Did they think I had really done that? Because how could anyone take seriously what she said when she was dressed like that?

THE TRUTH ABOUT THE ICE CREAM GIRLS! A 'concerned neighbour' of Poppy's parents described how she had seemed a nice girl until her teens when she started sneaking around, staying out late, getting out of different cars at all hours of the night, usually with different boys. They'd seen her scantily clad, smoking and drinking, and worried what else she got up to. They also wondered where her parents were in all of this. I did not like her but I knew this was pure fiction, what the neighbours wanted to believe about her, having heard what she was accused of, rather than the truth. None of that behaviour was Poppy.

THE KILLER IN ME! A psychologist explained in the newspaper how everyone was a potential killer but some, like The Ice Cream Girls, like Serena Gorringe and Poppy Carlisle, were closer to the edge of actually committing murder. We did not need much to tip us over; we actively sought the flimsiest excuse to hurt someone. We had probably singled *him* out because he was weak-willed. He hadn't been able to resist two of his pupils and then was stuck. If he ever left us, we would have ruined his life. As it probably turned out, when he decided to end it with us, we decided to seek revenge by first torturing then killing him.

I gorge myself on the stories, the headlines, the theories, the reports from the courts. I gorge myself until I feel nothing but sick: it swirls like a whirlpool in my stomach and at the back of my throat, it weighs heavy on my mind. This is what the world saw and thought. I do not blame the papers, they only reported what they were told by the people who supposedly 'knew' us, and the information they got from the police. But is this what my family thought? That I had seduced him? That Poppy and I were lovers because of the kissing picture he had made us pose for that the police found but never actually gave to the press? Did they really think that I was the one who went back and stabbed him through the heart? Did they read everything in the papers and believe it? Or think there had to be at least some truth to it?

And did they see that picture, the only picture the papers had of Poppy and I together, and think we really were lovers who had plotted this?

I hate that picture. It was used over and over and over again. And I hate it. If only the world knew. If only they knew what had really happened that day, maybe they wouldn't have been so quick to use it, so ready to condemn us in the various captions. Maybe they would not have used the inscription *he* scrawled on the back of the photo, *'My ice cream girls, 1987'*, to rename and brand us The Ice Cream Girls. To mark us in the world's mind as cool, calculating killers.

August, 1987

'Come on now, girls, you can do better than that.'

We had come to Littlehampton for a day trip. *He* chose Littlehampton because he said most people we knew would go to Brighton on a sunny day like today, so we'd come here instead. He had chosen our swimsuits – mine was a string bikini in white with red polka dots, hers was an electric blue one-piece with a plunging neckline and the legs cut so high you could see right to the top of her thighs and the smoothing of her abdomen into the v of her pelvis. We had this area of the beach to ourselves, we were there so early, so he told us to get our dresses off while he got us some ice creams so he could take a picture. We each held cones in our hands and were smiling at his camera lens.

For the fifth time he lowered the camera without hitting the button. 'Come on, you don't look like you're having a good time at all,' he complained. In unison we both fixed smiles to our faces. 'Stand closer together . . . that's it. Anyone would think you didn't like each other . . . Poppy, suck in your stomach, there's a good girl . . . Serena, stick out your chest a bit more, pretend you've got something to hang those bikini cups on . . . That's it . . . Now if you could just smile, it'd be perfect.'

Click!

'One more for luck.'

Click!

'That's it, ladies, thank you. Now we can all relax and enjoy our little beach adventure. I bring you to the best places, don't I?'

'Yes,' I said brightly, at the same time as she did.

We both knew it was easier, simpler, *better* to just play along.

August, 1987

'I don't know why you make me do these things, Serena,' *he* said. 'You shouldn't have worn her dress. And you shouldn't have got ice cream on it.' His footsteps came closer to me. 'We had such a nice day, why did you have to ruin it? Why?'

I watched his bare feet, standing in front of me, as if they were waiting for me to say something.

'You won't do it again, will you?'

'*No,*' I managed to whisper, as pain jack-knifed through me. My lip was split, my jaw ached, my throat hurt, my chest burned, my stomach was a caved-in mass of bruises. The smallest movement would light up another part of my body in pain like a Christmas tree. *No, I won't do that again.*

'Good girl, I knew you'd learn,' he said. He finally bent down and picked me up, causing more pain, more agony to ricochet around my nerve-endings. 'Come on, let me help you up, here.'

My body was too bruised, too heavy from what he had done for me to move unaided so I could not resist as he dumped me on the bed.

'It's over with now, baby, OK? Let's make up.'

'*No,*' I whispered again. I did not want to make up, I did not want him anywhere near me.

'We can still salvage the day, can't we?' he said. 'We can still fix this.'

I moved my head to shake it and a migraine of stars and bright lights popped behind my eyes. '*No.*'

He was lifting my dress, pushing it up around my waist. 'You can make it up to me,' he said.

'*No.*' I shook my head again, setting off the migraine but I did not care, I wanted to stop this. My limbs felt like lead, I could not move them to stop it, I had to tell him 'no' with my voice, with my headshake.

'You can show me how much you love me.'

'*No. Please. No.*'

He was tugging off my bikini bottoms, pulling them down over my legs.

'*No.*'

'Stop saying no, you owe it to me, Serena.'

He was unbuttoning his shirt, unzipping his trousers.

'*No. No.*'

He was looming over me, watching my split lower lip make the same movements over and over as I said the word over and over: '*No. No. No. No. No. No. No. No. No. No. No. No.*'

'You owe me,' he said through the twist of the smile that had taken over his face. 'You owe me this.'

He was pushing himself inside me.

'*No,*' I continued to whisper. '*No.*'

'Please stop crying, baby, we're only making up.'

I wonder if they would still have called me The Ice Cream Girl if they knew the real story, if they knew that because of that day I could never bring myself to eat ice cream again.

poppy

Sometimes I forget who I am. *What* I am. What I am meant to be doing.

It's been five days since I watched Serena. Since I went to see what she was up to. I didn't realise that until this morning, when I was trying to put together an outfit for my 'New York' lunch date. I really am crazy in love, I think.

Alain and I sit side by side in the booth of an American-style diner in Brighton, on the red seats, the Formica table in front of us, our table's jukebox playing a medley of fifties hits.

This is our second date to New York and I'm so glad we've decided to come back. This place does the best burgers: all thick and juicy and oozing with grease. The cheese is slabbed on top, the salad is fresh and the pickles have the perfect sharpness. And the French fries – *divine*.

I love this. I love sitting around, talking to someone, having him talk to me as if I'm an equal, replying without vetting every word I utter in case I make a mistake. Being able to relax with someone is another luxury for my list.

I must write to Tina and tell her. Tell her that in the outside world you don't have to be so cautious, you don't have to be wary of people who want to be your friend. You can let someone in, even if you have just met – because if you do, if you let that person in, you can open yourself up to a whole new, wonderful world. You can become like me. On the edge of love.

Yes, I am falling in love with him. And that does not scare me as much any more, because he has a good heart, a good soul, he is a man I can trust.

Maybe I won't write that to Tina. If I were still inside and she wrote that to me, I'd probably have done something hideous to myself.

Surreptitiously, I kick off my sandal and caress Alain's ankle with my toe, gently teasing him.

He swallows the mouthful he is chewing and raises his napkin to his mouth, wipes his lips, while he stares ahead at the opposite side of the booth. His eyes are slightly hooded and his gaze is slightly unfocused. Swallowing hard again, he reaches under the silver-edged Formica table and runs his hand up and down my denim-covered thigh. He turns towards me, his eyes even drowsier with desire as he unbuttons two of the middle buttons on my denim skirt and slips his hand inside the material. He uses two fingers to trace a path from my inner knee to the top of my inner thigh, and I have to stifle a loud gasp as a bolt of desire jolts me. That is what I imagine what being struck by lightning would feel like, how it would feel to plug yourself into an electrical socket and flip the switch. I only felt something like that *once* before. It was *only* like that once with Marcus. I can't believe that this is what other women feel all the time and I experienced it after the very first time Marcus kissed me.

Alain leans in and kisses me, his tongue pushing urgently into my mouth while his free hand snakes around the back of my head and his fingers entangle themselves in my hair.

'Let's go,' he says breathlessly as he pulls away a fraction, his hand on my thigh increasing in pressure. 'Let's go now before I change my mind and decide we still need to wait.'

He pays for a taxi to take us back to my parents' house from Brighton, and we kiss the whole way back. I was embarrassed at first because I was so used to doing that sort of thing in private, was rarely allowed to even acknowledge Marcus in public let alone anything else, that I wasn't comfortable simply kissing in front of the taxi driver, let alone what Alain was trying to do.

'He's seen a lot worse,' Alain whispered as he gently nibbled my earlobe, devoured my neck. 'Ain't ya, mate?' he called to the taxi driver. 'You've seen a lot worse.'

'Just keep your clothes on,' the taxi driver replied, unbothered. If he didn't mind . . . when Alain kissed me, I kissed him back and by the time we fall in through my parents' front door we are ready to start ripping clothing to get to each other.

We stumble up the stairs, still pawing at each other, tugging at clothing but hampered by buttons and zips and sleeves.

'Do you have a rubber Johnny?' I ask as we fall on to my narrow bed. He climbs on top and sits astride me, and I start on his jeans' buttons.

'A rub—? Oh, you mean a condom. Yeah.' He climbs off again and grabs his jacket, which is on the floor by the door. He picks it up and pulls out his black leather wallet, then pulls out the rubb— the condom. I sit up on my knees and, with him watching, I peel my white top over my head, then let it drop to the floor of my bedroom.

Rather than drive him wild with desire, as I thought it would given that we were practically doing it the whole way home, it seems to stop him, scare him, and he drops his wallet and then the condom as if they have burnt him.

'What's the matter?' I ask him. Instinctively, I cross my arms across my top half, hiding my white lacy bra, protecting my heart. He cannot change his mind now – we're both ready.

He reaches up and anxiously rubs his hands over his mouth. 'Performance anxiety,' he says. 'So much pressure.' He blows out a couple of times, like a weightlifter about to lift the big one. 'Pressure.' He is uncurling and curling his fingers into his hands. 'Real pressure.'

'You really know how to make a girl feel wanted,' I say, holding my arms closer around me.

'It's not you,' he reassures. 'It's just this is the first time you've . . . in twenty years. Twenty years. It's like taking your virginity. I've never done that. And I don't want to do it wrong.'

'Shouldn't *I* be worried about that?' I ask.

'Oh, Poppy. Poppy, Poppy, Poppy,' he says, again rubbing his mouth. In the language of the body, something I did quite a lot of reading on, this behaviour suggests someone is lying to you. They are trying to rub away the stain of their lie with that action. *Is Alain lying to me? Is he really feeling performance anxiety or has he just changed his mind?*

'I'll be right back,' he says then leaves the room, almost at a run. I hear the bathroom door shut and lock behind him. My parents are in London visiting my siblings again. We have the house to ourselves, and I hadn't actually been expecting this to happen. When I started to play footsie with him, I thought it'd be something nice and gentle to do on our New York date. I didn't expect it to so overwhelmingly turn him on, and I didn't expect taking my top off to so completely turn him off.

What do I do now? Do I get dressed, do I get undressed? Do I gather his stuff up and throw it at him the second he comes out of the bathroom? Do I open the window and chuck his stuff out and tell him to go mess with someone else's head? What do I do?

I pull back the covers and climb into bed. That's probably the best thing to do. If he does come back and has changed his mind, at least I'll be covered up; if he comes back hoping to pick up where we left off, I'll be part-way there and won't have to do the thing that so clearly put him off.

Time moves on and on, and nearly ten minutes pass before he returns to my bedroom. He shuts the door behind him, then leans heavily on it, his tall, wiry body like a book that has fallen against a bookend.

Something more than performance anxiety is wrong.

'I think you should put your top back on,' he says in a serious tone. 'I need to tell you something.'

'And I need to be dressed to hear it?' I ask.

He nods, and I watch the guilt creep like climbing ivy across his face. 'That would be for the best.'

poppy

'I've got something to tell you,' he says.

The dread starts to roll over me in waves, the knowledge that whatever he says will alter my life for ever. That scares me. I do not want to have this love destroyed. It has kept me going these past few weeks, I do not want to lose it.

'What, you're married?' I say, trying to sound flip, trying to disguise that my heart is already crumbling. There's a moment in any relationship when you know that it is over. For the most part you can ignore it and carry on but, in this instance, that is not going to happen. I know it. I know it like I know how to breathe. It's simply a case of finding out why it's over.

He does not laugh, and he does not flinch.

'You're married,' I state. Serious this time.

'No,' he replies, still frowning, still serious. 'No. I was, a long time ago. I got divorced five years ago. We got married and divorced quite young, it's not a new story. Not that interesting, either. But that's not what I've got to tell you.'

'Is it important?' I ask, trying to save this, save us.

'Yes.'

'Are you sure? Because we all think things are important and ninety-nine per cent of the time they're not. We could go our whole lives without knowing whatever it is. And I am not that curious.'

Alain is not playing, he is not interested in saving our

relationship, he is hell-bent on destroying it. He continues to speak: 'We didn't meet by accident,' he says. 'It wasn't Fate that brought us together.'

A cement truck dumps its load on my chest, crushing my lungs. 'What are you saying?' I manage through short bursts of breathing.

'I'm a journalist,' Alain says.

'What? What are you talking about? You're not a lecturer?'

'No. Well, yes, but no.'

What is going on? What is he saying? 'Is it yes or no? Are you a lecturer?'

'I lecture – well, I used to – in basic journalism at a night school. My main job, my real job, is writing. Investigating. Being a journalist.'

I bite on my lower lip, knowing that there is more to this. He has more to confess, more to unburden from his soul. 'What are you telling me?'

'Like I said before, us meeting was not Fate. I engineered those encounters to meet you.'

'Why?' I know the answer. It's pretty obvious, but I need to hear it to believe it.

'I wanted to meet you because I wanted to write a story on you. On The Ice Cream Girls and what really happened. I wanted to get close to you to find out the truth.'

'No, no, no . . .' I say, standing up and holding my head. 'No, no, no . . .'

'I'm not going to write the story any more,' he says above my moans. 'I can't. I didn't expect to fall for you. I didn't even mean to be anything more than a friend. But how could I not fall for you? You're nothing like the girl in picture and the girl in the stories. You're . . .'

'No!' I say to him. 'You don't get to explain this away. Just stop talking, OK? Stop.'

He does as he's told and stands still and silent against my door. I pace the room, my hand pressed over my mouth, my eyes wide.

'Is that why you didn't want to go further? In the sack, I mean? Is that why you kept stopping? Because none of it was real?'

'It was real. It was very real. Which is why I'm not going to do the story.'

'Just answer the question.'

He closes his eyes before he says, 'Yes.'

'So all along you've been grilling me to find out background for your story?' I hold my hand up to him before starts to answer. 'Just yes or no answers, no talking and trying to excuse yourself. Just yes or no. So all the concern and interest have been to get background?'

'Yes.'

'And you were using me all along to make a name for yourself?'

He moves in protest.

'Just yes or no.'

'Yes.'

Betrayal is such a dramatic word. It's the sort of word I would find in the bonkbusters I read in the early nineties. 'Betrayal' always reminded me of women who were meek and mild and had 'victim' scrawled across their foreheads in an ink only the worst type of men could see.

I am that woman. First Marcus, now Alain. Will I never learn?

I take my hands away from my face and stand up straight, running my eyes over him. I thought I loved him. I thought I had been given a second chance, a fresh start. I'd even let Serena start to slide off the hook. I thought Alain was my ticket to the future, to a life I never had the chance to live. And he wasn't. He isn't. He is this.

'Thank you,' I say to him, meaning every letter of those words.

He stares at me, bemused and bewildered.

'I . . . nope, that's it, thank you.'

'For?'

'For reminding me that I can trust no one. I'd actually allowed myself to forget that for one sorry moment. Well, thank you for reminding me before I got really hurt. Now leave.'

'Not like this. I have to explain. I have to . . . I . . .'

'GET OUT!' I scream at him. 'GET OUT!'

He scrambles upright, then grabs his jacket and wallet and rubber Johnny from the floor beside him and opens the door. He pauses, then turns to me. 'I'm sorry,' he says.

'GET OUT!' I scream again.

I'm not just screaming at him, of course – smirky, snidey Marcus is being shouted at too. I want him gone as well. I do not need to hear from him right now that I am stupid and gullible and basically useless; I do not need an 'I told you so' from the man I am using to haunt myself. I just need peace and quiet and solitude to clear my head and do what needs to be done.

After ransacking the mirrored cabinet that hangs on the wall opposite the door in the bathroom, the only blade I can find is the last one in the pack. Dad is old school, thank God. Getting rid of the line of fuzz that sits around his chin every morning is still done using an old fashioned razor and shaving foam. I remember one Christmas when I was maybe fourteen, I used my saved-up pocket money to buy him an electric razor from Bella, Logan and me. He was so chuffed with it, gave us all a massive hug and thanked us profusely, but never used it. Not once.

I'm grateful now that he's stuck in the dark ages, because I can do this. Now. And it has to be now. I haven't needed to do this for such a long time that I'd feel stupid having to delay so I could go to the shop. It's not ideal, though: the last razor in the pack. He might notice, he might wonder where it's gone and quite rightly blame me, the only criminal in the house. But I have no choice, it has to be now. I watch my face in the mirror as the edge of the blade finds its spot on my forearm and sinks in, just below the skin. The blade knows, it knows where it should go, how deep it should sink before it stops, when it should start threading its path into my skin. My eyes roll back in my head as the pain gushes through me, and the release, the sweet, sweet release gushes down after it. The blade slips from my fingers into the sink and I grab on to the sink for support as the gush of pleasure born of physical pain, a cocktail you have to get just right to be effective, floods every sense in my head.

I watch the spot-work pattern of red cover the blade, cover the smooth shiny surface of the white basin. The head rush continues: I'm hitching the ultimate ride without actually taking anything. I am high without narcotics.

My legs wobble slightly and I grab tighter on to the sink. Maybe I did too much, cut too deep, sliced too close because this is going on for longer than normal. This is just pain.

And that pattern in the sink reminds me of my sixteenth birthday.

May, 1987

He bought me a cake.

I couldn't believe it. It was a huge one with white and pink icing and huge 'one' and 'six' candles. I sat at the table and waited for him to hand me my present. The big, shiny white box with a big pink shiny bow on top had been sitting on the living room telephone chair when I walked in. And now he left the room, grabbed it and brought it into the kitchen and handed it to me with a small smile on his face. I pulled open the ribbon and took care to fold it up so I wouldn't leave a mess. Marcus hated messes. I didn't want him to get cross on my birthday. I didn't want to do anything to upset him ever, but especially not today. Excitedly I lifted the lid. I hadn't expected a present from him: he'd said only a few days ago, and he was right of course, that being with him should be gift enough. He was risking everything to be with me, I should think myself lucky. And that every day I had him was a gift. But he'd just been joking, because now I had this.

Inside was a mound of bright pink tissue paper, folded around something. I pulled apart the folds, again carefully so as to not make a mess, and from it lifted up a red and white spotted halterneck dress. It was ruched and pleated in the smoothest, softest cotton. 'It's lovely,' I said to him. I ignored the fact it would probably look better on Serena, against her dark skin and slender frame. On me it would probably look too bosomy, make me look a lot larger than I was. Red didn't really suit me, either, but none of that mattered – it was a present and he had chosen it. And he hadn't given it to Serena, he'd given it to me.

I looked up at him and crossing my toes and my fingers in my head, I clutched it close and said, 'It's really, really lovely. I love it.'

Marcus's handsome face smiled with pride, which made me beam back at him. Sometimes, when he was like this, I forgot he was twice my age, because he seemed so eager to please and to make me happy – he was like a little schoolboy.

'Put it on,' he said, excitedly, still smiling. 'I want to see what you look like in it.'

'OK,' I replied and leapt up. His excitement was starting to make me like the dress even more. I put the lid back on the box and placed the folded up ribbon neatly at its centre before I picked up the dress and moved towards the door.

'Where are you going?' he asked.

'To change,' I said.

'Do it here.'

I hesitated. The kitchen windows didn't have any coverings on them and it was broad daylight – any of his surrounding neighbours would see me without my clothes on if I did it here.

'It won't take me long to nip upstairs,' I said.

'Do it here, I want to see you,' he insisted. An edge, *the* edge, had crept into his voice.

I heard the edge but I continued to hesitate because I still wasn't used to him seeing me naked. We'd been sleeping together for many, many months, but I was always glad that the bit at the start, the bit with the lights on, didn't last very long – the moment the light went out, I would relax a bit, not be so tense about what was coming next. Marcus had once jokingly said that he preferred it with the lights off because he could imagine me looking the way I was meant to look instead of the way I did look. But that was only one of his little jokes.

'But . . .'

'*Now*, Poppy. Don't make me wait.'

Carefully, I laid the dress over the back of the chair I had been sitting in and pulled my batwing top over my head. With folded arms and his head on one side, his eyes piercing spotlights, Marcus stood and stared at me. I could feel a million eyes from all his neighbours staring too, burning into my white, veiny skin, the lingering rolls of puppy fat – Dad called them that when I complained about being a bit on the large side – around my middle, the white strapless bra I was squeezed into. Marcus insisted I wear strapless bras when I was with him, even though they weren't that comfortable for someone of my bra size. But he said it made things sexier for him. And all I ever wanted was to please him. I pulled down my black leggings and could feel the eyes staring at them, too.

'Take off your knickers,' Marcus said throatily as I reached for the dress.

Oh God, no. Not that.

'Take your knickers off,' he repeated.

Inhaling deeply, gathering all my strength, I did as I was told.

'That's it, good girl,' he said, his voice deep and rich with lust. 'Now put on the dress.'

Gratefully, I pulled it on and tugged up the zip at the side. He'd got my size just right, and the dress fit perfectly. I would not look good, but it fit.

'You look good,' he said. 'You look beautiful, Poppy.' His smile was genuine. 'I remember why I fell for you now. You're beautiful.'

'Am I?' I replied.

'Yes, yes, you are. God, I'm a lucky man.' He was smiling that smile I'd first seen in the park, when I was eating ice cream and he spoke to me. My stomach flipped and I fell in love with him all over again. He held out his hand and I went to him.

He took both my hands in his and stared down at me, our eyes never straying from each other. He smiled again, his gorgeous lips spreading across his face. 'I don't know what I would do without you,' he whispered and then lowered his head to kiss me. His lips pressed gently on mine as he raised his hand and stroked his thumb across my cheek while his tongue gently slipped into my mouth.

He broke away and moved only a few inches away. 'You make everything worthwhile. I love you, you know that, don't you?'

I nodded in reply. Except I didn't really. I'd feel better, I'd believe it more, if he finished with Serena, but I didn't say that. It must have taken a lot for him to say that. From what I heard from the girls at school, men rarely said they loved you first. You had to trick it out of them, or say it to them over and over again until they got drunk and said it back.

He kissed me again, longer this time, running his long fingers through the loose curls of my black hair. As always, I melted against him. I loved kissing. I loved kissing him. I wasn't so excited by the rest of it, but I could do kissing for ever if I had to kiss Marcus.

The doorbell interrupted us and, reluctantly, he pulled away, rested his forehead on mine as he sighed.

'Be a treasure and see who that is while I light the candles on your cake.'

'OK,' I replied happily.

I almost skipped to the door, wondering how this day could get any more perfect. I was smiling – grinning, actually – as I opened the door, so it was the smile that froze on my face.

Serena.

What she was doing here, I didn't know. The smile on her face froze as well when her eyes alighted on me. Not just because I was opening the door at his house, something neither of us were usually allowed to do, but because she was wearing the exact same white-with-red-spots halterneck dress as me.

It did look better on her.

We said nothing to each other, just stared and stared, then I turned away first and walked towards the kitchen.

'Ah, Serena, right on time as usual,' Marcus said and kissed her on the cheek as she followed me into the kitchen. 'I think I forgot to tell you it was Poppy's birthday,' he said. 'But it's good you're here because Poppy was just about to blow out her candles, weren't you, baby?'

I did not want my cake any more. I did not want this dress. I did not want to be here if *she* was here. My birthday had gone from perfect to hellish, in under five minutes, and that was all *her* fault. If only she'd disappear, if she'd leave him alone and stop being a burden on him, he and I could be together properly. He and I could be happy. Numb, I stepped towards the cake to do as I was told. *Did he buy the dress for me after seeing it on her, or did he buy it for her?* I risked a sly glance at her, and from the expression tugging at her eyes, I knew deep inside he bought it for her, too. Maybe for her birthday, too. Whether he'd bought it or not, he'd obviously told her to wear it today. Maybe it was another of his little jokes.

'Don't forget to make a wish,' Marcus said as I leaned towards the flames.

Serena and I locked eyes during my sly glance and I knew exactly what to wish for. Serena was wishing on my birthday candles, wishing the exact same thing too, as I took a deep breath in and blew . . .

Wow. I really am out of the habit.

I've done something wrong. I've done something terribly wrong and I'm going to pass out. My fingers can't hold on to the sink any longer and I'm going to . . .

May, 1987

They both clapped as the orangey-blue flames on the candles went out in one go.

'OK, Poppy, since it's your birthday, we'll go first,' Marcus said jovially as he held his hand out to me. Still numb, still working like a machine, I slipped my hand into his. 'Serena, be a love and clean up down here. Poppy was too excited to tidy up after herself. But be careful of your dress, you don't want to ruin it.'

She nodded and, with a strength I don't know where she got from, she smiled. *Is that what you do when your heart is breaking? You smile and do as you're told? And when does it start? At what point are you willing to put up with anything for him?* All these thoughts surged into my head and pooled in my brain like the water from a waterfall. The main one, the one that kept swirling around my head like a whirlpool as he pushed me down onto the bed and lifted my skirt, was: *Is it too late for me? Am I going to be like Serena and just put up with anything because I love him?*

I couldn't relax. The thought of her downstairs, listening, waiting, cleaning kept jabbing at me. It scared me that anyone could allow themselves to be led into a life like that. It scared me that I was going to go the same way if I wasn't careful. And I felt sorry for her. For the first time since I realised I had to share him with her, I felt sorry for her. Racing up behind the pity was guilt. Guilt that I loved him too. Guilt about what I was doing. Guilt about what I wished for on my birthday candles.

I turned my head and stared at the window as Marcus raced to the end of what he was doing. A thought buzzed into my head as I tried to mentally escape from there: maybe I had wished for the wrong person to disappear.

If I lie here, very still, I can feel the earth moving. I can tune in and feel it spin its way through space and time. I can understand the workings of physics and try to manipulate them so I can turn back time. I can undo it all. Then I won't have met

Marcus. And I won't have met Alain. I won't be lying here, in a pool of my own blood, wishing I was back in prison.

Inside, I knew everything about everything. My life was ordered, it was structured, I had nothing to worry about, except getting out and clearing my name.

Outside, I know nothing. I trust the wrong people, I am living in emotional chaos. I have parents who don't want me around. I have a boyfriend who was never a boyfriend.

When is a boyfriend not a boyfriend?

When he's Poppy's boyfriend, of course.

Dry and hacking and painful is the laugh I make to go with my unfunny joke – it reminds me of the way I used to cough some mornings after I first took up smoking for something to do. And also how I'd cough after being up all night in my cell smoking and thinking and trying to order my life.

If I do something bad, will they let me back inside?

Probably not, because this time I'd be guilty and, with my luck, they'd make me stay out here – in the chaos and uncertainty and betrayal.

I'm definitely high – only high people think such crazy thoughts. I need to focus. I need to get back on track. I need to make proper contact with Serena and I need to get her to confess. It was her who did it and I want her to tell the truth. Because once the truth is known, maybe this nightmare will finally – finally – end.

In the meantime, I'd better just lie here. I'd better just lie here and listen to the earth turn, and slowly but surely pass out ag—

poppy

This is what happens when you allow yourself to become distracted.

When you don't follow the path you are on.

If you are on a path, heading in a direction that you know will change your life, do not take a moment or two to smell the roses, no matter what those fancy self-help books say. Roses have thorns, and smelling them could end in serious injury. Could end with you cutting up after years of stopping all that and spending the night on the bathroom floor too weak to move. Smelling the roses on the path of your life could bury you under tonnes of accumulated memories of times and things you've done that you'd rather forget. Yes, it could end with you remembering that you have a purpose in life and forcing yourself to get back on track, but you'll also know that if you hadn't allowed yourself to be distracted you could have finished it by now.

It's odd, walking across this road when I have stood by this tree so many times, watching. I feel as if I know every brick of their house, every tile on their front path, every blade of grass in their front garden. I feel like I know everything there is to know about Serena Gorringe's family, I feel like I am part of the family.

I have picked Thursday for a reason.

Thursday is a good day to cross the road, to open the metal

gate, to walk up the tile path, to reach out and to press the bell. Thursday is a good day.

Her white shirtsleeves are rolled up to her elbows, and she has a pinny over her grey suit trousers and white shirt. Her hair is wild and spiky in the haphazard scrunchy she has shoved into her hair, her face is without make-up. She is harried, probably trying to get dinner on before the family arrive home. She's a good mum like that. Always thinking of them first, always putting them first. She'd do anything not to rock the boat, to keep the equilibrium of their lives.

I smile at her.

Smile and wait.

Her expression melts away and her body draws in, forcing her back and upright, moving away from the horror that is I.

I keep on smiling. Keep on smiling as I watch her fall apart.

'Hello, Serena,' I say, 'fancy seeing you here.'

serena

I am scared.

I do not know what she is doing here and I am scared. She is a killer, she is standing in my kitchen and I am scared.

I have only let her in because I do not want the neighbours to see her, for them to mention to Evan that a strange, gaunt-looking woman had started a row with his wife on the doorstep. People still gossip around here, especially about the doctor and his family.

There is a killer in my kitchen. She murdered *him*. She did not kill him by accident, as I originally thought, but deliberately, with thought – she went back and removed him from this earth. She is standing in my house and she might have the same thing on her mind. But that is not what is making me afraid. My fear comes from not knowing what she is going to do. If I knew she was going to hurt me and me alone and then go away, I could stand it. I would welcome it, but I do not know if she plans to hurt the kids, too. Because I could probably stand being hurt, but I could not tolerate someone hurting them.

She is an unknown quantity, a wild card I do not know how to play.

I did not expect her to show up here. What reason would she have for coming to find me? And *how* did she find me? I have remained carefully anonymous, but it seems the only people who have wanted to find me – her and the stalker – have done so with relative ease . . . *Her!* It was her. She was my stalker. I dismissed it before, but obviously it was her.

'Aren't you going to offer me a cup of tea or coffee?' she asks.

I shake my head. 'No.'

'Suppose I won't leave until you've at least *offered* me a cup of something?'

'Suppose I call the police?'

'Suppose you do. And suppose I wait patiently here to be arrested and your lovely husband comes home and I explain *everything* to him.'

'He already knows everything.'

'I'm sure he does. That's why you looked like you were going to have a breakdown when you opened the door just now.'

'Believe it or not, Poppy, it's not entirely pleasant seeing you. You're part of the past and I want you to stay there.'

She throws the back of her hand up to her forehead, and swoons mockingly. 'Why, Serena, you wound me so,' she says scornfully in a Southern-American accent.

My eyes go to the kitchen clock. Thursday is Evan's half-day. He will be here soon, with the kids. She cannot be here when they return.

'Oh dear, dear,' she says, standing up straight. 'That's right, isn't it? Thursday is Evan's half-day. He should be back with the kids any moment now.'

'You've been watching my family,' I state, feeling the fear drain away. I am not scared any longer. She can watch me all she likes, but to watch my husband, my *kids* . . .

'Had to see how awful life treated you, didn't I?' I remember a time when her words were always formed with a soft, slightly posh accent. Now she sounds as if gangsters would be afraid of her if she spoke. 'And boy, life really beat you up, didn't it?' She is running her eyes over the kitchen surfaces, the appliances, the pictures on the walls, the notes to each other on the fridge, the chopping board with the vegetables I was slicing up when she rang my doorbell.

'What do you want?' I ask.

'All in good time, Sweet Serena, all in good time. Let me just immerse myself in what family life is like. I don't know, you see, since I was locked up for so long. You do know that, don't you? I was in prison for a while.'

Whatever game it is she is playing, I am not going to take part.

'I only ask because you never wrote, you never rang, you never visited . . . I got damn lonely locked up in there by myself.'

'What do you want?' I ask again, more firmly.

'I want us to meet up, chat about old times, old lovers.'

'Not going to happen,' I say.

'OK, well, maybe Doctor Evan will know what to suggest to get you to change your mind about that.'

'I don't have any money, if that's what you want. There's no point in us meeting up and then you trying to get money out of me, I don't have any.'

'I told you, I just want to meet. One chat, have a catch-up.'

'OK, when?'

'I don't know yet. Give me your mobile number and I'll call and tell you where and when.'

What choice do I have when my family is about to walk in the door any second now? I scrawl down my number and hand it to her. She takes the piece of paper and looks at it for a very long time, almost as if it means something to her.

'I'll be in touch,' she says as she leaves through the front door. 'I'll be in touch really soon.'

After closing the door on her I lean against it, shaking. A few minutes pass without me moving, then I reach into my apron pocket and pull out my mobile. I push a button to call Mez, to have someone tell me that is going to be OK, and that she will leave me alone. Poppy might do this right now but, if I play along, she will eventually leave me alone.

Before my finger can hit the green 'call' button, I remember Medina and I are not talking. I am not talking to anyone who believes me a murderer.

I'm alone in this. I am alone in this and need to remember that. I have to gather my strength and remember that *she* can't do anything to me, not really.

part five

poppy

She'll turn up, of course she will.

She is a good mother, after all. And a good wife. The last thing she wants is for them to find out that she is a murderer. That she killed her former lover in cold blood. I couldn't be sure they didn't already know until the moment she opened the door and saw me again. She did not have time to fake a reaction; she did not have time to secret away from me the fact that her family think she is one thing, when I know she is another. I know she is Marcus's killer. *Murderer.*

I arrived early, because I have nothing much to do on Saturdays, especially not since . . . As if on cue, my mobile buzzes on the table in front of me. It's him. Calling to leave another voicemail. He's given up trying to actually get me to talk to him, now it's long voicemails apologising and trying to explain, trying to tell me he loves me.

Love is not meant to be this painful.

I feel the throb of my wound, hidden under a bandage, hidden under a top, hidden under my suede jacket. (I cut off the fringes and it looks noughties-passable now.) The dull ache is like a pulse, a reminder that I must never let myself get distracted again.

Dear Tina, (I start to write in my head)
You were right. The snake does have the prettiest smile. And I

fell for it. I wonder if all the people you meet first of all are not meant to be your friends? Do you really have to be cautious of everyone you meet until you have completely sussed them out? I thought I had it so right. I thought I had proved you wrong, but you're always right. You're also the friend who disproved the rule. But I'll forgive you, all right?

The jangle of the café door's bell drags me out of my daydream into the present. For a second I thought it was the start of the riot bell, the jangle that mutates into a constant, loud clang. My heart slows because it is just the door to a sweet little 'organic' café in Kemptown. I'd tried to insist on Preston Park where she lives, or even the centre of Brighton, but she was adamant, she didn't want me – *us* – anywhere near her family. Anyone would think she had something to hide.

She walks across the café and I notice she isn't walking confidently. She is nervous, clutching on to the bag on her shoulder as if she expects a mugging at any minute. She has dressed simply in jeans and a lightweight beige v-neck jumper, which is a good sign. If she had tried to power-dress that would show she is not scared of me and what I could do to her life.

I do not stand up when she arrives at the table I have picked: I stare up at her, reminded again how tall she is, how strong she always looked.

'Serena,' I say, as she pulls out the padded chair opposite and sits down.

'Poppy,' she replies. She pulls her bag on to her lap, a shield to protect herself and her life from me.

'Would you like a coffee or something?' I ask. I don't know if she drinks it, or drinks tea, or orange juice. I don't now anything about her. I don't know if I ever did.

'No. I just want this over with. Tell me what you want and then I will leave and we will both go back to our lives – and never see each other again.'

'Wow, Serena, you seem to have it all worked out. I will happily never see you again, if you do the decent thing.'

'Which is?'

'Confess, of course.'

She sits back in her seat, frowns and then screws up her entire face in incomprehension. 'Confess to what?'

'What do you think?' I ask.

'I don't know, that's why I'm asking.'

I had forgotten how good a liar she was. She must have been to get away with it. But I didn't expect her to be able to do it to my face. Lying to the person who knows what you have done takes some guts, some kind of innate steely, anti-social reserve. I lean forwards in my seat, and make sure she is paying full attention to me. She doesn't flinch away from our eye contact; her face returns my gaze without a hint of the fear she had two days ago. 'Confess to killing Marcus.'

She frowns again, opens her hands questioningly. 'Why would I do that?' she asks.

'Because it's the right thing to do,' I tell her. I am appealing to the good nature of the woman who has let me do her bird for twenty years. I might as well ask ice cream not to melt in the midday sun.

'It would only be the right thing to do if I'd actually done it,' she says slowly, carefully, as if she is talking to a small child who has trouble grasping even the simplest things. 'But I didn't Poppy, so I can't confess.'

I put my head on one side, observe her. She's a grown-up now, a proper grown-up with those near-invisible wrinkles only a mother has around her eyes and mouth. You get them, I've decided, from smiling at your child in a particular way, crying about your child in a particular way; you wear the love of your child on your face when you're a mother, even mothers like mine do. Her body is no longer firm and hard and slender, she's sort of doughy. Not fat, not even 'round', more doughy, spongy, a soft landing place for her children should they need it; the whole point of not losing fat so quickly after giving birth, someone in the nick once said. Serena is used to dealing with children, so she thinks nothing of talking down to people. But she should not be talking down to me. She should be fearing me; she should be fearing what I am willing to do to get her to confess.

'*Who do you think you're talking to?*' I ask calmly, but venomously. Another thing I picked up in nick. You can menace a person without raising your voice, you can get your point across in a low-toned manner. 'Who do you think is sitting opposite you right now?' I lean ever more forwards in my seat. 'Some two-year-old who still believes in Father Christmas? Some teenager who really believes you waited until you were married before you had sex?' I am almost out of my seat with leaning forwards. '*I* know you. *I know* what you did. And *I* am asking you nicely to confess.'

Surprisingly, for someone who has not done time, she is not scared or even moved by me. She sits still in her seat, stares at me with a closed expression on her face. Her eyes study me, but give nothing away. People who react like that, I've found, are the most dangerous. An unknown quantity. I'd prefer it if she'd looked scared, if she'd affected an unbothered expression that showed her real emotion, or even if she'd got angry and gone for me. Any of those reactions you can work with, you can play on. This, blankness, it gives you no kind of leverage.

'What if I don't confess because I have nothing to confess?' she asks calmly. Even her hands, the part of the body that often gives people away, rest calmly on top of her bag.

I sit back in my seat, trying not to show that I feel a bit defeated and deflated by her lack of response. 'I'm sure your family would love to know what you got up to at the end of the eighties,' I say with a smile. 'Verity might pick up a few tips, and darling Dr Evan might find it super sexy to be married to a woman who had an affair with her teacher. And, of course, sweetie Conrad might think it's cool his mother is a murderer.'

As I talk, her fingers curl tighter and tighter around her bag. I imagine she is pretending the bag is my neck and that she is squeezing the life out of me. I've heard murder gets easier after the first time.

It's her turn to lean forwards in her seat.

'You stay away from my family,' Serena says, even more convincingly menacing than I was. She has more to protect after all; that's what mothers do, apparently, they do anything to protect their young. 'You stay away from me, you stay away from my family. I did nothing wrong. So, *leave me alone.*'

I have her. Threatening *her* does no good, threatening her family – even with the emotional danger of finding out Serena's true identity – is the way to get to her, to start to pile on the pressure until she does the decent thing, the honest thing.

'Sorry, no can do. I want my life back, I want to be someone respectable again, and I need you to come clean to do that.'

'Go to hell,' she says and stands, hooking her bag on her shoulder. 'Just go to hell.'

'Been there, done that,' I say. 'Can't wait for you to try it out, too.'

She says nothing as she turns away.

'We should do this again sometime,' I call to her retreating form, waving my mobile phone at her. 'It was such fun.' I don't care that everyone in the place is watching me. I just need to get through to Serena that I'm not going anywhere. Not until she has done the right thing. 'I'll call you really soon.' The door slams shut behind her.

A feeling bubbles up inside me. *This isn't me. This isn't what I'm like,* I think, as the feeling spreads throughout my body. *I don't like being like this, I don't like threatening people, even her.*

'*Is there any other way?*' Marcus asks me. I glance up and he is sitting in Serena's seat, his elbows resting on the table, his face cupped in his hands. He used to be so kissable when he sat like that. I could never imagine his face twisted in murderous rage, ready to punch me in the back of the head, kick me in the ribs, knee me in the stomach, when he looked like that.

No, I reply to him in my head. *There isn't any other way.*

serena

Conrad and I are having a kind of Mexican stand-off at the supermarket checkout.

He is staring at me, while the things he wants – wine gums, marshmallows, full-fat oven chips and sweet popcorn – wait at the bottom of our trolley to hear their fate, to find out if they are coming home with us or if they are being returned to the shelves. I am holding the note that says he can buy whatever he wants and staring down at my son.

One of us has to give in.

The note is from Evan, of course. A doctor's note. *You are to allow Conrad Gillmare* – it says – *to buy anything he wishes as they are for me, Dr Evan Gillmare. This note is valid for 28 days from the date at the top of the page.* He rather helpfully adds a list of the items he might require, allowing Conrad to use his own judgement. That's actually how he motivated himself to help teach Conrad to read – so that he could get him to do his dirty work.

He only does it because he knows I let Con get away with pretty much anything he wants. He's my little baby, after all. It used to be Verity he sent to do his dirty work: to get his favourites made for dinner, to get his favourite T-shirt and jeans ironed so he could go out, but when she started to asking for kickbacks – often payment in cash *in advance* – he moved on to using Conrad. The first time he'd done the note business, I'd

289

asked him if he was serious. *'People have to pay to get a note from their doctor, you know,'* he replied. *'Of course I'm serious.'*

'People also have to pay to get divorced from their partners when they're being silly,' I told him.

'Well, it's a good job I don't want to divorce you, then, isn't it? I couldn't afford a doctor's note and a lawyer. Now, come on, Sez, you know a local doctor can't be seen to be buying junk food.'

'But it's all right for the doctor's wife?'

'Oh yeah. That way, if I keel over, they'll blame you instead of me.'

I'd balled up one of his notes and threw it at his head, knowing it'd miss because he'd duck.

Today's note has the usual list of required items at the bottom and from it Conrad has chosen four items instead of the three as per the rules I imposed upon the whole 'note' system.

Conrad, eight years old and a fiend like his father, is not happy because his big soulful eyes and pet lip haven't worked and I have told him to put one item back. He looks away from me, at the trolley, trying to decide the fate of his and his dad's favourite junk food. I am being a little mean, but if I do not stand firm the pair of them will continue to run rings around me. It's what they do.

'But Mummy,' Conrad says, bringing out the big guns with 'Mummy', 'I don't know what to choose.' I can almost hear him subliminally transmitting into my brain, *I'm only eight, please don't make me choose.*

'I know, sweetheart,' I say sympathetically, 'none of us like to choose.'

He turns his big eyes on me again, looking up at me through his long eyelashes. 'Please don't make me choose,' he actually says. I remember when he was about ten months old he used to flirt with every woman we saw on the street, on the bus, on the train. He would turn his big eyes on them, then would smile and look away, then look back to see if they were watching him. Which they were, of course. He was a good looking baby, and the pitch-black eyelashes around his eyes would make his already large brown eyes stand out even more. Even then he knew the effect he had on people, especially me.

I'd had to steel myself against it. Like right now, when I actually want to give in.

'I'm not making you choose, sweetie,' I say.

His face brightens. 'You're not?' he asks.

'No, your dad is. He's the one who gave you the list. If he'd just given you three things to buy, you wouldn't be in the situation.' I hand him my mobile. 'Maybe you should call him and make him choose.'

Reluctantly, Con takes the phone and I smile to myself as I start to load the conveyer belt with the week's shopping. Evan would have told him to get four things because I'd probably let it slide. In a few weeks, it would be five things, then six, etc., etc. I want my husband, like my daughter, to know that I was on to them. I wasn't born yesterday.

Verity is waiting for us in the car. For the first time in ages she showed an interest in shopping with us but, when we pulled up in the car park, she decided to sit in the car listening to her music with her feet up on the dashboard. Chewing gum, no doubt. She'd said I could leave my bag behind if I wanted. 'I'll look after your bag' was teenage speak for: 'So I can use your mobile, then erase all the recently dialled and texted numbers, as well as the received ones'. I don't have an itemised bill, either, so I'd never know who she was calling.

'I'll take my mobile and purse, then,' I'd said to her and she wasn't quick enough to hide the disappointment that pirouetted across her face.

I am pretending that this morning did not happen. I did not sit down opposite Poppy Carlisle in a café and listen to her accuse *me* of killing *him*. I did not hear her ask me to confess. Confess? She is on another planet. What do I have to confess to apart from extreme stupidity? And for allowing that stupidity to ruin my family's life?

As I left the café, I kept wishing that I had already told Evan, then this would not be an issue. She could not use that against me, to get me to keep meeting her. She could not set about destroying my life by being around all the time like she was with *him*.

I want to tell Evan. I have to tell Evan. I'm scared to tell Evan. He might think like the rest of my family – he might think, despite what I say, that I did it.

While I wait for my turn to pay, and for Conrad to finish on the phone to his father, I glance across to the next checkout. Ange. I whip my eyes away, hoping she doesn't see me.

Ever since I saw her black eye that morning she has avoided me as much as possible and often pretended not to see me. I haven't exactly gone out of my way to make contact, either.

I casually look around the whole of the shop, before briefly casting my gaze her way. I do not want to make eye contact, but I do want to see how close she is to being served and if we're likely to run into each other in the car park or even at the end of the checkouts. Because that would mean talking to her. And that . . . my stomach tingles at the thought of that.

Ange is who I was until Poppy killed *him*.

I sneak another glance at her from the corner of my eye. The first fresh bruise is a bracelet of purple, blue and black around her left wrist, visible where the thick cotton of her sleeve rides up. The next – a thumbprint seared into her flesh by an angry hand – is below her left jaw, on her neck, where the waves of her blonde hair fall away. The third is on the crest of her cheek, faint and almost transparent under a near-perfect make-up job. The other bruises, old and new, are hidden beneath her clothes. Because he knows what he is doing. He knows how and where to do it so that no one else can see. So that she can play her part and cover it up with her clothes, with her make-up, with her strong faith in his ability to change and to never do it again.

I know those other bruises are there because I have X-ray vision. It comes from knowing that, once, my body had a con-stellation of bruises just like that. From knowing that no matter how many layers you wear, how clever you are with make-up, they're still there. They're still there and once they heal, they'll come back. They'll find a way back on to your skin, into your muscles, because faith in someone's ability to change just isn't enough protection to stop it happening again. Faith, on its own, is never enough.

'Dad says it's a shame because we could all have shared the chips,' Conrad's voice jolts me back to him, back to this life.

He hands me my phone and shoots me another look, just in case.

'You know, it's funny, because he often says that but, for some reason, those chips only seem to get eaten when Verity and I aren't around,' I say.

'But that's because you two always go out at chip time,' Conrad says, reminding me again that he really is his father's son. His big brown eyes are staring forlornly at the four remaining items languishing at the bottom of the trolley.

'Or maybe it's only ever chips o'clock when Verity and I aren't around,' I say.

I grab the wine gums, the marshmallows, the popcorn and finally the oven chips and throw them on to the conveyer. Evan is a good man. He would never hurt me. He once got very drunk – Max and Teggie's fault – and called me from Barcelona where they'd gone to watch football. 'You three are my whole life,' he slurred. 'If any of you hurt, I hurt. I've just finished telling the lads how much I love you all.' He'd immediately thrown up very loudly on his favourite Adidas trainers, but I never forgot the sincerity in his words – that even when he was very drunk and away with his friends, all he wanted to do was talk to me.

He deserves a treat now and then. He deserves to 'get one over' on me every now and again. Especially as it's only a little junk food. Especially as that clock is ticking ever louder now that Poppy is back in my life. Especially as I need to find a way to tell him.

'*Especially as you've been getting one over on him since the second*

293

you met him, eh, Serena?' says my conscience. I do what is best for all concerned and ignore it.

October, 1987

'I got you this,' *he* said, holding out a wide, flat velvet jewellery box. He'd bobbed down beside me as I was reading for my A'Level homework at his house.

'Thank you,' I said automatically, knowing I had to show my gratitude straight away or . . .

He gave a little laugh. 'You haven't seen it yet, you might not even like it.'

'I'm sure I will,' I said.

I opened the lid, braced myself to put on a happy face, no matter what I found inside. Where a watch or a bracelet would normally rest, lay a white, star-shaped flower with five petals. It had long stamens that were topped with red. It was a pretty little flower, but I did not understand what it meant, why he had given it to me. Panic spiralled inside: I didn't know what to say.

'It's a Stonecrop,' he said, before I could think of how to hide my ignorance and not ignite his temper. 'It grows in warm rocky areas. It took me ages to find one. In the language of flowers, it's the symbol of tranquillity. And your name means the same thing. I wanted you to have it.'

'It's lovely,' I said. 'Thank you.'

'I thought we could press it between the pages of a book so you could keep it for ever.'

'Yeah, yeah, that'd be great,' I said.

He reached out towards my face and I flinched, closed my eyes as I waited for it – I hadn't sounded grateful enough and now he was going to make me pay. I was grateful. I loved it. It was a thought-filled present, but I hadn't been grateful enough. 'I love it,' I said desperately. 'I really love it.'

His hand stroked gently on my cheek. 'I'm sorry,' he said. 'I – I haven't been very good to you lately, I'm sorry.' I said nothing, I did not want to say anything that could be used against me later.

'I'm going to try really hard, you know, Serena? I'm going to try not to get so angry about little things. I've hurt you, and I'm sorry. I'm so, so sorry. I won't let it happen again. I've never loved anyone the way I love you. I've never given up anything for anyone – not even Marlene – before, let alone a job I loved, but when it came down to the choice between you and the job, the job lost.

'I could find a job any time, but you, you're it. You're the one for me. I could never find another you. I don't want to lose you. I really mean it. OK?'

I nodded.

'You know, whenever Marlene shows up here, shouting and ranting at me, I'm always tempted to tell her that I want nothing to do with her because I have you. Someone as beautiful as you.'

I nodded again.

'It'll never happen again. I promise you.'

I nodded. 'OK.'

He leant in to kiss me and I kissed him back. He had said everything I needed to hear. Everything that told me he was going to change and everything would be all right between us. He had reconfirmed for me that I was the most important person in his life and he would change for me, he wouldn't hurt me any more, and I could trust him again.

He was telling me that he was the man I fell in love with, the man of my dreams.

We both knew I had heard it all before.

Princess Verity thinks that, if she closes her eyes and turns her music up loud, she won't have to help load up the boot. I sometimes wonder if she remembers who her parents are, what we are like. Verity and Con have a list of chores they have to complete every night, as well as their homework. They watch minimal TV – if any – during the week, and they have an hour every Sunday to tidy their rooms. Helping out, being part of the clockwork that is our family, is not optional.

Con is keen to get started in loading up – he loves that part. I suspect it's to do with feeling a bit like his dad, scrabbling around in the boot – the area he's only ever allowed to go near when there is shopping to be loaded or unloaded. I tell him to wait a second and go over to the front passenger window, tap on the glass. Verity keeps her eyes closed and her music loud, her head bobbing in time to the music. Like I hadn't tried that ploy with the radio when I was her age. Like I didn't get busted for it every time till Mum just took away my radio.

I open the door and she almost spills out because she has been half-leaning on it. I reach out, my fingers brushing her ears as I pluck the earpiece from her left ear. 'Your other mother might do all the work, but not this one,' I tell her. Knowing she has been caught out, she reluctantly pulls the other white earpiece from her ear, stops the music and tucks the player away in her bag. She climbs out of the front seat and I'm taken back again at how tall she is. She's almost as tall as me. I'm sure I didn't reach her height until I was about fifteen.

We start to work at putting the green cloth bags into the boot and just as I pull my upper half out from having rearranged them to make them all fit together snugly and securely, I see Angie coming to a stop beside the huge Land Rover that is parked beside us. My car is dwarfed by hers.

'Oh, hi,' she says.

'Hi,' I reply, awkwardly.

'Doing the shop?' she asks.

'Yeah, you?' I reply.

'Yeah,' she replies.

'Yeah,' I say, because I don't know what else to say. I don't know how to extract myself from this. For once, the kids are both silent as they stare at her. It's usually them who save me in such situations. They'll do something that will call me away from the person I need rescuing from. But, for some reason, they are suddenly The Angelic Twins.

'Look,' Ange says, 'I wanted to apologise about never arranging that coffee properly. Life, you know?'

'Oh, that's OK,' I say. 'We've had a lot on, too.'

'Are you feeling better now, Mrs Ryan's Mum?' Conrad asks.

Her eyes widen a fraction and she swings her gaze to the eight-year-old glued to my side. 'I haven't been sick,' she says, a little confused.

'What are you talking about, Conrad?' I ask, looking down at him. 'Where did you hear that?'

'Luc told me. He said his mum told his dad that Ryan's mum had another one of her accidents and this time she'd had to go to hospital because her husband couldn't keep his fists to himself.' I curl my toes into my shoes with embarrassment. I wish he'd run that piece of information past me, so I could tell him that he shouldn't really ask people about it. Especially not the people involved.

While I am embarrassed, Angie is terrified. Her eyes are wide and fixed and she is running scenario after scenario through her head about what will happen if her husband ever hears this. It's obvious my other neighbour has been gossiping, that's what she does, which means it may come back to him. And he will most likely go for Ange if and when it does. That's what you do in those sorts of relationships: you don't worry about the humiliation and embarrassment you're feeling at someone saying something about your situation, you worry about what is going to happen to you if he ever finds out that someone else knows. That's why you are so careful to hide your bruises and lie about cuts because you know that if he finds out that someone else saw, someone else questioned you, then he will get upset. And life will not be worth living if he is upset. Everything is easier for everyone if he is not upset. So you do everything in your power to make sure he is not upset.

'Are you?' Conrad asks again, just in case he hasn't embarrassed me enough. 'Are you feeling better?'

Verity is wide-eyed in incredulity. Conrad hasn't shared this information with her either and she is agog at this woman whose husband tried to kill her.

'Come on you two, into the car. The frozen stuff will be melting. Let's hit the road.'

They both drag their feet getting into the car, stealing long, curious glances at Ange as they go. Even when they are belted in inside the car, they stare at her through the window. She must feel like an extraordinary special exhibit in a carnival freakshow.

'I'm sorry about that,' I say to her. 'I didn't know he knew that, nor that he was going to say it out loud.'

'Please,' she says trying to sound dismissive, 'kids make things up all the time, I wouldn't worry about it. We both know he's got it wrong.'

'I'll make sure he doesn't repeat any gossip about you when I'm out with him,' I say in a tight voice. 'But, Ange, we both know he hasn't got it wrong.'

I wish I could tell her that there is only one way this is going to end: badly. Unless she gets out now it will only end in someone getting really hurt. But she won't listen to me. Why would she? I know what I'm talking about, but I'm pretty certain that if someone had tried to give me that advice when it was necessary, I wouldn't have listened.

Why would I? Why would I listen to someone who told me to walk away from *him* when he was the love of my life?

'Did I do something wrong, Mum?' Conrad asks as I get into the driver's seat.

'No, sweetheart,' I say, as I watch Angie get smaller and smaller in the rear-view mirror. 'You told the truth as you knew it, and that's the only thing any of us can do. It was just that she didn't know that you knew.'

'I'm sorry, Mum,' he says, 'I didn't mean to make her cry.'

'You didn't. She wasn't crying.' *Yet.*

I glance at him in the rear-view mirror – his face is scrunched up in concern and worry – and, because I cannot pull over and go to hug him, I'm glad I let him have all of the treats. 'I'm sorry, anyway,' he says.

'I know you are. And that's because you're a good boy.'

'You're not a good girl, are you Serena?' my conscience says in my head.

'And since you're such a good boy, which one of the treats are we going to have when we get home?'

'What did you get?' Verity asks.

'Marshmallows, wine gums, popcorn and oven chips.'

'Wine gums,' Verity says.

'Marshmallows!' Conrad says.

'I'm with Conrad,' I say, 'it's gotta be the marshmallows.'

'No way!' Vee exclaims.

We argue about the best choices on the way home, while, *'Are you sure you don't want ice cream, Serena? Are you sure, are you sure, are you sure?'* plays on loop in my head.

poppy

It's Dad's sixty-third birthday today.

And my parents do not want me around for it. They haven't said so outright, they'd never do that, but it has been made clear to me.

Last week I casually asked Mum if they were up to anything the following weekend. I didn't let on that I remembered it was his birthday. I just wandered into the kitchen where she was making shepherd's pie for dinner and sat down.

The atmosphere in the room immediately shot up a volt or two: charged, tense and uncomfortable. 'I love your shepherd's pies,' I said, trying to be nice. Mum wasn't the world's best cook. It stemmed from the days when she was unwell; she couldn't really do much except lie in bed most days and Dad had been given a crash-course in feeding himself and a baby, then a toddler. Ever since then, Mum had been trying to cook and bake – and having varying levels of success. Numerous times as I was growing up Dad would coach me and the kids to say something that was disgusting and barely edible was delicious. He was desperate to spare her feelings, to keep encouraging her. We got quite good at lying about her awful food.

Her cooking hasn't improved much over the years, but prison food makes her seem worthy of one of those Michelin Man Gold Star thingies.

Mum struggled to hang a smile across her face; it sat uncomfortably on her thin lips and merely glanced off the edges of her eyes. My heart ached, actually physically ached sometimes, that she was so uncomfortable around me. It didn't seem fair when I had done nothing wrong. *I bet Serena's family all love her despite everything she's done*, I thought as I watched Mum struggle to mash up the potato topping in the pan – it was obvious what the problem was: she hadn't cooked the potatoes properly, some of them were still virtually raw.

'So, Mum,' as usual, she flinched when I used that word, like I had called her a whore or something, 'what are you up to next weekend?'

Her hand paused for a second in its mashing duties, before continuing. 'Nothing special,' she said innocently. 'Why?'

'Oh, no reason,' I replied. 'I was just thinking of maybe going to see some friends in London if you weren't doing anything? You know, unless there was any other reason I might want to stay around here?'

This was my olive branch, my way of saying, 'Include me, *please*. Give me another chance to be your daughter.'

'Your father and I were thinking of going out for dinner, maybe catch a show in town.'

'Sounds nice, any special occasion?' I asked. She must know that I knew it was his birthday. Every year I sent him a card and every year it was returned to me. But that should tell her that, because this is the first one since I've been out, I'd want to try again to get through to him. To get through to them. I want my parents back.

'No, no special occasion,' she said, her eyes fixed on the disgusting mash in front of her.

'OK,' I said, sitting back in my seat. 'What about Bella and Logan? What are they up to these days?'

'Oh, they never tell me anything about their lives, you know how youngsters are,' she said.

'Are they not coming down for a visit soon, maybe next weekend?'

'Not that I know of,' she said. She was working up a real sweat, trying to mash up her pan of under-boiled tatties – it'd be funny to watch if it wasn't a way of her avoiding looking at me.

'Oh, OK. Well, could you give me their numbers? I might visit them if I'm up in London next week.'

She faltered in her mashing, almost knocking the pan off the table. I have never asked directly, before. From prison, I would write them letters asking for them to be sent on, and I'd often get a reply weeks later saying Bella and Logan didn't want to be in touch, to leave them alone. Now I was out, I wanted to hear it from them myself. I wanted them to look me in the eye and tell me they wanted nothing to do with me. Even if they had been brainwashed by Mum and Dad, it'd take nerves of steel to tell someone to their face that you had disowned them.

'Come to think of it, Bella said she was going on a hen weekend to Amsterdam and Logan said he was visiting his girl-friend's parents up in Scotland next weekend. There's no point in trying to call them, they won't be there.'

'Funny that they're both away the same weekend that I'm going up there.'

'Yes, I suppose it is,' Mum said. She was back in her stride, demolishing the potatoes to top her only half-browned mince. It's a wonder none of us got food poisoning growing up. 'Coincidences happen all the time.'

She couldn't be lying – that was too smooth, too quick a reply when I brought it up. Mum could deflect an enquiry very easily, but not in that much detail. If she was lying, she'd say something like, 'Oh, I don't think they're going to be there.' But to provide details meant it was true, or she had turned into a pretty expert liar.

'So, you won't mind if I go to London?' I asked, hoping that since the other two wouldn't be around, they might want me instead. I was grasping at the thinnest, wispiest of straws but I had to. I had to try everything.

'No, not at all. Why don't you stay overnight?'

Like a tap that hasn't been properly closed and drips slowly into a plugged sink, tears collected slowly in my eyes. Not only did she not want me here, she wanted me gone completely. She might as well have told me that the best present I could give Dad was to stay away. To remove myself from the house and his life.

'I might do that,' I said and got up.

She looked at me. 'You do that, Poppy. You stay overnight in London. It'll be good for you.' For the first time since I came back, Mum smiled at me because she would be getting rid of me for a night. It must have been so much easier for them when I was under lock and key elsewhere. They could pretend I was dead, that I didn't exist any more. They could pretend that they only had a daughter called Bella, they only had a son, called Logan, and that the first child, the problem child, was gone, taking with her all the mistakes they made.

I do not believe in coincidences, not any more. Like meeting Marcus was not coincidental. I am convinced he saw me in the park, and recognised me from teaching at my school. Remembered me as timid and a little lonely-looking. I was in his sights from the moment he stopped to talk to me. He wasn't sure it would work, of course, if I was naïve enough to wait for him, to call him, to come to his house, but it was a chance he was willing to take and it paid off.

I do not believe in coincidences, which is why I am waiting on the street corner near my parents' house, waiting to see who will come for lunch. When a blue car that looks like the space age version of the Beetle pulls up outside the house, my heart catches in my throat because instinctively I know who is inside, where they are going. The driver's door opens and out steps a young man with a muss of dark hair, a strong jawline and muscular frame he inherited from his father. The passenger door opens and out steps a young woman with loose curls of dark hair that reach down to her shoulders and a slight, almost bony frame she inherited from her mother. She carries a silver-wrapped box topped with a giant blue bow that fills her arms – she obviously can't come to her father's birthday lunch without a gift.

I leave my watching spot at the bottom of the road and walk casually towards the house. I don't know what I'm going to do, I haven't thought that bit through, but I have to get a closer look, I have to be as near as possible to them. They walk up the path, the woman first, laughing at something her brother has said and the slight dig with his elbow he gave her before they left the pavement. Her face, creased in laughter like that, reminds me of someone I used to know. Someone called Poppy Carlisle, the girl I used to see in the pictures of myself. The girl who used to be in the mirror.

I near the house as the door is opened by their mother; she grins when she sees her two children, she could not love them more. The mother's gaze strays to the street as she steps aside to let them in and her face falls as she sees the stranger who is approaching her house. Her look of shock and anxiety stays in place as she locks eyes with the stranger, expecting the stranger to stop and turn into her gateway, to come up the path. But the stranger only keeps the eye contact for a second or two, and does not stop. The stranger instead moves on, continuing her path past their house, continuing to walk on and away from this mother's precious home.

poppy

There was a time when Sunday afternoon meant the Carlisle home would be drenched in beautiful smells: roast chicken, roast tatties, Yorkshire pudding, stuffing, gravy, veg – the works. After midday mass, we would come back to the house and the smells of the lunch Dad had cooked would surround us as we opened the door. We would all sit around the table, eating and talking and laughing. Even if it'd been an awful week, even if we'd fallen out with each other, Sunday was the day of forgiveness. Sunday, sitting around the table together as a family, was what fixed everything.

Something in me still expects to smell this when I step across the threshold and shut the door behind me. There is nothing, of course. I don't know when the Carlisle Sunday roasts stopped, but there have been none since I have been back. There has been nothing family-like since I returned.

Mum appears at the doorway of the kitchen as if by magic: she must have heard me close the front door, she must have been waiting for me.

'Where did you stay last night?' she asks, voluntarily allowing her eyes to focus on me directly, braving the dangers of being burnt by my image to see me for the first time.

'In a B&B in Brighton.'

'You could have come back here, you didn't have to waste your money like that.'

'I didn't know how long your guests were staying; I didn't want to intrude.'

'They only came for lunch,' she says.

'Oh, right. I wasn't sure. If you'll excuse me.' I start up the stairs, I have a mission to complete and it won't do itself.

'Poppy, can I talk to you?' Mum says before I have cleared the second step. I pause there because that's all I've wanted since I arrived home – for her to talk to me – but I'm now finding it hard to work out if I want to listen. I don't think I need to hear anything; her lie has told me everything I need to know: I will never be welcomed back into this family. I killed that chance when they believed I killed Marcus.

'It's OK, Mum,' I say, not feeling her flinch this time, 'you don't have to say anything.' I risk a look at her, scared that if I do I'll lose the composure I put together to allow me to come back here, and I'll start to cry. I thought I'd be angry – anger seems to be the emotion I have felt the most of since I heard the word 'guilty' all those years ago. Anger and fear. But last night all I had was sadness. A deep, abiding sadness that I had been cast out of my family, the people who I used to be a part of no longer loved me and there was nothing I could do to change that.

My mother is wringing her hands, twisting them over and over as her thin frame stands rooted to the spot. A memory pops up. My first day of school; she and Dad both took me to the school gates and, while Dad gave me a pep talk, Mum stood perfectly still, wringing her hands. I ran through the gates to join the other children, then changed my mind and came back, ran to my mum and threw my arms around her, while still holding my lunchbox and my satchel, and squeezed her as tight as I could. 'I miss you, Mummy,' I said. She stopped wringing her hands and hesitantly laid one hand on my head. 'I'll miss you, Poppy,' she said. As I let her go, she got down on her knees and bundled me up in her arms, her handwringing suddenly forgotten. 'I'll miss you, Poppy,' she said again and kissed my cheek. I wasn't as scared then. I wasn't scared of the other children, I wasn't scared of the teachers, I wasn't even scared any more that Mum and Dad would forget about me and not come back. Well, Mum. I knew Dad would never forget, but after she told me she'd miss me I knew she wouldn't forget to come back, either. 'You wait right here, OK?' I said to her.

'OK,' she replied. 'OK, Poppy, I'll wait right here.'

I don't want my mum to wring her hands any more. She did that the whole year in the run up to the trial. She wouldn't sleep, she could hardly eat, she just wrung her hands and paced. I was scared the stress would bring back her 'illness'. I knew what it was, of course, I just liked to pretend to myself I didn't. I could feel less guilty that way: she had a breakdown brought on by untreated post-natal depression.

'Please, Poppy, I just want to talk to you.'

I give in and come back down the stairs, allowing her to lead the way into the kitchen to a seat at the kitchen table. Marcus had a kitchen table like this one. I used to think it was romantic and sexy and oh-so grown up when we would make love on it. Then he had sex with me on it in front of Serena. Ordering me to keep my eyes open and making her tell him if I closed them. She lied to him, said my eyes were open when they weren't. But I hated the kitchen table after that. Every time I went near it, I remembered Serena's face – an emotion-less mask. He probably beat her afterwards, too. Not only did she have to watch, she had to suffer physically, as well. Serena's experience of Marcus is like the uglier version of my experiences, the future I was headed towards because she had six months or so on me. Maybe if I had stayed with him a bit longer I would have thought I had no choice but to kill him, too.

Mum is talking. I am watching her thin browny-pink lips move, but I have not heard a word she has said. I have submerged myself in thoughts of Marcus, thoughts of Serena, thoughts of the reasons for murder – because it is easier than listening to my mother explain why she doesn't love me.

'Mum,' I say to her eventually, genuine, sorrowful regret in my voice. 'You'll have to start again because I haven't heard a word you've said. I'm sorry, my mind drifted away.'

Inhaling deeply, expanding her bony frame in the process, she once again looks directly at me.

'I want you to understand what it was like for us, Poppy,' she says. 'To me, you were still a little girl, you still wore bunches in your hair and danced in front of your mirror pretending to be a popstar. And then in the middle of the night we get a phone call from the police station saying you had been arrested for killing your boyfriend. I remember almost laughing when your father told me – I said to him that it must be some other Poppy Carlisle because our daughter was asleep in her bed and wasn't old enough for a boyfriend. But it was you. My little girl was really facing prison for killing a man.

'And the more we found out, the more we heard, it was like we never knew you at all. You had slipped away from us and we hadn't noticed. You were there all the time, physically, but you had gone from us two years before. Two years of living in the same house as you and we had no idea what you had been up to. It was worse for your father because he thought you and he were close, he thought you told him everything.

'It was like a nightmare that would not end. I kept seeing your photo in the paper, in that swimsuit cut up to *there* and wearing make-up. Over and over, this picture of my little girl looking like those tarts you see on television. And the stories about the things you had done.' Mum sags, as if memory after painful memory is piled on top of her. 'Imagine what it was like to have to read about the things your daughter has done with a man twice her age, to hear that she had been with a woman.' She covers her heart with her hands as if trying to stop it from trembling its way out of her body, as if protecting it from the worst of the memories. 'The neighbours were all whispering, people would stop and stare at us in the street and we started to get hate mail. Whenever we thought we had seen the worst of it, something else would happen – like the stories from the people we knew and thought we could trust. Everyone in our lives was potentially a source for the papers. The police were here all the time and I was sure we were being followed.

'We had to do whatever we could to protect the three of you, especially Bella and Logan. And the whole time I was so tormented because it was all my fault.'

That brings me up short, makes me sit up in my seat. 'How could it possibly have been your fault?' I ask.

'I was never a proper mother to you, I know that. And killers always blame the mothers. They always say their mothers were bad or absent or not loving enough. I had my . . . problems . . . after you were born. I thought I had done this. I had not protected you enough and so I caused this. A mother is supposed to protect her child against everything. Even when they are old enough to go out into the world you still want to protect them. You still try to protect them and I didn't do that with you.'

Serena comes to mind – I can say anything I like about her, but the second I mention her family, she flares up. She becomes a creature capable of doing almost anything to protect her young. I wonder what would happen to her if she failed in that. If, despite how hard she fought, her children were still hurt, still damaged, what she would do. How she would turn it in on herself. How deeply she would blame herself.

Because of Serena, I can understand what Mum is saying.

'When you were found guilty, all I wanted to do was take you and hide you. I would have helped you escape if I could, you have to believe that. But it was too late for you, you were gone from me, so I had to concentrate on Bella and Logan. We left the court so quickly to get to them before someone else could tell them the news. We had to tell them in our own way before they found out in a nasty way, which a lot of people were desperate to do. They were so upset that we couldn't leave them for too long. That's why I didn't come in when I dropped off your case, I had to get back to them. They were so upset, love, that I promised myself there and then to try to avoid the same mistakes again. I focused everything I was on them and on

311

trying to make them happy and protect them from the outside world.'

'And that world included me, didn't it? That's why you never passed on my letters.'

'Yes, unfortunately it did. As long as you were around, we couldn't forget and rebuild our lives. And people would try to use them to get to you. But I couldn't just shut you out, you're my little girl. That's why I came to see you.'

Not in a long time, I want to say.

'I hated seeing you in that place. I would cry inconsolably every time I left, and your father started to forbid me from going. He couldn't stand what it was doing to me, but I had to keep coming. When you said not to come again I was devastated. I cried for a week. I thought you were finally blaming me and my punishment was not to see you again.'

'I told you to stop coming because you looked so uncomfortable. You could barely focus on me you were so scared. I decided to put you out of your misery.'

'You're my little girl, of course I hated seeing you in that place, but of course I would come to see you no matter where you were. After that, your father said we were to have nothing to do with you again. Because he knew it would start upsetting me and it would do the same to the kids, probably worse.'

'So that's why you wouldn't let them write to me or visit and wouldn't pass on my letters? You made them forget me because it might upset them?'

'They could never forget you, Poppy. Yes, your father and I decided that they were too young to understand properly, and we forbade Granny Morag from telling them the truth, but they were always asking for you. Bella sat on the step day after day for weeks, waiting for you to come back. Logan kept asking his teachers how he could find out which prison a person was in. Bella wanted to send you Raggy, her doll, so you would have someone to hug at night. They wrote you letter after letter, but we didn't want them seeing you in that place. We just wanted them to forget so they wouldn't go through the pain your father and I were going through. Eventually they stopped asking, stopped talking about you. Not because they had forgotten but, I think, because they thought it would be easier on your father and I if they stopped talking about you.'

She pauses to look at me again, her eyes moving over my face as if this is the first time she has had the opportunity to see me since I turned up on their doorstep.

'We were too hard on them, growing up. We didn't let them have any freedom as teenagers in case it happened again. No parties, no sleepovers, no holidays with their friends. Nothing. It seemed the only way to protect them from what happened to you and give them the best chance to get to adulthood unscathed. I don't know if we did the right thing but it was the only way we could think to—'

'To stop them turning into me.'

'No, to stop us feeling like failures. It's a painful thing to know you have failed your child, to see them struggle and flounder and then to lose them. We both just wanted to have done better by you. We both wanted better for you.'

'So why can't Dad even look at me, let alone talk to me? He doesn't seem to want better for me, more like for me to not be here.'

'Poppy, your father has cried every single day since you were sent to prison. He thinks I don't know, but he has. That's what he does when he shuts himself in that office of his, or in his shed. Sometimes it was at the beach hut. But it almost killed him losing you. He was so angry after the trial. With you, yes, but also with himself for not guessing what all those cuts and bruises and broken bones were about. For not seeing what was going on and not protecting you. You, all three of you, are his life.

'It was him who put your room back together exactly as it was in London. He wanted you to have something familiar to come back to. After all those years away, he wanted you to be able to find comfort in something that was yours.'

'So why have you been so awful to me since I came back?'

'I don't know how to be with you,' she admits. 'I don't know if I should ask you about prison, if I should just pretend it didn't happen, if I should talk to you like I did back before all this happened. I don't know Poppy. The last time I saw you you were barely more than a teenager, now you're a fully-grown woman. How do you relate to someone you haven't seen in so long who basically moves in with you out of the blue? We just have to try to rub along together until we can find a way back to where we were. But we're still your parents, we still love you. We never stopped loving you. When you become a parent, you never stop loving your children. And there is nothing you wouldn't do for them. Please believe that.'

I do believe that. And I believe every word that she has said.

'I do believe you, Mum. Of course I believe you.'

From her apron pocket she produces a slip of paper, reminding me instantly of the paper that Marcus wrote his number on. I kept that piece of paper, I stuck it in my diary because it was the first thing he ever gave me. She looks at the piece of paper, places it on the table, slides it over to me, then almost reluctantly removes her fingers from it.

'I think it's time I stopped trying to protect Bella and Logan – they're old enough to make their own decisions.'

She gets up from the table and goes back to the stove. While she bends to look in the oven at whatever she has sitting in there, waiting to be baked, I look at the piece of paper she has given me. It has Bella and Logan's addresses and phone numbers.

I stare at the information for a long, silent moment, not sure how to respond. I wanted to make contact, I wanted to speak to them, and now I can. Now it's all up to me and I am terrified. What if they're like Dad and can't bring themselves to look at me, or what if they're like Mum, scared of me? Or what if they just can't bring themselves to let me back into their lives?

I push aside these worries and stand up. 'I'll talk to you later, Mum,' I say. Again she doesn't flinch, she simply nods without looking round.

Pocketing the piece of paper, I go back to the mission I had when I came back here: to dismantle that bedroom, that mausoleum to a time long gone, that decayed monument to a life that existed a long, long time ago.

I kept it as it was because I did not want to destroy all their hard work; I think a part of me also believed that it would make my parents love me again. Would make them want me around. No matter what Dad's reasoning for rebuilding the room, it has become another cage by being a constant reminder of the past I destroyed by becoming involved with Marcus. It is as if they were doing what they wanted to do all those years ago – sending me to my room to think over the consequences of my actions.

What's that quote? *I put away childish things?* Something like that. I do not know where it is from, I must have read it over the years, but it is what is apt for me. The sooner I destroy all evidence of the child I was, the sooner I can start to move forwards as an adult.

Mum's words, her explanations, her reassurances, are whirling around my head like the blades of a helicopter: fump, fump, fumping in my mind. I do believe her. I believe and even understand most of what she said. But in that talk, in all those reassurances, at no point did she say she thought I was innocent. And that's because they both still think I'm guilty.

They may love me, but they still think I am a liar and a slut and a murderer.

poppy

'You know, Poppy, I suffer from gaps in my memory,' she tells me.

'Good for you?' I reply, unsure what I'm supposed to say.

This is our second meeting. When I call her, she answers the phone straight away – no hesitation, no ignoring me – almost as if she has been waiting for my call. It's probably because she is scared of what I might do. That moment she realised I knew about her family must have given her a jolt, the kind you get from stepping on the live rail on a train track.

We are back in the Kemptown café again, and this time she hasn't arrived looking so cool and removed. This time she is almost friendly, for want of a better word. She seems more relaxed, as if I am an old friend she hasn't seen in years and she is looking forward to catching up. I do not know what her game is, but she says this out of the blue, and it sounds very much like she is trying to share with me.

'I don't know if the gaps are from getting smacked in the head so many times, or if they were a way of coping with what went on, but I've been thinking – maybe you suffer from them too?' she says.

'No, my memory is fine, thank you very much,' I reply. 'I haven't forgotten anything at all about that time.'

'What I mean is, maybe you don't remember what happened afterwards? Which is why you think I did it.'

The laugh bubbles up and out of me, rumbling my belly. She has got to be kidding. That is the funniest thing I have ever heard. 'You think that you can convince me that I did it with that lame theory?' I laugh some more. 'You've got more chance of convincing me the Sun is made of butter!' I laugh even harder. 'Memory gaps! You'll be telling me that raindrops are God's tears next.'

Serena, so pure and untainted by life, sits back in her seat. 'I was only offering you a possible explanation for what happened,' she says calmly, reasonably. 'It's fine if you don't want to accept it as a possibility.' I sometimes wonder how she can consistently remain so cool and together. She does not seem to react in the way that most people would. I have just ridiculed her, laughed in her face, all but called her pathetic and she doesn't seem upset, or even slightly ruffled. She is like a brick of ice, inured to everything I throw at her. She was like this with Marcus, too. Sometimes he would goad her, he would do things like kiss me in front of her, plainly doing it to get a reaction. And she wouldn't comply. I always reacted, I always hated seeing him touch her, talk to her sweetly, even look at her sometimes. I always wanted her to go away, probably until my sixteenth birthday. She wasn't like that. The only times she reacts now are when I mention her family. Then she becomes something close to a wild animal – ready to attack me. Is she made of ice in the places that other people have warm blood? Is she so shut off that she cannot care about the things normal people care about? Is that what made her capable of murder?

'Why didn't you get upset when Marcus kissed me and stuff?' I ask her. I have to know. Even if it puts me at a disadvantage to ask, I have to know why she is not like other people. Why she is not like me. 'Why didn't it bother you?'

She frowns at me, and her confusion is genuine. 'What makes you think it didn't bother me?'

'You never acted it. Like on my sixteenth birthday, when you had to tidy up while we went upstairs, you smiled. You actually smiled at us. How could you?'

'Do you always take everything at face value?' she asks.

'No.'

'Then why did you take me at face value?'

'It's not normal to not be jealous. It's not normal to smile when your boyfriend goes upstairs to fuck another woman.'

'Those weren't norm—' She stops speaking then sighs. 'What's the point? Look, if you must know, if I reacted to anything like that he would be incredibly loving when we were alone. He would cuddle me, tell me that he didn't like hurting me and he was going to finish with you soon. He'd explain that you were just something he had to get out of his system, that you were fragile and if he dumped you just like that he was scared of what it'd do to you. And if you were hurt, you might tell everyone about the pair of you and that would ruin things for us. This – the kissing and cuddling and telling me he loved me – would go on for ages.

'Then, it would switch. He'd have lulled me into a sense of security, into believing that it would be all right, and then he'd turn on me. Sometimes it'd be after he left the room and come back, sometimes it'd be just like that!' She clicks her fingers. 'Slap! Right across the face as he yelled who did I think I was, making him justify himself to me. Then slap!' She slams her hand down on the table. 'Another one, to drive his point home. And if I didn't say sorry quick enough, as in within seconds of the first slap, when my head was still reeling, he'd lay into me properly.

'So I learnt my lesson, and I stopped reacting. I stopped letting him see that it bothered me, because then he wouldn't have any reason to hurt me, right? No, it got worse. Because I didn't react, it showed I didn't love him enough. He had given up so much for me, he'd stopped teaching at the school he loved for me and I didn't love him enough not to feel a little jealous when he *had* to be with someone else.'

Marcus used to slap me whenever I reacted to him being with Serena. If I twisted my lips or rolled my eyes or looked sad for even a moment he would be on me: slap, slap, slap. Saying the same things. Almost word for word. But unlike Serena it never occurred to me to hide my feelings. It wasn't something I could do. I'm just not made that way. Not until I went inside, though, when I learnt that I had to hide everything all the time.

'Which left me with a choice,' Serena continues. 'I react and get beaten, not react and get beaten. I chose not to react because it defied him. In a small way, it defied him. He wanted me to react so that he could see he had hurt me twice, meaning he was in total control. If I stopped reacting, he lost just that bit of control and he didn't get full satisfaction. The night of your birthday, he broke two ribs by kicking me with steel-capped shoes for that smile.'

I cannot help but take a sharp breath. That is what he did after I had gone home. While I sat at my parents' dining table, blew out candles, cut cake, drank lemonade and ate crisps and sandwiches with Bella and Logan and Mum and Dad, Marcus broke her bones.

'I haven't thought about that properly in a long time,' she says. 'I've certainly never talked about it.'

'Did you go to hospital?' I ask her, wondering if it was like it was with me. We never compared notes, but from what was said at the trial we could have written our stories from the same main script and just substituted our names at the relevant points. When he broke my wrist by accident – he slapped me at the top of the stairs and I fell down them and my wrist snapped halfway down – he took me to hospital. To one in another part of London because I'd been to the one nearer to him before and he didn't want people to see me coming in twice. He didn't want people to start to get suspicious. He waited outside in the car and drove me home afterwards.

'Yeah,' she says, 'he drove me. But you knew the drill: different hospital every time, waiting outside in the car, driving you home afterwards. That time, he cried. He cried and cried, real tears. He cried and said he hated himself and he didn't understand why he did it. He begged me to forgive him, he begged me to give him another chance, he cried and he begged me not to leave him. He cried so much I had to comfort him. It broke my heart he was so upset.'

'It was always easiest after a big thing like that because he was so remorseful, I genuinely believed he wouldn't do it again,' I say.

'And he was so lovely afterwards. For days, sometimes weeks, he'd be kind and considerate and thoughtful. He'd be loving.'

'He'd buy things and say he loved me.'

'He'd plan our future.'

'Plan for that time when we could tell the world about us and he wouldn't care about the consequences.'

'I'd always believe him.'

'I would, too.'

'And then it would start again . . . God, it was no wonder he went after fifteen-year-olds, we were so gullible. He was a terrible human being.'

'Yeah, he was. But he didn't deserve to die for it, Serena.'

'No, he didn't, Poppy. And even though I understand more than most why you'd want to do it, you shouldn't have done it.'

'I shouldn't have done it? *I* shouldn't have done it? Do you think I'm soft in the head or something? I know you did it, Serena. I know it was you. And I'm going to make you confess.'

'Are we going to keep having the same conversation every time? Are we? Because no matter what you threaten me with, it's not going to change anything. It's not going to make it the truth.'

'I might run your little memory-loss theory past Evan, see what he thinks. See if he believes his wife has enough gaps in her memory to commit murder and then get away with it.' The anger is visibly rising through her body. 'You might actually want to try that theory out on why you kept it from him. You never know, it might work.' She is going to blow at any second. I need to leave first this time. Whoever leaves first has the power, the ability to control the situation, to say stop. And it has to be me this time. Last time her anger ambushed me and

321

left me sitting alone at a table for two. Now it is my turn to balance the scales.

I get to my feet and scoop up my hat and mobile phone, shove them deep in my jacket pocket. 'I'll see ya, Serena,' I say. 'Or should I call you Sez?' Her already tense body and demeanour become rigid. But I cannot stop myself leaning down and pouring more discomfort into her ear: 'Give my love to Evan and the kids.'

I do not look back as I leave. I want her to know for once what it is like to be free of Marcus but to still feel completely powerless.

serena

That shakiness is back. I cannot get my legs to work properly and I have to stop and lean against the wall outside of the café, hold my chest and calm my breathing. I have to force air into my lungs because I am breathing too fast, too shallow. Evan once described a panic attack for me and this is it.

She's going to ruin my life. I have to stop her by doing it first.

Evan would rather hear it from me than from her. Or from anyone else.

No matter what happens tonight, once the kids are in bed, I have to tell him. I have to tell him and make him understand that I didn't do it. I am not the smiling vixen killer of the press, and I am not a silent killer who snuck back to finish what Poppy started earlier that evening. I am not that person.

I am Serena Gillmare and I have never killed anyone.

serena

I can tell by the way Evan is sitting at the kitchen table that he knows.

Did she do it, then? Did she tell him? I came home knowing I had to tell him but she has beaten me to it. He sits slumped in his seat in the dark kitchen, tapping the pads of his fingers lightly against the tabletop in a slow, rhythmic manner as he stares at the table. He did not move when I entered the kitchen a moment ago and that was how I knew something was wrong. Even when he is furious with me, and wants to shout at me, he at least looks at me.

The fear from the fact he cannot even look at me throws a blanket over all of my emotions except for dread and fear.

'Where are the kids?' I ask him as I stand beside him at the kitchen table. First things first, the most important things first. We cannot do this if they are likely to return at any moment.

'At my mother's,' he says without looking up. Another tumble of my stomach, another streak of terror across my heart. 'They're staying the night. Maybe tomorrow or until the weekend, I'm not sure yet.'

'Don't you think you should have checked with me first before making such big decisions for our children?' I say. I don't care what's happened, you don't make those kinds of decisions without their mother being at least told.

'Don't you think you should have told me you were a

325

murderer before making me marry you?' he replies. He is not shouting. Shouting, I could understand. Yelling, I could defend myself against. But quiet attacks are more deadly, they are the ones that have a habit of getting nasty on so many levels that you find yourself cut in several places all at once.

'Who told you?' I ask.

'Why, trying to work out which lie you're going to have to tell me to cover up what you did? Huh, Ice Cream Girl?' he asks.

'Don't call me that.' It wasn't Poppy. She would never have used that name. Despite what she acts like, how aggressive she can be, she hates that label as much as I do. It damaged her, it hurt her, she would never willingly describe herself like that. I'm relieved in many ways that it wasn't Poppy. Despite what she is like now, despite the hard lines of her face and the hair-cut that makes her look scary when she scowls, I'm glad she did not to do it. Because, out of everyone in the world who could have told him, she would have made it sound a million times worse than it was.

She would have made me sound guilty. I have a lot of hazy memories from that time, I have stuff that I have blanked out in order to be able to carry on living, but I know for sure that I did not murder him. It was Poppy, not me.

I pull out a chair and sit down, the wooziness from earlier is starting to circle my head again and my legs feel like rubber on springs. At least I can breathe.

'Why not, Ice Cream Girl, isn't that what everyone used to call you? Or was it plain old "murderer"?'

'I am not a murderer. I did not kill anyone. And *don't call me that.*'

The edge in my voice makes him turn slowly to look at me. I am gritting my teeth between my clamped-together lips. He can say what he likes, but I will not have him calling me that as though it is a fair weapon. I will not have him call me that and then try to maintain the higher ground. Every time I hear that, I am back in that room, on the floor, exhausted and all but extinguished from trying to fend off his punches and kicks. I am whispering because my throat has almost been crushed from where he tried to strangle me. I am lying on the bed, powerless to move and stop him finding a new way to hurt me. I will not have Evan, the man I have given my heart to, take me back there. I will not go there with him.

'Are you seriously getting an attitude with me after what you've done?' he asks.

'Yes, I am, if you are going to call me that.'

He shakes his head. 'You are unbelievable. After the day I had . . . Imagine, Ice— Serena, what it's like to have a patient come to see you, not because she wants to talk about her wheezy chest as she usually does, but to tell you that every time she's visited you for the past ten years or so she's been convinced that she's seen your wife somewhere before, and then, after a piece in the paper the other week, she realised who your wife was. Imagine having to then look at this newspaper clipping from twenty-odd years ago about a murdering tart called Serena Gorringe. Imagine that, eh? And imagine being me, sitting there, reading about a Serena Gorringe who got away with murder and who dropped out of sight after the trial where her best friend – and lover – went to prison in her place. Imagine that, eh?'

Oh God.

'And imagine me having to tell her that I think she's mistaken and it's just a coincidence that my wife is called Serena and she looks a bit like the girl in the picture. And imagine getting a call from the practice manager and the other partners who suggest I take a bit of time off to spend with my family until this whole thing blows over because that patient has been showing people in the waiting room the article and patients are starting to cancel their appointments. Imagine that, eh, Serena? Imagine.'

I'm floating. Above my body, above the room, above everything. I am light and floaty and I do not need to deal with this. Not now, not ever. I am free and floaty and light.

'I'm sorry,' I tell him.

'You're sorry?'

'I should have told you. I'm sorry I didn't. I came home wanting to tell you today, but it was too late.'

'You're sorry?' he repeats.

'I don't know what else to say.'

'How about why? Why did you kill him? Why did you lie to me for all these years? Why aren't you in prison?'

'I didn't kill him. And I'm not in prison because a jury found me not guilty of killing him. And . . . I'm sorry. I should have told you. I wanted to tell you. But . . . Look, aren't there things about you that you haven't told me? Like you smoking cigarettes every now and again? You kept that from me. You kept that from almost everyone. We don't always tell the people we should everything.'

'Yes, Serena, because me having the odd fag now and then is the same as you concealing your murderous past.'

'I am not a murderer. Stop saying that.'

'And what about this Poppy character? Do you still see her?'

I shake my head.

'But she's out of prison now?'

I nod.

'So you mean she hasn't shown up trying to rekindle things?'

'We were never like that. I didn't even like her. We were never friends, let alone anything else. All that stuff in the papers was lies. All of it lies. That's one of the reasons I couldn't tell you – it's all still so painful. We were young and they had this one photo of us holding ice creams looking a bit glamorous and the papers couldn't help themselves. And there was this other picture, this one that they never published but . . . but it showed me and her kissing. *He* made us do it. It was nothing more than a quick peck but he took a photo and it got leaked and that's why they thought we were . . . We weren't, I promise you we weren't.

'But only the people who knew us really well knew it was all lies and I didn't want to risk you reading those stories and for one second thinking they were true. I mean, look what happened when you saw one clipping. Imagine seeing the same type of thing over and over for months and months. I just had to forget about all of that to carry on with day-to-day life. I did not want to dredge it all up again by talking about it.'

'So it's not because you're a coward.'

How could he call me that after all these years? 'Go to hell,' I say to him.

'You first, murderer.'

'I did not murder him. Or anyone. I did nothing to him.'

'This is why you've fallen out with your sisters, isn't it?'

'Yes.'

'And why you thought I'd thrown my drink in your face on purpose.'

'Yes.'

'And why that policeman was so nasty about you speeding.'

'Yes.'

'And why you won't eat ice cream.'

'Yes.'

'You're a liar,' he says simply.

'No. No, I'm not.'

'YOU'RE A LIAR!' he roars in my face. 'YOU'RE A LIAR!'

'I'm sorry,' I say, trying hard not to cry.

He calms himself, then says, 'You're a liar and I want you out of my house – tonight.'

'What do you mean, your house? This is my house too. I pay for half of it. I found it. I'm not going anywhere. I'm not leaving my kids; what sort of mother do you think I am?'

'Well, I'm not living with you and I've done nothing wrong so why should I go? I want you gone.'

'No. I've told you, I'm not leaving my children.'

'Serena, listen to me. I want you to move out. You can stay nearby, you can come over every day and spend time with the children, feed them, put them to bed, etc. But I don't want you under the same roof as them or me. You're not the person

I thought you were. And the person I thought you were is a great mother. You, you are a stranger and I don't want you here.'

'Why can't you see that I've done nothing wrong? I don't deserve this.'

'People who have done nothing wrong don't keep secrets like this. People who have done nothing wrong have nothing to hide.'

'You don't understand what it was like. Why I couldn't tell you.'

'You're right, I don't understand. And I don't much care. I'm going to the shed for an hour – by the time I come back, I want you gone.'

'Where will I go?'

'Not my problem.'

Evan pushes out his chair with much scraping of wood on tile, and stands. He is made of stone, suddenly. My soft, comforting, gorgeous husband is made of a substance I cannot get close to. He is hard and unyielding. He is someone other than the man I fell in love with.

'I didn't do anything wrong,' I say to his retreating form.

He shrugs as his fingers close around the back-door handle and he pulls it open.

'I love you,' I say. I want him to know that. Even if he won't change his mind, I want him to know. And aren't they the words that are meant to fix everything? To make everything that is wrong, better?

'Again, not my problem,' he says and closes the door softly behind him.

part six

serena

I left him a note saying I would be back the next evening to give the children their dinner.

He sent me a text saying 'fine'. He wasn't going to stop me seeing the kids, he was just going to remove me from being there when they needed me. Which in many ways was worse. Babysitters, nannies, au pairs – they gave children their dinner, they gave them breakfast, they took them to school. They were not there in the middle of the night for the stuff only a parent would want to do. I loved being a parent for the moments in the middle of the night: the watching over them, the talking to them after a nightmare, the hushing them back to sleep, the sharing your bed. They were the things that tired you out, left you drained and snappy, but they were the necessities, the stuff I loved. I lived for them because, apart from Evan, no one else had those moments. And now, Evan has removed that from me. He's made me into little more than an unpaid caregiver.

And I only have myself to blame.

I sit outside in the car for a long time, hands gripping the steering wheel, staring at the front of my house. *Our* house. Eventually, Evan returns to the house, switches on the living room light and flicks shut the blinds. I'm sure he saw me, parked in the residents-only parking bay outside our house, but he pretended he didn't.

It's time to go. To leave. I need some sleep. I have work in the morning even though I do not have to get up as early to the take the children to school. I wonder what he will tell them. What he will say about me not being there in the morning? Actually, they'll probably never know, because his mother will take them to school. But afterwards, when I'm not at home, when I have to leave and return in the morning to act the role of nanny and feed them, ferry them to school, they'll know.

I could so easily drive to his parents' place in Haywards Heath. Tell the children it's OK. Say goodnight, God bless, sleep tight. But that would be all about me, what I want, how I want and need to hold them, to cling to them because they are the two best things that have happened to me. I would be scaring them to make myself feel better.

I pick up my mobile, dial Evan's parents' number. His mother answers on the second ring.

'It's Serena,' I tell her, waiting for the coolness to blast down the phone. 'Can I speak to Verity and Conrad, please?'

'Of course,' she says, cool but not unpleasant. Evan obviously hasn't told her everything. Maybe he's said it's just a row. 'They've been waiting for your call.'

'Mum?' Verity is first. Her voice is high, strained. She'll be anxious because her nan won't let her use the computer for anything other than schoolwork, and she'll have to go to bed at the same time as Conrad.

'Hello, gorgeous,' I say with a smile on my face, but tears in my heart, eyes and throat. 'Are you OK?'

'What's going on?' she asks.

'Nothing, sweetie. Your dad and I needed to do something tonight, it was very last minute, so your nan and granddad had to look after you. That's all.'

'Oh,' she says disappointedly, 'that's what Dad said. I thought something was happening.'

'I'm not surprised,' I say. 'Now, I've got to go, so big kiss and cuddle goodnight.'

'I'm not a baby!' she says contemptuously.

'You'll always be my baby. Even when you're forty-five and a mother yourself, in my mind, you'll always be my baby.'

'Goodnight, Mum,' she says, resigned to her fate since I say this to her all the time. 'See you tomorrow.'

'Yes, I'll see you tomorrow.'

'Here,' Verity says, handing the phone to Conrad. 'Don't stay on there for ever, OK? She's busy.'

'Hello gorgeous boy,' I say to Conrad, feeling the wrench again. I want to be with him. I want to be with both of them. The world doesn't feel the same knowing I'm not going to be with them any time soon, that we won't be sleeping under the same roof, sheltered by the same bricks and mortar.

'Mum, Mum!' he says, urgently. 'Nan let us have fish fingers AND sausages AND chips that weren't made in the oven for dinner. AND we had chocolate mousse on top of chocolate cake.' I love that Conrad will always tell me things like that. Neither set of grandparents is ever able to get away with anything because he can't help but tell. Verity was never like that, she was – is – like me, always good at keeping secrets.

'Wow, that sounds like a big dinner,' I say.

'Not really. It's real food, Nan says. She says that we need to eat real food sometimes because you're—' He turns away from the phone suddenly. 'Nan! NAN! What did you say Mum was? A health fantastic?' I hear my mother-in-law in the background, dying of mortification. She'll be standing in the kitchen doorway, tea towel in hand, waving her hand frantically, shaking her head, her white hair bouncing wildly, trying to convey to him that he shouldn't be telling me that. Those words of dismissive condemnation were not meant for my ears. I have no sympathy: she's known Con all his life, she knows he's a veritable tape recorder. 'Nan said you were a health fantastic,' he says, having not persuaded his nan to repeat what she said.

'I think you mean fanatic,' I say.

'Yes!' My whole chest expands when I hear my little boy smile. 'She said you were always feeding us rabbit food because you were a health fan—'

'Fanatic,' I supply.

'Is that true? Do you always feed us rabbit food? I thought we were supposed to eat lots of vegetables and fruit every day. Is that what rabbits eat? Cos I want to eat horse food if we have to eat like an animal. My teacher at school says you have to eat lots of fruit and vegetables to be healthy. Are you doing something wrong if you're not giving us real food like Nan does?'

'No, I'm just giving you different food to your nan, that's all.'

'Oh, OK. Are we coming home tomorrow?' he asks.

'Yes, sweetheart,' I reply.

'OK. Goodnight, Mum. I have to go to bed now. I have to see if I have the sea horse dream again. The horse swam all the way to Australia! And I was on its back. And I didn't get wet. I want to have that dream again, so I have to go to bed.'

'OK, gorgeous. Love you, big kiss and cuddle goodnight.'

'OK, bye.'

And then he's gone. They're both gone. My mother-in-law doesn't bother to speak to me again, I just have the chilling brrr that is the dialling tone.

I know tears are falling down my cheeks, but if I give in, if I have a proper cry now, I will not move from this spot. I will sit here and cry the night away. And that would antagonise Evan further. It's important I do not do that. If I want him to take me back, if I want to rescue our marriage, I have to do whatever he wants me to. Because if our marriage fails and Evan goes for full custody of the kids, I doubt any court in the land would award them to me with my history. In fact, they may even question the wisdom of anything other than the most basic access. I have to fix my marriage. I love my husband, and I do not want my relationship with my children to become little more than the phone conversations we just had.

I am sitting in the centre of a bed in a hotel near Brighton seafront. It is comfortable enough, the décor is dated but clean and in good repair. It isn't too pricey – I have to be careful with costs because I don't know how long I'll be staying and I'm not sure how Evan will react to me putting it on the joint account.

I sit in the dark, my legs pulled up to my chest, my arms wrapped around them and my head resting on my knees. I am staring at the bundle of silk beside me on the bed. It's my red silk shirt, wrapped around the sharp knives from my kitchen. Evan wouldn't hide them every night like he should, so I had to take them.

He's going to be so mad if he wants cheese on toast for breakfast tomorrow. But if he would put them out of harm's way like he should, then I wouldn't have been forced to steal them.

I hide the knives because of *him*, of course. Sometimes it seems everything I do for safety is because of *him*.

January, 1987

'If you ever leave me, I'll kill you,' *he* whispered, his eyes narrow, slitted peepholes to the venom in his soul. He held a small all-purpose kitchen knife with a serrated edge and black wooden handle against the smooth piece of skin at the centre of my throat, so close I was too scared to swallow in case it caused the knife to peel back my skin. 'I'll slice your throat wide open. No one else will ever have you. Do you hear me?'

I did my best to nod without moving my neck or throat. I could not manage it and I felt the cool touch of the blade on my skin. 'Yes,' I managed to push out through my stiff, scared lips.

'Good.' He whipped the knife away suddenly and was laughing, his big, booming laugh. 'I'm only messing with you!' he said while tossing the knife on to the kitchen table. 'I'm only joking. Oh, God, Serena, you know I could never hurt you. Never in a million years would I ever do anything to hurt you,' he continued as he played with one of my plaits, twirling it around his little finger. 'Darling, I love you. I could never, ever hurt you.'

337

We both knew that wasn't true. And we both knew he wasn't joking about the knife. He was messing with me, but he wasn't joking. I couldn't say anything. All I could do was paint on a smile, force out a laugh and let him put his arms around me. Even nowadays he was still sometimes lovely to me. Those times were precious. Those times were what made the rest of it bearable. And now I knew he had a back-up plan for the times when it wasn't bearable. The times when I thought about escape. He had found a way to make sure I would never leave him.

For five days, I have been visiting my children.

I make them breakfast, I take them to school. After work I go to my home and make them dinner. I supervise homework and baths and story time and long-winded goodnights. I would clean the kitchen before I leave but my husband does it while I am upstairs – he does not want me there any longer than necessary, I suspect. He has spoken to me very little. In fact, only once – on that first night I came over. 'The knives,' he said sotto voce as the children changed out of their uniforms. 'You took the freaking knives. *Are you mad?*' Con's arrival prevented my answer, which we both knew would have been: 'Probably.'

'You're getting divorced, aren't you?' Vee says as I perch myself on her pink-duvet covered bed on that fifth night.

Am I? a part of me wonders. *Does she know something I don't?*

'Am I?' I ask her.

She blusters while shrugging her shoulders, 'Yeah, it's obvious. One person moves out and then they get divorced.'

'No one's moved out,' I say confidently, even though each day I have been taking a few more things with me. These things have moved beyond necessities and comforters, now they're sliding into everyday items that I'd normally do without on holidays or short stays away from home. When I was packing I wasn't sure what to take, having never had to pack before for my husband throwing me out for an unspecified amount of time. I'd already taken the large bottle of body moisturiser to use at the hotel. And a normal-size tube of toothpaste. My pack of cotton wool, my large face moisturiser and face wash had come with me yesterday. Today I was planning on taking a couple of towels and my dressing gown. The longer Evan didn't initiate conversation, the more things I found I needed to bring.

'But you're not living here any more, Mum,' Verity points out. 'I know cos I see you leave at night and come back in the morning wearing something different. Even Conrad knows. He saw you weren't in the big bed the other day.'

If Conrad knows, I'm surprised he hasn't said something. Or has he, silently? He's been clingy and ever so slightly baby-ish at night recently. Not wanting to let me go when I hug him goodnight, constantly asking me questions that are designed to prolong the night-night process, climbing out of bed to get things to show me. Of course he knows. Of course they both know. You can't create the atmosphere that Evan and I have and not expect the kids to know. They're children, not stupid.

'OK, I'm not staying here at the moment.'

'When are you coming back?'

I'm loathe to say, 'When your father will talk to me' because it *will* sound like the start of divorce to them. Especially to Verity. And we're not there, we're nowhere near there.

'*Not yet, anyway,*' whispers that little voice of my conscience.

I don't even bother to argue with it, I just ignore it. '*Like your oh-so wonderful husband is doing to you,*' it adds smugly.

'I don't know, Vee,' I say. 'I just . . . it's complicated. Your father and I just have a few things to work out.'

'See?' she says, tugging the covers right up under her chin. 'That's what parents do. Eliza James's parents did the same thing. Except her dad moved out cos her mum caught him kissing someone else. I think it was a man but Eliza won't say. But her mum said they were "working a few things out" and her dad never came home and they got divorced. That's what parents do. They say it's complicated and then they get divorced.'

'Really? How many parents have you had then? Because you seem very experienced in all this,' I say, silently wishing she'd stop using the 'D' word in such a familiar, comfortable manner. The way Vee speaks, it seems we're halfway to the courts already.

'Ha ha, Mum,' Vee says. I watch her stare intently at the poster on her wardrobe door, as if seeking comfort and understanding in it. Where most girls her age would have a band member or band or movie star, she has the periodic table. She likes the look of it, she said. The pretty colours and straight lines and orderliness are lovely to her. That is her excuse – the real reason is that my daughter is a big girly swot. Just like I was. She is just better at hiding it. 'Did you kiss someone else?'

'Much as I love you, sweetheart, you shouldn't be asking me questions like that.'

'Why?'

'Because it crosses the line. It's not the sort of thing you should ask me, as your mum, and it's not the sort of thing I should answer.'

'Why?'

I remember wanting to ban that word from her vocabulary when she was a toddler. Every child goes through the 'Why?' stage, but Verity's was relentless. Even the ubiquitous, 'Because it is' was not good enough for her. 'But *why*?' she'd persist until Evan and I were ready to pull our hair out. We were each constantly throwing each other to the wolves of Verity's whys, finding ways to get out of the questioning, and it was almost always me who had to do the extra research to find the answer.

'Look, Vee, love, if I did answer that question and you didn't get the answer you wanted, it would just upset you. You'd start to worry on a whole new level to the one you're worrying on right now, and that's not for you to do. Not until you're an adult and married and can at least stay up past nine o'clock on a school night. Do you see what I mean?'

She shrugs her shoulders; they are small compared to adult shoulders but they seem to be carrying a heavy burden right now. 'I suppose so.'

'I love your father so much. I would never do anything to intentionally hurt him. And kissing someone else would be doing something to intentionally hurt him.' Her body relaxes a little at that. Poor kid, she actually thought I'd been cheating. If I had kissed someone else, maybe Evan would have got over it a lot quicker. Maybe I'd be able to know when I could put our family back together again. 'But, Vee, we have a lot of things to work out, your father and I. It *is* complicated, not the stuff for you or Con to worry about. It might take time, but we'll get there. And whatever we decide, it'll be the best for all concerned – especially you and Con. OK?'

She shrugs.

'Shrug is not an answer,' I say and launch myself at her, tickling her. She struggles and giggles and kicks, but I feel her relax as we play and that's what I want – for her to relax.

I stay with her until she is asleep, and think about how I was going to search her room. I didn't, I couldn't in the end. I had to trust her, and I had to watch her. The second she started to show any signs of being any different, the moment I felt something shift in her, I would take her room apart looking for clues. Then I would take her school locker apart looking for clues. I would do anything, but first she had to give me a good reason. Until then, I had to trust she wasn't like me, she wasn't stupid.

As her eyes slip shut for the final time, I kiss her forehead, stroke my hand over her headscarf, before I leave her to dream the night away.

Downstairs, instead of shrugging on my coat and texting Evan a goodnight – which he never replies to – before I leave, I go into the living room. This surprises him because he jumps up out of his seat and turns towards me for the first time in a week.

'Yeah?' he asks, burying his hands in his pockets and planting his feet hip-width apart. 'What do you want?'

'We have to talk,' I say.

He shakes his head. 'No, we don't.'

Is this really my husband? The most reasonable man in the world? *Really*? 'Yeah, we do. The kids think we're getting divorced.'

'Right,' he says.

Mild panic flutters inside my stomach: he didn't dismiss the idea, but at least he didn't confirm it.

'We need to talk about what to tell them. How to reassure them.'

'OK, we'll talk about what to tell the kids, but it might not be reassuring to them. I'll meet you in your car.'

'Fine,' I say. For someone so reasonable, who is loved in his profession for his empathy, Evan is very good at quietly torturing me.

'So, what do we say to them?' I ask. I have to keep things on topic, anything that deviates from that will obviously antagonise him.

'I don't know. Probably not that their mother is a cold-hearted killer who kisses girls. Nor that she got herself pregnant so she could con some poor sap, *me*, into marrying her and giving her a new name.'

'I'm sorry,' I say quietly, fixing my line of sight on the house, keeping an eye on it in case a light goes on in one of the upstairs bedrooms. 'I should have told you.'

'Yeah, you should have.'

I do not know what else he wants. He clearly doesn't want me to explain, he doesn't want me to be around him, he does not seem to want my apologies. I do not know what else he wants me to do, how I'm supposed to fix this if he doesn't want it to be fixed, if he cannot step outside of his hurt and anger and rage for a few moments and give me a clue.

'What should we tell the kids?' I repeat. 'I've already said that there are some things we need to work out, but we can't keep saying that for ever. We need some idea of what to tell them about what is going to happen next.' *I* need to know what is going to happen next.

'If you're angling to come back, don't bother. I'm still too angry to even . . . Just don't bother.'

'OK, you decide what to tell them and they can tell me.'

'Yeah, maybe that's for the best,' he says.

'No, that's not for the best, but it's the best that's going to happen right now.'

A dull click is followed by a rush of air as Evan opens the passenger door.

'I'll see you tomorrow,' I tell him, still staring at the house. Still not able to turn around and look at him. The heat of his anger might burn the skin on my face. It's been a week and he is still angry. It seems to be getting worse, not better. That's probably because he is fanning the flames by reading old newspaper and news reports rather than talking to me. Rather than getting the truth from the person who was there, he is winding himself up with the half-truths and outright lies. This is what I didn't want to happen.

'Right,' Evan states and shuts the door.

He would be loving seeing Evan and me in pieces. *He* would laugh and say this is what he meant every time he held a knife up to my throat: *if I can't have you, no one else will either.*

poppy

'Poppy, it's good to see you.'

'You too,' I force out through gritted teeth hidden behind a fake, close-lipped smile. It is not good to see Mr Fitch, my parole officer. Although technically I have to have regular meetings with this man if he deems it necessary, since he got me the job with Raymond he hasn't deemed it necessary. In fact, the last time I sat here in his tiny office – which is so stuffed and lined with files and books and paper, paper, paper, I wonder how he breathes – he said we could 'play it by ear'. *'If you have any problems call me. But otherwise, I'm pleased with your progress so we can play it by ear.'*

I didn't think for a moment he would be calling me in for 'a chat'. Or, as he called it, 'just a quick catch up, to see where you are with everything'.

I know that parole officers only call you in 'for a quick catch-up' when there is a problem. And I suspect the 'problem' lives in Preston Park. If she reported me to the Old Bill for stalking, I would have been arrested and sent straight back to prison to serve the rest of my sentence, so she must have just found out Fitchy's name and asked him to warn me off. Which would be a monumentally stupid move on her part. I will ruin her if she has grassed on me. I will ruin her and I will ruin her family. Sod clearing my name slowly and carefully, if I'm going down, I'll take her down with me.

'How are you getting on? Raymond tells me you've been great for his business. Which is good; it's nice to hear something so positive about a parolee. Especially an ex-lifer like yourself. It's usually a struggle for them to adjust to the outside world.'

I nod at him as I'm expected to do. I cannot say anything because it'd be either: 'It's a breeze,' or, 'Yeah, my life is pretty much ruined since my parents hate having me around, I still haven't had the guts to call my siblings, I fell in love with a man who wasn't really my boyfriend and I'm no closer to getting the person who actually committed "my" crime to confess.' I doubt he'd want to hear either of these things. Better to just nod and find out what he wants.

He sighs suddenly, a dramatic sigh, the signal to something grave being discussed. I am ready, though. I'm fully armed with explanations for turning up at Serena's, meeting her for coffee twice now, even for knowing so much about her life. I can deflect, divert or lie my way out of anything he throws at me.

'I'll get to the point,' he says. I shuffle in my seat, making my body taller and straighter to show I really have nothing to hide. 'You were friends with Tina Wynard, weren't you?' he says. 'I believe you shared a cell for a while.'

'Yes, we were roommates,' I say. 'And we're still friends.'

'When did you last speak to her?' Tina has escaped. That's the only thing it could be – although I'm surprised it's not the Old Bill questioning me. I can't believe she's done it. Or how she's done it. She is so straight-laced, a totally by-the-rules person. *'Know de rules an' stick to dem,'* she told me when she was still hiding behind her 'Jamaican' accent. *'Den, you work out how to divert attention away from de rules you no wanna keep, y'know. But you so good in every udder way, dem not tink it you at-all-at-all-at-all.'*

'I don't know, a few weeks maybe. She wrote to me just after I got out. I keep meaning to reply. Why all the questions? What's happened?'

'Tina had her meeting with the parole board last week.'

'Oh, yeah. She mentioned it was coming up in her letter. I

didn't know when, though.' I meant to reply but I was hanging on, hoping I'd be able to tell her that Serena had confessed. That it had finally worked and I could clear my name, that I had finally managed the ultimate rescue and saved myself.

He shifts in his seat, clears his throat, tries to moisten his lips. 'Her application was unsuccessful.'

'But why?' I ask, my voice rising a notch or two in indignation. 'She was the model prisoner. She was polite, she never got into fights, and she was always looking after new prisoners. I can't think of a person more suited to parole than she was. She even admitted and showed remorse for her crime, for God's sake; you don't get much more suitable than that.'

'It was felt that although she was a very strong candidate for parole and, as you said, she admitted her crime and showed great remorse, there was a real danger that she would fall back into drugs and prostitution.'

'She'd knocked all that on the head before she got sent down,' I say. 'And she was a grown woman, not the naïve youngster she was when she got into all that.' If I race ahead, if I skip to nearer the end of this conversation, I can hazard a guess at what is coming, what is waiting for me. But I am not going to race ahead, I am going to see where I am being led, because it is possible I might have it all wrong.

'Maybe so, but the board felt—'

'They hadn't quite got their pound of flesh from her yet?' I say, then mentally snap the air, trying to bite those words back into my mouth. I have to be careful – this man could make my life not only difficult but impossible. He is one of *them* after all. He is nice, he treats me with respect and kindness, he helped me out with a job and spoke up for me with the board, but he is, at the end of the day, a screw in a suit. His keys are his pen and paper, the tools with which he could get me locked up again. If I am not careful, he could have me sent back.

Mr Fitch bristles, but not overly so. 'They were just doing what they felt was right for her, Poppy. Not everyone is out to hurt prisoners, you know. We do care about what happens to them. And it was genuinely felt that Tina could become a danger to herself or the public if she were allowed to fall into the habits she had in the past.'

'If she was going to go back to drugs, don't you think she would have done so in the last twenty-five years?'

'She has been in prison for the past twenty-five years.'

'Exactly. It's easier to get drugs inside than it is outside and there are more reasons to turn to drugs inside than outside.'

'I don't think you're right there, Poppy.' The official denial of the drugs problem inside is a beautiful, full and rounded creature. Most people in charge from the Big Luv right down to the everyday screws seem to have the attitude that if they pretend drugs aren't a huge problem inside then they aren't. They have their searches and policies, after all – there is no way drugs could get in, is there?

'Whatever you say, Mr F,' I say to him. 'How is Tina doing? It must have been a blow to her.'

His hands move papers around the desk; shuffle, shuffle, go the white sheets in my file, which he has open but has hardly glanced at since I sat down, but he now seems very engrossed in. There is a pale patch of skin showing through the fine covering of his mousey-brown hair on the top of his head. Slowly he raises his head and meets my eye. 'Were you aware that Tina suffered from depression?' he says.

I want to clamp my hands over my ears and scream 'Lalalalalalalalala' at the top of my voice. If I can't hear him, this won't happen.

'Everyone suffers from depression inside,' I say. 'Everyone sane suffers from depression.' In my head, I am still screaming 'Lalalalalalaalalalalalala'; my hands are still clamped over my ears. In my head I am protected from what he is about to say.

'I'm sorry, Poppy,' he says. 'I'm sorry to have to tell you this, but Tina took her own life on Saturday night.'

Lalalalalalalalalalalalalalalalalalalalalala.

'She became very depressed after the board's decision.'

Lalalalalalalalalalaalalalalalalalalalalalalalalalalala.

'But we believe she might have been thinking about it for a while because she used sleeping pills that she had obviously not swallowed when they were given to her in the infirmary, and she'd been storing up.'

Lalalalalalalalalalalalalalalalalalalalalalalalalalalalalalalalalalalalalala.

He fumbles in his drawer and pulls out one of the clear plastic bags they put prison belongings in. Embossed all over it are the words HMP Colfrane. Wrapped up in the bag is a Good News Bible. 'In the note she left, she said she wanted you to have this.' He holds it out to me but I cannot move to take it. I cannot move to breathe. He eventually places it on the area of desk in front of me. 'She left you a note inside.'

She'd done it again, she'd broken one of the Commandments she held so dear, she had broken the First Commandment: thou shalt not kill, again. But this time she had accomplices. This time she'd been egged on by a whole group of people sitting around a table debating what was best for her life.

'We don't think she suffered,' he says, to be kind because he is kind. He does try. But we both know that is a lie. Of course she suffered. She suffered and suffered and suffered. Tina had paid her debt to society, I don't care what anyone says. She wasn't a danger to anyone.

'I'll give you a few minutes,' he says and excuses himself, shutting the glass door behind himself.

The inside cover of the bible bears the inscription, *A gift to Betina Wynard from the nuns at St Angela's Convent School, 1981.* The note is tucked in between the inside cover and the first page of the Bible. It is sealed, but the lack of my name on the front of the envelope tells me that it has been opened and checked as per the rules. Even in death a prisoner has no privacy. Even in death those in charge need to know everything. If she had put something incriminating in there, I would not have seen this, I'm sure.

Don't be angry with me, Ice Cream Girl, (she has written in her neat, rounded handwriting.) *I'm tired. Just plain old worn-out. If I had been allowed to go then maybe this story would have turned out different but, either way, I had to leave here. I could not see another Christmas or New Year behind these bars. I sometimes wonder if I was ever meant for anything more than this? But then I remember you and how you weren't stupid and I think, I hope, that you were my reason. Looking after you kept me here longer than I would have otherwise stayed. So you looked after me, too. You did know about rescuing people. Make me proud, Ice Cream Girl. Live your life well. Live your life in peace and happiness. Live your life in the best way you know how.*

Love, Tina.

P.S. I hope God will forgive me. I think He will. (John 3:16).

My fingers flick through the pages of the Bible until I come to the passage she has quoted. *'For God loved the world so much that he gave his only Son, so that everyone who believes in him may not die but have eternal life.'*

The words float in the tears in my eyes. I wish I had her faith. I wish I could believe what she believed, then it would not hurt. I would read those words and I would feel comfort, I would feel sure that she is safe and happy. I would feel something other than this. It is pain, it is loss, it is anger. I refold the note, slip it back in its envelope, slip it back in its place in the Bible.

It was not meant to be like this.

We were meant to have our happy ending; we were meant to start our lives again together. I have not had one drink of alcohol because I have been waiting for her. Waiting for us to sit outside a pub and have our first proper drink together, like those young professionals I always see relaxing without a care in the world, outside Brighton pubs and bars. She was meant to coach me to stop smoking while taking blatant drags from the fags I'd lit. We were meant to talk about the men we met and ask each other's opinions on whether they were good enough. We were meant to be friends on the outside too. We were meant . . .

I close my eyes and call up her slender face, her short Afro hair, her big insightful eyes, her soft voice, her gentle spirit, the smile that was never far away from her lips. *'Tell me what it's like out there,'* she'd written in her last letter to me. *'Tell me if I'll like it.'*

I cover my face with my hands, trying to hold back my gushing tears.

I don't know if you'd like it, Tine, I say in my head. *I know that I'm not liking it. I'm not liking it at all.*

serena

'Don't hang up,' Mez says. She has blocked her number from my work's caller ID, knowing that I would have to pick up the phone. 'It's me, but please don't hang up.' I don't know why, but I've always been able to tell my sisters apart on the phone. Mez's voice is ever so slightly higher, with a slight lift at the end; Faye's is a fraction deeper and stays much more close to her normal register even when she is asking a question.

'Verity called me; she's worried about you.'

'What's she worried about?' I ask, for the sake of my daughter. I thought I had reassured her last night, but obviously not. And Evan has failed to convince them things will be fine, too.

'She said you'd moved out. She's worried that you're not taking care of yourself. She said you told her to call one of us if she couldn't talk to you.'

'What did you tell her?'

'I said I'd call you to find out how you really are.'

'Tell her I'm fine.'

'And are you? Are you fine?'

I say nothing. I am not fine. How can I be when I have destroyed my life? When my husband won't speak to me, my daughter and son are living apart from me and I hate myself for the choices I've made, how can I possibly be fine?

I also do not say anything because I do not want to talk to Mez. It's all too hard, too difficult for me at the moment. I do not know the right thing to do any more. I do not know how to fix my family. I ruined it and I do not know how to fix it. But I do know I cannot pretend that I don't know what they think I am.

'What can I do to help?' she asks.

Get my husband to talk to me. Help me rewrite history. Believe in me. 'Just be there for Verity if she needs you.'

'Are you and Evan going to be OK?'

'I don't know. He thinks I'm a murderer and he hates me for lying to him, and he won't tell me if he wants to divorce me. So I don't know.'

'Sez, about what Adrian told you—'

'I don't want to talk about it.'

'But—'

'I. Don't. Want. To. Talk. About. It.'

'OK, OK,' she says. 'We won't talk about it. But I love you, little sister.'

'Please take care of Verity if she needs you again. And please be convincing when you tell her I'm fine. I don't want her or Con to worry too much.'

'Will do.'

'And I love you, too.'

That's my problem, isn't it? I've always found room in my heart to love the people who hurt me.

poppy

Every day I get out this slip of paper and I try to make those calls.

I long to talk to Bella and Logan, but what if the feeling isn't mutual? How would I feel about talking to a person who I've been brought up to believe is evil personified?

I run my fingers over the lines of their names before I carefully refold the piece of paper and slip it back in my pocket.

I'll do it another day. Today is not the day for using the phone.

serena

I probably shouldn't keep meeting her.

Especially since she – her release – has precipitated what has been the decimation of my life, but I can't really help myself. I could pretend it's because I'm scared of what she might do, if she'll show up at school one day and tell the kids. Or that I'm scared of her – that she'll do something to me if I don't show up or if I turn her down. I have seen the rage in her.

The aggression she keeps flashing at me is simply the surface of what she is feeling. It is a cover for the true anger that burns like a volcanic fire deep inside her. She is going to explode one day if she does not find an outlet for it. She is going to erupt and could destroy herself and all those around her if she does not find a way to let it out in little chunks. That is part of the reason – the real reason – I meet her. I fear for her. I feel sorry for her and the state she is in: what she has probably endured in prison, what she is probably putting up with now that she is out. I feel for her as one human being feels for another, as an acquaintance might feel for someone they once upon time knew. I don't like her, but I feel for her.

The main reason, the main *real* reason I feel for her, is that I feel responsible. Since that night, since what happened, I have felt a weight of responsibility about the choices I made, and it burns like Poppy's volcanic rage. That responsibility, culpability – *guilt* – created the conscience that mocks and ridicules me, it makes me lightheaded and woozy. It, I'm sure, causes the memory lapses and the moments of hyperventilation.

I feel guilty for so many little things, and I feel responsible for the big things. I feel responsible for what happened to Poppy. And, of course, I feel guilty for *his* death. I feel guilty about why he died, how he died, that . . .

Poppy enters the café and she reminds me again how different she is from the girl I knew. She walks slower, almost as though dragging her feet will stop her from getting where she is going. Her shoulders are slightly hunched, as if ready for attack. Whenever she enters somewhere, I have noticed, her eyes dart around, taking in the scene, checking where everyone and everything is, almost as though she needs to know where the exits are, where the most potentially dangerous people are, where she needs to be should something happen. Prison has done that to her.

She saunters over to me, pulls out a chair and sits down – after a quick look around to see how the environment has changed since she entered. She tugs off her brown leatherette cap and shakes out her hair, running her fingers through it. It's growing back: the waves are starting to be seen.

'Serena,' she says, formally.

'Poppy,' I reply.

'Now we're sure of who we are, let's get down to business,' she says.

'You mean, you're finally going to tell me what you want?' I say. Her aggression is disconcerting. Not scary, per se. I think it's the absence of any other emotion in her speech sometimes, as if she doesn't know how to be anything other than this angry, that unsettles me. Sometimes all that Poppy sounds is angry.

'You know what I want,' she says and sits back, puts her head to one side as she sizes me up. She's wondering if she can take me. Wondering if she leapt at me across the table and started a grappling match on the grubby black and white lino tiles beneath our feet which one of us would gain the upper hand most quickly.

She is prison-tough, I'll give her that. But doesn't know what I am like in a fight between equals, what I am capable of. She's never known, that's why she found it easy to be with my boyfriend. She thought I would walk away. That I *could* walk away. It didn't occur to her that I had been so brainwashed and demeaned, so broken and damaged, that – until that night – walking away was not an option.

'If I did, I wouldn't have said that.'

'You need to tell the truth about what happened. What you did.'

'I did tell the truth, Poppy. I told the police, who tried to twist it. I told the court, who found me innocent. I told the people who mattered.'

She sits forwards, leans across the table and hisses, 'You killed him. Admit it, you killed him.'

The guilt flames up inside me. 'I didn't,' I say calmly, even though inside I am shaking. Trembling, and woozy; the palpitations – the latest element to how I've been feeling – start up. I place my hand on the centre of my chest and try to breathe. It's nigh on impossible with the guilt flaming up inside. 'I didn't.'

'Stop lying!' she continues to hiss. 'Stop *lying!*'

'If you carry on like this,' I pause, trying to quell the fire inside, 'I'll leave. I don't have to come here, you know.'

'Yes, you do,' she says with a smug snarl that stops her from erupting. 'If you don't, I'll tell your darling hubby all about you and me and the murder.'

'He already knows,' I reply, relieved to be taking that card away from her.

'No, he doesn't,' she says, looking unsure, unsettled and a little afraid.

'He does.'

'And, what, he's been loving and supportive and believes in you one hundred per cent? Pull the other one, Serena, it's got bells on.'

'Hardly. He asked me to leave.'

'He threw you out?'

'Yes, if that's how you want to put it. Nearly ten days now. So, you see, I have nothing left to lose.' That is not true, of course. The kids don't know. And I am hoping to get him back, but she doesn't need to know that. Because right now, I have been thrown out.

'So why did you come here, then?' she asks.

'Because you obviously need someone to talk to. And I thought I might be able to . . . I don't know. Not help, exactly, but . . .'

Her face twists dramatically. 'You came out of *pity*? *Pity!*'

If she wants to look at it that way, then she can. I came because I can't help myself.

Poppy used to look at me at lot with resentment. She wanted *him* all to herself and she wanted me to disappear. Around the time of her sixteenth birthday she changed. I think it started to get to her. She started to see that *he* wasn't perfect. Or maybe she knew and she stopped thinking I was the cause of *his* imperfections.

October, 1987

'Serena,' he barked, 'into the kitchen.'

I did as I was told, too emotionally exhausted to even ask why. He held Poppy's hand tenderly as they followed. He went to the side of the kitchen table nearest the sink and pulled out a chair. 'Sit,' he ordered me, his tone reminding me of Barbara Woodhouse. *Good dog*, I expected him to say any second. *Good dog, Serena.*

Ten minutes earlier, before she arrived, he had held a knife to my throat, and reminded me that leaving him wasn't an option. I had felt the bite of the knife as he pressed it to my flesh, then he took it away. Now, he was caressing her, stroking her, reminding me he had someone else. I did not want to watch. I did not want to watch because I did not want to feel jealous over a man who wanted to kill me. It was not logical, it was primordial. He was supposedly my mate and I wanted to leave him, but I still felt bad when he went with another woman. When he went with her.

He was torturing me to get a reaction. I would not give him one, I would not show him how I felt about what he was doing. He would hurt me no matter what I did, but I would rather I got beaten for not reacting than reacting. He would get less satisfaction from that.

Suddenly he was pushing her forwards and lifting her white pencil skirt. Confusion and embarrassment exploded in Poppy's eyes. We locked gazes, and I realised she was asking for help. She wanted me to do something to help her. I felt sorry for her, I really did, but the last time I helped her he discovered a new way to punish me. After last time, 'let's make up' had entered his repertoire of torture, his latest way of prolonging the suffering of a beating. I could not risk making him that angry again.

'Make sure you keep your eyes open,' he told Poppy as he started to move inside her.

She nodded and stared at me for a second, then she screwed her eyes up tight.

'Are her eyes open?' he asked me.

I nodded. Even though they weren't. She had found a way to escape what was happening, a place to hide while he humiliated her in front of me, but I didn't have that place. I couldn't do anything but watch.

'Good girl, Poppy,' he said tenderly, afterwards. He stroked his hand over her hair, and kissed her neck, kissed her cheek. 'Good girl.'

Whenever he was that nice, that loving to her in front of me, it meant he intended to hurt me as much as he could later.

It didn't matter as much, though, because I had managed to defy him. He would never know it, but I had defied him and that was all that counted. Because that meant I could slowly find a way to escape from him completely. I could maybe find a way to set myself free.

★

After that incident, Poppy was a little bit nicer towards me. She started to act as if she wanted to be my friend but it was a little too late for that. And that's why I feel responsible. I wonder sometimes if I had tried to be friendly back, if we had found a way to be friends, could I have stopped her from doing what she did? Could I have stopped her from killing him?

'Now isn't that the joke to end all jokes?' Poppy's bitterness spews out of her like lava. 'Serena pities me. She lets me rot in prison for two decades for something she did, and then manages to feel pity for me.'

'Poppy, I didn't do anything.' Even with my unstable memory I know I didn't do it.

She slams her hand down on the table, rattling all the cutlery and crockery, making everyone around us turn and stare. 'STOP LYING!' she screams at me. 'JUST STOP LYING!'

I stumble to my feet. I have already paid, so I do not need to hang around here a moment longer.

'WHY WON'T YOU TELL THE TRUTH?' She is on her feet, too; she is raging, flaming, her body rigid with anger. I have woken the volcano. By trying to do good, by trying to help her, I caused the volcano to erupt. 'WHY ARE YOU STILL LYING? JUST TELL THE TRUTH. JUST TELL THE WORLD YOU DID IT.'

The wooziness comes over me in huge waves, I am floaty and lightheaded, my head feels as if it is a giant balloon that will float away from my neck. But my chest is tight and small and I cannot get air into it. I cannot breathe. I push my hand on to my chest again, feel the wild gallop of my heart beneath my fingers, the tensed muscles of my chest. *I cannot breathe. I cannot breathe.*

My legs stop working, stop being capable of holding up my body and they give way. As I fall, I hear a loud *CRACK!* That's my head hitting the table. That's my head ushering in the blackness . . .

poppy

Please don't die, Serena. Please don't die.

Everything is moving so fast and people are talking at a million miles an hour and I feel like I am on a television set, starring in an episode of *Casualty*.

I have a single mantra repeating and repeating itself in my head: 'Please don't die, Serena.'

I do not care at this moment in time if she confesses and clears my name. I just do not want her to die.

Please don't die, Serena. Please don't die.

I am clinging on to her handbag and know that inside is her mobile phone and I should go through it and find her husband's number and call him and tell him. But I don't know what to tell him. I don't know how to explain who I am. And I do not want to speak to him. Not like this. It was all very well threatening her with telling him, but doing it is another matter. If pushed I would have done, I'm sure. But this is not such a time. I am not being pushed, I am being punished; being threatened with having another death on my conscience.

I am told by a senior-looking nurse to wait in the waiting area and to give details to the receptionist about my friend.

She fires questions at me:

'Name?'

'Serena Gillmare.'

'Date of birth?'

'Twentieth of September, 1970.'

'Address?'

'93 Blues Point Road, Preston Park, BN3 VCZ.'

'Next of kin?'

'Dr Evan Gillmare.'

'Any children?'

'Yes, two: Verity, thirteen; Conrad, eight.'

'Any known illnesses or allergies?'

'She sometimes suffers from lapses in memory, and she's only really allergic to button mushrooms.'

As I speak, answering each of the questions without having to think, a nest of snakes has been crawling and slipping and sliding inside me. I know too much about Serena. I have been *stalking* her. I have been doing a horrible, horrible thing. And I knew what I was doing. I *knew* and I thought nothing of it. I felt justified because I wanted justice, I wanted a confession; I wanted to clear my name. And so I have managed to justify violating someone's space and life. Who am I? *What* am I?

'Have you contacted your friend's next of kin?' the receptionist asks.

I shake my head. 'We're not really friends.' I have to come clean now. She is a complete stranger and has no idea what I have been doing, but I have to start being honest somewhere and she will do. 'I knew her a long time ago.'

Such anger that could drive me to do what I have done was never part of my life until I entered prison. Now, I feel anger all the time, I'm always about two minutes from snapping. That has to stop. Right now. And I need to start putting things right. I need to be a better person: first by being honest, second by doing the right thing.

I push Serena's handbag through the little plastic cubbyhole behind which the receptionist sits. 'I think her mobile will be in there,' I say. 'I think it's better you look. You're a complete stranger, she probably won't mind as much.'

Efficient and calm, the receptionist unzips the black leather bag and reaches inside, while twisting the bag towards the not overly bright light hanging in her office area. It doesn't take her long to locate the small black square of Serena's mobile and flip it open. 'I wonder if she's got Ice on her mobile?' she says.

That's probably a cool new programme that everyone has these days that I've never heard of. That wouldn't surprise me. I'm still playing catch-up with the whole mobile thing. When I was with Alain I'd be looking around at other people when my mobile rang because I wasn't used to having a phone ring when I was away from home. I'm still a little 'witchcraft' about them, if I'm honest. I don't get how they work or why they're such a good idea – except maybe at times like this. But how many times in an average person's life do they have times like this? The receptionist twiddles with a lock of her grey-smattered red hair as she presses buttons and comes up with something, because she says, 'Good woman. She has Ice right here.'

'OK,' I say. *Weird, weird time to be playing a game on someone else's mobile, but who am I to judge?*

She smiles endearingly at my blank expression. 'It's a new thing: you put an entry on your mobile under "ICE" – which stands for In Case of Emergency – with the number or numbers of people to be contacted in such situations. That stops a lot of faffing around for us trying to work out who to call. She has this entry, which is very useful.'

'I see,' I say. *You mean faffing around like you've just done in telling me all that when you could have been dialling?*

The receptionist picks up her phone and dials a number. I take a few steps back because right now I do not want to be in hearing distance when the fall-out from her call begins.

Dr Evan Gillmare is not a happy man when he strides into the casualty department. His brown eyes dart around him, taking everything in, but I'd imagine he's been here several times before – he is a doctor, after all. He has rushed here, maybe run all the way, because his broad manly-man chest is heaving as he walks, and his face is set in a grim, determined expression.

Last time I saw him, he seemed so gentle and kind and concerned – everything you want from your GP, really. Now he is not a GP, he is a concerned husband of a woman who may or may not be at death's door, who may or may not be dead.

He speaks to the receptionist and I'm sure he's asking lots of technical, doctory questions, and receiving answers that may or may not be satisfactory. At the end of the conversation, the receptionist points to me. He turns and strides towards me, and I stand to greet him.

I should not be here. I should be at home, at my beach hut, on the beach, at the bottom of the sea, anywhere but here. I should not be about to speak to the husband of the woman I was stalking and, who for all I know, collapsed because of me.

'What happened to her?' Evan Gillmare asks brusquely. No greeting, no let up in the grim – almost aggressive – expression on his face. Not the bedside manner I was expecting of him after last time but, then, he is talking about the wife he recently split up with and he has no idea what my role in her collapse has been.

'We . . . we were talking and she collapsed. I don't know much else. They won't tell me because I'm not family.' *I'm not even a friend.*

He frowns a little, then says carefully, suspiciously, 'Don't I know you?'

'Erm . . .' *Why did I decide to become a better person thirty minutes ago? Why can't I still be the person who lied and stalked, because then I wouldn't be forced to tell the truth right now.*

'You came in to see me recently. You'd just moved to the area. Penelope . . . ? Penelope . . . ? Penelope Argyle?'

'I said my name was Penelope Argyle. It's actually Poppy. Poppy Carlisle.'

His body stiffens as a dozen little memories click into place as he matches the name to the face to the situation. I'm sure mine is a name he never wants to hear again, a face he'd never wanted to see in the flesh. And now he knows what I was doing, he would be well within his rights to have me arrested. If I'm arrested, I'm going straight back to where I came from – whether I deserve to be there or not.

'What happened?' he asks through gritted teeth, obviously deciding that finding out about Serena is more important than dealing with me. 'What *really* happened?'

'Like I said, we were talking . . . OK,' I sigh, I can't keep this up. 'OK, we were arguing. Things got a bit heated because I was trying to get her to confess. And right in the middle she just collapsed. That's the truth. She got wound up, and the next thing I knew she was lying on the floor, not moving. I don't know why. I swear, Sir. I didn't touch her. I swear.'

'And did she? Confess?'

'No.'

'Did it ever occur to you that she's innocent?' he asks.

'Did it ever occur to you?' I reply. 'She told me that you'd virtually thrown her out of the house. Her home. You wouldn't have done that if you didn't think she was guilty.'

'You know nothing about my marriage or my wife,' he says, tersely. I have not only touched a nerve, I've clawed at it with long, jagged nails. 'I haven't got time for this. I'm going to see how she is. Don't be here when I get back.'

'But I need to know if she's going to be OK,' I protest.

'So that you keep on stalking and harassing her and her family?'

'I haven't done that!' I object. It sounds so sinister when someone says it aloud. I can think it and it is bad, but it is far worse reflected back at me in the words of others.

'What would you call it then?'

'I . . . I just . . .'

'Go away, Poppy, or whatever your name is. Just leave my wife and my family alone.'

Before I can complain, he has turned his back on me and is striding towards the inner area of casualty. I stand where I am, not sure of what to do next. I do not want to go home. I do not want to be alone. I want someone to tell me it's going to be

OK. That she isn't going to die and I will be OK. That it's not too late for me to become a good person again.

The large, glass circular doors at the entrance of Brighton A&E hush as they open to expel me into the warm air.

I don't want to be alone. I've spent so many years alone and I don't want it now. I'm tired of it. I'm scared of it. Alone makes me cut up. Alone makes me do things I do not want to do. Alone makes me remember that Tina is gone.

I reach into my pocket and my hands cover my little box of witchcraft and I pull it out, hold it up in front of me. My fingers go to 'I' on the keypad, hoping that when I press it I will find an entry has been added under ICE, an entry that will be there for me to call in case of emergency. But there is nothing. Of course there is nothing.

I type in another letter and a number comes up on the screen. I stare at the number, I stare at the name. This is an emergency – there would be no way on earth I would be calling otherwise.

'Hi,' I say when the phone is answered after two rings that seem to last a lifetime. 'It's me. I really need your help.'

serena

Evan is sitting by my bed. His fingers are steepled together and he has a very serious, deep-thought-induced look on his face. He smiles when he sees I am awake, then he remembers he's furious with me, that we've separated and that he basically thinks the worst of me, so he tucks away the smile and instead wears his serious face again.

Sighing, I shift my line of sight to the ceiling. I'd like to move, but I can't. I feel like a herd of elephants has danced the chorus to 'Come On Eileen' on my body over and over again, and my head has been inflated with a canister of helium gas.

'What are you doing here?' I ask, not moving or breathing too much because it hurts. It hurts like the time *his* fist slammed into me over and over because I'd left a smear of lipstick on a white towel, and I'd ended up with three bruised ribs. But it's not as bad as the two broken ribs. That is how I judge pain sometimes, from the pain *he* caused me and how I managed to endure it.

'You collapsed, do you remember?' Evan says in his best doctor voice – reassuring, kind but ever so significantly removed.

Poppy. Shouting. Cement in my stomach, pain in my helium-inflated head, car parked on my chest, peace. 'Yes, I remember,' I manage.

'They think you fainted as a result of an extreme panic

attack. But they're going to run more tests to make sure it's nothing more serious.'

'OK,' I say, still not looking at him. He's my best friend, my husband, my soulmate – and he is talking to me like I am a patient.

'How long have you been having panic attacks?' he asks. 'Because this sounds like it's the end of a whole series of them, not a one-off.'

How long have I been having panic attacks? How long have I been on the edge of terror? 'Long enough,' I say. That's the sort of answer I'd give to a stranger, which is what he wants to be from the way he is behaving. I've known him visit patients in hospital, and I'm sure he isn't like this with them. I'm sure he is kind and caring and human.

'And how long have you had lapses in memory?'

'Long enough,' I say again.

'Long enough,' he repeats, quietly. I don't think he even realises he's spoken it aloud.

'How did you know I was here?' *Did she do it? Did she call him and compound my troubles?*

'The hospital called.'

Relief comes in a small, gentle wave that doesn't shake my bruised head and body too much.

'I met Poppy outside in the waiting area.'

My body sags, my eyes close.

'She's very worried about you.'

'I'll bet she is.'

'Her concern did seem genuine.'

'Hmmmmm,' I say.

'Look, I think you should come home. At least until you're better, then we can talk about it again. OK? I can sleep in the spare room.'

'No.'

'What do you mean, no?' He is confused and the confusion strips him of his cool voice and demeanour.

'I mean, no, I'm not coming home.'

'What?'

I turn my head, ignoring the tug of a thousand nerve endings being lit up with pain. 'I'm not coming home, Evan. I'm not coming back to the house where you walk around like you're allowing me to be there under sufferance, while I lie in bed dreaming up more and more elaborate ways to get you to believe I'm sorry for not telling you everything sooner. It's not going to happen.' I take a deep breath and hold on to my ribs as I do so. 'I'm not living like that again.'

'Again?'

'That's . . . that's what *he* was like.'

'He?'

'Him . . . *him* . . . the man who died.'

'Marcus Halnsley?' It feels like an abuse of love to have Evan say his name, to have the man I love humanise the man who almost killed me.

'Yes. I was scared all the time. On edge all the time. Trying as hard as I could not to upset him. Trying to anticipate the things that might enrage him and trying to fix them so he wouldn't go off on one. And I'm not doing it again. I was so worn out. Exhausted and scared. I can't . . . I *won't* do it again.'

'You need looking after, you can't rest properly in a B&B.'

'I'll survive.'

'Was he really that bad?' Evan asks.

I'm sure he's seen it all the time in his work. He's experienced it and counselled on it but still Evan wants to ask why I didn't just walk away. Leave. Move on from him. And the answer is always the same: I couldn't. Until the night he died.

That was why no one believed us. When Poppy and I tried to explain what he was like, tried to tell that he wasn't our victim but we were his, no one believed us because no one could really understand why one of us – let alone both of us – would put up with it. Would tolerate being so beaten down we would have done almost anything for him. Almost anything. It was the 'almost' that was important in the end. The things he did, the fact that Marlene refused to talk about him, made it easier for people to believe that we were a couple of spoilt vixens who seduced, abused and ultimately killed a decent, if flawed, man rather than that we were capable of putting up with so much.

'I don't want to talk about it,' I say.

'What about the kids? They'll be worried if they find out you're ill and not at home with them.'

'Don't do that, Evan. Don't use the kids. You didn't think of them when you were sitting on your high horse and throwing me out. Don't try to use them against me to get what you want now.'

'I'm sorry. That was a bit low. I just want you to come home is all. Even if the atmosphere isn't great, I don't want you to be too far away in case something happens to you again.'

'I'll be fine. Maybe time apart is what we both need right now. So that you can process stuff and I can . . .' I don't know what I'll do. I buried myself in my family, in being a wife and being a mother. I don't know much else. That's why I clean my B&B room every night and hide the knives; I can't break that habit.

'I don't want time apart. The past few days have been hell. I gave myself a glimpse of what life without you is like and I hate it, Sez, I really hate it.'

'I hate being without you and the kids, but I can't come back if you're going to be awful to me.' I swallow, the pain moving in waves down my throat and chest. 'I'm not saying you don't have a right to be angry. God, you'd be a bit of a freak if you weren't. But I can't be there with you treating me like a subordinate.

'One of the things I love about you, about being with you, is that we're equals. I'm not saying we can do exactly the same things as each other, but we're equals in every other respect. When we make decisions we make them together. When we argue it's as equals – not because one of us thinks we're better than the other and the other has to feel bad and accept they're wrong and start kowtowing to avoid trouble . . . You have no idea how difficult it is living like that. I never had that with you, I was always free to say what I like and think what I like and know that even if you don't like it, or you shout at me, you're not going to follow it with a punch, a slap, a kick, or withdrawing your affection. Until now.'

'What, you're scared of me?'

'No, but I was starting to be because I was starting to do things to make sure that I didn't upset you. It's no way to live a life: walking on eggshells in case you set someone off.'

Evan reaches up with his left hand and scratches his left eye. Verity used to do that as a baby, when she was tired or about to start a marathon cry. I used to pull her hand away and tell her no. A few times, in the middle of the night, when I had picked her up to resettle her I would scratch my eye, she would take my hand away as if to say, if she wasn't allowed to do it, then why was I?

'I'm sorry,' he says. 'I was just so shocked and hurt. I couldn't understand why you didn't tell me. And I just wanted to shout at you. I didn't mean to make you scared.'

'Evan, I'm not saying if I come home you have to forgive me or pretend you're not cross with me. I just want you to act as though you're cross with me as an equal and not expect me to creep around feeling bad.' I gingerly touch the centre of my chest. 'I could not feel worse about not telling you, believe me, and I will apologise and apologise and apologise – till the end of time, if I have to, but I won't come home and apologise if you're going to use it as a way to treat me badly. I'd rather suffer in a hotel and apologise from afar.'

'Come home,' he says immediately. 'We can work everything out later, once you've got the all-clear, just come home with me.'

'I'd love that. Honestly, I can't think of anything better.'

'You say that now,' he says. 'Wait till you see all the washing up, laundry and tidying that needs doing.'

He doesn't kiss me, or hold my hand. There's a long way to go before that can happen. It might not happen ever again, but at least at home I can be with the children and I can start to pretend I'm a boring old Brighton mother without a real-life skeleton buried in my past. At least at home I can be something approximating Serena again.

poppy

'I've been stalking Serena,' I finally admit to Alain.

'Serena? *The* Serena?'

I nod.

'Oh. OK. OK. Why?'

'To get her to confess to killing Marcus, of course. To get her to clear my name.'

'And did she?'

'What do you think? Fucking hell! If she had cleared my name, don't you think I'd be celebrating? I wouldn't have fucking called you, would I?'

'I guess not,' he says, moving his lithe body forwards in the armchair and linking his hands together as if in prayer. 'What's happened?'

'She's in hospital.'

'Oh . . . Oh, fuck. What happened?'

'We . . . we were arguing. And she . . . she fell and hit her head.'

'Is she all right?'

'I don't know. Her husband wouldn't tell me. He told me to go away. You have to find out for me. I have to know that she's OK. You have to help me.'

'She just fell?'

'Yes.'

'You didn't . . . You didn't hit her or anything?'

'What?! NO! Why would you ask such a thing? I wouldn't . . . I *couldn't*. What makes you think . . . ? What?! I mean, *what?*'

'Sorry, sorry,' he says, raising his hands in surrender. 'I had to ask.'

'Why did you have to ask? How could you think such a thing of me? I've never hit anyone except in self-defence. And that was cos some silly bint thought that I was an easy mark. She was a grass and, to throw suss off her, she tried to make out I was the grass. Got herself a room spin and blamed it on me. When I wouldn't bite she came at me, tried to make it look real. I only shoved her to get her off me. It wasn't my fault. That was the only time. I talked myself out of all sorts of trouble. I'd never hit someone first. Why would you think that I would?'

Alain gets up, crosses the wooden floor of his Hove living room and comes to crouch down in front of me. Gently, he reaches out, covers my hands in his in a warm, tender embrace. He looks up at me with his head to one side, like a man studying a painting he can't quite see properly in a gallery, like a climber wondering if he can really reach the summit of the mountain in front of him. 'Poppy, please, please don't take this the wrong way – because I think you're incredible. You are gorgeous, and generous and funny, and beautiful and kind,' he says. 'But you can also be *terrifying*.'

Me?

'I love you. I absolutely love you but sometimes without warning you switch into what I can only guess is prison-mode. You rant and start in with the prison slang, your body sort of toughens and you hold yourself in a covertly menacing manner, while your eyes seem to start scanning the room for danger or for a weapon. It's . . . terrifying.'

He is talking gibberish; I am only 'terrifying' when I need to be.

'And when you're like that, it's easy to believe you capable of anything.'

'Anything,' I repeat in a monotone. 'Including murder?'

He sighs and glances away for a moment, before increasing

his hold around my hands and refocusing his attention on me again. 'Anything,' he says, with a slight, resigned nod of his head.

'But I didn't . . .'

'I know, I know. Poppy, I believe you, that's why I never asked. After spending two minutes with you I knew you weren't a murderer, but there is something about you that is capable of causing harm. I'm sure you weren't always like this. I'm sure it's happened as a result of prison, but it's there. It's who you are sometimes. That's why I had to ask.

'I didn't mean to hurt your feelings,' Alain continues, gently. 'I have no idea what you've been through, and what has caused this in you. But, Poppy, it's there. And it's scary.'

'She gets to live this wonderful life and I . . . I get this. I get all of this. And even when I try to put things right, I'm the one who ends up in the wrong.'

'I'm not saying you're in the wrong. Hell, I'd want to clear my name, too. But I'm just not sure this is the way to go about it.'

'How else am I going to go about it? After my second appeal was rejected, I wasn't allowed to appeal again because there was no new evidence. Nothing to show and prove that I didn't do it. Do you understand what that means?'

He nods. Naturally, he nods because he thinks he does. But he doesn't, how can he?

'It means, it meant, that they didn't want to hear the truth. No one wanted to hear the truth. I was guilty as far as they were concerned – the evidence said so. But the evidence was wrong. I didn't do it.'

'I know.'

'No, you don't!' I scream at him. 'How can you know? I had all these years of being told I did it. People offering me the chance to change my plea to manslaughter so I'd get less time. People wanting me to go on courses where I talked about my crime and the impact it had and to be rehabilitated. But I wouldn't. I *couldn't*. How could I plead guilty to manslaughter

377

when I didn't do it? How could I talk about my crime when I didn't do it?

'They all kept wanting me to face up to it or they hinted that they wouldn't recommend me for probation, etc. But at the same time, because I wasn't like the other girls my age, because I kept working hard and I didn't get involved in the fights and the drugs and all of that, they kept trusting me with the important jobs. They knew I was trying to unofficially study for a degree, and they encouraged me to take an Open University course. But *still*, I was just a prisoner to them. I was a *murderer* to them. It was as if they knew on the one hand that I didn't do it, but on the other hand kept badgering me to admit I did.

'Twenty years of that.'

'I'm not surprised you're angry,' Alain says reasonably. 'I would be, too. Anyone would.'

'You don't understand!' I wail. 'You just don't understand.' How can he understand when he sums up things like that, when twenty years of that can be summed up with essentially, 'Anyone would be angry'?

His thumbs caress the palms of my hands and he leans as close to me as he can without touching me. 'Make me understand,' he says. 'I want you to talk to me until I do understand. OK?'

I stare at him. Wondering how I can do that.

'First, I'm going to call the hospital, find out how Serena is. And then you and I are going to sit here and you are going to talk to me until I understand what you've been through.'

I shake my head. 'It won't do any good. I can't make you understand.'

'You have to try because this can't go on, Poppy.'

'What?' He sounds like he is threatening me.

'You can't keep stalking Serena.'

'I'm not going to do that any more,' I say. 'I decided earlier I had to stop.'

He presses his lips together; there is something he wants to say but is scared to. What, in case I turn into Prison Poppy again? In case I become 'terrifying'?

'What you did,' he says, again with the gentle tone, 'what you did was compulsive. You did it because you felt you had to, not because you wanted to. I'm worried that you're going to feel like that again. That you'll start to watch her again because you won't be able to help yourself.'

'I will be able to help myself.'

'Poppy, you are innocent. You think the only way to prove that is to make Serena confess. How are you going to do that if you stay away from her?'

'I . . . I don't know, but I'll find a way.'

'That's what I mean. In a few days, when the horror and shock of all of this fades a little, when your feelings of resentment towards her start to resurface, you'll want to go back to how it was before. You'll want to be in control again. She was responsible for your world being destroyed, for you being powerless, so you are going to need to feel in control – *powerful* – again. The easiest way is to go back to what you've been doing.'

'You're wrong.'

'Maybe. But hold that thought. I'll just go get my mobile. It's got the number of someone at the hospital who may be able to help, OK?'

I nod at him. He is wrong. I may be a monster, and I may want the monster-maker to pay, but I won't do that again. Today was the wake-up call I needed. Serena's accident, her husband's face . . .

A shudder scuttles through me when I think of it all. I can't go back to that.

Alain's house is cosy, a nice place in Poet's Corner. It's all swish and posh, with fireplaces and floorboards and large windows.

I stand up, shake my legs out and walk the length of his room towards his work area. It is where most people have their dining area in similar houses I clean around here. His work area is a chaos of papers and books and in the middle, at the eye of the work storm, is his computer.

I've almost forgotten that his job and the fact he was originally 'researching' me is why we broke up. It's also the reason why I called him. After his questionable behaviour, he wouldn't be in any position to judge me. Although now I wonder if he would have judged me even if he hadn't done what he had done.

His computer swirls with a pattern of coloured lights that twist and turn on themselves. His desk is a mess. I don't know how he manages to work in all of this. I glance down at the notepad on his keyboard and my name jumps out at me. He has sketched my name in block capitals over several lines in blue biro. Some of the letters are filled in with sketchy blue biro lines, others are not. Inside the 'O' of my name he has drawn a little blue angular heart which has been coloured in, filled over and over until that section of paper is heavy with blue ink; until his heart is full.

I reach out to touch it, run my finger over the little blue angular heart. Touching it unhitches a new fear inside me, causing my stomach to spin. *'I love you. I absolutely love you.'* Alain said that to me.

How can he? How can he love a monster? *What is wrong with him?* I ask myself.

I did it, I loved a monster. I loved Marcus. And look where that got me. Look how it all turned out.

I hear the creak of Alain's footsteps as he paces upstairs, the murmurs of his voice as he talks on the phone.

What is wrong *with him?*

I snatch my hand away from the notepad and decide to leave.

I have to get away from here. From him. From this. I have to be on my own to think about what I'm going to do next. I'll find out about Serena some other way.

I just have to get away from this.

I ease the door shut on my way out. I do not want him to know that I've gone because he'll probably come down the stairs and try to stop me. Try to be nice to the monster. And we all know that you should not feed monsters, it only makes them want more.

★

'She's going to be fine,' he says to me.

I suppose I didn't try too hard to hide. Outside the beach hut, the world is crying, a torrent of tears is falling from the sky, bouncing down on the smooth skin of the promenade. I have been listening to it patter down on the roof, counting the tears as much as I can.

'They think it was a panic attack. She hyperventilated which is why she was unsteady on her feet and then hit her head. But she'll be fine.'

I am sitting on the green table – I didn't have the energy to unfold a deckchair – and I continue to stare at the floor as I nod at him, relief ebbing slowly into me.

His trainers are wet. They look expensive and they are wet. So are his trousers, and what I can see of his beige raincoat. The world has cried on him. What does the world have to be so glum about?

'Do you want to fuck me?' I ask him, not bothering to look up to watch his reaction.

His immediate response is silence. The kind of silence that says he does not know if there is a right answer to that question, if he is just being set up to fail.

'We could do it here,' I say. 'Or at your place. Even at my parents' house. Anywhere, really. If you want to.'

'Yes, I want to,' he says, carefully, as though stepping through landmines. 'But what I want more is for you to make me understand what you've been through.' He sits on the floor in front of me, ignoring the tiny puddle that has collected on that part of the floor from him and from the slight leak in the roof. 'I *need* you to make me understand.'

'Why?' I ask, knowing that if he says he loves me, I will probably throw up on him. The word doesn't mean anything. Marcus used to say it all the time, and I used to lap it up, so stupid and naïve was I. Marcus did not love me. He said he did. And then he did all those things. What he loved about me was being in control. You can say the word 'love' until it is the same as 'sand' or 'boobies': it doesn't mean anything if there is nothing behind it.

'You can't go on how you have been,' Alain says. 'You need to do this for you. All this rage is not going to leave you until you start to make yourself heard. Forget about Serena, forget about Marcus, just think about Poppy. And tell me. Tell me about Poppy. Tell me about her life. Tell me what you've been through. Tell me. I want to understand.'

I shake my head. 'I don't know how.'

'You do. Just start at the beginning.'

'The sky isn't a square of patchwork quilt,' I eventually tell him. 'Sometimes with two or three black bars running down it, sometimes with wire mesh upon it. The sky is vast and deep and capable of smothering me.'

part seven

serena

Evan wants me to tell him about that time. About what happened and why I got involved in it all.

He came into the bedroom three nights ago and lay down on top of the covers and started to talk. About nothing in particular and then suddenly he asked: 'What was *he* like? Beyond what you've hinted at and said, what was *he* really like? Why don't you ever say his name? What happened that night? The night *he* died.'

I had been stroking the fine bristles on his head and had to stop. My current life, the one I loved, had already been contaminated enough by the past. By coincidence after coincidence, by Poppy and her crazy demands, by my decision not to tell Evan, by my guilt that made me try to help Poppy. I had contaminated this life enough with the other life: I wanted it to stop. I wanted this life to heal, and that wouldn't happen if I made what happened a part of now.

I wanted separate compartments for everything and for that time − everything about *him* − to live in a compartment that was locked, with the edges glued shut and the keyhole blocked and the key lost for ever. I wanted *him* to stay gone. When I told Evan this, he seemed to understand. He still slept in the spare room, but he understood. Or so I thought.

Because right now, I am sitting on the bed watching him pack. He is leaving me. Not the kids, not our family, just me.

I cannot talk to him, I cannot be one hundred per cent open with him and he cannot take it any more.

It's an odd thing, watching someone leave you. Maybe that's why he had to stay in the garden that time he made me leave. Odd is the wrong word. Horrendous is probably closer to the reality.

I want to reach out and stop his large, gentle doctor's hands from moving. I want to take everything he has neatly folded up into his bags and put them back in the drawers and hang them up in the wardrobe. I want to stop him, but I cannot do so physically. I am frozen. I could do it with a few words. I could stop him, I could stop the dissolution of our marriage but that is something else.

'Don't you love him?' Mez had asked when I told her what he wanted on the phone.

I told her I did.

'Then why won't you just tell him?'

I explained it all, how I felt, why I had never told anyone let alone him.

'Ah well, I suppose it's your marriage. If you don't want to do everything in your power to save it, then there's nothing any of us can do. For the record, I think he's right to ask. I've always wanted to, but couldn't bear to hear it all.'

I had said to her that what she meant was that she couldn't bear to hear something that would confirm to her that I am what she thought I was, a killer.

'I thought we said we weren't going to talk about this,' she said.

She was the one who brought it up, I reminded her. She was the one who wanted to know what was happening with Evan, and I had told her.

'Fine, let me put it like this: if you're innocent, then you've got nothing to hide. Tell him.'

Which is not true. I do have something to hide. And I want to hide it from him. Of all the people on the earth, I want to hide it from him. I do not want Evan to judge me, to be horrified by what I have to tell him. I do not want him to be horrified like I am, every time I think about it.

'I think that's it,' he says, looking at his two holdalls, sitting by the bed like giant brown pebbles stolen from the beach.

This really is what *he* meant when he said he'd kill me. He meant he would kill everything good in my life. If Evan goes, *he* will have killed the children's happiness as well. Killed their chance to a happy family home with two parents. I'm sure we can find a different happiness without Evan, but they will be divided. They will have to live with one parent here, one parent there and the knowledge that I did not do everything I could to make it work.

Some things are irretrievable, irreconcilable, but not this. Some marriages and relationships become broken with no hope of being fixed. Not this marriage, not this couple. All I have to do is own up. Confess.

What is it the Americans say? I have to own my truth.

I have to own my truth so that I can try to make my husband not leave me. Even if he still does leave me, even if he can't understand or bear what he hears and still leaves, at least I'll know I tried. I tried everything to make him stay.

'I loved him,' I say.

Evan moves slowly, pivots on his sock-covered heels and turns to me. I am sitting cross-legged on the bed, unable to look away from the spot on the wall by the light switch. One of us has swatted a fly and not cleaned its dead body away.

'I'm ashamed of that,' I continue. 'I'm ashamed because after everything *he* did, I still loved him. I hated him, but I loved him, too.

'I can't talk about it because right up until the end, even afterwards, after he was gone, I was still in love with him. And I'm so ashamed of that. I'm so ashamed to admit that. He was awful. He was an awful, terrible person. For more than two years he mentally, physically and emotionally terrorised me; I watched him do the same to Poppy and I still . . . I could still love him.'

Evan sits on the edge of the bed. Listening. Listening to me tell him why I think so badly of myself.

'I could never admit that to anyone, not even Poppy, and I know she must have felt the same because she was there almost as long as I was. The things he did, and neither of us walked away. Even in court, when we were both fighting for our freedom, part of us, part of me certainly, but I assume it was the same for her, was protecting him. We told what he did, but not the full horror. No one would have believed us, anyway. How could anyone in their right minds love a person like him?' I shrug. 'I don't know the answer to it; all I know is that I did. And what happened that night only happened because of Poppy. I thought he was going to kill me, which was bad enough; I'd been prepared for that, I'd been willing to fight that, but what actually made me react, what actually made me fight back, was Poppy. I hated her, I really hated her, but the only reason I reacted, fought back, was because he was going kill Poppy, and I could not let that happen.'

poppy

I leave Alain sleeping and slip out of his bed, grab his grey dressing gown from the bedpost as I creep out of the bedroom, and put it on over my naked body outside the room. It's a chilly May, so the wooden treads of the stairs are cold underfoot as I go down.

We have been in each other's company non-stop for nearly forty-eight hours and most of them have been spent talking. In between we've eaten, drunk, showered and slept. Nothing else. I've been tempted to go home to get some clean clothes and my toothbrush and other everyday knick-knacks, but I know that once I step out of the door, once we open ourselves up to the outside world, the magic will disintegrate. I won't be able to talk any more, I won't be able to explain, I won't be able to make him understand.

I move in the darkened living room to the window and crack it open a fraction, not so much that the magic will start to leak out, just enough to let some of my smoke out. I curl up in the armchair by the window, and pick up my cigarettes and lighter, settle the ashtray on the arm of the chair, and slip a cigarette between my lips.

The past two days we have not talked about that night. I just didn't want to. It's hard enough to recall it, so I always avoid going through it in detail, picking over the carcass of my misguided notions of love, but now I will.

I flick shut my lighter and inhale life into the cigarette.

I'm going to allow myself to think about it because I am all talked out. All the stuff that was inside me is outside, so there is space, room for the memory to breathe. Room so I don't get crowded and panicked when I think about it.

My eyes slip shut and I whirl the clock back. My mind goes with it. Racing back to that night.

It didn't begin that night, of course.

No story begins the night it ends.

serena

June, 1988

I'd had enough. I'd had enough and I was leaving him.

It wasn't, as I thought, that I couldn't take any more. Of course I could. I could take more and more and more. I could take whatever he piled on top of me, the last two years had shown me that, but I'd decided enough was enough.

If it meant that he was going to kill me, then so be it. He could kill me and I wouldn't have to suffer any more. He had done that to me. I had nowhere left to turn: I could not talk to my sisters, I had no friends to speak of because he didn't like me hanging around with other people – I spoke to the people I worked with in the supermarket but never socialised with them. My whole life had become about him and pleasing him and not angering him and waiting for him to get rid of Poppy. It wasn't a life, I realised. I had finally grown up. I had finally stopped being the naïve fifteen-year-old he'd relieved of her virginity, who he had moulded into his willing puppet.

When he opened the door to me, he knew. He knew that whether he beat me or ignored me or told me he loved me it would do no good. I was not going to be with him any longer. One way or another we were over.

Looking back, I know I should not have gone there. I should have called and told him. But for some reason I went. I went to tell him and I went to tell him clearly and openly. Like the adult I had become.

His face, usually a mask of confidence, slipped for a moment when he saw my face and he said nothing, just stepped aside to let me in.

'And to what do I owe this dubious pleasure?' he asked as he led the way into the living room and threw himself on to the sofa. He lounged back, his head on one side as he stretched his arms wide along the back of the sofa and sat with his hips thrust slightly forwards.

'I came to talk to you,' I said, amazed that my voice, which had been small and timid and quiet for so long now, sounded different. It sounded like my real voice. The voice I used to speak with before him. It was normal and ordinary. Just like I was. Like I had been before this.

'So talk, baby. Got another appointment soon. You do know that tonight's Poppy's night, don't you?'

He said that, I think, to test me. To see if it would get a rise out of me, because that would be a weakness he could exploit, that would be proof to him that I wasn't completely free. I hadn't completely had enough. Disappointment circled his eyes and mouth when I just stared at him. For a moment, I'd wondered who Poppy was – so determined was I to do this, I'd forgotten that I shared him. That he probably wouldn't care that one of the people he tortured would no longer be around. Except, he might but only because he hadn't done the chucking first.

I cleared my throat, to make sure that I wouldn't stutter or pause, to make sure everything I said was clear and concise and to the point – like he always used to say my essays should be. 'I don't want to go out with you any more,' I said. 'I want this to be over. Tonight. I don't want to be with you any more.'

His eyes narrowed and the right side of his top lip curled upwards in a sneer. Slowly his eyes crawled over me, from the top of my head to my feet. I had tied my hair back, and I was wearing jeans, a loose white T-shirt and my stonewashed denim jacket. He hated those sorts of clothes on me. My biggest crime, though, was wearing my black plimsolls. He hated them most out of anything in my wardrobe. His eyes lingered on the plimsolls for a long time before they crawled their way back up to my face. The sneer deepened.

'Who is he? I presume this sudden bout of disobedience is down to some little oik you've picked up along the way. Who is he? Tell me, so I can kick the shit out of him.'

'You,' I said. '"He" is you. I don't want to be with you any more.' I would never have said something like that to him six months ago. Not even a week ago. But now I didn't care and I'd had enough so I could say whatever I wanted. When you don't care, you don't worry about being hurt, about being damaged. You are foolish and reckless and do the things that need to be done.

'You don't mean it. I wish you did, but you don't. You'll be back before the end of the week, begging me to take you back.'

'If it makes you happy to think that, then think it. I'm going, now. I just needed to tell you that.'

'Hey, wait.' He sat forwards, his arms open in surrender, it would seem, if I didn't know him. 'Is that it? Don't I get a say? Don't I get to talk to you about it? Try to change your mind, at least? I mean, what is it? Is it Poppy? Because I can finish with her tonight if you want me to. What is it? Because, baby, I love you. I can change.'

That was the whole point. He couldn't change. He wouldn't. He'd said it before, over and over and over again. And it always ended up the same: me in pain from a beating. Me lying to people about how I got hurt. Me trying to work out how to avoid it happening again. I was sick of it all.

'I don't want you to change,' I said. 'Because I don't want to go out with you any more.' Someone had once told me that if you kept repeating the key phrase in any speech it would ensure that your core message would stick in your audience's mind and it would make you believe one hundred per cent in what you were saying.

393

'But I love you, Serena. I *love* you. I've never felt like this about a woman before.'

His heart wasn't in it, I could tell. He was just saying the words with no feeling or emotion behind them. Or maybe that's the way it had always been; he'd always just been saying the words but with no emotion, no feeling, no love or sincerity behind them, and I hadn't been able to see that. I'd always been so wrapped up in the fear of not upsetting him, enraging him, not doing anything to make him hit me that I did not notice before. Everything about him was one-dimensional. I had only just seen that.

A knock on the door followed by a short ring of the bell interrupted us. That was Poppy's signal – mine was a ring and then a knock. 'Hold that thought, baby, hold that thought,' he said, leaping to his feet. Instead of going straight to the door, he went to the kitchen first. In that time, Poppy didn't knock and ring again. She wouldn't dare. She, like me, knew what was good for her.

What would be good for me would be to leave now. I'd told him, and I was sure he understood, so I should leave. Nothing here was mine: all the clothes and underwear were all stuff he had bought me. I did not want them, I did not need them. I could go back to dressing like the teenager I was now. I could stop dressing to please him.

'Poppy,' he said as he finally let her in. 'Go straight through. We've got a surprise guest – you'll never guess who's here.'

She was a little startled to see me. She stared at me, her eyes as wide, round and wary as an owl, but it was not because I was here. It was because of how I was dressed. It was because, in her wide-open owl eyes, I could see that she was where I was. She had come to finish it too. And she was scared that she'd not be able to do it with me standing there. She must have guessed from how I was dressed, from the plimsolls on my feet, that I was doing it too. That I had got in there first.

I decided to stay. I'd been about to duck out, to leave him to it, but I knew if I left he would take it out on her. And she would probably be trapped for ever. She would never be able to leave because even though she had reached her decision, even though she was going to do it too, my being there had thrown her. Thrown her to the point where she might decide to do it on another day. And if she did that, she'd never do it. I did not want to be the cause of her staying more than one second with him. I did not want her to suffer another beating at his hands. I hated her, but I didn't want anything bad to happen to her again.

When he entered the room, I realised that whether I wanted to or not, I was staying. From behind his back, I saw the glint of it. I saw the glint of the knife.

'I'm glad you're here, Poppy,' he said to her, still holding the knife behind his back. I wasn't sure if she had seen it or not, or what she thought he was doing, but from where I was standing I could see its outline, its dark brown wooden hilt, its wide, flat, sharp blade.

Poppy stood very still, not sure whether to ask why he was glad she was here, or to blurt out that she was leaving him. She clearly hadn't seen what he had behind his back, and knowing her as I did, I knew the second she did see it she was going to panic. Maybe not scream, but definitely panic. She wouldn't pretend not to see, she wouldn't start mentally chasing a plan of escape for us both, she wouldn't even try to see if she could communicate with me telepathically, she would hurtle headlong into a panic and we would both be lost.

He strode to the centre of the room, his eyes fixed on me, trying to intimidate me into not making a run for it until he was ready. I was probably meant to see what he had in his hand; I was meant to know that he intended to keep that promise he made to me.

'Poppy, darling, I've decided that the time is right. I know you've been mostly patient with me, but I've decided that you're right; I should dump Serena.' Poppy's owl eyes seemed to double in size.

'I've found a way for us to be together, and to make sure that Serena stays gone from our lives. Because you know what she's like. Even if I dump her, she'll just keep coming back and coming back, trying to make trouble for us. She might even tell people – it'd be lies, of course – that I started seeing her when she was my pupil. And you know how mud sticks. It'd ruin me. No, it wouldn't be fair on me to do that. So I've decided the only way forward is to make sure she never comes back. And never tells.'

Poppy's body was growing more and more still with every word he spoke. She had finally twigged what he was saying. She was starting to guess what he had in his hand. I don't know if he had ever threatened her with a knife – it's not as if we ever talked, compared notes, compared bruises, we disliked each other far too much for that – but if he had then she would know. She would know what he was about to do.

Of course, I didn't think he would do it. Not really. It wasn't as simple as slapping someone, or kicking her when she was down on the ground after a beating. It wasn't as easy as wrenching arms from their sockets, or punching her in the back as you tell her to walk away from you. Killing someone could not be that easy. He wasn't going to do it. He might threaten it, he might try to show he was serious by doing this in front of Poppy, but he wasn't going to do it. Not really. He couldn't. He wasn't that evil.

Moving slowly and carefully, he brought the kitchen knife into view. It was one of the larger ones. Sharpened by me just over two weeks ago. Its blade so fine it could cut clouds into thin, neat, even slices, ready to be topped with a thick layer of sunshine.

'I want you to remove her from our lives,' he said to Poppy. 'I want you to put an end to her and her blight on us. I want you to kill her.'

He was offering the hilt of the knife. Involuntarily, she took a step away.

'Come on, baby, it's the only way, you know it is. I want to be with you, and if you do this one thing for me, just this one little thing, we can be together for ever. We could . . . we could even get married.'

Yes, Poppy, you could get married. Why don't you ask Marlene how well that worked out for her? Why she's always calling, always showing up to tell him face-to-face to leave her alone. Why she told him last week she's going to take a restraining order out against him. Yes, Poppy, why wouldn't you want to marry someone like that?

The worst part was, of course, that if he had brought up marriage, I would have considered it. Even after all he'd done to me, I would have thought it'd be the fresh start we needed; I would have convinced myself that things would change after we got married, he wouldn't hit me any more, we'd go back to how we used to be. It wouldn't occur to me that how we used to be only existed because he had manipulated me into being with him. Slow and subtle, but definite. He had probably decided to seduce me from the moment he worked out what I was like: quiet, studious, a little bit of a loner – someone who could obviously keep a secret. There was never anything loving or real about our relationship, there was nothing to base a marriage on.

He held the knife out more forcefully, obviously surprised that she hadn't immediately snatched it from his hand and plunged it into my breast. *He won't let her do it,* I thought. *He'll just let me think he's going to let her, scare me into submission. He won't want to kill me, not really. Not really.*

'Isn't us being together what you've wanted from the start? What you've constantly dreamed of?' Again, his words were hollow and flat. Each of them said in his honey voice that used to convince me of anything – convinced me that he was sorry and it wouldn't happen again – but my ear had been tuned out of his frequency now. I could hear the truth. And the truth was he felt nothing. I should have been scared by that. Because a man who can do what he did to me and still live with himself rather happily must feel nothing. And someone who feels nothing will have no problem killing. But I did not feel scared.

Deep down, I knew, *knew*, he was good. He had some good-ness inside him.

I was still a fool, you see. Even though he had shown me time and time again who he was, I was still convinced he had a heart. It is thinking like that which got me to where I was. Which got me to standing in a man's living room while he tried to convince his lover to kill me. That convinced me to stay with a man who had another lover.

'Don't worry about the police; we'll tell them that she broke in, she attacked us, and we had to kill her to subdue her. We had to do it to stop her.' He moved the knife towards her again. 'Don't worry, I'll protect you. I'll lie for you.'

No. Poppy shook her head: no. I don't know who was more surprised – him or me. She followed her firm, clear headshake with words, a word: 'No.'

He took a few more steps into the middle of the room so he could see her but was nearer to me. 'What did you say?' he asked. I was about to ask the same thing. It was a revelation. To hear it. To know it could be done. To know it could be done to him: someone could and did say no – and it was heard.

'No,' she repeated, sounding, if it was possible, even more certain. 'And I'm leaving you. It's over. I don't want to be with you any more.'

I had never seen him so surprised, so taken aback – shock and disbelief were chiselled into his features.

'Did you just say no to me?' he asked. His voice was low, his tone dangerous, a viper about to strike.

'I don't want to be with you any more. And I'm not going to hurt Serena.'

He swung round to me, his eyes as narrow as possible. 'You bitches have cooked this up together,' he snarled at me. 'You bitches think you can do this to me?' His knuckles were yellow from his hold on the knife, his face bulging with red, the veins in his neck standing out like pythons wrapped around a tree.

'Me?' He jabbed himself with the knife to emphasise who he was talking about. He jabbed himself with the point of the knife, slitting a little line through his T-shirt and into his chest. He was so enraged, he did not notice. He did not stop. 'ME?!' he roared, jabbing himself again. Over and over. Screaming at us. 'YOU BITCHES THINK YOU CAN DO THIS TO ME?!' Jab, jab, jab. 'YOU ARE NOTHING WITHOUT ME.' Jab, jab, jab. 'I MADE YOU WHO YOU ARE.' Jab, jab, jab. 'IT'S NOT OVER UNTIL I SAY.' Jab, jab, jab. 'YOU HEAR ME?!' Jab, jab, jab. 'I SAY WHEN IT'S OVER.' Jab, jab, jab. 'I SAY. NOT YOU.' Jab, jab, jab. 'I SAY!'

I moved before he did. I knew, you see. I knew what he was going to do.

'AND I SAY NOW!' he screamed and lunged at Poppy, knife aloft. I had moved first; I grabbed hold of his T-shirt and pulled at him, my hands clamouring at him until they were on his shoulders, pulling him back and away. As he fell back on his heels, he dropped the knife. Quick as anything, Poppy swooped in, picked it up, to take it out of harm's way, I think. She gripped it, holding it tight and trembling slightly.

'GET OFF ME YOU UGLY BITCH,' he screamed, wrenching himself out of my hold, while his hand flailed back and caught me full in the face. The pain from my nose shot stars behind my eyes, my lip burst wide open and I tasted liquid iron in my mouth, felt it dribbling down my chin.

He slapped me again for good measure, throwing the whole weight of his body behind it and knocking me off my feet.

Poppy, shaking on the spot she was frozen to, finally moved as if to come to me, just as he turned to her. She was so close to him and he stumbled forwards as he swung back from putting me on the ground and the two of them came together. Him and his knife. It sliced its way into his side, stopping him in his tracks.

She looked as if she was going to scream. Scream with the horror of what she had done. Scream because he was stuck to her via a metal and wood object. Shaking and still on the verge of her scream, she stared at him with horrified eyes.

He stared at her with a startled expression on his face. From where I had fallen, I could see he was staring at her. Twice she had shocked him tonight. First by saying no and that she was leaving, now with this. Stabbing him. It was an accident, but it was still at her hands. Still something she was a part of.

His head moved down, to inspect the damage that had been done to him, to see how he had finally been opened up to the world.

Poppy's head moved down as well, and when her gaze alighted on the knife she let go of it, pushing herself away, as far away as she could get in that one step.

Nausea turned me inside out as he fell first to his knees, the instrument of his destruction still embedded in the space just to the right his abdomen. Nausea and horror petrified me as I watched him take the knife in his hand and then tug it out in one jerky move, and drop it on the floor beside him. Nausea and horror and terror punched me as blood pumped out of him, staining his white top, drenching the carpet and his jeans.

He made a soft thud as he fell to the side, rolled on to his back. Then stopped moving.

'I'm sorry. I didn't mean to. I'm sorry,' Poppy said, her voice shaking as much as she was. She was staring at her hands. Then her gaze flew to me. 'I didn't mean to. You saw. It was an accident. I didn't mean to. I'm sorry. I'm sorry. I'm sorry.'

I returned my gaze to him. Waiting for him to move. For his chest to go up and down, for him to breathe. Or move. Or show me that he was going to be OK, he was going to live not . . . Because things like this did not happen to people like me. I did not see people die in front of me. I did not. I did not.

He was so still. And calm. Calm. For the first time in so very long, he was calm. He had seemed so angry with the world, with the rage that used to eat him up and make him lash out physically, emotionally and mentally, that he did not know how to be calm. But there he lay. Still. Silent. Calm.

I got to my feet, my eyes glued to him the whole time. He did not stir, not even to breathe. He was really . . .

I almost ran across the room to Poppy, avoiding him,

avoiding going anywhere near him. I grabbed her bicep, feeling the muscle underneath my fingers go limp. 'We have to go,' I told her. 'We have to go.'

'I'm sorry,' she continued to whimper. 'I'm sorry.'

'Poppy,' I said, forcing myself to be calm. Forcing myself to ignore the bitter taste of fear dissolving at the back of my throat, the blood in my mouth, the spiky pain of my split lip. 'Poppy,' I repeated, calm and quiet and gentle. 'Poppy, look at me.' Something got through to her and she stopped saying she was sorry and lifted her gaze to me. 'We have to go, OK?' I said to her, brushing her sweaty hair from her face. 'OK? We have to go. Now. OK?'

She nodded quickly in return.

'Good. Good. Come on, let's go.' I slipped my arm around her shoulders and led her away. She could not stay to watch this. She was too delicate, it would drive her crazy. She would lose her mind if she stayed here, trying to apologise to whoever would listen. It was not her fault, it was an accident.

Outside, in the open air, I let go of her, and let her walk down the path on her own. She had stopped speaking, had stopped saying sorry, her shocked apologies stemmed by being away from him, I guessed. We stood outside, staring at each other.

Poppy was talking at me. Asking me things. I told her I did not know what I was going to say or do. I told her I did not have the answers. I blamed her for this happening. I tried to throw up. Tried to dislodge the horror that was jammed underneath my ribs. I couldn't shift it, it wouldn't move. I told Poppy to stay away from me. To leave me alone. And then I ran away. I could not stay a second longer in the road, near that house, near that man or near that woman. I wanted out. Away. I never wanted anything to do with any of them again. I ran and I ran until my lungs became a smouldering mass in my chest and my heart was almost still from beating so rapidly. I ran until my legs threatened to give out. I did not know where I was, I had not been paying attention. I stopped and I was outside a church. The lights were on, they shone out from the stained glass windows. There would be peace in there. I needed peace. I needed to not be on the streets. I needed to be somewhere that was inside and safe.

I pushed on the large oak door, hoping but not expecting it to be open. It gave way under the weight of the gentlest push and allowed me to enter, snuggled me up from the harshness of the outside as I stepped inside.

Moving slowly, my body now like a heavy weight, I genuflected to the altar before going to a pew. It was a habit of being in Church all those years of going with Mum had ingrained in me.

That was when Father Gabriel found me. He spoke to me, told me whatever I said to him in confession he would keep to himself. I told him then, that I had killed someone.

'Can you tell me what happened?' Father Gabriel asked.

I shook my head. No, I couldn't. I couldn't talk about it. I couldn't say any more than I had already said. And even then, I'd said too much. Who was this man who I had entrusted with this awful thing? He said he would not tell, but how could I know that he'd keep his word? Even if he did swear to God. Didn't the First Commandment override all other things? It was the first thing that God told us we mustn't do; how could I expect him to keep that to himself?

'I have to go,' I said.

'Serena, you are safe here. You don't have to tell me what happened. You don't have to do anything you don't want to.'

I leapt to my feet. Father Gabriel stood too. 'I have to go,' I told him. 'I have to go.'

He would know what happened in the morning. When someone found *him*. And Father Gabriel would be able to tell the police that the person responsible was called Serena. And they would find me. I had to leave now. I had to go home and tell my parents.

'Are you sorry for what you have done, Serena?' Father Gabriel asked in a serious tone he had not used since he sat down with me.

'Yes,' I said. 'Yes, I am. I didn't mean to do it. And I'm sorry.'

'God the Father of mercies, through the death and resurrection of his Son has reconciled the world to himself and sent the Holy Spirit among us for the forgiveness of sins,' Father Gabriel said. 'Through the ministry of the Church may God give you pardon and peace, and I absolve you from your sins in the name of the Father, and of the Son, and of the Holy Spirit.' He made the sign of The Cross as he spoke.

He could not absolve me. No one could. I had done the worst thing on earth. He could not absolve me.

'You will be fine,' he said. 'I know you will do the right thing.'

I ran all the way home. I was a bundle of heat and sweat and burning pain; my body felt like one huge strained muscle, my mind was whirring and spinning and I could not catch my breath as I came towards my house. The living room light was on, the brown nylon curtains drawn and the corridor light out.

I should go in and tell them everything. Ask them what to do next. I should tell them and let them look after me.

'Hello, Serena,' Mum called as I shut the door behind me.

'Hi, Mum, hi, Dad,' I called back. I started up the stairs on shaking legs.

'Where are you going?' Dad asked.

'*Dallas* is on,' Mum added.

'I – I need the toilet,' I said. 'And I'm really tired. I think I'll go to bed. Let me know what happened tomorrow.'

'Goodnight,' Mum called.

'Goodnight,' I replied.

They didn't call me into the room, so I must have sounded normal. My legs managed to work underneath me as they carried me up the stairs. In the bathroom I slammed and locked the door, then collapsed behind it.

This is a nightmare. This is a nightmare I am never, ever going to wake up from.

I didn't even realise I was crying until I went to splash water on my face and discovered it was already wet. Discovered that

I didn't know when I started crying, and I didn't know when I would stop crying.

I didn't know much of anything.

Except that *he* was dead.

poppy

June, 1988

Marcus had been the focus of my life for two years. Everything had been Marcus, Marcus, Marcus. From when I first met him in the park, to *that* night, it seemed that everything I did was for him.

But in the end, I could not take any more.

He wasn't always violent and nasty. If he was, then it'd be a no-brainer – I'd have to leave. He started off as sweet as pie. He made me feel special and wanted and loved. He told me I was pretty, he made me feel clever, he seemed to think the world revolved around me.

Obviously Serena was around, but he explained all that and I was so in love with him so quickly that I lapped up everything he said. And he said a lot. Then he did a lot.

Still, I kept thinking that I could fix it by being perfect, by being the person he said he wanted me to be. I was careful with what I said, what I wore, what I did. I tried not to mind about him and Serena and I never told anyone anything about us. I did everything he wanted but he *still* found things wrong with me, he *still* found reasons to hurt me, to batter and brutalise me physically and emotionally. He had me so convinced of my worthlessness, my inability to exist without him, that I knew he was right when he said no one else would look at me. I accepted it when he told me that I was the lowest of the low. I believed him when he said he would show my parents and my brother and sister, and anyone else he could think of, pictures of Serena and me kissing.

That was the only reason I went there that night: I wanted the photos so no one could see them. I was sick to my stomach every time I thought about them, and how they could have been a million times worse if Serena hadn't refused to do anything after that kiss. He probably kicked the living daylights out of her after I left but she had told him he could do what he liked but she wasn't going to. That was another thing I was grateful to her for, because I would not have been strong enough to say no. Those photos were going to ruin my life – I had to go there to get them back.

That night was 'my' night with him. He'd decided that to spare us the pain of not knowing who he wanted to see when, and to stop us just turning up – like we'd ever do that – he gave us 'nights'. The reality was, of course, it controlled how we felt when we weren't with him, because we'd always know that he was with *her* and would spend the night wondering what they were doing together.

As I walked towards his house, I thought again about how I was tired of being scared all the time, of watching what I said and did and felt. I knew I had to end it. I was terrified, of course – every step was a shaky, nervy movement towards the most dangerous person I knew. But I had to do it.

With my heart in my throat, and my whole body shaking, I rang the doorbell, then I knocked.

There was a look in his eye that threw a band of cold, naked terror around my core. The last time he had looked that crazed, I had needed five stitches at the base of my head. He was also standing funny, his body tense and jittery, while he held something down by his side, just out of my line of sight. I didn't dare provoke him by trying to catch a look at it, that would be a bad way to start this.

He had been on the verge recently of spilling over into becoming a constant terroriser. It was a slow build up to the worst times, when he would find little things that irritated him to complain about. I would be on edge more than normal. Tense and fretful, jumping every time he spoke, shaking every time he came near me. Sometimes it would get so severe that I would wish he would just do it, he would just hit me so it would be over with. He could hit me and I wouldn't have to teeter on the edge waiting for it to happen.

His eyes had a new level of wildness about them, I realised. This was not like the five-stitches time, this was far worse. He would probably kill me if he caught me looking for the photos – from the look in his eye, it might just be a miracle if I walked away unscathed. 'Poppy, right on time. Come in, come in. Guess who's come for a surprise visit?'

I was suddenly scared. I had the urge to turn and run back the way I had come, to try to escape, because something didn't feel right. Things rarely felt right around Marcus nowadays, but this time it was worse. Whoever his surprise visitor was, they had set him off and I would be paying the price.

What's she doing here? I asked myself when I saw Serena standing in his living room. My insides flipped over when I looked at her properly. *What has she done? What has she done?* I started to fret as I took her in. She was standing up straight, for starters, and had clearly grown in the past two years because she seemed even taller than usual. Her long plaits were swept back into a ponytail, which sat at the base of her neck – Marcus would hate that. He liked her to wear it loose around her face, or pulled back into a high ponytail; this ponytail he would consider slovenly and casual. She was wearing denim – jeans and a denim jacket over a loose white top. At his house, we always had to dress like girls and wear tight clothes. If we ever went out without him – a rarity in itself – we had to dress down, but still like girls.

I stopped breathing when I saw the flat, black plimsolls on her feet.

She'd done it. She'd gone and done it. *No! No!* I was screaming inside. *I was meant to do it tonight. I was meant to leave him.*

Now, he'll never let me go. As long as he had her he might have let me go, but now he won't. Now I'll be stuck with him for ever.

Marcus, the crazed look still in his eye, moved to the centre of the room so he was between us. He was going to hit her in front of me. For the first time he was going to hit her as I watched and I wasn't sure I'd be strong enough to stop him. It had taken every piece of courage to come here and to do this, so how could I do anything else against him?

'I'm glad you're here, Poppy,' he said, while my mind was tearing around like a caged animal, scared and desperate to escape. I didn't know what I was going to do. I stared blankly at him, listening to him with my eyes because my ears were not sending the messages to my brain. I could not understand anything except the overriding need to escape. Not only from this room, but from this life I had become entangled in. I had almost been out until Serena derailed it.

He was staring at her, but talking to me. He was talking about a way for us to be together, I realised after a few more seconds. Which was the last thing I wanted. I just wanted – *needed* – my life back. He was talking about dumping Serena. 'Even if I dump her, she'll cause trouble for us. She won't leave us alone, and she'll start rumours about me seducing her when she was a pupil of mine. It'd be a lie, of course, but mud sticks. It'd ruin me. Which I don't think is fair. So, I've found a way to make sure that she never bothers us, never tells or comes back.'

Oh God, oh God, he's going to kill her. He's going to kill her and he's going to make me watch. It had hit me what he had in his hand, what he was going to do. My whole body solidified with the horror of what I was about to see happen. I could not let it happen but I was not strong enough to stop him. The ice cream day exploded in my mind. How she took a beating for me because I had been clumsy. The day in the kitchen came to mind – how she lied to him that I had my eyes open. I did not know Serena, I did not like Serena, but I did not want her dead. I did not want anything bad to happen to her.

He seemed to be moving in slow motion as he brought what was by his side – a large kitchen knife – into view.

'I want you to remove her from our lives,' he said. And my heart stopped beating. 'I want you to put an end to her and her blight on us. I want you to kill her.'

He was offering the knife to me. *Me*. He wanted me to . . . I stepped away from him and away from *it*. I needed to put as much distance as I could between me and it and him. Did he really think I could . . .

'Baby girl,' he encouraged in his sweet, soft voice, 'come on now, it's the only way, you know it is. I want to be with you, and if you do this one thing for me, just this one little thing, we can be together for ever. We could . . . we could even get married.'

I did not want to be with him for ever. I did not want to be with him at all. I stared at the knife. It was probably the largest knife I had ever seen. It probably wouldn't even fit in my hand, even if I wanted to take it. Which I didn't. How could I? Was he mad? Did he think that I would be capable of doing that? Or was it that he saw me as so brainwashed that I would do anything he told me? Probably, because, up until this moment, that's all I did. Everything he told me to do I did. It had started with asking me, then telling me, then ordering me. It had all been leading up to this moment; it had all been pushing and dragging me to this moment when he would order me to do the unthinkable and I would do it without question. I would do it because that's what I did.

More firmly, he offered me the knife. 'Isn't us being together what you've wanted from the start? What you've constantly dreamed of?' *Not in a long while,* I wanted to tell him. *What I've been dreaming of lately is getting away from you, never having to be around you or have anything to do with you again. I just want my life back, I want me back, to be the person I was before I fell into this thing with you.*

'Don't worry about the police; we can convince them that we had no choice. We'll tell them that she broke in, she attacked us, and we had to kill her to subdue her. We had to do it to stop her.' Even more decisively, he pushed the knife towards me. 'Don't worry, I'll protect you. I'll lie for you.' What you would do is blackmail me until the day you had no further use for me, then you would call the police and tell them the truth.

No, I do not believe you and no, I will not do it.

I shook my head. Then I said the word that was often at the back of my tongue with him but was never said because of the consequences. I said the word and it fell off my tongue like light fell on water: gentle and beautiful. 'No.'

He reeled back a little, as if I had hit him because he had never expected to hear that word from me. He moved a little backwards, so surprised was he, unintentionally, I think, putting himself closer to Serena. 'What did you say?' he asked, his voice and face both dripping in shock.

Having done it once, I could do it again. Louder, more definite, more meaningful. 'No,' I said again. 'And I'm leaving you. It's over. I don't want to be with you any more.'

He was floored but standing up; as if Mike Tyson had delivered a knockout blow to a Weeble – he wobbled but he did not fall down.

'Did you just say no to me?' he asked. He had turned from a coaxing man to someone who looked ready and capable of murdering me with his bare hands.

But I had to finish this. If I backed down now he would kill me – not tonight, maybe, but at some point in the future. He would know that I was not strong enough to see an escape plan through and he would increase the torture and the pain until he had nowhere left to go but to kill me. 'I don't want to be with you any more,' I said to him. 'And I'm not going to hurt Serena, you can't make me.'

His eyes became angry slits as he turned violently towards Serena. 'You bitches have cooked this up together,' he said, his voice so full of anger he could barely get the words out. 'You bitches think you can do this to me?' I had never seen him incensed before, I realised. I had seen him angry; I had thought

I'd seen him incensed, but this was it: his usually beautiful, smooth features were swollen and red and almost pulsating with this new, never-before-seen ferocity. His whole body was taut and he could barely move with the rage that was burning him up.

'Me?' He stabbed himself with the knife and I gasped inside as the cut it made sprang blood. 'ME?!' he screamed suddenly, and stabbed himself once more. 'YOU BITCHES THINK YOU CAN DO THIS TO ME?! YOU ARE NOTHING WITHOUT ME. I MADE YOU WHO YOU ARE. IT'S NOT OVER UNTIL I SAY. YOU HEAR ME?! I SAY WHEN IT'S OVER. I SAY. NOT YOU. I SAY!' The screaming was not as scary as the way he kept stabbing himself in the chest, stomach and abdomen with the knife to punctuate what he was saying. Stabbing and stabbing and stabbing. I fixated on that, more than his screaming. More than his words, what he was physically doing was more terrifying.

'AND I SAY NOW!' he shouted suddenly.

I didn't have time to be scared, I didn't have time to react when he went for me, the knife moving in a smooth arc towards my chest. Serena was quicker than him, and she grabbed him from behind, yanked him away. As he stumbled backwards, the knife flew out of his hands, clattering on to the floor in front of me. They were fighting and he was trying to get free from her. And if he did, he'd go back for the knife and use it – on me or on her. Without thinking I snatched it up, moved it out of harm's way.

He was shouting as they struggled and I didn't know what to do. I should help her, I should stop him, but the loud *SMACK!* he delivered to her face freed him from her and made me jump. *SMACK!* He slapped her again, and she was on the ground, her mouth gushing bright red blood all down her face.

Marcus twisted back towards me and stumbled, still unsteady on his feet but ready to rip me into pieces, to tear me apart. He stumbled forwards again, this time with a silent thud; a short, sharp, heavy jolt at the end of it.

A short, sharp, heavy jolt that embedded the knife in his side.

A moment of stillness passed. Nothing happened, nothing moved, nothing breathed.

He looked like an earthquake had opened up on his face with his mouth gaping and his eyes wide.

I heard myself screaming. No one else could hear because I could not move enough to actually make the sound. But inside, at my core, I was screaming. I was screaming and screaming because something had happened and I didn't know why or how. Something had happened and now Marcus was . . . Inside, deep inside me, I screamed. I screamed and screamed and screamed. I screamed because I did not know what else to do. But it did not leave my mouth, nor my body. I was screaming inside because in my hands I held a knife, the knife on which Marcus was impaled. I had done this. I had put a knife in him. I didn't mean to. I didn't mean to and I couldn't stop screaming inside.

His eyes, so wide and white around his blue pupils, began to fill with red; his mouth still hung open as he stared at me. He stared and stared at me, silently asking me what I had done. How I could I have done it.

I watched his head move, lowering to stare down at what was sticking in his side, at the redness that spread outwards like red shockwaves from the epicentre of the wound, linking up all the tiny little stab wounds he'd made. I dared to look down and saw that my fingers were still curled around the hilt of the knife, my body was still a part of his.

I tore my hand away, the horror of the situation causing me to back away as well.

Another soft thud as Marcus dropped to his knees.

A third soft thud as he closed his hand around the knife and yanked it free of his body.

A fourth soft thud as he dropped the knife, then fell on to his side before eventually, with the final soft thud, he flopped over on to his back.

'I'm sorry,' I said to him. 'I didn't mean to. I'm sorry.'

I turned to Serena: I had to make her understand that I didn't mean to. He walked into it, fell into it. I didn't do it to him, I didn't mean to. 'I didn't mean to. It was an accident. I didn't mean to. I'm sorry. I'm sorry. I'm sorry.'

She didn't respond; she didn't tell me she knew it was an accident, she didn't say it was OK, she didn't even seem to know I was there. She was staring at him, just staring and staring at him.

'I'm sorry,' I told her across the room. 'I'm sorry. I didn't mean to.'

She was standing beside me. 'I'm sorry. I'm sorry. I'm sorry.'

'Poppy, Poppy.' She was saying my name. 'Look at me. Come on, Poppy, look at me.' She was still bleeding from the lip, and a trickle of red was coming out of her nose. Her ponytail was awry, her face was wet and she looked as if she had been in a fight.

'I'm sorry,' I told her, holding out my hands. 'I'm sorry.'

'We have to go, OK?' she said to me. She gently moved my hair away from my face, and my face felt cool again, instantly better. 'OK?' she said, her voice soft and kind. Kind, she was being kind. She had saved me and she was being kind. I had to do whatever she said. And she was saying we had to go so I had to do that. I had to go.

I nodded to her that I understood. I understood that whatever she said I would do, because she was nice to me.

'Good. Good,' she said. She was kind again by putting her arm around me. She was being lovely to me. Serena wasn't as cold as I thought. She was lovely and she was lovely to me, even though I had done that thing that was an accident. 'Come on, let's go.' She moved me towards the door. I moved my legs but she moved me, gently telling me with a slight nudge or tug where I had to go.

Outside, the air was cold and sharp against my face. Another welcome cooling moment. What month was it? Why was it so cold? What day was it?

I was going to ask Serena, but she had let me go. She had stopped holding on to me, something that I needed more than anything, and stepped away.

'What are we going to do?' I asked her. Because whatever she said, I would do. I owed her that. I owed her everything, so all she had to do was tell me and I would do it.

She didn't say anything. She didn't look as confident as she did back in the house. Now she was shaking, and she looked small and scared; her eyes were leaking and making her face even more wet.

'Serena,' I asked again. 'What do we do now?'

'I don't know, Poppy,' she said. 'All I know is that we had to get out of there.'

'Do you . . . do you think he's . . . ?'

'Yes,' she said. 'Yes, I think he is.'

My whole body lurched at the thought of what I had done.

'What are we going to do?' I asked her.

'I don't know,' she said.

'Are you going to tell?'

'I don't know.'

'What about the police?' I asked her.

'I DON'T KNOW!' she suddenly shouted back. 'I don't know anything. Stop asking me questions because I don't know.'

I covered my mouth with my hands, as my breaths started to come in short, gasping bursts. 'Oh my God, M—'

Serena was suddenly bent over, twisted towards the evergreen bush outside his house and she was retching, her body moving in violent jerks, but she was throwing up air, just dry heaving.

She stood upright and rubbed at her dry mouth with the back of her sleeve. 'I can't be here,' she said out loud. 'I just can't be here.'

'Can I come with you?' I asked. I didn't want to be alone and she was the only person I knew who would understand why.

'Do you understand what happened?' she asked. 'Do you?

Why would I want you to come with me? Why would I want you anywhere near me?'

'It was an accident.'

'I don't mean that. None of this would have happened if you'd just left us alone. We were doing fine until you came along.'

'But that's not true. Serena, just—'

'Leave me alone. Just leave me alone.' She took off so suddenly, so fast, I didn't have a chance to stop her, to beg her to let me come with her. She ran away from me, from where we were, as fast as she could, leaving only the sound of her plimsolls slapping on the paving stones behind her.

I turned in the other direction, heading for home. I had nowhere else to go. I had no other friends because I had no friends – Marcus had seen to that. I had to go home, tell my parents everything, warn them about the photos, tell them I was sorry and have them listen and love and comfort me.

I knew they'd protect me, they'd look after me. I started to walk faster as the thought of them holding me, kissing me, telling me it was all going to be OK grew stronger and larger in my mind. I had to get home. I would be safe and loved and looked after there. Home. My legs moved faster, faster and faster until I was running, pounding the streets, tearing them up so that I could get home as soon as possible; I could get to safety as soon as possible.

The house was in darkness when I arrived. Everyone had gone to bed early and I was alone. I stood in the blackness by the front door, listening. If I heard even a creak from my parents' bedroom I would go in, tell them everything. I didn't want to wake them to tell them this; it would be too distressing to wake from sleep to find your daughter has killed her boyfriend you knew nothing about. I could not do that to them.

I waited and waited and waited. But nothing, not even the slightest, tiniest creak. *In the morning*, I decided. *I'll tell them in the morning.*

In my bedroom, I ripped off my clothes and bundled them up. They had spots of blood on them. I had to hide them for now – I didn't want Mum or Dad or, worse, Bella or Logan to come in in the morning and find them. I pulled back the carpet from under the window and removed the two loose floorboards. I pushed the clothes in with everything else Marcus-related I kept there.

Still shaky and shaking, I used my pot of Pond's to remove the grime and the invisible spots of blood on my face, the drops of wetness I had felt in my mind splashing on my face. I could not run a bath without waking everyone up so I cleaned myself as best I could, then I climbed into my bed and pulled the covers up over my head. I was safe under there, no one could find me or see me. No one would know what I had done.

In the morning, I would tell Mum and Dad everything. They would know the best thing to do and I would be all right. All I had to do was get to morning and then I could tell them.

Morning came and went and I could not find the words to tell. Morning after morning came and went, until I ran out of mornings and Mum and Dad found out everything from Detective Inspector Grace King, ringing from North West London CID.

And the nightmare that was the story of The Ice Cream Girls began.

serena

'I'm going to tell you something that I haven't ever told anyone else. It is the reason why I have a conscience that taunts me, it is why I feel so guilty all the time. But when I tell you, I want you to try not to judge me too harshly. I want you to try to understand why I did what I did.'

Evan and I have moved into the back garden. I wanted to talk out here because the words, the secrets I tell him, will rise up into the night air and will be scattered by even the smallest of breezes; they will not stay in our house, locked into the bricks and mortar of our home, distantly echoing to us what I have done whenever they get the chance.

Out here, we can talk and the truth will be set free. We were laying side by side on the grass, staring up at the night sky. Now, because of the gravity of what I have said, Evan is sitting up, he has crossed his legs and he is sitting in front of me, waiting to hear my confession.

I sit up, too, match his position by crossing my legs in front of me. I gently reach out for his hands and take them in mine, slip my fingers into the spaces of his. I want to hold on to him while I tell him this bit. I want him to know that what I say was then, it is not now. It is not me.

My lips are dry and parched under my tongue as I try to wet them, my throat is tight and taut. I do not want to say but I have to. I have to be honest.

'About an hour after I got home, I got up and I got dressed.'

Evan's face gives nothing away, no sign at all of what he is thinking. His fingers have tightened around mine, though, which tells me he is scared of what I am about to say.

'I sneaked out of the house.'

Evan's fingers tighten like mini vices around mine, clamping my fingers to him, holding me secure.

'I walked for a while – it was late and it was dark and I was scared – but I had to do it. I want you to understand that I had to do it. No matter what it meant about me, I had to do it. I walked and walked until I was far away enough from home, then I found a phonebox and called an ambulance. I told them that someone was hurt, I told them the address and then I hung up.

'I know he was a despicable human being and he had terrorised and abused me for years, but I could not stand the thought of him being there all alone. I . . . I still loved him. And the thought of him lying there for days on his own was too much to bear. It was bad enough, distressing enough, that I would never see him again. I had to make sure he was all right. As all right as could be.

'When the police told me he had died later, from a stab wound to his heart, I realised that if I had gone out earlier to make the call, he would probably still be alive. It was my fault. I let him die. I've hated myself ever since.'

'You weren't to know,' Evan says. 'You weren't to know that Poppy would go back and kill him.'

'No, but I had . . . I wanted it to end.' I press my hands on my face, my fingertips pushing on to my closed eyelids, trying to hold back the tears, trying to hold back the flood with a thimble. 'I wanted him gone. I just wanted him to stop. To be out of my life, to leave me alone. And I knew, deep down, I knew the only way that would happen would be if he was . . . I just wanted him to stop hurting me, so I wanted him to stop being. I feel so guilty because I wished it. I willed it.' I shake my head, my fingers dripping with the tears that run down them. 'In more than one moment, I wished him not here any more.

And then it happened. Because of that fight, because he stumbled after he hit me, it happened. She could go back and kill him because he couldn't fight back. I wished him gone and it happened.'

'You weren't to know that he'd die, Serena. You can't blame yourself for that. And you called an ambulance, you didn't just walk away and forget him.'

'It was too late, though.'

'I know, love, I know. But why didn't you tell anyone that you called the ambulance?'

'Because when Poppy and I both went in to tell the police what happened, to tell them it was an accident, they wouldn't listen to me. They kept jumping to conclusions; they kept telling me that I had killed him. If I told them I had left the house that would mean the only confirmation from Mum and Dad that I had come home when I said I did would be gone. And if I told Mum and Dad, they might have had to lie to save me. And I had caused them enough pain already.'

Evan nods in understanding.

'I did want to go back, you know? I wanted to go back and stay with him until help came. I wanted to be with him because when he was on the floor he looked so peaceful, so gentle. He hadn't been like that in so long, I just wanted to be with him like that one last time. He was like *him* again.'

Unexpectedly, Evan asks me, 'Why did you love him?'

'I—'

'Not why did you stay with him; why did you love him? What was it about *him* that made you love him in the first place?'

'I can't remember,' I admit. 'I remember that I loved him. I remember that it was this hideous, achy feeling every time I thought about him not being with me and him being with her, but I can't remember what I felt for him. I can't put my finger on something and go, "Yes, that's it". You know? I can't say with any sort of certainty that he was kind, because I don't think he was. I can't remember one instance of him being kind.

419

I remember him being nice, although that got less and less often as time went on. I remember him being so proud of me when I did well at school and in my exams. I remember feeling safe with him at the start, but then that went away.

'You see, that's where my memory loss is worst. I can't remember anything that would make him special and worth everything he put me through. It's one of the biggest things that's fallen through the memory gaps in my mind.'

'Maybe it's not memory loss,' Evan says.

'What do you mean?'

'Maybe you don't remember because you didn't really love him,' he says gently.

'But I did. I know I did.'

'Maybe you've spent all these years trying to convince yourself you did because that would explain why you stayed with him after he beat you and raped you and terrorised you.'

I look away, look down at the grass beneath us, rather than look at my husband, my mirror of truth.

'Sez, he traumatised you for years. My guess is that you were so scared of him telling your family, of him going through with his threat of killing you, that you found the only way you could cope with staying with him was to try to convince yourself that you loved him.

'And maybe you did in the beginning. You were a teenager, he was your first love, he was probably the first male to show any real, genuine interest in you. He knew what he was doing – older men who go out with young girls always know what they're doing. What sort of girls to pick, who will keep a secret, and who can be manipulated into doing whatever they want.

'He picked you and you fell for him, that's nothing to be ashamed of. I'm sure he'd done it to several other young women. Telling yourself that you loved him to explain away being scared of leaving is nothing to be ashamed of, either. Sweetheart, you did the best you could. I truly believe that. You found the strength to walk away in the end. So many women – grown women – don't.'

Evan's words creep over me, climb over my skin and sink into my body like a host of twinkling stars – they light up my blood and make me hot all over. *Maybe I didn't love him.*

'You're a good person, which is why you feel guilty for what Poppy did. But, Serena, you've got to let *him* go now. Let him go and get on with your life.'

'I have.' *Maybe I didn't love him.*

'No, you haven't. You are letting him rule your life, still. You are protecting him, still. You almost let our marriage fall apart rather than tell me the truth about him. You need to let him go, and you need to let the person you were when you stayed with him during his abuse go.'

'But how?' *Maybe I didn't love him.*

He shrugs. 'No idea. That's something you've got to work out for yourself, because if I tell you you'll be doing what I would need to do to let someone and my past go. You need to do what *you* need.'

'Maybe I didn't love him.' I say to myself. 'Maybe I didn't love him.' Which means it's OK to hate him for what he did.

It's OK to not feel sorry every second of every day that he isn't here.

It's OK to want to let him go.

It's OK to decide to live in my present rather than be shackled to my past.

poppy

I finish up the final cigarette in the packet, and breathe.

In and out, in and out, in and out. Breathe.

I never got to see Marcus again. That hasn't occurred to me until now. He was such an important part of my life, he *was* my life for nearly two years, and then suddenly he was gone. My last image of him was of him laying on the floor, the look of shock and agony on his face.

He might have survived if it wasn't for Serena. He might have survived to continue to haunt me. Because now, looking back properly, I can see that he would never have let me go. He would have kept on and on until he had me back under his control or he had ruined everything about my life.

I did not want him dead; I did not want him gone like that. But was there another way? Did Serena think the same thing? Did she realise that he would never let her go, he would never leave her alone because nothing was over until he said so?

Is that why she did it?

During the trial, she said he used to say he'd kill her if she ever left. Did she see this as her only chance, her only way out, as a simple case of 'me or him' and he lost?

I do not know. I'll probably never know, because this is almost it for me. This is my chance to leave prison for good. To shake off Marcus and the shockwaves he sent through my life to the lives of everyone I knew. When Marcus hit me, everyone got bruised. I have to stop living my life for him, about him, around him.

I have to find the way to move on. To stop being the naïve fifteen-year-old he met, to stop being the terrified eighteen-year-old who went to prison, to stop being the angry thirty-eight-year-old who came out into the world.

If I don't, I'll wear myself out; I'll become tired of the world, just like Tina. I'll start to believe that the only way out, the only way to free myself of the yoke of the past, is to do what she did.

'You all right, babe?' Alain asks as I slide back between the cool sheets, and wriggle towards him, ready to rob him of his heat.

'Yup, I'm going to be,' I say. 'I need you to take me some-where. I need to go and see some people.'

'OK,' he mumbles.

'Thank you,' I reply, hoping he knows I don't just mean for the lift he is going to give me.

part eight

serena

'I come bearing sketches and fabric swatches,' Medina says the second I open the door. She holds up her large A3 sketchpad and her fabric book, just to prove it.

'And I come bearing wine and cake and chocolate,' Faye says, indicating to the overflowing wicker hamper she is cradling in her arms. 'All of them samples of the items I'd like to contribute to your wedding, if you'll let me.'

Without a word, I open the door wider to let them in and I lead the way to the kitchen and stand by the cooker, where I had been heading when the doorbell rang. Vee is at Zephie's house and Con is at his friend Mattie's house, and for the first time since I had them I am not obsessively worrying about what is happening to them without Evan or I there. I believe they can be safe away from us.

I have started to let *him* go. I have started to let fifteen-year-old Serena go, too. I am starting to let go of the past because, for the first time since I did not tell my parents a teacher had stroked my face, I am in control.

Evan is out doing something. Probably seeing Max and Teggie for a few afternoon drinks, but I didn't ask. He does what he does when he does it. I've found it so much easier these days to not worry about it. He is, after all, scrupulously honest.

I wait for it. Wait and wait and wait. But it does not come. My conscience does not chime in to taunt and abuse me, to needle me and remind me how bad I am. Not completely gone, but fading. It is only a whisper at the most extreme of times. It will be a murmur soon, and hopefully then silent.

Faye dumps her hamper, which looks heavy and cumbersome, on the kitchen table and Medina dumps her stuff beside it, followed by her bag and mobile. Faye takes off her glasses and balances them on top of the chocolate in the basket. This must be serious if the glasses have come off.

'So you two think you can buy me off with a wedding dress and wedding food?' I ask my sisters.

I am not in that position I used to be for all those years. I am not indebted to them any more. Telling the truth does that. I do not have to accept their gifts without comment; I do not have to accept anything they offer me – good or negative – because they can't intentionally or unintentionally ruin my life any more. And I do not feel as guilty any more for almost ruining their lives. I lied to them as a teenager, when I was naïve, young, scared and thinking I knew it all. They have lied to me all our adult lives. They have treated me like they have, not because of what I did to their lives but because they think I am the lowest of the low, a killer, a murderer. Which is bad enough. For neither of them to have ever said it . . . That is what I am most hurt about. They have just thought it and never challenged me on it. We are meant to be close, the three of us. We are not. Because they have lied to me over and over and over. They have resented me. They have feared me. They have branded me killer. And all in secret. Families, especially ones that went through what we did, are not meant to have those kinds of secrets.

'We also come bearing apologies,' Medina says.

'Big, huge apologies,' Faye adds.

'What for? Aren't I the criminal? What do you two have to apologise for?'

The two of them share the same shamed expression. 'Evan called,' Faye says.

'He asked why we thought you were capable of ending someone's life.'

'And said he was more curious than anything, not demanding we change our minds. He was just asking.'

'And when I thought about it, I realised that I didn't think you were. I really didn't,' Medina explains.

It's going to be one of *those* conversations. Where the two of them start and finish each other's sentences and I get so confused that I might as well be talking to one person. In fact, if I close my eyes, with their similar voices, it could almost be like talking to one person. It's incredible that after twenty-odd years of living apart, they can still do that.

'Neither did I.'

In unison, they pull out a chair and sit down. I remain standing by the cooker, unwilling to join them, unwilling to pretend that this is anywhere near settled.

'The thing is,' Faye says, 'you're my little sister. *Our* little sister. And we're meant to look after you.'

'And we didn't.'

'I felt so guilty, not insisting on meeting him that time. Helping you to keep it secret from Mum and Dad.'

'And there was me, giving you advice on make-up and how to get a boy to like you and, all the while, I was sending you off into the clutches of that pervert.'

'We both felt responsible. He was beating you up and neither of us noticed.'

'I was very good at hiding it,' I stated. Because that's what you do in those situations: you hide it.

'That's exactly it, Serena – you weren't. You became so secretive, hiding things, when you'd never been like that. We should have noticed that you'd changed, that you weren't being as open and relaxed as you usually were.'

'But we didn't.'

'We just accepted all those excuses you had for how you got hurt.'

'When I found out, I wanted to hurt him for what he'd done to you.'

'Really hurt him. I mean, *really* hurt him.'

'But I couldn't. We couldn't. And I suppose I started to believe that you'd have been justified if you did do it.'

'It would make it all seem better somehow. That you didn't just take all those beatings and let him get away with it.'

'And it became part of my way of handling the situation. Believing you did it to defend yourself, to make it all stop, made me feel as if I had done something.'

'And that I'd protected you when you needed me to.'

'But we were angry with you as well – for making us feel like that. For making us genuinely think at any point that murder is the answer. When it isn't.'

'And we were angry with you for lying to us. For keeping things from us.'

'One way to deal with that anger, and the guilt of feeling that anger towards you when you'd obviously been the victim, was to believe you'd done it.'

'So, over the years, it became a reality. That you'd killed him. When, really, the crime we were punishing you for was lying to us. Because when Evan asked me that, my instinctive answer was "I don't think she is".'

'Me too. We both know you could never kill someone on purpose. You could never murder someone.'

They pause, the one-person conversation staged by two people takes a hiatus, and they both stare at me. I stare at them.

'You thought I was guilty all this time,' I eventually say. 'You and Mum and Dad. All this time.'

'Not Mum,' Medina says. 'She's always believed you were innocent. Always. She's never had a moment's doubt. She said she would understand why you'd be pushed to it but you never could.'

That eases the pain a little. Knowing that means I have not lost all my family because of *him*.

'The hardest bit is knowing that all this time you've thought I was a liar,' I tell them. 'I thought you believed me and even if you hadn't, if you'd said so, I could handle it. But you've resented me for all these years and I had no idea.' The emotion rushes to my face, to my eyes, to every nerve ending in my body. I want to be strong and firm and indignant. I want to show them that I am capable of existing without their approval. 'All these years, all the things you've both said, the arguments you've had with me and each other, it's all because you thought I was . . . That's what hurts. You hated me for lying but you did the exact same thing to me all these years. For longer.'

'I never hated you,' Medina says, almost knocking over her chair to come to me. Even though I stiffen in her hold, she throws her arms around me and squeezes, resting her head on my chest. 'I never hated you.'

Faye is slower off the mark because, in general, she is more reserved. But she throws her arms around me and Medina, then rests her head on my shoulder. 'I never hated you, either.'

'Even if you had done it, we could never hate you.'

'You're our sister, we could never hate you.'

'It was about us, how the situation made us feel. We weren't really thinking about you.'

I wipe angrily at my tears. Some indignant, hurt woman I turned out to be. At my big moment, when I am called upon to make a damning speech about family loyalty and standing by each other and being honest at all costs, I turn to mush. I cry. 'Tell me something,' I ask. 'Did you believe the stuff that was written about me? In the papers. Did you believe it? Even for a minute?'

'No,' they both say at the same time. They're lying, of course. It was so persuasive, so pervasive, I started to believe it. I started to believe I was a vixen who seduced an innocent teacher and, together with my lover, tormented and toyed with him for weeks, months and years before we finally got together and tortured then killed him.

'You're lying to me again.'

'No, we're not,' Faye says.

'Sez, if we believed the stuff that was written, how could we then be so angry that you didn't tell us you'd been abused by that man?'

431

'Either we believed you were a cold-blooded killer or we believed you were his victim.'

'It would be oxymoronious to believe both things.'

'It would be *what*?!' Faye and I ask together.

Mez throws her hands up in the air. 'Don't start on me. We're meant to be sorting out our relationship, we're not going on about my use of words.'

'Or non-words,' Faye says.

'I said don't start on me.'

She moves back towards me, bringing the warmth and soft, cushiony comfort of her body. 'I'm sorry,' Mez says.

'I'm sorry as well,' Fez says.

'So am I,' I said. 'I wanted to tell you. I just couldn't. First of all I couldn't because I thought it would be OK, and then because I was scared. I knew if I talked about it, *he'd* come and get me. There were so many times I thought it would be OK. Those were the times when he was sweet to me, told me he loved me. And I thought I could make it OK if I did everything he wanted, exactly how he wanted it. And it never was. I'm sorry I kept it from you. I'm sorry.'

'Don't say sorry,' Medina says.

'Never say sorry. Not for that. Not for being too scared to leave,' Faye says.

'None of us know what we'd do in that situation. Especially when you're fifteen.'

'None of us,' Faye echoes.

I move my arms to encompass them, to hold them closer to me.

'We're going to be OK,' one of us says. 'We're going to be OK.'

'What's all this?' Evan asks of the items spread out on the table in front of me. Medina has left all her wedding-related paraphernalia and will return very soon to get on with it. She is planning on working through the night to get it done, especially now that Adrian is helping out more.

'Wedding stuff.'

Evan comes over from the fridge, where he's grabbed the milk and is downing the last of the carton. I decide to pretend I didn't see him do that. He picks up a bottle of the wine that Faye left in her hamper. 'Wine?' He examines the label and his eyebrows shoot up and he gives a long, low whistle. 'You know how much this stuff costs a bottle?'

'No idea,' I reply.

'About too-much-pound-fifty.'

'Faye wants to give it to us as a present. Medina's going to virtually kill herself to get the dress done. She's paying for the material as well. And to get my shoes made to match.'

'Ahh, the Witches of Ipswich are back together. I'm glad.'

'Thanks to you,' I say to him.

'Now, what would my life be like without the witches?' he says, dropping a kiss on my nose. 'I'm glad it's all sorted with you three. I didn't like to see you so unhappy.'

'It's not completely sorted. It'll take more than a chat and a bottle of wine to undo twenty years of pain and resentment, but we'll get there. That's what families do, isn't it?' I run my hands over Medina's books and magazines, as well as the big file that I'd started and compiled. It is bursting with pages and coloured section dividers and magazine tears and vital info. 'You know, I've been thinking,' I say.

'Ah, but have you been reading the streets?'

I roll my eyes but don't comment. 'I was thinking, this –' I indicate to the wedding in front of me, 'this isn't really us, is it? It's all a bit flash and showy and we're not like that. We're more . . .'

'Private and low-key.'

'Yeah.'

'I've been thinking that, too. But I thought you wanted this.'

'What I really wanted was the proposal, I got that.'

'So you don't want to get married again?'

'Yes and no. Not like this, I suppose is the real answer. And we could do so much with that money.'

'Yeah, we could.'

'I knew saying that would speak to the real you,' I say.

'I've got an idea.'

'What's that then?'

'I can't tell you, but I want you to trust me. We cancel all this and I put my idea into motion, what do you say?'

'I say, if you decide we're going to use the money to buy you a flash car, you'll find yourself a very unhappy man. Very unhappy.'

'Trust me, sweetheart. Trust me.'

'Can I just emphasise the *very* of the "very unhappy".'

'Trust me.' He flashes me his crooked grin. I love this man. I'm amazed that I can forget that sometimes. That in the everydayness of everything, I can forget to remember that I love him. And I love the family we've made. I almost let all of that go – I almost allowed my guilt to let him walk out. A shudder runs through me. Never again.

'Here we go,' I say, hefting up the file into his arms.

'What's all this?'

'The wedding you need to cancel. I totally trust you to do that. Have fun, I'm off to pick up Con.'

His face is crumpled in dismay as he stares at the file in his arms. 'This isn't fair, you know,' he calls at me as I go to find my car keys.

'Oh, yeah, speaking of fair,' I call over my shoulder, 'don't forget to call Mez and tell her I won't be needing the wedding dress.'

'Ahhhh, *man*! She's your sister.'

'And you, apparently, are the wedding canceller. It's in the job description. Right up there with, "gets to decide what we do with the money".'

'This still isn't fair,' he shouts, as I open the front door. 'It's not fair at all.'

I love you, I tell him in my head.

serena

Ange is leaving her house as I drive past and I see that she is moving stiffly, awkwardly, as though she is in pain. As though every tiny bump that is walking is causing her agony.

I hit the indicator and pull over. I get out of my car and barely remember to lock it behind me as I run to cross the road. If I think too much, I won't be able to do this. I won't be able to give her the chance to change her life. Maybe if someone had done this for me, *he* would still be alive. And I would not have been living with all this guilt for all these years. Maybe I would have been able to escape.

'Ange,' I call to her as she heads for her big posh car.

She stops and looks up at me, confusion in her eyes and fear on her face as she glances around. Scared that someone will see us together. Scared of what will happen if he finds out she was talking to someone.

'Ange,' I say, standing in front of her. She looks thinner, paler, too much make-up piled on to hide the bruises, her hair too straight and pulled too far forward to hide the marks on her neck. 'I know you're scared,' I tell her.

'Scared? Of what?' She almost convinces me that I am delusional, that she isn't constantly on edge, she isn't constantly chasing that perfect, impossible equilibrium that will keep him happy and stop him from erupting.

'I know you're scared and I understand. I've been where you

are. Except I didn't have kids who had to watch me get beaten up. But I want to tell you my story so that, hopefully, you can get out before things end for you the way they did for me.'

'I really don't know what you're talking about,' Ange says.

'He ended up dead, you see,' I say. 'He tried to kill me and because I fought back, he ended up dead. I wish I had found the strength to walk – run, actually – away from him before it came to that. But I didn't. And because I didn't, he ended up dead. And if it hadn't been him, it would have been me. He told me often enough he was going to do it and, that night, I believe he would have.'

Ange is stilled now. She is no longer searching for spying eyes that are going to tell on her, she is staring at me. Something has hit a chord. Something has resonated so closely with her, she knows that I do understand. I really was where she is.

'Do you want me to tell you?' I ask.

She gives a brief, stiff nod of her head.

I inhale, drawing strength from the fact I've told this story once now. The second should be easier. The second time should remind me I have finally escaped *him*. I am not protecting him any more and because of that, because I can tell the story again to a complete stranger, I have begun to bury him for good. 'I thought I loved him. And I thought it was my fault he was so angry. His name . . . his name was Marcus . . .'

poppy

'Of all the cemeteries in all the world, we had to meet in this one,' I say to her.

I'd know her shape, her outline, anywhere. And after I walked around and around looking for the right place, the right plot, I'd been only a little surprised to find her here. It is, after all, where this story ends. Where our story ends.

Her whole body became uptight and rigid when she heard my voice and, when I come to stand next to her, her profile is tense from her clenched jaw and her eyes are staring hard at the earth in front of her.

'Are you still following me?' she asks.

'No, Serena, I am not still following you.'

And I'm not going to follow her any longer. I've come to realise that even if I was cleared, vindicated, there would always be people who would still think I was guilty. And if not guilty of murder, culpable in its execution. And the two people who I would be doing it for, the two people who I would want more than anything to think me innocent – Mum and Dad – would still think I was guilty. They will always think I'm guilty – because I was there. Because I wasn't the perfect little girl they thought I was. That was a hard pill of reality to swallow but, now that I've swallowed it, I realise that I can stop. I can stop this, and start again.

'So how come you're here at the exact same time as me?' she asks.

'Because I had the exact same need to come here and lay his ghost to rest at the exact same time as you?' I reply.

Her body relaxes a little as she says, 'That wouldn't surprise me.'

'It's weird, isn't it? How we keep doing the same thing at the same time? We finished with him at the same time, we went to the police at the same time. We're clearly so basically similar, it's strange that we were never friends.'

She turns her head to face me, incredulity on her face. 'We were never friends because you were sleeping with my boyfriend,' she reminds me.

'Oh, yeah,' I say. 'I suppose that would put the mockers on most friendships, wouldn't it?'

'Just a bit.'

We stand in silence for a while, staring at the patch of green in a stone plot in front of us. The grass is slightly overgrown, but is not unkempt; I suspect it is cared for by the cemetery, not by anyone else. There are no flowers. The inscription is simple:

Marcus Halnsley
Devoted father

I wonder if his son ever visits, or if he tries to hang on to memories of his father in other ways. I wonder if anyone visits? Over the years, I got about six letters from other girls – just like me, just like Serena – who said they knew what he was like, they had also fallen for him at a young age, and he had brutalised them, too. They got out, they said, but if they hadn't, they might have had to do what I did.

I threw those letters away because I did not do it but, thinking about them now, I wonder if any of those girls came to visit? Came to lay his ghost to rest.

'Do you miss him?' Serena asks.

How am I supposed to answer that? What is she really asking me?

'I'm just interested to see if you do,' she adds to my silence.

'I do sometimes. And it freaks me out. Even now, I'll see something or hear something and I'll think, I have to tell him, and then I'll catch myself and what I'm doing.'

Marcus has been haunting me for years or, rather, I've been revisiting all my mistakes, all the dark, scary places of my personality through him for years. So I don't miss nasty Marcus, he has been with me all the time, but do I miss the other Marcus? The one I fell in love with?

'I used to miss him a lot at first, after it happened. That freaked me out. Because sometimes, in my mind, it was like he wasn't how he was. All I could remember were the good things about him. How sweet he could be, the special little presents he'd buy, those paper boats he'd make, and the way he'd be so excited when he was helping me to study. I'd miss that. I'd crave that again.'

'That's the worst part of missing him, I think,' she says. 'I kind of remember those things, but then I don't. I remember the presents and the help with studying, but in a haze, really. I'm still trying to work out why it took me so long to walk away.'

'Because you didn't know any better,' I say to her. 'Neither of us did.'

'I suppose not.'

'And that's why I can sort of understand why you did it – you thought you had no choice. When you're in that situation, it's hard to see a way out. I do understand. I have been there, literally.'

She turns fully to me, faces me square-on. 'Poppy, I'm only going to say this one more time. I didn't do it. There, I've said it. Never to be repeated. If you don't believe me, there's nothing I can do.'

Memory loss. That's the only explanation. She told me herself that she has it sometimes, she's had it since she was with him and needed a way to cope, so I believe her when she says she didn't do it – because she genuinely doesn't remember doing it. Doing something like that is so hideous, so gruesome, your mind wouldn't have any choice but to erase it from both long- and short-term memory. That's why she sounds so convincing, why she believes she is innocent: she doesn't remember doing it. It had to have been her.

Because if she didn't do it, then it was me.

'Does your husband know you're here?' I ask.

'He drove me here.'

Alain, my boyfriend, drove me here, and is waiting for me, too. Waiting to take me where I need to go next. 'Oh, good. Good. I'm glad. He seems like a good guy. Really nice.'

Her head creaks around to look at me again, her gaze a hard stare. 'You stay away from him,' she says.

'Oh, no, I didn't mean . . .' I open my hands in surrender. 'All that's over, Serena. The stalking, trying to get into your life, all done with. I promise you. I am going to get on with my life, what is left of it. I can't promise not to hate you from afar, but I'm not coming near you again. In fact, if I never see you again, it'll be too soon.'

'Feeling's mutual,' she replies.

Dr Evan obviously hasn't told her that I went to see him, and I'm grateful for that. I'm eternally grateful that she doesn't know how bad, how obsessed, I got.

She crouches down, and reaches for the smooth, simple lettering chiselled out of the grey smooth stone. She runs her fingers over it, taking his name and his description in by touch. Then, slowly, she takes her hand away and stands.

'Goodbye, Sir,' she whispers as if she were talking to her teacher. 'May you rest in peace.'

As she turns away she gives me a smile, probably the first genuine one she's ever aimed at me. 'And may you live in peace, Poppy,' she says over her shoulder before she walks away, and out of my life.

serena

'All done?' Evan asks as I climb back into our car.

'Yup,' I say. 'All finally done.'

'Where did you go, Mum?' Conrad asks, as if he didn't ask when Evan pulled up just down the road from the cemetery. Sometimes I think he asks questions more than once to try to fox us, to catch us out.

'She told you already,' Vee says. She doesn't like sitting in the back but, on a family trip, she has no choice. And this family trip is being taken with the aid of the wedding fund.

'Someone I used to know died a long time ago and I went to visit their grave and to say goodbye.'

'Oh, right,' Con says.

'Right, so is everyone ready for the trip of a lifetime?' Evan, the only one of us who knows where we're going, asks.

'Yes!' we all say together. All he would tell us was to pack for a hot summer and a cold winter – in other words bring as much as possible. Con, of course, has no trouble showing his excitement; Vee is far better at hiding it, but not from me. I'm excited, too. Now that I have finally said goodbye to Marcus and to Poppy and that part of my life, I can immerse myself fully in the people I have sitting around me. I still hide the knives – and did so before we went away – and I still can't eat ice cream, but change takes time.

'Right, so where are we going?' I ask my husband. He also

told me to pack a dress I wouldn't mind wearing to get married in.

'OK, you're going to love this,' he says, turning to us. 'We're going to . . . pick up our new motorhome!'

He is greeted with silence.

'Our *what*?' I say.

'I thought, what can I spend that money on that will be for all the family, and will mean that we can always afford to go on holidays? So I invested the cash in a motorhome.'

'Mum, is Dad joking?' Vee asks me desperately. Not as desperate as me, I'll wager.

'Yes, Vee, your father is joking. Because he has known me for ever and he has to know that I am not the type of person who uses a "chemical toilet" – especially not a second-hand one.'

'It is going to be fantastic,' Evan says. 'We can go off on holidays whenever we like: we don't have to worry about hotel bookings, we can sleep wherever we fancy. We can read the streets whenever we like. It's going to be fabulous, I promise you.'

'Wow,' breathes Conrad, 'we have a chemical toilet?'

'We certainly do, son, we certainly do.' Evan slaps and rubs his hands together, then reaches for his seatbelt. 'Let's go, let's go. I can't wait to get there.'

'And where is "there" exactly?'

'Wales: well, Portmeirion. Where there is a lovely little church, right by the beach, where we could get married tomorrow if you want?'

'So, that's the choice: motorhome and wedding, or no motorhome and no wedding?'

'Yup.'

I reach for my seatbelt. 'Portmeirion, here we come.'

'Ah, Mum!' Vee complains.

'Mum, are there whales in Wales?' Conrad asks.

'I don't know,' I reply. 'Why don't you ask your clever big sister? I bet she'll know.'

'Vee, are there whales in Wales?'

'I'm not telling you.'

'Mum, she said she's not telling me.'

'That's probably because she doesn't know.'

'I do, too.'

'She does, too.'

I reach over and squeeze my husband's knee as he begins to take us into our future. 'We made two good ones, there,' I whisper so as not to disturb the arguing in the back. 'I can't think of anywhere else I'd rather be.'

poppy

They open the door the second I unhook the gate and they come running at me, flying into my arms, almost knocking me over as our bodies connect halfway up the path.

None of us even attempt to speak, we just cling to each other: holding on and holding on.

My precious, precious sister. My precious, precious brother.

My arms do not seem wide enough to hold them as close as I want to, my words would not be deep enough to tell them everything in my heart. For nearly twenty years I've wanted nothing more than this. To hold them. To be near them.

Now is the time for us to set things right, for me to concentrate on what is truly important. Not *that* past, *this* future.

They're here now, we're here now, we do not need anyone or anything else.

Bella slips her hand in mine and Logan wraps his arm around my shoulders and we head back into the house, so close that every step we take is a step in time, a step that sews up the years we were apart, pulling the seams together until they can barely be seen, and we can pretend that they never really existed.

marcus

marcus

June, 1988

I never thought she had it in her.

After those bitches left me bleeding, I knew I had to get to the phone. It was on the other side of the sitting room, but I knew I could make it. It was only really a nick in the side – looked worse than it was. But I wasn't going to tell those two that. I was going to tell them I'd nearly died, make them feel as guilty as they should.

Who did they think they were, saying no to me? To me! I was going to teach the pair of them a lesson they'd never forget. And I was going to make each of them watch while the other got her lesson.

I managed to roll on to my front, even though it hurt like hell. It hurt like nothing on earth. I really did need an ambulance before I lost any more blood. I slammed my hand down on to the carpet, dug my fingertips in and then heaved myself forwards. It worked – I moved. Only a small distance, but I was that bit closer to the phone. It wouldn't take long to get help. And once I was at the hospital, I would think it over slowly, clearly, soberly. I would find the perfect punishment.

Suddenly she was standing there, framed in the doorway, staring down at me. I should have known, by the look on her face, but I didn't ever think. Not her, not her of all people.

'Marlene? How did you get in?' She'd obviously turned up

on one of her 'leave me alone or else' visits, but that didn't matter right now. She was there and she could get me help. 'Arggh,' I groaned, clutching my side and willing the pain to go away. 'Never mind, never mind,' I gasped. 'Just get me an ambulance.'

She did not move and she did not speak. She stood still and watched me. Maybe she was in shock, seeing all that blood.

'Marlene!' I shouted, trying to snap her out of it. 'The phone. It's over by the window. Call me an ambulance. NOW! MARLENE! NOW!'

She nodded and then the stupid bitch went towards the sofa. No wonder I divorced her. Couldn't take an order that one. I never did manage to knock any sense into her, either. 'Not the sofa. The window. The window!' I told her.

I couldn't see what she was doing so, screaming out in pain, I rolled over on to my back as she came towards me again. She had my knife in her hand. And then she was holding it up above her head with both hands.

'What are you doing?' I asked, even though it was obvious.

'Goodbye, Marcus,' she said.

'Marlene? Marlene?!' I screamed. I couldn't move. I couldn't stop her because I couldn't move, I had no strength left in my body. She said that about me once. During the divorce, during the pack of lies she told the judge to get full custody of Jack, she told the court that I had *forced* myself on her. Me, her husband, had forced her. And when my solicitor had rightly asked why she didn't stop me, she replied, 'I couldn't move. I couldn't stop him because I couldn't move. It was as if all strength had left my body.'

'I'll make sure Jack remembers you as a good man,' she said. 'Not the low-life, violent, rapist scum that you are.'

'Marlene?! Marl—' I hate that I died with tears on my cheeks and her name on my lips. *Her* name. After all those girls who had adored me over the years, she was the one I was with when death us did part.

From right beside her I watched her lean over and use the

hanky in her pocket to wipe the handle clean. To erase all evidence that she was ever there and she did this.

She wasn't good enough, of course. Like I always told her, she wasn't good enough: she missed a bit. The little bit that Poppy had touched. I could see into the past, into the present and into the future, now that I didn't need to. I could see that Poppy would be blamed, Poppy would be convicted. I could see that Poppy would always think it was Serena and Serena would always think it was Poppy. And no one, not even Poppy and Serena, would think to ask Marlene if she killed me.

Marlene would have admitted it if anyone had ever bothered to ask her. She was that weak, she would have cracked. But no one did, because all the evidence pointed to Poppy with Serena's help. What they asked her was where she was the night of my murder. And she told them. She told them that she came to see me to tell me to leave her alone, but I did not answer the door when she knocked. Which was true. And she told them that she went home. Someone even remembers her going back to Birmingham on the 9 p.m. train. She had already killed me by then, but only she knew that.

Marlene wiped down the door handle and checked she had not stepped in any blood.

She even remembered to wipe her fingerprints off the spare key and return it to its place under the mat. She looked around and around, and was quite calm considering what she had just done. Maybe it was true what she said in court. Maybe I had broken her. Maybe living with me had turned her into a person she did not recognise. I did not recognise her, that's for sure. She never looked at me again. Once she had done it, once she had stepped back, she did not survey her handiwork; she did not look at me for one last goodbye. But that is understandable. If she had, she would not have been able to walk away. She would have called the police, she would have confessed. In her mind, the reason she never did confess was because she did not want to leave Jack.

I could see the years ahead, and I could see that she would

451

allow Poppy to take the blame. First she would reason that Poppy was innocent, so they would find out the truth. And after Poppy was sentenced, she would think that Poppy was not a mother, Poppy didn't have a young child relying upon her, so it wouldn't matter as much as it would if she went away. Jack's life would be ruined to know that his mother had killed his father and then she would not see him outside of jail until he was an adult.

But, in all honesty, she was a coward. She was scared of prison, she was scared of being labelled a murderer, and most of all she was scared of Jack hating her for what she had done.

And what she had done, stupid cow that she was, was to unintentionally commit the perfect murder: she had killed someone and someone else had been arrested, tried and sentenced for it.

I was glad in the end that it was her who did it. Because she would never sleep again. Every single night for the rest of her life she would wake up in a cold, terrified sweat. She would spend the rest of her life looking over her shoulder in case she got caught. She would always hear the sound I made as I called out her name that one last time, and she would always feel the sickening give as the knife went in.

Marlene thought she was getting rid of me by doing what she did but, in truth, she was doing the opposite. She was making sure I would haunt her for ever.